GHOST

BAEN BOOKS by JOHN RINGO

Ghost

Princess of Wands *(forthcoming)*

A Hymn Before Battle
Gust Front
When the Devil Dances
Hell's Faire
The Hero *(with Michael Z. Williamson)*
Cally's War *(with Julie Cochrane)*
Watch on the Rhine *(with Tom Kratman)*

There Will Be Dragons
Emerald Sea
Against the Tide

Into the Looking Glass

The Road to Damascus *(with Linda Evans)*

The Prince Roger Saga with David Weber:
March Upcountry
March to the Sea
March to the Stars
We Few

GHOST

JOHN RINGO

GHOST

This is a work of fiction. All the characters and events portrayed in this book are fictional, and any resemblance to real people or incidents is purely coincidental.

A Baen Books Original

Baen Publishing Enterprises
P.O. Box 1403
Riverdale, NY 10471
www.baen.com

ISBN-13: 978-1-4165-0905-9
ISBN-10: 1-4165-0905-4

Cover art by Kurt Miller

First printing, October 2005

Library of Congress Cataloging-in-Publication Data

Ringo, John, 1963-
 Ghost / John Ringo.
     p. cm.
 "A Baen Books Original"–T.p. verso.
 ISBN 1-4165-0905-4
 1. United States. Navy. SEALs--Fiction. 2. Retired military personnel–Fiction. 3. Terrorism–Prevention–Fiction. 4. Florida Keys (Fla.)–Fiction. 5. Siberia (Russia)–Fiction. 6. Middle East–Fiction. I. Title.

 PS3568.I577G48 2005
 813'.54–dc22

                                                              2005019119

Distributed by Simon & Schuster
1230 Avenue of the Americas
New York, NY 10020

Production & design by Windhaven Press, Auburn, NH (www.windhaven.com)
Printed in the United States of America

10   9   8   7   6   5   4   3   2   1

DEDICATION:

To the service men and women of the United States Armed Forces.

> People sleep peaceably in their beds at night only because rough men stand ready to do violence on their behalf.
>
> —George Orwell

Stay safe and come home with mind and body intact. Our prayers go with you all, even the ones that don't officially exist.

And to Tammara. You fly with the angels now.

Acknowledgments:

Besides all the authors and singers of songs that I use to drown out the world around me, I'd like to specifically mention a few people who helped in the writing of this book.

Ryan Miller, former petty officer, for helpful advice on a range of topics. Leave it at NONEL and "You've got to be shitting me!"

Mike Massa, former Navy LT, for extensive professional content correction. Any mistakes in flavor or language, however, are mine. Nice trick with the shirt, by the way.

Kacey, Cassie and Casey, for more professional input. See you next year if you're not somewhere dusty, dirty and dry.

Doug Miller, my best friend and a helpful source of information on electrical systems and combat instruction.

And my Shepherd, Boadicea, for not getting too upset when I'd make weird hand movements like I was shooting or something.

John Ringo
Chattanooga, TN
abn1508@mindspring.com

BOOK ONE
Winter Born

PROLOGUE

Hamid Halal stepped past the two teenage mujahideen, pushed aside a flap of rotting canvas and ducked to enter the low doorway. The room beyond was small, no more than three meters on a side, dark and dirty with a litter-strewn, packed-clay floor and granite walls covered in Arabic graffiti. The only light was from the doorway, blocked by the canvas and his body, and a small paneless window on the south wall. Despite the size, five heavily armed mujahideen were packed along the sides leaving only a narrow spot in the middle. In this narrow spot a tall, spare, figure squatted behind a low table, typing on a laptop computer.

"Great One," Halal said, dropping to both knees and bowing his head. "It is good to see that you truly survive!"

"Did you believe that Allah would permit the forces of the Great Satan to kill his most valiant leader?" the man said, soberly, his piercing eyes meeting those of Halal with a real question behind them.

Halal recognized what the question implied. Only true belief could bring about the Final Jihad and the destruction of the Dar Al Harb. Questioning the survival of the Great One, surely Allah's most important sword in the battle against the Dar Al Harb, implied a lack of faith in Allah Himself. And the slightest trace of lack of belief, in this place, in this man's presence, could lead to immediate martyrdom. Halal bowed his head and nodded in submission.

3

"Great One, my faith has been tried by the events of the last two years," the mujahideen commander admitted. "We battle the Great Satan daily and yet our numbers dwindle. Again and again the mujahideen fearlessly attack them as we are instructed in the Words of the Prophet. To put aside fear of death and think only of the Will of Allah. Of the Glory of Paradise and the spread of the Dar Al Islam. And, again and again, we are not only defeated, but destroyed. Their technology, their training . . . their faith in their false Gods, seems to be beyond even the Will of Allah to defeat. But, your presence fills me with renewed hope. If you can survive when all their forces search for you, anything is possible. Forgive me my trial of faith and look upon my actions. I have sought battle without fail. As Allah is Merciful, have mercy upon his true servant."

"Very pretty," the tall man said. "And very common. Everywhere I go, the faith of the mujahideen is tried. And, everywhere I go, they profess renewed faith. It is with these weak tools that Allah's Will must be worked. But, Halal, the Jihad has need of you. You have skills that are needed in a great mission. We still can bring the Great Satan to its knees and teach the Lesser Satans of Europe and Asia that Allah's Will is great and powerful beyond even that of Satan. And you will be the tool that shall show that will. In one stroke, we will break the will of the Dar Al Harb, which is divided even in the lands of the Great Satan, and bring the banners of Islam, once again, to the lost Dar Al Islam. And all the jihad needs is your skills."

"I live in submission to Allah," Halal said, nodding. "What is the mission, Great One?"

"We shall strike at the Satan's greatest weakness," the tall man said, his eyes lidding heavily. "The love of its whores."

CHAPTER ONE

Mike Harmon stuck his laptop in his jump bag and tossed the latter over one shoulder, standing up and stretching his back. He had been sitting in the coffee shop for nearly three hours and he wasn't as young as he used to be. Fifteen years in the teams had left him with degenerative damage in half the major joints in his body and a back that was compacted enough for a fifty-year-old.

As he wandered out of the shop, he glanced at his image in the plate glass window and grimaced. Brown hair, brown eyes, a "regular" face, neither handsome nor ugly, shoulders a bit wider than the norm, middle beginning to bulge a bit despite regular exercise. Not the most prepossessing figure and certainly not, by any stretch of the imagination, a big man on campus.

He'd thought that going back to college would be a cinch. With both his career and his marriage foundered on the rocks, time to go find some time in the sun. After years of eighteen-hour days, how hard could homework be? And then there were the lovely young coeds, long legs flashing by, skirts swirling and flirting, practically begging to be snapped up by a not particularly bad looking former SEAL.

Well, the homework wasn't actually that bad, or it wouldn't be if it weren't for the classes he had to take. History. How bad

could it be? Greeks and Romans and Persians and the Renais-
sance. Egyptians and feudal lords and maybe memorizing a bunch
of dead guys' names.

Little did he know. That was "old history." His current major
course was "An Introduction to African Pre-Colonial History."
As far as he'd been able to determine, his definition of what
constituted "history" and the definition used by the University of
Georgia History Department didn't come from the same diction-
ary. Sure, the old time historians made stuff up. Livy read like
something written by Tom Clancy and Julius Caesar's *Gallic Wars*
was written with political image in mind with only brief touches
on reality, something like a Democratic stump speech. But it had
brief touches on reality and it was at least *written*. Prior to the
"colonization" period, Africa *had* no writing and, apparently, no
problems worth discussing. His professor attributed every ill of
Africa to the colonialism of the White Man, ignoring the ongoing
tribal wars that dated back thousands of years, not to mention
the Arab slave traders that benefited from them. He'd had to see
the first episode of the mini-series *Roots* and had been loudly
shushed when he started laughing in the first fifteen minutes.
Slave traders didn't get off their boats and go chase bush-bunnies
around. They *bought* them from Arabs, not fucking "Islamics,"
Ay-rabs. And the Arabs bought them from the tribes, who were
constantly at war with each other.

Sometimes it was all Mike could do to not stand up and punch
the stupid bastard, especially when he got started on "modern
colonialism," by which he meant the War on Terrorism. Mike
wanted to scream "Have you ever *been* in Mogadishu you ignorant
son-of-a-bitch?" Hell, the conditions in Africa were *better* when
the English and the Germans and even the French and the Belgians had been in charge. He'd read Conrad's *Heart of Darkness*
a couple of times during down time on the teams. And he'd been
in Congo, not that there was any trace of it going in or out. And
Congo now was "Heart of Darkness" on fucking steroids. The
only thing worse than having the Belgians in charge was having
the fucking gomers handling things.

But, of course, the problem with the gomers wasn't that they
were totally fucked up gomers. Oh, no, the problem with the

gomers was all the fault of colonialism and "western military adventures." Well, he'd been on one "western military adventure" in Congo and as far as he was concerned the best thing to do was spray the whole damned place with anthrax, including the fucking gorillas, shoot anyone that tried to leave and start over.

Attitudes like this, of course, didn't sit very well with his professors. It also didn't fit very well with the pretty little airheads that were being fed a steady diet of leftist propaganda bullshit. And no matter how he tried, he'd always end up opening up his mouth and pointing out that it *was* leftist propaganda bullshit. That the problem with the gomers was their fucking culture, which was totally fucked up and had been *before* colonialization and was going to stay that way until somebody beat some sense into their heads. At which point terms like "militarist" and "baby-killer" and, with the real intellectuals, "myrmidon" would start getting tossed around.

What was funny was that some of the most leftist, ball-busting, bitches seemed to get off on his being a former team guy. There was one little brunette wearing a beret just like that fucking terrorist Che that he swore was getting ready to go down on him right in the middle of the damned argument. But he'd blown her off instead. The hell if he'd get told he was a mindless myrmidon and then fuck the little bitch.

Sooner or later, something was going to give. His *really* bad side was starting to peek out and that was something he feared more than failure. It violated the warrior code. Courage in Battle, Loyalty to the King, Protection of the Innocent. Sometimes it seemed it was the only thing he had left. He was *not* going to become a fucking rapist.

He'd always managed to restrain that side of himself, even with the Filipino B-girls and the Thailand whores, when it didn't matter what you did, as long as you paid the mamasan. One of the reasons he'd just left the little bitch in the beret hanging was if he'd taken her home it would have been a grudge fuck, with emphasis on "grudge." And she'd have gone home sorry and sore. Which was all well and good if it was lined out in advance and agreed to by both parties. But that wasn't where that particular relationship was going.

So his right forearm got overdeveloped, his anger got hotter and hotter and there didn't seem to be any release in sight. He very much needed to kill someone. Just about anyone would do, but one of the little airhead bitches was getting even farther up the list than his professors.

Thoughts like that had carried him, unthinking, to the areas by the library and the English department buildings. His path wasn't even vaguely in the direction of his apartment; in fact it was in the opposite direction. But there were quiet pathways where occasional young ladies wandered by, most of them so totally fucking oblivious they wouldn't have noticed if he threw a rock in their direction. It was a sick addiction with a very specific name: "stalking." He'd pick a dark spot, stand still as if he were simply drinking in the night and wait. Sooner or later some brainless bitch would walk past, totally defenseless.

Sometimes, just to get a rise out of them, he'd cough. And they'd notice the dark figure in the shadows, their eyes would get wide and they'd hurry past. He never looked at them then, he'd totally ignore them, but he could tell by their hurried steps, quite often clicking away in their high heels, how much he'd frightened them. Sick, but oh so very fun. And he considered it to be instructional for the little idiots. It might teach them to keep some situational awareness.

He also considered it keeping in training. There were plenty of *non*-idiots among the girls on campus, girls who knew damned well that college campuses had the highest rate of rape in the U.S. And, nine times out of ten, even with the ones who were alert, he could avoid being seen even standing in plain sight. His team name was "Ghost" and it had been hard earned. It was an ability he'd had even before he was on the teams and one that he'd raised to a high pitch in various third world shitholes. He could just . . . blend.

If he put on local clothes and spent some time watching local moves, he could move among the populace of half the world unnoticed. A little heavy-set, jaw a little square, shoulders a little broad, but nobody seemed to take that into account. Grow a little stubble, cover his haircut and he was anything from an Arab to an Afghan. As long as he didn't open his mouth: he'd never had

language training and his Arab extended to "where's the bathroom" and "lie on the floor and put your hands on your head."

The spot he'd chosen overlooked Baldwin Street, which ran between the English building, Park Hall, and the Military Science Building. He'd thought about going ROTC and maybe bucking for an Army commission. But even with his background his physical damage—he was paid for being "50% disabled" and might go as high as 100% in time—made it unlikely that even the Army would give him a commission. And if he did get one, at his age, he'd probably end up in supply or civil affairs or some such bullshit. Better to eat the shit at the college, get his history degree and go looking for a teaching job. Coach track or swimming, teach history and just . . . veg.

He stopped vegging as he spotted a nice young quarry, blonde, nice tits in a midriff top, ruffled miniskirt revealing long, shapely legs and black high heels clicking along on the sidewalk heading west on Baldwin. The fashions had come together nicely in the last year with just about everything a heterosexual male wanted to see women wearing being the "in" thing. It was like some over-sexed ancient Greek god had told fashion designers exactly what he wanted them to push. She was probably coming back from some of the clubs over on Broad—she was "club" dressed—headed down to the dorms along Lumpkin. And too stupid to stay to the more traveled and lighted ways. *Probably a freshman,* he thought.

It was as professional a snatch as he'd ever seen. The late-model custom van slowed down, the door opened, a man stepped out in a trot, the bag went over the blonde's head, she was lifted into the van before she could even start kicking, the door closed and the van started to accelerate. It took no more than a couple of seconds. As far as Mike could tell there was no one in sight of the snatch, certainly no one in easy view and if you hadn't been looking right at the girl you probably wouldn't have been able to process it. Whoosh. The girl was just . . . gone.

Except the van had to stop at the west end of Baldwin Street, where it intersected Lumpkin, and Mike realized he was already down the hill in a sprint, off the low wall by the sidewalk, his jump bag banging on his back as he accelerated down the middle

of the road, no cars in sight and it kept him out of the view, mostly, of the driver. The van started to pull out onto Lumpkin and Mike leapt upwards, landing lightly on the ladder at the back of the van, crouched. If he lost track of the van the girl was going to disappear, probably into an unmarked grave.

He knew that, at heart, he was a rapist. And that meant he hated rapists more than any "normal" human being. They purely pissed him off. He'd spent his entire sexually adult life fighting the urge to use his not inconsiderable strength to possess and take instead of woo and cajole. He'd fought his demons to a standstill again and again when it would have been so easy to give in. He'd had one truly screwed up bitch get completely naked, with him naked and erect between her legs, and she still couldn't say "yes." And he'd just said: "that's okay" and walked away with an amazing case of blueballs. When men gave in to that dark side, it made him even more angry than listening to leftist bitches scream about "western civilization" and how it was so fucked up.

The van was an older modern custom van like Mexicans tended to drive and from inside he could hear the struggle going on and the muffled cries of the girl followed by slaps. While it made one side of him angry as hell, another side was so turned on he could barely stand it. But the good news was unless somebody saw him on the back of the van and vectored in the police, he stood a good chance of being able to kill someone and not go to jail. This was probably a bunch of fucking illegales who'd decided they wanted to party with a coed. And they were going to be seriously fucked up, armed or not, as soon as this damned van stopped. He might even get laid out of it, if not by the blonde, who was going to be pretty fucked-up from this experience, then by some girly who'd take pity on the poor hero.

The van headed south on Lumpkin through the university area and towards the south side of town. It was late and if anyone saw him he couldn't tell. There weren't even any cars behind the van or he'd have waved at them or something. He wanted to get his mad out by killing some of the bastards in the van, they were ripping cloth now, but he figured at least *trying* to be the "good citizen" instead of the "vigilante" would be a good idea. He couldn't bring in the police himself; he'd left his cell phone charging by his bed

before going to class and hadn't been home to pick it up. And unless someone saw him soon, the van would get into darker, and less populated, areas where he might never get spotted.

He kept hanging on to the ladder, swinging through turns, crouched down to stay out of sight, half hoping some cop cruiser would pull up behind them and half hoping it wouldn't. Most of the cops stayed up towards the center of Athens on Friday and Saturday, closer to the action. And, proverbially, there was never a cop around when you needed them. This time, especially. Not even any fucking *cars*. The van had gotten off of Lumpkin and into neighborhoods that were mostly dark this time of night. Neighborhoods with speed bumps that were a real *bitch* to hang on through. The route appeared to be planned and he started wondering if he was really dealing with a group of Mexes. The snatch looked professional, to his trained eye, and the egress also looked professional. Which either made it a group of long term serial rapists, even funner to kill, or . . . something else.

The van finally pulled into an industrial complex, closed and dark, and slowed through a series of turns. Mike got a look at a dead end, a parking lot with a few cars, a person standing in the shadows and . . .

He was off the back of the van, tumbling as quietly as he could into a roadside ditch, before his mind fully processed the MP-5 the sentry was holding. He hadn't seen any phone booths in miles; the buildings around the guarded one were all dark which meant no getting to a phone easily. And a sentry meant that this wasn't just a simple snatch for pussy, this was . . . something else.

He dropped the jump bag and leopard crawled down the ditch, heading for the building. The sentry was at the front and his brief glimpse hadn't spotted one on the side. But there were some windows. He needed more intel before he figured out how to call in support and the windows might tell him something.

As soon as he was around the side and out of sight of the front sentry he leopard crawled across to the wall of the brick building and crouched in the shadows at the base. The window was about eight feet up, which was a long damned jump for a guy who was five ten and a bit out of shape, and he knew he didn't dare make much sound. He squatted and then sprung upward, his hands

clamping onto the narrow sill, the entire evolution completed in near perfect silence. He waited for a moment to listen for reaction, then slowly chinned himself up to the window.

The room was mostly open with some metal boxes that looked a bit like coffins lining the walls. The van was parked inside and there was a container vehicle pulled in with its doors open. The blonde, now sans everything but bra and panties, tied hand and foot with fast-strips and with a gag stuffed in her mouth, was on the ground near a table in the middle. One of the boxes was being loaded into the container vehicle and, as he watched, the doors were closed and the vehicle pulled out. It was a red container with "OCCP" on the back and a symbol like a flower. The doors were dented towards the top. The license plate was out of view. He got all of that in one brief glance and then went back to examining the room.

There were seven subject males of apparent Middle Eastern extraction in view. One was at the table, talking on what appeared to be a satellite phone. Three were standing by the van, between it and the blonde. A fourth sitting in the open side door. There was an additional subject female on a metal table like a surgery or butcher table, naked. She appeared to be unconscious, had had an IV inserted and something like a cloth diaper put on her lower regions. As he watched, two more subject males lifted her up and lowered her into one of the "coffins." The IV was inserted into a pouch in the top and the top closed and latched from the outside.

Mike started to lower himself, having seen enough, when he heard a light hiss to his lower right. He closed his eyes, willing his night vision to come back, and then looked down. A man in a light jacket was pointing an MP-5 at him and gesturing for him to come down.

Mike, briefly, wondered why the guy hadn't shot him already. In a way the former SEAL wished the target had done so. He was embarrassed. He'd mentally been bitching at the girls on campus about their security and here he'd gone and completely lost situational awareness. It was . . . annoying.

He nodded at the man in agreement, smiled nervously, dropped down, apparently stumbling on the fall, and rolled into the man's

legs. Reaching up, Mike gripped the barrel of the submachine gun and rotated it upwards, ripping the grip out of the man's hands at the same time, then slammed it into the target's stomach before he could cry out. As soon as he had partial control of the weapon, which was attached to the target's body with a friction strap, he rotated it, pressed it into the man's chest, rotated the safety lever to burst and triggered three rounds.

The entire action had taken no more than three seconds and the whole noise had been a grunt from the target and the sound of the MP-5's action. In the middle of taking down the target Mike had noticed, from the ribbed feel of the barrel shroud, that the weapon was an MP-5 SD, one of the quietest silenced sub-guns in the world. Highly illegal in the U.S. without the appropriate permits and uncommon among terrorists. On the other hand, Mike had spent more time with one in his hands than he had with school books, including high school. He searched the target's body and retrieved three more magazines, checked the level in the one in the weapon, reached up, tugged the collar of his T-shirt down hard, then snugged the weapon into his shoulder and ghosted towards the front of the building.

There was a sentry at the front and this one was apparently a rover. He knew he'd made two mistakes, one in not checking for the rover and one in losing situational awareness. Part of it was eagerness. He really wanted to kill these sons-of-bitches and he wanted to save the girls. From what he'd seen, they were being transported. Where was a big question. But terrorists, as these clearly were, weren't going to negotiate. If the police tried to handle this like a normal crime, all the girls were going to die. Terrorists of this type would only negotiate so as to get maximum news coverage and then kill the girls in the worst way they could manage.

He did a mental check and decided that this constituted a mission that he could do with a good conscience, if not legally. "Protect and defend the Constitution of the United States against all enemies foreign and domestic." Kidnapping was a de jure and de facto stripping of civil rights, and local authorities, however much they were the legal group to handle it, were not going to be competent to do so.

Mike knew it was so much bullshit. But he also knew that if he managed to extract the girls, nobody was going to give a shit how he'd done it. The prosecutor that tried him would get tossed out of office so fast the door would hit him, or more likely *her*, knowing liberal bitches and their incredible stupidity, in the ass.

Fuck it. If he went for commo, the sentry would be found, the two girls would die and so, probably, would the others, wherever they were going. Then the whole operation would just up and disappear. It was take-down time.

With that in mind, he shouldered the MP-5 and ghosted forward along the wall. Nearing the corner he actually let himself make some noise, as if he was the roving sentry coming up to the corner. No reason to startle the guy until he had to.

When he came to the corner he stepped outward, still at tactical present, and leaned to the left. The target was standing by a personnel door, smoking a cigarette. Marlboro from the drifting smell of the smoke. The cigarette spun out of his lips and into the grass by the side of the entrance pad as the three nine-millimeter rounds impacted with the side of the target's head.

Twenty-one rounds left but only two spare magazines. Mike stopped at the target and found three more, including the one in the target's weapon, and stuffed them in his back pockets. The night was quiet, still no sound of alarm from the terrorists in the building. There was probably some sort of rotation schedule for the sentries. Time to get inside the decision cycle.

He gently checked the handle on the door and determined that it was unlocked. Then the decision had to be made, slow or fast. He finally decided on slow and casual. One of the sentries coming in for some reason. He pulled the door open and stepped through looking unconcernedly to either side. The view from the door into the room was blocked by a stack of the "coffins." When he cleared them to either side, he'd be in view of the terrorists. Time to go tactical again. He lifted the MP-5 to his shoulder and stepped to the side quickly.

Party time.

CHAPTER TWO

"Yes, Hamid," Hazzah Bud said, nodding as he talked on the phone. "The delivery has been made on time, on my honor. The shipment will be at your warehouse no later than tomorrow night. We had trouble finding sufficient stock, but at the last moment we found a significant amount and not only have fulfilled the first order but have stock left over to start the second. Yes. Yes, we will ensure that the cargo arrives in good condition. Go with God, Hamid."

Hazzah had been a member of Hezbollah since the outbreak of the civil war in Lebanon. A member of the Joharra tribe, he had fought the Amal and the Hamas, the Irish and the American Marines. He had been one of five potential drivers for the attack on the Marine barracks but at the last minute his best friend, Murtaza Batatu, had been chosen for martyrdom instead. Over the years he had waned in his faith in the jihad and these days he was just happy to awake each morning alive. Martyrdom was for the young. But a job was a job and failure in this one would mean martyrdom for sure.

Bud looked up at Abdul Mohiuddin and shook his head.

"Halal is unhappy that it took so long to round up the full cargo and he already wants more. In good condition."

"That means we cannot rape these infidel bitches," Kahf Shishakli

said, angrily. Kahf was a youngster among the mujahideen and full of the work of Allah and the chance for martyrdom. A student from the Emirate of Kuwait, majoring in business, his family was fiercely Wahabbist and he had been raised to believe that death in the fight against the Dar Al Harb was the highest of callings. But he was young and the bitch on the floor was pretty. Like all the American whores she went not much more clothed than she was now. All such whores deserved to be raped.

"Are either of them virgin?" Bud said, grinning at the girl on the floor.

"The one who is packaged was not," Abdul said, settling into the open door of the van, then gesturing at the blonde. "These are all whores, are they not? None of them have been virgins."

"He said in good condition," Bud replied, pulling a pistol out of his waistband, and walking over to the blonde. "He didn't say unraped. I think we'll rape this one. If she is in bad condition when we are done, we'll send her soul to Satan and find another."

"In'sh'allah," Shishakli said, reaching down to grab the girl's hair and twist it. "It is as Allah Wills. Women taken in battle are allowed to be raped and these women are taken in the Great Jihad against the Americans. Let us rape them to the Glory of Allah."

As Mike stepped to the side he heard males speaking in what he was pretty sure was Arabic and then a muffled scream from the girl. He stepped around the coffin, at present, and targeted a male holding the hair of the girl. Three rounds to the chest put the target down, the silenced 9mm rounds punching into his chest cavity and blasting blood and bone out to cover the cowering girl.

Hazzah Bud had been fighting one group or another most of his adult life and had the scars to prove it. But it was a long time since he had had to fight for his life and the attack was unexpected. As Kahf's chest erupted in blood, he turned towards the faint "thocks" from the silenced submachine gun, raising his pistol as quickly as he could. In his haste, he actually triggered a round into the floor and he prayed to Allah that it would disturb

this djinn who had appeared long enough for him, Hazzah Bud, Allah's servant for most of his life, to live.

Mike shifted to a male holding a pistol in his hand. The male was rotating to the side to fire and actually triggered a round into the ground in his haste. Mike ignored it and serviced the target with a burst, then shifted to the group by the van.

Abdul Mohiuddin grabbed his AK and rolled into the body of the van for cover. If this was an American police assault team they would soon find that those who did not fear death were dangerous to battle! Allah would be with them in this battle!

The one that had been sitting in the doorway was gone, presumably into the cargo area; the other three had reached for weapons that were scattered on the ground. One was raising an AK variant assault rifle and was serviced as was a second reaching for another AK. At that point, an automatic part of his brain told him to cover and reload so he pulled back behind the coffins, ejected his magazine down the front of his shirt, and slapped in another. He wasn't standing still while he did it, but moving counterclockwise behind the cover of the coffins, looking for another shot.

Murtaza Saqqaf was amazed. He had gotten but one brief view of the assailant and it was not the heavily armored tac team they had expected. Indeed, there appeared to be but one American who had already killed many of his brothers in Allah. It was infuriating!
"There's only one of them!" he shouted. "We can trap him! Come around the coffins; he is hiding in there!"

There was shouting from the coffins behind him and he ducked into a space between two stacks, waiting a moment. After shouting the person was trying to move stealthily but it was nearly impossible in this echoing room. Mike followed the cautious movement and then took a coin from his pocket and tossed it over the coffins beyond his present position. The metal coin

made a loud bong as it hit, too loud really, but the target sped up, actually passing his position in a quiet trot. Mike waited a moment and then leaned out . . .

There was a metallic sound, like a magazine being dropped accidentally, well down the south wall, and Murtaza sped up, closing on his quarry. Allah was with him and he smiled.

"Allahu Akbar!" he shouted as he spun around the corner and emptied his magazine into the space where the sound had occurred. But there was nothing there and as he realized that, over the ringing in his ears from the firing, he heard a faint sound behind him. . . .

Mike wanted to laugh at the actions of the target but, instead, as the tango turned to check behind him he fired a three-round burst into the "sniper triangle" of the head and upper body, where there were numerous critical blood vessels, then began moving again, heading clockwise to his previous firing position.

Ahmed Rabah nodded as he heard the shout from Murtaza. There had been no flood of police into the warehouse, which meant it was likely to be only one American, thinking he was Rambo and trying to save the Satan's whores. Well, the mission was probably a failure, they would have to pick up and move elsewhere at the very least. But the purpose of the Warriors of Jihad was to spread fear amongst the infidels of the Great Satan and killing the bitch would do that well enough. So he darted out of the cover of the coffins towards the bitch on the floor. Let the American continue to battle, but even if he was victorious it would be as ashes in his mouth. He had just reached her when he heard the squeak of a tennis shoe from among the coffins and looked up into the barrel of a submachine gun. . . .

When he reached his firing position he saw one of the terrorists preparing to terminate the hostage and he put two bursts into the man's chest, the blood flying out onto the already blood-soaked girl screaming into her gag. Since there was a significant threat to the hostage, Mike decided to go for a thunder run and see what

he could get directed at himself. He moved to a different opening and then darted into the space in the middle of the room.

Abdul Mohiuddin had considered killing the whore on the floor but even if they moved she could still be smuggled out of the country. So he continued to wait in the concealment of the van, knowing that sooner or later the American would have to come into view. Suddenly a man in jeans and a shirt darted into the open area, moving fast.

Abdul had been waiting for that and opened up the back door of the van, dropping to the ground in a crouch and placing his AK against his hip, firing off the clip in a long burst at the running figure.

As the door opened on the van to his left Mike turned, then rolled on his right shoulder, coming up in a kneeling position and targeting the muj as 7.62mm bullets cracked the air around him.

Abdul Mohiuddin felt the 9mm rounds thudding into him as so many punches to the chest and stumbled to his knees. He tried to lift the rifle again but it was far too heavy. He tried to mumble a prayer to Allah, but his lungs were full of liquid and he couldn't get a breath. His vision darkened and all he could feel was fury at this one djinn American who seemed to be invincible. Allah had deserted them. . . .

Mike didn't even ensure the target was down, just sprung to his feet and sprinted across the area, bullets cracking around him, to dive behind the desk, reloading as he ran.

Sidi Al-Radi looked at his friend Khalil Medein in fear. Both were students from Pakistan at the University of Georgia. They had met at a student rally in support of the Palestinian cause and been recruited as warriors of the jihad that same day. At the time it had seemed a great cause and they had shouted with the others that they were willing to die for Allah.

However, now that they faced death, had seen the blood from

their fellow warriors staining the floor, knew that death came for them on squeaking feet, all they could do was crouch behind the desk and hope that it would pass them by....

As he cleared the top of the desk in a one-handed lift, he discovered to his annoyance two of the terrorists crouching down behind it and not even looking for him. They were as surprised as he was, and far, far slower. In a second and a half, two more warriors of Allah had been sent to have a conversation with their God. He suspected that it was not going to be a good one.

His position, however, was very exposed and he lifted himself up again, sprinting forward. There was an open gap in view and he headed for it like a goal line, ricochets whining off the floor around him. Suddenly most of the shooting stopped and he heard a lot of reloading which caused him to grin even in the middle of the mess he'd started.

Terrorists, even trained terrorists, used the "spray and pray" technique of combat. Point the gun in the general direction of the enemy, generally held somewhere near the hip, close your eyes, pull the trigger and hope that you hit something. It wasn't just terrorists, everyone in the region except the Israelis tended to use "spray and pray." Which was why, besides body armor and superior training, Western militaries, including the Israelis, didn't tend to take many casualties from rifle fire while, at the same time, racking up kills by direct fire. Westerners could, and would, target their shooting. Arabs didn't. And, at the moment, it was saving his life. He just hoped like hell they wouldn't accidentally, or intentionally, shoot the hostage.

He paused in the gap and counted on his fingers. Started with nine and the two sentries. Sentries down. One with a gun, one holding the hair. One in the back. One in the van. Two behind the desk. Three to go? No. Two. One trying to kill the hostage makes seven.

Rouhi Karim was one of the imported mujahideen, another member of Hezbollah. He had not fought as broadly or fiercely as Hazzah Bud, but he was an experienced street fighter and thought that surely he could kill *one* Allah-damned American. But twice

he had seen the infidel djinn cross the open area in the middle
of the room and twice tried to shoot him, emptying two full
magazines in his anger to no avail. Now he decided that there
was a better way. The infidel feared death and *always* negotiated
for hostages. He reloaded again and left his cover, running into
the open area and grabbing the blood-covered bitch by her hair
to lift her from the floor. She screamed at the pain but he felt
nothing but joy at the sound. Soon the American would be dead
and he would give her far more pain. . . .

"American! We will negotiate now!"

Mike peeked into the open area and shook his head at the
sight. A teenage muj was holding the blonde by the hair, an AK
pointed in the general direction of, well, the floor. Not *at* her.
He shook his head, targeted the terrorist, who was looking in the
wrong direction, and put three rounds through his head.

The blonde was in bad shape, covered in blood and apparently
choking. He had a choice of helping her or taking down the last
tango. Helping her meant exposing himself, and the hostage, to
hostile fire. But . . . choking could kill just as sure as a bullet.
The gag was a cloth band with, apparently, cloth in the mouth.
He looked at it and clicked out his locking-blade knife. Taking
it in his right hand he ran to the girl, slid the razor edge under
the gag and cut it off. He hadn't taken any fire doing so but he
ghosted over between the coffins again.

Silence. The last target, if he was counting right, seemed to be
playing the waiting game. Okay, time to see how stealthy "Ghost"
could be. He started to move along the wall, heel rolling to side
of the foot and then to the ball, one slow step at a time, checking
the gaps between the boxes and occasionally getting a glimpse of
the now crying, and still choking a bit, blonde. She at least was
keeping quiet and down, other than the crying. She'd probably
puked at all the blood and been choking on that, and that sort
of choke could take your voice away pretty quick. Whatever the
reason, he appreciated her not yelling for help or whatever. It
would be distracting.

He smelled him before he saw him, the distinct smell of urine
with a hint of shit. There was a fair bit of both in the room, the

offal and sulfur smell of battle. But this was close and sharp. As he got closer he could hear the breathing, fast, high panting. Sworn to die or not, this was one muj who was scared as hell.

Karem Majali was an agronomy student who had been born in the mountains of Yemen where his father was a minor sheikh. He had been raised to do battle, showing no fear, a warrior for Allah. But while he had sometimes fired his weapon at other Yemeni, and even participated in one of the numerous kidnappings of foreigners in that land, he had never truly faced death. And he found that his belief in Allah was not as strong as he'd thought. All he could think was that this one American had killed, as far as he could tell, all of the other mujahideen, even Hazzah Bud and Abdul Mohiuddin, who were well-known warriors of Allah. He seemed to not be human, but some desert-formed shedim, an evil demon. Karem tried to lift himself from his hiding place, to rise up and charge forth, screaming God is Great as he should. But his knees would not support him and he realized that he had shit his pants. He could only crouch in his hole, shaking and crying faintly and wishing that he had never left Yemen, had never agreed to join the jihad, had stayed in his dorm instead of going to that Allah-Be-Damned rally. The hell with the Palestinians, anyway, they were filth unto Allah. . . .

Mike peeked around the coffins and tried not to laugh. The tango was huddled by the coffins, AK gripped with white knuckles, shaking like a leaf, looking towards the open area. Mike leaned forward and gently but firmly pressed the warm barrel of the sub-gun into the back of the subject's head.

"Lie on the ground with your hands behind your head," the former SEAL said in his very best Arabic.

The target froze for a second, then the AK slid into the open area and he flattened himself to the ground, legs spread and hands on the back of his head, fingers interlaced.

"Clearly you've been watching Fox," Mike said, trying not to chuckle. He grabbed the tango by the back of his collar and yanked him to his feet, pushing him into the open area with the barrel of the MP-5.

"Oh, God. Oh, God!" The blonde had slid as far away from the bodies as her bonds permitted her and now was bent in a fetal position. But she'd looked up at the steps and now her eyes were wide. "Oh, thank you!"

"You're welcome," Mike said, kneeing the muj into a kneeling position, then lowering him back facedown on the floor.

"Who are you?" the girl managed to gasp between coughs.

"No one of consequence," Mike said, then barked a laugh. "God, I always wanted to use that line. Do me a favor, and be quiet for a second, okay, honey? I need to talk to this young gentleman."

There was a pile of tie-ties, plastic handcuffs derived from cable ties, on the table and Mike used two of them to secure the terrorist.

"Is there any way you could let me *go*?" the girl asked as he rolled the muj over.

"Not at the moment, I'm in a hurry," Mike said, sliding the barrel of the MP-5 down to point at the tango's balls. "You speak English?"

"Yes!" the kid said, quickly. "I am speaking good English! I am student!"

"Great," Mike said, sliding the barrel down to the terrorist's knee. "Now, here's the deal. The first time I think you're lying to me, I'm going to shoot you in the knee. Now, that *really* hurts and you'll be permanently crippled. So try *very* hard not to lie to me. Okay? I'm basically a very bad man and I'd like to hurt you. A lot. But, I'm also an honorable one and if you don't lie to me, if you give me good answers, I won't shoot you. Okay?"

"Okay," the tango said, desperately.

"Where did they take the girls?" Mike asked, mildly.

"I do not know!" the boy said. "All I know is an airport."

"Hmmm . . ." Mike murmured then fired a round through the kid's leg. "Don't believe you."

He waited until the screaming, from both the tango and his erstwhile rapee, died down, then pointed the barrel at the other leg.

"Care to go for two?"

"I don't know!" the kid screamed. "They not tell us, tell us not to ask! Maybe is in papers. Hazzah is handling papers! A file, on the desk!"

"Hmmm . . ." Mike said, going over to the desk. "What's your name, Blondie?"

"Ashley," the girl said, whimpering. "Oh, please tell me you're not going to hurt me!"

"Hell, no," Mike snorted, searching through the papers. "I'm one of the good guys. Sort of. I'd like to, mind you. Girls all tied up and covered in blood are a real turn-on."

"What . . . who are you?" Ashley asked, desperately. "What the hell *are* you?"

"Nobody you want to remember," Mike replied, picking what looked like a bill of lading out of the pile. "Look, the police are going to be on this like flies on shit. I'd really appreciate it, as the guy who just saved your miserable cheerleader ass, if you'd tell them you have no clue who I am. I'm a short, tall, fat, thin, blond brunet with greenish brown eyes. Got it?"

"You're not with the police?" the girl said, totally confused.

"Oh, come on," Mike scoffed. "I know you're an airhead, but use at least one brain cell. Do the police *commonly* shoot people through the leg to get information?"

"Well, they beat people up," Ashley said, with relentlessly liberal logic.

"Did those guys beat you?" Mike asked, gesturing at the dead terrorists.

"Yes," Ashley said, sobbing gently.

"Would you like me to shoot you through the knee so you can tell the difference?" Mike asked, puzzling over the load list.

"NO!"

"Then, trust me, police don't kneecap people for information. It's *really* obvious. It looks like they were taking them to the Atlanta airport," Mike said, dropping the manifest. "Okay, I'm going to cut part of the way through your bonds," he continued, pulling his knife back out. "As soon as you work yourself free, call 911 and report all of this. When they get here, remember . . ."

"Short, fat, thin, tall, blondish brunet?" Ashley said, nodding. "Got it. What about him?" she asked, gesturing with her chin at the gently sobbing and moaning muj.

"What about him?" Mike asked, pulling her upright and applying

his knife to the tough plastic. "If he bleeds out or dies of shock, it's no skin off my nose. Let me ask you, do *you* really care?"

"No," Ashley admitted after a moment's thought.

"Congratulations," Mike said, changing his mind and cutting the bonds on her hands completely free. "You're halfway to conservative already. Remember, Vote Cliff."

"I'm not *that* far," Ashley said, smiling faintly. "Why'd you cut me free?"

"Give me ten minutes," Mike said. "After I'm gone. Then call. And tell them Atlanta airport."

"You're going to get in trouble for this, aren't you?"

"It is not inside my normal mission parameters," Mike admitted without *really* lying. Let her suggest to the police that he was some sort of spook. "Yeah, if they figure out who it was, I'll be looking at, well, murder one, torture, you name it. They'll probably throw the book at me. So . . . be uncooperative, okay? Just tell them you want to talk to an attorney or, barring that, the news media."

"What's your name, please?" Ashley said, leaning forward to drift a kiss across his cheek as he worked on her ankles.

"Look, killing makes me really horny," Mike said, tightly. "So do tied-up half-naked, damned good-looking blondes. And if you really must know, it's the Dread Pirate Roberts."

"What?" Ashley said, pulling her ankles up to her as soon as they were free and rubbing at the marks from the strips.

"Haven't you ever seen *The Princess Bride*?" Mike asked, aghast.

"No?"

"Good Lord, woman." He stood up, shaking his head, and headed for the door. "Rent it. You owe me."

"I will," Ashley said.

"Ten minutes," Mike said, then paused. "Crap."

"What now?" Ashley said, looking around wildly.

"Well, two things," Mike admitted. "No wheels and I need to check on the other girl."

The coffin had not been hit and the girl, who was apparently drugged, was fine. Mike checked her pulse and had to really restrain himself from copping a feel. It wasn't like anyone would

know. Then he looked at his hands, which were covered in cordite residue and blood, and shook his head. Okay, so they'd know. He was already looking at murder one. No, down.

He left the top propped up and searched the pockets of the terrorist who seemed to be the boss on the basis that he'd be the most likely to have his own vehicle. Sure enough, he turned up a set of keys, with an electronic opener, for a Ford. He hunted around and found a couple more MP-5 mags and came back to find Ashley collapsed into the station chair that had been rolled away from the desk. It had a couple of bullet holes in it but she didn't seem to mind.

"You okay?" he said.

"Now you ask?" she replied. She'd been crying again, but she tried to smile.

"Yeah, now I ask," Mike admitted. "I'm coming off mission-high. You okay?"

"I will be," Ashley said. "I don't want to wait here alone for the police."

"Five minutes," Mike said, noticing for the first time that she had a really distinct cleft in her chin. It just made her cuter than before and he had to force down a wave of lust that was truly overpowering. On a whim he decided to take the satellite phone; there was a land-line she could use. Satellite phones couldn't call 911 anyway, and if she tried she'd get really confused. "At least. I can't stay, you know that?"

"Yeah," she sighed. "I really want to know who you are."

"Well," he said, grinning, "if you ever see me again, for the first time, be overwhelmed by a wave of lust and need to give me a blowjob right then and there, even if it's in public. Okay?"

"Sure," Ashley said, shaking her head. "Men. Maybe not in public, but we'll talk, okay? This has . . ."

"Don't let this put you off of men, God damnit," Mike said, firmly. "I didn't risk my fucking life to have you go lesbo. All men aren't these filth. And if you decide they are, you're spitting on what *I* did. Because the *good* guys want to get laid, too. Understand?"

"Understand," Ashley said, nervously. "Christ, you sound like my dad."

"Oh, that's *really* what I needed to hear!" Mike said, spinning away. "Five minutes. Minimum!"

"I don't have a watch," Ashley said as he disappeared behind the coffins.

"Plenty of them on the bodies."

CHAPTER
THREE

The keys turned out to be for a dark green Explorer and he pulled out of the park quickly, stopping only long enough to grab his jump bag where he'd left it. He thought about evidence he'd left behind. Probably enough to convict him. Fingerprints on the back of the van, if they dusted that. Yeah, they would; he'd left footprints on the bumper for sure. And not even Athens PD was going to miss those. He'd kept all his magazines, expended and unexpended, but there were sure to be prints somewhere. On the coffin, too, come to think of it. Damnit, he wasn't a natural criminal type. Well, he might as well be hung for a sheep as a lamb; he wanted to find the container vehicle and make sure he'd read the documents right.

To get to Atlanta from there the quickest way was to get on the 10 loop and take it to 316. That led to I-85 and a couple of ways to get to the airport. He'd never been to the cargo side of the airport but he wanted to eyeball the damned thing.

He took the bypass fast, pushing the Explorer up to nearly a hundred and weaving in and out of traffic. He was going so fast that he nearly missed the exit for 316 but caught it just in time, the vehicle swaying perilously as he decelerated for the cloverleaf spiral. He'd decided that if he spotted the vehicle he was going to do *something* to attract police attention. Ever since 9/11 aircraft

had been heavily controlled. But if the aircraft was controlled by the muj, as it probably was, if it got off the ground it was a flying bomb filled with hostages. Better to make sure the truck got stopped before much more could be done to them.

He was headed down 316, fighting the light traffic and, more importantly, the traffic lights, when he passed the turn for Ben Epps Airport. He was concentrated on the road ahead of him but out of the corner of his eye, as he blew through the red light, he caught a glimpse of truck lights up the slope to the airport. A fast head check and he cursed luridly.

"Okay, did the fuckers lay a red herring?" he muttered to himself as he pushed the vehicle up to speed, looking for somewhere to do a U-turn. "Or did I read the damned things wrong?" He was sure the truck he'd seen was the same cargo container. It had the logo and in the brief glance he'd gotten he'd thought he saw the bent part in the door.

There was an opening in the median and he pushed the SUV into a tight turn, cutting off a truck that nearly went into the median with a blast of horn, and heading back to the airport.

There was a sign for cargo, which he hadn't even realized went in and out of Ben Epps, and he followed it. However, as he passed around the end of the runway he could see a guard post. He wanted to call the police, wanted to report what was going on and direct the proper guys to the right place. But he also still hoped he could avoid arrest. He could probably walk, even on torturing the kiddie tango. But "probably" versus twenty years, maybe life, maybe even death . . . that "probably" was looking mighty thin.

He took a Y corner to the right and continued past the guard post, headed for an apparent circuit of the airport. He could see the cargo container and this time he got a clear view of the back and the dent. It had stopped by a jet and was already unloading coffins onto a lift-truck.

"Motherfuckers," Mike muttered. Once that plane got into the air, if anyone tried to catch it, it was going to be bad. Fifty dead girls, by his quick estimate. Maybe 9/11 all over again. Muj weren't supposed to be able to get control of aircraft coming into the U.S. And he'd spend forever and a day trying to find a number

that he could use with a satellite phone. *"Hello, overseas operator? I'm trying to find the emergency number of Athens, Georgia, police department. No, Georgia, not Greece. No, the state in the United States, not the country..."* No.

He was in a portion of the circle road that was partially screened and he cut his lights and pulled to the side using the parking brake. He put the satellite phone in his jump bag and did a quick mental check of the contents. Besides some notebooks, his laptop and the like, it had an eclectic selection of material. Bottle of water, two power bars, toiletry items, a small thermal survival blanket, small flashlight and a change of underwear and T-shirt.

He opened the door, slipping a toothpick into the stud to keep the interior lights from coming on, and dropped out of the vehicle to the ground, closing the door quietly. He knew what he was planning and he didn't like it. But he couldn't contact the police in time to keep the plane from taking off and once it was out of American airspace, tracking it would be problematic. It wouldn't be headed for anywhere in the Americas, that was pretty certain, so it would have to refuel somewhere. And it was likely that anywhere it refueled, it could get its tail number and transponder changed.

It was pointed basically towards him with most of the activity taking place at the back. There were no lights on in the cockpit so the pilots wouldn't be looking in his direction. There was a perimeter fence, but that was no problem. The guards might see him, the tangos might see him. Either would probably keep the plane on the ground, good, but also put him in prison, bad. But if he could figure out where they were going, he could vector in a rescue op.

He paused just a moment to think about that one as he crawled to the fence. He had trained for rescue ops, but never actually done one. However, in his training, he'd never *once* done one clean. No matter what, the hostages always ended up shot to shit. It was one of the team mantras: "It sucks to be a hostage."

But that was probably how it had to go down. If the police reacted right now, the plane could probably force its way off the ground. Police didn't think in terms of "it must not take off."

And even if they blocked it, the pilots were probably aware that it was a potential "martyrdom operation" and they'd slam the plane, somehow, and kill the girls.

Follow, recon, lead in support. If he could call 911 direct, he would. But as it was, there just wasn't time for anything but . . . stupid heroics.

He'd gotten to the fence and cut the lower section with his knife, then wriggled under, pulling his jump bag and the MP-5 behind him. He was in a dark portion of the field; it was dark most of the way to the plane. Slow or fast? There didn't look to be many more coffins to load and the pilots might turn up, and look out or turn on their landing lights, at any time. Fast.

He sprinted across the open area, staying low, willing no one to see him, until he reached the nose-wheel. No shouts of alarm, no change in the regular action of loading. The plane was a 727 and he'd briefly studied it, and other, aircraft with a view to taking them back from hijackers. Again, not a primary mission but one that they trained on occasionally. If he recalled correctly, there was a hatch behind the nose-wheel assembly that led to the cargo compartment. From the cargo compartment, the plane could be accessed through a small tunnel, and another hatch. If the compartment was pressurized. They'd have to pressurize it to ensure the girls lived; the coffins had not been pressure sealed nor did they have air. Okay, get into the cargo compartment and he'd be golden.

He lifted himself up into the nose-wheel assembly and found a ledge to stand on. As he did he heard the engines start to whine.

"No pressure, we're good," Mike muttered. There was the hatch, appropriately marked. There was just one problem. There should have been an operating lever, actually a sort of horseshoe thingy, on the outside. But this hatch was smooth. Either he'd messed up on his recollection or this one was a different design.

"Motherfucker," he muttered. "What now?"

He heard an engine approaching and ducked up into the darkness, looking around wildly. When the nose-gear raised, he was going to be squashed like a bug. Even if he avoided that, the way that planes like this climbed, he'd not only be in an anoxic

condition, without enough oxygen to stay conscious, possibly so little that he'd take brain damage, but it was likely he'd get the bends. Sudden reduction in pressure is sudden reduction in pressure and just as a SCUBA diver can't come up quickly after a certain amount of time because of nitrogen saturated in his tissues, being exposed in a plane in a fast climb can cause the bends. In a HALO jump, the cabin was slowly depressurized. This bird wasn't going to ascend slowly.

There was a ledge that had half of it marked in yellow with the words "Stay Clear" and the rest was just plain metal. With any luck, at all, the plain metal part wouldn't be filled with nose-gear. The truck sound had been a follow-me that hooked up to the nose assembly and turned the plane around.

He lay down on the metal and pulled out his thermal blanket, wrapping it around himself. Then he hooked the MP-5 to the jump bag and put the latter under his head.

"This is a *truly* bad idea," he muttered as the plane started to taxi. He thought about what he could have done. Instead of going into the airport, go to a convenience store and call 911 from a payphone. That might have worked, if they'd reacted quick enough. Too late now. Try the sat phone? They'd just shoot down the plane. Lots of dead girls. He didn't want that on his conscience or the conscience of the pilot that had to take the shot.

He pulled the jump bag around and fumbled out an aspirin tablet and his water. He took the tablet and washed it down and then put everything away as the plane moved into takeoff position. Sometimes aspirin helped reduce the bends. Anything would help. Oh, his poor abused joints; they were *not* going to like this.

"God . . ." he muttered as the engines revved and the plane started to move. "No, St. Michael. St. Michael, patron saint of all warriors of the air and of the sea, we've got a really screwed up situation here. These girls don't deserve what they're in, no matter how bad they've been. And, well, I could use a little help here. I know I'm not the greatest example of your name, but I'm on a pretty good mission and I think that should count for something. St. Michael, patron of paratroopers, protect us all. And *please* don't let me get so bent I can't do my job at the other end!"

The last was shouted over the blast of wind coming through

the open nose assembly and Mike really hoped that he wasn't going to simply be picked up and washed out by it. There wasn't anywhere to hold on, just smooth metal. Suddenly, the nose came up and they were in the air. Then there was a sound of hydraulics and he could see the assembly coming up.

"And please don't let me get squashed like a bug!"

"Holy shit."

Special Agent in Charge Barry Conway had seen his share of murder scenes. The FBI didn't have murder as one of its jurisdictions, but they got called in on special cases. And this case had "special" written all over it.

"What do we have so far?" he asked the detective from Athens PD.

"We've got two witnesses," Detective Sergeant Jason Nix replied with a shrug. "The female victim, Ashley Winters, is being remarkably uncooperative. Her description of the perp keeps shifting around and she's not sure she really saw him shoot anyone, including the torture victim."

"That's because she's protecting him," Conway replied. "Wouldn't you?"

"I'm not particularly happy with the unknown perpetrator," Nix admitted. "I've got ten dead bodies on my hands, one torture victim and two females who had been kidnapped, one of them drugged, the other one beaten and molested. I want to know what his connection is to all of this."

"His connection appears to be that he killed most of the terrorists that were involved." Conway sighed. He liked bank jobs. Tracking down a bank robber was straightforward FBI work. Domestic terrorism, that was okay. You got somebody on the inside, got your intel and rolled them up. Foreign terrorism ops got really complicated really quick. The Patriot Act had helped, at least he wouldn't have to jump through hoops figuring out which particular action was simply illegal, kidnapping for example, and which was terrorism . . . kidnapping for example. The way things used to be structured, it was like he had to have two separate brains that were *not* permitted to link the national security information with the criminal information.

If for no other reason, he was a big fan of the Patriot Act. It also meant he could say . . .

"We've got jurisdiction over the case from here. We've got terrorism and kidnapping with transit, possibly across state lines."

"The girl said the perp said that they were going to Atlanta airport," the detective replied. "It's the one thing she's clear about."

"And did you put out that alert?" Conway said, quietly.

"Not yet," the detective said. "We're waiting for some corroboration."

"Do it," the FBI SAIC said, bluntly. "Do it now. Before the damned plane gets in the air."

"Okay, if you say so," Nix said with a shrug. "But, again, I want to know how this guy knew. I think he was working with them and they had a falling out. That fits the situation better than an unknown superhero rescuing the damsel. That shit doesn't happen."

"There you have a point," Conway admitted.

"This looks more like . . . well," Nix stopped and shrugged. "This looks like a really violent bad drug deal to me. I think he was getting shafted by them, maybe he was their lookout or something, and he decided that he could get away by offing all the witnesses."

"Why keep the torture victim alive?" Conway asked.

"Maybe he didn't know enough to bother?" Nix said, shrugging. "I'm going to go call in the all points on a cargo container heading for the Atlanta airport, possibly carrying hostages. You know how many cargo containers move through Atlanta?"

"I've actually got that number on my computer, somewhere," the SAIC admitted. "It's just part of the background of how lovely my job is since any one of them could be a truck bomb. Call it in; I want to talk to the victim."

"The torture victim?" Nix asked.

"No, the *kidnap* victim, the *victim* victim. The 'torture victim' is a fucking terrorist. Period. So he got shot in the leg. See me crying."

He walked over to where the young lady was sitting in a chair, a frustrated police woman by her side with a notebook open filled with obvious gibberish.

"Hi," Barry said, smiling as pleasantly as he could. "Officer, could you give me a moment alone with the young lady?"

"Not alone," the police woman said with a sniff. "That would be a violation of procedure."

"Then stand across the damned room," Conway said coldly. "Among other things, we have jurisdiction now and your 'procedures' are *my* procedures."

When the woman was gone he perched himself on the desk and shook his head.

"You look, frankly, like you've been through hell."

"Thank you, so much," Ashley responded, pulling the blanket around her more tightly. "I don't know anything about the guy who did the shooting. I didn't get a good look at him. Sort of short, sort of tall, medium build, maybe a little thin. Sort of . . ."

"Spare me," Conway said with a chuckle. "I'm not after him. I could give a rat's ass about dead terrorists, miss. Tell me anything you can about what was going on. We've got missing girls, girls just like you. These days, the FBI tries *really* hard to stop this sort of thing and this time we screwed up. They got through. I want to know where the girls are going, how, anything you can tell me."

"There's probably a piece of paper on the desk," Ashley said cautiously. "That might have information. It was a container thing, a truck. Like they load on ships. But . . . somebody said it was going to Atlanta airport."

"That somebody might have read that off of the paper or he might have heard it after shooting the terrorist in the leg? Or is that too blunt of a question?"

Ashley looked at him for a moment and then shook her head.

"I don't know anything about that. Just that you should be looking at Atlanta airport."

"Ashley, your name is Ashley, right?"

"Yes."

"Ashley, I swear to *God* I'm not looking for whoever shot up these . . . assholes," Conway said, waving around. "But I need hard information. Would you *please* tell me what happened to get the information so I can verify it and check it?"

Ashley lowered her head and shook it, slowly.

"I think I need to talk to a lawyer," she said, softly. "Or the news media."

"Ashley, *please*," Conway said, getting off the desk and dropping to a knee. "I've got a *time* issue, here. The girls are being moved. You say to the Atlanta airport. Fine, we're checking on that. But I need plate numbers, container numbers, a plane number if it's available. I want to make sure we're not missing something. Think about the other girls, please. I won't use the information you give me against whoever saved you, if there was such a person, who might have been a short, tall, thinnish-fat man with a full head of receding hairline."

Ashley looked up at that and faintly smiled, then shrugged.

"Okay, the terrorist said the girls were being transported to an airport," she said, getting up and walking to the desk. "But he didn't know which one."

"You're sure?" Conway asked.

"I'm really, really sure," Ashley replied. "And there's a paper, somewhere, on this desk that said Atlanta airport. It was some sort of form," she said, reaching for the papers.

"Let me," Conway said, holding out his hand. He reached into his suit pocket and pulled out a set of rubber gloves. Then he glanced over the top papers and picked up a cargo manifest.

"Says that they're being sent to the Atlanta airport," he said with a nod. "One problem."

"What?" Ashley asked.

"It's got so much bogus information, I can tell it's a fake a mile off. The weight of the vehicle is wrong, way too high, the container number is the wrong number of digits, the license plate doesn't match the standard parameters. It's a red herring."

"Damn," the girl muttered. "I guess Mr. Wonderful didn't know it all, then, did he?"

"Not that I know who you are talking about," Conway replied. He lifted some more of the scattered paperwork then pulled out the drawers. The top, center, drawer was locked but it opened to a screwdriver. He pulled out the file folder in the drawer and opened it, scanning the paperwork. Then he looked at his watch and grimaced.

"What's wrong?" Ashley asked.

"They left from Ben Epps Airport two hours ago," the agent replied. "Even if we could figure out what airplane, quickly, they're going to be out of radar coverage. And five gets you ten, the listed destination for the plane is going to be bogus."

"What's that mean?" the girl said, worriedly.

"It means they're gone."

"I just love waking up to good news in the morning," President Cliff said, leaning back in his chair and looking around the Situation Room. "What do we know, what don't we know and what do we suspect?"

"We know that fifty females from the Athens, Georgia, area have been kidnapped and transported somewhere," the FBI director answered. "One of the persons who was involved in the operation has admitted to being in a terrorism cell. He says that it's an Al Qaeda cell, but he's very low level and that information would be suspect without other items. One of the dead terrorists is on the terrorism watch list and has ties to Al Qaeda. We suspect the subject females were loaded on a 727 at Athens airport. The 727, tail number R2564F, had a listed destination of Rota, Spain. We know that it is outside our airspace at this time and we do not have a lock on its transponder nor did we have a lock by the time the information came out. The females were transported in coffins. One of the two rescued females had already been loaded in one. She was connected to an IV that had a mild dose of Rufinol in it, enough to keep her sedated for up to twenty hours. We suspect that the plane will not head for Rota but for some other location. We suspect that it may have its tail number changed at that location or the girls may be transloaded. We are tracking down the ownership of the plane as well as the background of the pilots. We have alerted Interpol to look for the plane."

"What about the shooter?" Secretary of State Powers asked. "Do we know where he is or who he is?"

"We have not, yet, identified the shooter," the FBI director admitted. "We're still lifting prints from the scene. The one witness, Ashley Winters, is being notably uncooperative...."

"She's protecting her rescuer," Dr. Minuet Kern, the national security advisor, pointed out.

"Obviously," the FBI director said, dryly.

"I don't blame her," Minnie said. "I'd do the same thing in her position."

"Well, it's not helping the investigation," the FBI director said, bluntly. "We need to find this guy and ask him some questions. Notably, how he was aware of the operation."

"I heard he went through the room like a buzz saw," Donald Brandeis said. The secretary of defense looked as if he'd had a full night's sleep, unlike the FBI director and the President, and he grinned at the image. "Just blew them away like they were cardboard cutouts."

"The shooter appears to be highly trained," the FBI director said. "Possibly a member of a SWAT team or military."

"Ten dead terrorists? All of them armed? One of him?" Brandeis grinned again. "That's not a SWAT team guy, that's SEAL or Delta. Maybe Ranger. There's a Ranger base near there."

"Whoever he is, we'll find him," the FBI director said.

"Just like Eric Rudolf," Brandeis jibed.

"Enough," the President said.

"Sir?" Minuet said. "This person, whoever he is, has killed ten terrorists and broken up a major operation. If they find out who he is, he's a target."

"Good point," the President said, nodding. "This case goes under national security restrictions as of now. No further investigation by local authorities, all investigation at TS Code Word level only. Understood?"

"Understood," the FBI director said. "The news media has already gotten wind of the shooting and that kidnapping was involved. What do we say?"

"Just that," Edward Travali, the chief of staff, said. "There was a shooting involving terrorists who had kidnapped one or more females from the Athens area. Talk to the victims and tell them that it's really important that, for the time being, they not say anything else."

"Don't threaten them with U.S. Code," the President interjected. "Just try to reason with them. If your SAIC can't reason with

them, have him call *me* and *I'll* tell them why they have to be quiet about this. We don't want the name of the shooter coming out."

"And, in a way more important," Minuet pointed out, "we don't need them to know that we're trying to track the shipment. We don't even want them to know we're sure there *is* a shipment."

"And *find* the plane," the President said, definitely. "Find the girls. Where's the CIA director?"

"The acting director is out of town," Minnie pointed out. "His deputy was called but he lives out in Reston; he's still on the way in."

"Well, he's missed the meeting," the President said, glancing at the clock on the wall. "Tell him to find those girls. Call the NSA, the CIA and every other acronym down to the DEA and tell them that their number one priority is to *find* those girls. Don?"

"Mr. President?"

"We all know that they're probably headed for one of about six countries," the President said harshly. "I want plans dusted off for going into any of those six countries, with anything it takes, to get them out alive. Send out some sort of warning order. I want jets warmed up, I want Delta up, I want FAST and the SEALs and Marines and Rangers and everybody down to the *Cub Scouts* ready. Understood?"

"Understood, sir," the defense secretary said. "If it's Iran, Syria or Lebanon . . . well, it's not going to be easy, Mr. President."

"I don't care about easy," the President said, his face hard. "I'm not going to go through one hundred and forty-four days of 'the hostage crisis' on my watch. Understood? We're getting them out or we're taking down the country. We're not going to negotiate. Nobody does this to the United States. I don't care if they're in *China. Nobody* does this to the United States. Not and lives to talk about it. If they're in Iran, we're going to take the mullahs *all* the way out, once and for all. If they're in Syria, Basser Assad is going to be buried in an unmarked grave. If they're in the Hezbollah camps I will *nuke* those camps to the ground to get them released and if one *hair* is harmed on their heads those raghead bastards are going to wish that Allah had never let them be brought into the world. Religion of peace my ass."

CHAPTER
FOUR

Mike woke up once on the trip, when the plane landed, somewhere, to refuel. "Somewhere" as far as Mike could see could
have been anywhere from New Mexico to Afghanistan. There was
a whole strip of the world, where he'd spent a good part of his
professional life, that looked exactly the same. Even the people
all looked the same: dirty, slow and uncaring. He was cold as
hell, hyped out for sure. He'd had hypothermia a couple of times
before and he knew what it felt like. He slid the thermal blanket
back and spent the time trying to warm up before the next flight.
It was daylight and hot so he warmed back up pretty fast. He
had what felt like a touch of frostbite on one ear, so he pulled
his spare T-shirt out of the jump bag and wrapped it around his
head. Then he pulled out his power bars and bottle of water and
ate and drank it all. Better to carry it in the body than in a bag
that might get lost. He'd toss the litter on take-off; in an Islamic
country littering was a way of life; nobody would notice.

With that done, there wasn't much else to do. There was no
sound of the girls being unloaded so the plane was going to
refuel and go on somewhere else. Where that might be he had
no idea. What he would do when they got there . . . he had no
idea. He just hoped it would be at night.

No, there was something he could do. He pulled out the satellite

phone, which looked like one of the old "brick" cell phones, extended the antenna and pressed 0.

"International operator, how may I direct your call?"

"Person to person to the duty officer of the day, Special Operations Command, MacDill Air Force Base, Tampa, Florida, United States of America."

Bingo! We've got a prints match on the Athens shooter. Michael R. Harmon, social 477-98-9023, United States Navy petty officer first class. End of active service is about two years ago. Fifty percent disability pay. That's all I've got from the print run. I can do a standard request for his service record. . . ."

"Pass it up," the agent in charge said. "And forget you ever heard it. This is all TS Code Word level now."

"Petty Officer Michael 'Ghost' Harmon," the briefing officer said.

Colonel Bob Pierson was the Office of the White House liaison officer from Special Operations Command. When the FBI had forwarded the information on the shooter, it had been passed to his desk with a priority to, quietly, find out everything he could about one "Michael Harmon" and prepare a brief. Now he was sweating as, for the first time, he was briefing the full "War Cabinet" on one minor, separated, petty officer. "Two years of college at the University of Georgia in Athens, mediocre to poor grades, quit and joined the Navy with stated intention of becoming a SEAL. Graduated from Basic Underwater Demolition/SEAL school in class 201, was assigned to SEAL Team Three, Charlie Platoon. Operational in Mogadishu, Congo, Sudan. Towards the end of his second enlistment, requested transfer to a training position, which was granted."

"Why?" the secretary of defense asked.

"That's not clear, Mr. Secretary," the colonel answered. "It's not stated anywhere in his records."

"Go on."

"Transferred to the Naval Special Warfare Center, at Coronado, assigned to second phase training. Promoted to First Class Petty Officer while a trainer, after having a real problem with passing the bosun's course."

"Explain that," the President said.

"Yes, Mr. President," Pierson replied, thinking. "SEALs are trained as commandos. But their actual military skill is in something else, in the case of Petty Officer Harmon it's as a bosun, which is the guy who handles ... well, 'real' Navy stuff, how to bring in a small boat to a ship, how to do an underway transfer, how to rig stuff for a storm. Winches and boat driving and paint. It's not SEAL training by any stretch. So the SEALs have to take time off to study up for the tests that they have to pass to get promoted. And since they don't do it as a regular skill, they often have problems."

"Okay," the President said, nodding. "I'm too smart to get into *why* they're doing one skill and listed in another. Go."

"He spent four years in the training school; his evaluations are mostly top of the list. Various advanced schools, good words from his commanders about his training ability and personal skills. Less ... stellar comments about peripherals. If I may?" He picked up one of the sheets of paper and cleared his throat. "Quote: Petty Officer Harmon is an erect petty officer of excellent bearing whose skills as a trainer are beyond reproach. His technical skills in all areas of his primary specialty are of the highest class. He is well liked by peers and respected by his students. Petty Officer Harmon's greatest weakness is perhaps his greatest strength, a blinding determination to do his duty and an inability to choose his battlefields. Petty Officer Harmon needs to work on his interpersonal and leadership skills. End quote. That was from one of his last evaluations as an instructor."

"Can somebody translate that for me?" the President asked plaintively.

"He's a great operator and a great instructor," Brandeis replied. "And it sounds like he can't play military politics worth a damn. The kind of guy that when he sees a brick wall, can only try to shove his head through it instead of going around."

"Colonel?" the President asked. "Agreement?"

"Yes, Mr. President," the colonel said, swallowing. "I'd concur in the secretary's evaluation." He paused for a moment and took a chance. "Even if he wasn't my boss."

There was a brief chuckle from the room and the President nodded. "Keep going."

"He requested transfer back to an operational platoon near the end of his third enlistment," Pierson said. "Anticipating the question, it's hard to get promoted to chief if you're not an LPO, leading petty officer, in an operational unit, and by that time the War on Terror had kicked into high gear. Guys he'd trained would have been coming back from Afghanistan and Iraq telling stories about kicking doors and wasting bad guys. Any SEAL worth the name wanted in on that. He transferred to SEAL Team Five, Alpha Platoon as an LPO. He completed retraining with the team and was evaluated. Again, there was a note about using his chain of command skills. Then, while they were actively deployed, he was relieved from the LPO slot and returned to the States. His subsequent evaluation stated that he had failed to demonstrate leadership skills of a level necessary to be an LPO at this time but that he had potential as a future leader. This, in effect, killed his career. He was transferred back to the local training detachment, but not as an active instructor and subsequently ended his service on terminal leave two years and three months ago. He has drawn fifty percent disability based upon widespread occupational damage, primarily to joints and back, and veteran's educational benefits for attendance at the University of Georgia for the last two years. His grades were not immediately available."

"What happened with the 'leadership skills,'" the defense secretary asked.

"I did as much digging as I had time for, Mr. Secretary," Pierson said. "There was an accidental discharge of a weapon and a wounding of one of the SEALs from the AD. In the report, Harmon stated that he had previously counseled the shooter about weapons safety on entries. From the . . . tone of some of the other statements, notably from the shooter and the chief, I would venture to guess that it was something like the following. Harmon was a trainer for years and he came back to a platoon that had been working together for some time. The shooter had been in the platoon for his entire career. There is no written counseling statement about his weapons control immediately available but having Harmon, some jerk trainer,

tell a guy with lots of operational experience he was doing it all wrong, probably didn't sit well. Especially since Harmon, apparently, has limited tact. When, in fact, the shooter turned out to be wrong, and Harmon right, the team leadership probably had to make the choice between removing the guilty party from the team or Harmon. They chose Harmon."

"Politics," the President said.

"At that level, I'm unwilling to judge, Mr. President," Colonel Pierson replied. "I'm not going to say, from what I've seen, that they were, overall, wrong in their decision from the standpoint of the good of the team and of the military. Sometimes, just being right isn't enough."

"There's that," the defense secretary said. "I've seen it often enough in the Pentagon. A guy who's *right* but such an asshole that nobody wants to listen to him. Sometimes *I* don't but I know the information's important, so I team him up with somebody that's got some political skills. That wouldn't work on a SEAL team. And it doesn't matter to this brief."

"No, sir," Pierson admitted. "Petty Officer Harmon is a qualified instructor in close quarter combat, survival and evasion, clandestine insertion and extraction, unarmed combat, sniping, international small arms, land and underwater demolitions, Combat Diving including open and closed circuit equipment, airborne operations including military free-fall and static line. He is, from his evaluations, considered high level expert in each."

"Well, that explains Athens," the national security advisor said. "Those guys never stood a chance."

"Agreed," the President said. "So where is he? I want to shake his hand."

"We obtained his home of record," the FBI director said. "There was no one home when our agents went there and his personal vehicle was parked nearby. I've authorized a covert entry and search under national security guidelines but I think it's a moot point. There was a vehicle, registered to the cover name of one of the terrorists, discovered at Athens Ben Epps Airport. It had bloodstains on the seat, secondary it appeared, not from a bleeding person, and a magazine from an MP-5 was on the floor. There were prints matching Petty Officer Harmon on the SUV and on

the magazine. It was concealed near the pad where the 727 was loaded. Petty Officer Harmon was not found in the area."

"He's on the plane," the President said. "He got *on* the plane."

" 'Clandestine insertion,' " the defense secretary said, grinning. Then his face cleared. "Can he *survive* on the plane? Won't he get cold? What about air?"

"Mr. Secretary?" Colonel Pierson said, clearing his throat. "I'm trained in HALO: an instructor for that matter. It depends upon how high they went and how fast they climbed. He would be subject to bends from rapid decompression in the climb and anoxia at altitude. Petty Officer Harmon would be aware of both issues and must have been willing to risk it. He may have entered the pressurized cargo bay for that matter. I don't have a design on the aircraft available at this time."

"The surviving terrorist has been cooperative," the FBI director said. "He stated that, besides ammunition, the shooter picked up a satellite phone that had been used by the terrorist commander. I suspect we may be getting a call from him. Hopefully soon."

"Now *that* is a conversation that I want to hear," the President said, smiling faintly.

"Major Roberts, Command Duty Officer, U.S. Special Operations Command, how may I help you, sir?"

Jack Roberts was a Special Forces officer now imprisoned, from his point of view, in durance vile in SOCOM headquarters. He knew that, at this point in his career, doing a staff rotation was a must if he wanted to get any sort of high rank before retirement. But being the "Assistant Deputy Joint Air Delivery Coordinator" was a far cry from running a group of former muj in southern Afghanistan, tracking down remaining Taliban. Which was what he *had* been doing. And enjoying the hell out of it, frankly. Being a tribal warlord was just like having a command, but with less paperwork. He'd considered banking some of his pay and going back when he retired. All he needed was about fifty grand in capital. He figured he could get the U.S. government to pay his band to keep doing what they had been doing for income. But he'd also need his retirement pay

to live a reasonably decent lifestyle and be able to get back to The World from time to time.

So he cooled his heels and took odd calls from international operators.

"Major, this is not a prank call," the man on the phone said. "Can you do a trace on me?"

"Who is this, please?" Roberts replied, tersely. "I don't have time for games, buddy."

"This is one very lost former operator who is sitting in a damned plane in some third world shithole tracking some kidnapped girls. Have you heard any news from Athens, Georgia?"

"Yes," Roberts said, sitting up and waving to the staff duty NCO. Calls were automatically recorded but he made a motion to do a trace.

"I don't have much time. The plane took off from *Athens* airport and is now on the ground. They're refueling somewhere in the desert area. It's day, maybe afternoon local time, I can't get much of a look around. Just . . . fucking desert shit, you know what I mean? You got any experience?"

"Lots, son, who is this?" Roberts said, frowning at the SD NCO who shook his head and shrugged. The trace wasn't locking yet.

"No names, Major," the man said. "I think I'm looking at murder one, okay? And I'm going to try very hard to avoid going to the slammer. So no names. Call me . . ." There was a long pause and then a sigh. "Call me Ghost."

"Ghost," Roberts said, nodding. "Okay, Ghost, what's your situation?"

"I survived the first flight," the man said. "I'm in the nose compartment with the wheel. It's tight and I passed out, but I don't think I'm bent or too loopy." He paused then whispered. "Wait."

Roberts waited, impatiently, hearing faint breathing from the phone, then a sigh.

"Thank God for shitty mechanics," "Ghost" muttered. "They were checking the nose-wheel assembly but didn't bother to get off the ground. Just kicked the tires and wandered off."

"Well, that means you could be anywhere from Morocco to Mongolia, buddy," Roberts said with a chuckle.

"Tell me about it," "Ghost" replied with a faint note of humor. "I'm going to try to track and report. What's your number?"

"813-715-4279," Roberts replied.

"Got it on my arm," "Ghost" said. "They kicked the tires, now they're lighting the fires. I got to go back to my hide."

"Hang in there, buddy," Roberts said. "We've got a warning order on this. The whole fucking world, at least the good part of it, is going to drop on them as soon as we know where you are going."

"Good to hear," "Ghost" said, then snorted. "Go tell the Spartans, right?"

"Yeah, man," Roberts replied, his face set in a hard grin. "Go tell the Spartans. Well, the Spartans know and they're coming, unlike the damned Athenians."

"Please, no French," "Ghost" said. "Out here."

Roberts leaned back and looked at the SD NCO with a raised eyebrow.

"Satellite phone," the E-7 said, shrugging. "Couldn't get a positive lock on position. The satellites it used were generally servicing the western Mediterranean."

"NSA will be warmed up for the next call," Roberts said. "Well, we have contact. The day just got much more interesting."

"Well, you got to listen to the phone call, Mr. President," the defense secretary said, smiling. "What do you think?"

"Spartans?" the President replied. "I know, in general, who they are. But what is that about 'go tell the Spartans?' The colonel seemed to recognize it. Minnie?"

"Two history buffs," Kern said, turning her face away for a moment and taking a breath. "In fifth-century BC, a group of three hundred Spartans were dispatched to the pass in Thermopylae, Greece, to hold off an oncoming Persian army. Thermopylae, by the way, translates as 'The Hot Gates.' They were to briefly delay the Persians until reinforcements from Athens arrived." She paused again and shook her head, looking at the table.

"The Athenians debated," Secretary Powers said, his face hard. "And the forces were never sent."

"What happened to the Spartans?" the President asked.

"They were outnumbered . . ." The secretary of state paused and shrugged. "Well, it depends upon which history paper you believe. But they were outnumbered by between ten at the low end and a thousand at the high end, to one. And . . . they held the pass. For three days. Fighting all day long, every day, in that high, unbearably hot, place. I've been there, I've seen the tablet." He had to pause, too, and shook his head.

"I take it they didn't survive," the President said, looking at the faces.

"They were betrayed by a Greek who led the Persians around the position," Powers said, nodding. "Each day they would rise, polish their armor, comb out their hair and bind it up, and then do battle all day long. For three days. Until they were finally encircled and destroyed."

"It's . . . legend in . . . call it the military circle," Brandeis, the secretary of defense, said, nodding, his eyes bright. "I'm surprised you've never heard of it, Mr. President. The tablet translates in various ways. But I think I like Byron's translation best."

"'Go tell the Spartans, passerby,'" Minuet said, quietly, her head still down, "'that here the three hundred lie, obedient to their commands.' The Athenians never came."

"Well, we will," the President said. "By *God* we will."

CHAPTER
FIVE

The second time he woke up it was much worse. He had degenerative damage in both knees, his right hip, his right elbow and his left shoulder. Which was *why* he was on fifty percent disability. All of those joints, and his back, and his head, were screaming. He knew that pain was weakness leaving the body. He'd been in worse pain in his life. Rarely, but he had. Unfortunately, this pain was crippling enough he couldn't move.

The plane was taxiing through a blacked out airport. That was as much as Mike could tell from his position. He managed to pull his jump bag around and rummage in the medicinal portion. First he pulled out a handful of Pepcid Complete and chewed them up, swallowing them with just about the last of his saliva. Then he took two eight hundred milligram ibuprofen "horse" tablets. He'd taken so much ibuprofen in BUDS that he'd ended up throwing up blood and his stomach was still sensitive to it; the Pepcids were a necessity not a nicety.

When he'd swallowed the pills, he forced his body to move, grimacing against the stabbing pain in his joints. He wasn't sure if he'd been bent or if it was just the joints reacting to the pressure change. That was a "mild" form of the bends he'd have for the rest of his life every time the weather changed. More damage or

simply pain? It didn't really matter, he had a mission to complete and he had to drive the fuck on.

He had a feeling this was the final destination. More than one refueling stop would be problematic for the terrorists. They'd probably refueled in one of the "lawless" regions of Algeria. That would make this somewhere in the near Middle East. He wasn't sure 727s had enough legs to make it from Algeria to, say, Pakistan or Iran. Iran was top on his list of probable spots for the girls to be taken. Not only were the mullahs getting really crazy lately, they'd done the "hostage" game with America before.

The plane coasted to a stop and a follow-me hooked up and turned it around, backing it into position. Mike could hear echoes and realized they were being backed into a hangar. Which would be a pain in the ass to egress. The follow-me stopped, though, before the plane was fully in the hangar. The doors were partially closed and he could hear voices shouting in Arabic. That changed things. Iranians spoke Persian, Farsi, and it was close enough to Dari, which he'd heard a lot, to tell the difference between it and Arabic. Farsi was more . . . liquid. Arabic was a really guttural language like Hebrew with a lot of hawking up loogies involved. These guys were hawking loogies so he probably wasn't in Iran.

He stood up, quietly, and worked his joints, then got down on his knees and took a quick peek, upside down, out of the nose section. Group of guys in blue jumpsuits, like airport workers, unloading the plane from the back, using another one of those lift-trucks. Another cargo truck the coffins were being stacked in. A couple of military-uniformed guards hanging around watching. Two or three civvies watching as well, maybe muj. No guards on the front of the hangar. Why weren't there guards on the front of the hangar?

He looked at his clothes and rubbed his chin. Not enough stubble, clothes not shabby enough, hair too long. For that matter, the clothes were too well made; the reason everybody in the third world wanted American jeans was that Levis were just *better* than anything made overseas. But they didn't "look" right. He couldn't really pass for a local. A T-shirt was not a normal item to wrap around the head. It disappeared into the jump bag. Jump bags weren't normal items, nor were MP-5s. Too frickin' bad.

He took another look, then lowered himself out of the nose assembly and onto the pavement, keeping the nose assembly between him and the work at the rear. The front of the plane was in darkness, probably deliberately to try to keep the Americans from noting it by satellite and wondering.

He shifted his bag to his left and just slowly sauntered towards the doors. Once he was past them, nobody in the group at the rear was going to see him. And, still, no guards in view. Maybe they were trying to act like it was no big deal, unloading a plane in the dark of night with no lights on.

Past the doors he headed for the side of the hangar, MP-5 down. The worst possible thing he could do was kill someone. If the terrorists, and whoever was supporting them, knew the op was blown, they might kill the girls on a whim. Or speed up whatever their plans were. Al Qaeda generally killed their hostages if their demands weren't met quickly. Nick Berg had found that out. The Philippines had caved but he couldn't imagine the American government doing the same. Especially since Al Qaeda would make the demands *high*. And he was pretty sure that they wouldn't simply slit their throats in front of a camera. There were other things they could do to make the experience more uncomfortable for both the girls and the American public.

But they were being transported, again, "somewhere else." He had to find out, somehow, where the truck was going. If he called it in they *might* be able to track it on satellite, but satellites had to be in just the right basket to get a good view. Probably they were retasking all the Keyholes for just that reason, but they still had to be in the right basket.

There was another hangar next to the one where the girls were being unloaded, also unlit and unguarded. He could see guard towers in the distance and a control tower bulking against the sky. He cautiously checked the corner of the hangar, but there wasn't anyone in the dead space between the two, just a slight channel for water run-off and a bunch of litter. Typical.

He moved down the wall of the hangar cautiously. There would be, were from what he had seen, guards on the far end of the hangar. That end of the hangar, north from looking at the stars which were bright in the clear sky, was near the perimeter fence

of the airport. Like most in the gomer zone it looked as if it had
been put up in the 1950s and never repaired: sagging and rusted
chain link with a single strand of concertina tacked on the top
that dangled almost to the ground in places. He slowly moved out
from the wall of the hangar, moving over to the adjacent hangar,
hunting for a glimpse of what was happening at the front. What
he saw, first, was that there was a guarded gate about fifty meters
from the back of the hangar. He squatted down and considered
the view, thinking. The girls were probably going to be driven
out there. The road beyond the gate curved to the left, his direction, then climbed up some low hills towards barely glimpsed
mountains. At least that was how it looked from the darkness
between the hangars.

There were side doors on the hangars and he was just considering backing up and trying one, to get out of sight and call in if
nothing else, when one of the blue-clad workers walked around
the corner and lit up a cigarette. The man was no more than
thirty meters from him and glanced down the narrow alley but
didn't register his squatting figure in the dark. Moving, however,
was out of the question. All Mike could do was squat there,
catching a faint whiff of tobacco smoke and BO, and hope like
hell the guy never spotted him.

One of the guards eventually drifted over and cadged a smoke,
the two of them talking in low tones as they puffed on their vile
local cigarettes. If there had been a roving guard he would have
been done, but the security all seemed to be focused on the rear
of the plane and, probably, the perimeter of the airport. As he was
squatting there in the dark a small truck drove past, just inside the
fence. He guessed that there were more guards out in the other
direction, looking for a reaction. But a small team could infiltrate
this place in a heartbeat and take down the guards by the plane.
Holding the spot would be tough, though, and he considered Panama
and rethought the situation. In Panama, in a similar situation, two
really good shooters had managed to take down most of a SEAL
platoon and had more or less stopped it cold when the SEALs tried
to advance across the runway. Fighting on airports needed a special
assault mindset, given their lack of cover, and such an assault would
probably kill some or all of the girls.

Finally the two gomers left the corner and Mike backed up to the door of the unused hangar. It was locked but the blade of his folding knife sufficed to force the lock and let him in without too much noise. The hangar was dark as pitch and he waited for his eyes to adjust as much as they could. There was some sort of jet, a fighter he thought, in the hangar with various parts pulled off. It looked as if the engine had been yanked. There were a lot of parts strewn around the floor and he moved across the big room carefully. He had to get in a position to cross the open area between the hangars and the perimeter fence. If he could get onto the hills, by the road, he might be able to hitch a ride on the truck as it slowed to climb the first hill. At least he could if he hurried. Still no time to call in. Maybe once he was in position, given time.

He crossed the hangar and found another door on the opposite side. He cautiously opened that one and saw that there was a blank building face on the far side. Not a hangar, maybe a maintenance area or something. No windows on the alley, though. He moved cautiously down the alley and checked the far side. No guards in that area but the open area was a great place to get spotted.

He considered the crossing carefully and really didn't like it. But. The area was built on a slight rise and he could, vaguely, see that there was a dip between the fence and the hills. And it looked as if it was designed for rainwater run-off. The alley was dipped in the middle to catch water, but it would form a pond if there wasn't a way out. And he'd seen some storm-water grates in the alley. *Probably* there was a culvert that led from the alley to the dip.

He backed up and found one of the grates, pulling it up cautiously to avoid too much noise then looked in the hole. Given third world maintenance he really wasn't looking forward to getting in that hole. The culvert was probably going to be at least partially blocked. He might miss the truck and never know it until he got out. But it was a way out of the airport that was less likely to get him caught, and the mission blown, than even a slow creep across the open area. If he had time for a slow creep.

He dropped into the hole and pulled the grate back over, ducking down and looking in the hole. It was black as the inside of

a stomach and it looked as if it was finally time for some light. He pulled the Surefire light out of his jump bag and carefully put the red lens on it, then twisted it on. The culvert was clear as far as he could see so he got down on his belly, rigged up the sub-gun and jump bag to drag behind him and started crawling, knife in one hand and flash in the other.

About the middle of the road he hit his first obstacle, a mess of trash that was too complicated to find even one item that was recognizable. There were a couple of rats rustling in the debris that wanted to contest his right-of-way but he wasn't in any mood for it. He waved them away, bopping one of them on the head with the Surefire and forced his way past the garbage. It was pretty wet and smelled like hell, but he could live with that. The air was pretty close as well, but there were more grates to let in fresh air. As he approached one by the road he flicked off his light and kept it off, using the faint light from the grates to find his way. He didn't want a mysterious red light giving him away.

He moved down the sewer as fast as he could, given the need to remain stealthy. The sub-gun clinked against the metal sides from time to time but that was the only major sound he gave off. And except for that one pile of trash the culvert was remarkably clear. He found the far side easily enough but was balked by the fact that it had galvanized metal bars over the end. He should have considered that. They were pretty old, though, they looked as if they'd been installed when the airfield was built and the galvanization had worn off of most of them leaving them heavily rusted, and after a wrestle that left him sweating one of them finally gave way with a slight ping of breaking metal and a grinding noise.

He slid out the narrow gap, ripping his shirt and cutting his skin on the torn metal, then lay in the dip, checking his surroundings. He was below the view from the guard gate but as soon as he tried to climb the hills he would be in view. He also had to consider that perimeter vehicle. He cautiously lifted his head and got a glimpse of the hangar. The truck was still there, the plane, apparently, still being unloaded. The perimeter vehicle, either the same one or another, was in sight but more than a kilometer off. The guards on the gate were looking out as well, but at the road.

He moved cautiously down the gap, in the direction the perimeter vehicle was coming from, looking for a covered way into the hills. As the perimeter vehicle approached he flattened himself behind some low rocks and thought about being invisible. It apparently worked since the truck rumbled past without alarm. As soon as it had gotten a few hundred yards away, on the other side of the gate, he started crawling again.

Finally he reached a point where a shallow wadi came down out of the hills. He was nearly opposite the airport control building, which had some lighted windows and, presumably, people in the tower. But he figured it was as good as he was going to get. He took the wadi in a combat crouch, moving up it as stealthily as he could. He was getting worried about time, though. He had to find the road into the hills and get a good hide position before the truck pulled out. And it would be nice to find time to call in.

Carefully, cautiously, feeling his way in the dark and still trying to hurry, he made his way into the hills.

"The plane was spotted in southern Algeria by a routine KH-11 flyover," the CIA acting director said, sliding pictures of the plane, being refueled, across the table. "However, when it took off, NSA assets say that its transponder codes had been changed. The new transponder codes were picked up by a Navy destroyer headed towards Italy for refueling. The plane was moving west to east, headed in the general direction of the Levant."

"Levant?" the President said, looking at the picture.

"Lebanon, Damascus, Israel," the national security advisor said. "That coastline area."

"Please not Lebanon," the President said.

"Well, it was headed in that direction," the CIA director pointed out. "That doesn't mean it would land there. Our analysts say that the range of a 727 loaded with only the estimated weight of fifty coffins and girls averaging one hundred and thirty pounds has a range of nearly 2500 miles. That puts it at the edge of range to land in Iran from Algeria. Also, obviously, back areas of Yemen, Sudan, Somalia, what have you, if it turned south and headed down over Libya. The most likely target, however, is either Syria

or Lebanon. We're redirecting what assets we have on the ground to start looking for it in both countries as well as retasking satellite assets to search for it. NSA has not picked up the satellite phone in use, either to us or others."

"So, 'Ghost' is out there, somewhere," the President said, "maybe alive, maybe dead from the second flight. And so are the girls. And we don't know where."

"We will, Mr. President," the CIA director said. "Somebody will give off an electronic emission we can decrypt or track. Just the plane taking off again in the footprint of a ferret satellite and we'll know."

"What's the status of the armed forces?" the President asked.

"All special mission teams have been put on lockdown," the secretary of defense said. "Special Operations Command and CentCom have been informed of the nature of the mission. They're working on a series of possible joint operations. If it's Iran or Syria, or even Lebanon, penetration of air-defense networks is going to make the mission tricky. It's going to be hard, for example, to simply sneak a team into Syria or Iran and bring the girls out. Both have significant armed forces of their own and air defense networks that have holes but not huge ones. We're looking at a series of plans. It all depends on where the plane lands or has landed."

"But they're ready to go?" the President asked.

"As ready as they can be without knowing the target," the secretary said. "The bases in Qatar and Iraq are dialed in and there's everything from SEAL teams to armored divisions ready to respond. I've started a movement of heavy forces towards the borders of both Iran and Syria in the event we need that much support. Bombers are standing by, fighters are standing by, *Marines* are standing by and a Marine Amphibious Unit has been shifted towards the Levant in case we're talking about Lebanon."

"We need to get some sort of statement out," Edward Travali said. "There's a lot of speculation about these kidnappings and a lot of fury. The parents of the girls suspected of being kidnapped are on all the networks. Most of them are from conservative backgrounds. Some of my people who have been looking at the conservative political boards . . . well, you're looking at a

spontaneous war if a planned one doesn't happen. Not to mention this has raised hatred levels back to where they were post-9/11. The liberals aren't reacting the same, of course. They're almost saying it's the girls' fault."

"Typical," the President said, letting out an angry breath. "Okay, we need to know what we can say. The shooter in Athens was . . . ?"

"Not a common citizen," Travali said hastily. "Not just some guy who stumbled on the op and broke it up, although I think that might be what happened. The person has been identified but for reasons of national security and the ongoing kidnapping investigation we cannot reveal his or her—"

"His," Don Brandeis said. "The news media has at least that much."

"His name," Travali said, nodding. "We're not even willing to discuss the person's connection to the United States government except to say that he is a former special operations soldier and he was not a member of any U.S. government program. That is, the U.S. government doesn't pay his salary. We also cannot discuss the investigation except to say that it's ongoing and the full assets of the United States government are focused on getting these girls home safely."

"Secretary Brandeis, given all that we spend on intelligence and defense, don't you have *any* idea where the girls have been taken?"

Brandeis leaned forward, his hands on the podium, and looked at the newswoman who had asked the question.

"Young lady, is English your birth language?" he asked, his brow crinkling in puzzlement.

"Yes," the reporter replied, surprised. It was her first attendance at a Brandeis press briefing. She had been sent because of the "human interest" in the current hostage crisis and wasn't a regular Pentagon reporter. In fact she'd mostly been sent because she looked as if she would have been a target if she was in the wrong place at the wrong time and her network felt that viewers would, therefore, identify with her. She knew something was going wrong, though, by the faint snorts in the room and how

her associate, a regular Pentagon reporter, groaned, then subtly shifted away from her.

"And did you go to *college*?" Brandeis asked very slowly and distinctly, as if talking to a four-year-old.

"Yes," she said, her lips thinning in anger.

"Then perhaps you could *try* to parse out a sentence like: 'We cannot discuss the investigation except to say that it's ongoing and the full assets of the United States government are focused on it.' Do you *remember* me saying those *exact words*, young lady? Or are you just drawing pretty pictures in that notebook in your hand? A brief of my comments was handed out in advance. Maybe you should look it over and get help with the tougher words from Bill there. But for those of you who can neither read nor understand simple English, I'll make it *simpler*. We're not going to discuss the details of the investigation. If *that's* too complicated, we're not going to talk about what we know. We're not going to talk about what we don't know. We're not going to talk about what we may or may not be planning. We're not even going to discuss what we know about the weather, just in case you manage to divine something from that comment, correct or incorrect, and give it to whoever stole these girls. Now, young lady, is that *clear* enough for you or do you have to write it a thousand times on a chalkboard?

"And, by the way, 'given' is the stupidest word a reporter can use. It does not discuss any objective reality of a situation but invariably points to the personal bias of the reporter. And, as we both know, reporters are *supposed* to be unbiased. Fair and balanced and all that. No one ever says: 'Given that the sky is blue.' They say: 'Given that American soldiers eat babies for breakfast.' One is not debatable in rational everyday terms. Sky. Blue. Sometimes gray, but blue if there aren't clouds and it is day. An effect of oxygen in the atmosphere. Scientifically provable. Neither is the second worth everyday debate, it is provably wrong, but it's certainly debated among the press in my experience. So if you're going to continue to attend these briefings, first learn to read, second learn to listen and third, remove the word 'given' from your vocabulary. Otherwise it is 'given' that you will not enjoy yourself. Next question."

CHAPTER
SIX

In the first couple of minutes after he'd secreted himself on the truck, Mike knew it was a bad idea. In five minutes he knew it was a *really* bad idea. After the first hour, he wasn't sure he was going to survive the really bad idea.

The truck with the girls in it was led and followed by open trucks mounting a heavy machine gun in the back. He had made it to the top of the slope just before the convoy of vehicles reached it. No time to call in, no time to do anything but pick a good hide position and wait. The road switchbacked right at the top of the hill and for just a moment the left side of the truck was out of sight of the trailing gun-truck. And it was going slow, no more than five miles per hour, as he darted out of the darkness by the side of the road and crouched under the bed of the truck.

Container trucks, like this one, had a solid metal support running the length of the container bed. In two places there were narrow gaps, and Mike grabbed one and swung his body up into it as the truck changed gears to negotiate the turn and descent.

He started with his arms and legs wrapped around the metal support but as soon as the truck hit the first pothole his chin slammed into the steel. Then he tried just perching on top but the second time he nearly fell off he rearranged. His stomach was being hammered, his chest was being hammered and given

the nature of third world roads it just went on and on. Then the truck got into the flats again and really picked up speed, hurrying down the highway as if there was no tomorrow and slamming over potholes the size of small cars.

The best position Mike could find was with his right hand clutched under the support, his left hand on top, pressing downwards, both legs wrapped around the support and his body flat on it. His balls were being slammed up and down like drumsticks, he was pretty sure he had a crack in his pelvis bone, his chest was being battered, his stomach was being battered but he managed to hold on. He wasn't sure how *long* he could hold on, but he was going to stay there till he passed out or the truck did something *really* stupid. At which point he'd get run over either by the truck or the following gun-vehicle.

Fortunately, before either event occurred, the truck slowed for another guarded gate. It didn't stop, it was clearly expected, but simply slowed to negotiate the gate, then turned into a large complex. Mike could see what looked like barracks and a large building of unknown purpose. The truck pulled up to a loading dock at the building and Mike heard the door opening. Then he saw feet move along the side of the truck, not just the driver but guards as well.

He desperately wanted to get out of this metal hell, but with guards all around that wasn't likely to occur. Instead he pulled his legs and right arm up and perched on top of the metal like a leopard in a tree. It wasn't exactly comfortable, but it was one hell of a lot better than being there in a moving vehicle. And he was at least mostly out of sight. He could see guard feet and legs and that was about all.

After a few minutes, the guards dispersed and he took a chance and lowered his head, looking to both sides. The loading area was about forty meters long and a guard had been stationed at both ends. The right-hand one was back by the loading dock, leaning against the concrete wall and smoking a cigarette. The left-hand one, however, had moved out about ten meters and was standing in what he apparently thought was a military manner. He was carefully watching the darkness beyond the loading dock. Mike briefly considered trying to sneak past him, but if anyone looked

down from the loading dock, likely, or if the guard turned around, also likely, he'd be spotted.

Instead he just hung on in his perch and tried to fight going to sleep. Not counting unconsciousness, he was on a solid thirty-six hours so far and sleep beckoned. He'd done longer times both in BUDS and in training, not to mention on operations, but he was still tired. And sore. And hungry. And thirsty. And cold, the thin air meant that it was damned cold. But he'd put up with all of it before and he slowly put all of it out of his mind and concentrated on maintaining vigilance and waiting for an opportunity to egress his current, lousy, condition and find a better position. With his jump bag and weapon on his back, he couldn't even call in.

The unloading seemed interminable but finally they were done. He expected the truck to pull out as soon as the doors closed but it didn't. Instead, the doors behind him, presumably to some sort of warehouse, closed and the two guards were recalled. He found himself more or less alone in an ill-lit loading dock.

He dropped down to the ground, trying not to groan at all the aches and pains he'd acquired, and looked around. Away from the loading dock was an open area, then a chain-link fence about a hundred meters away. There were guard towers along the fence, spaced about three hundred meters apart. To his left was another open area that had the vague look of a helipad. To his right was an open area but he could see the ends of buildings that paralleled the loading area. There was a faint scent of chemicals in the air, harsh with sulfur. He guessed that it was some sort of petroleum processing plant.

He moved left, ducking into the shadow of the concrete wall, until he got to the end of the building, then looked around the edge. The building was about a hundred meters long, maybe a bit more, with concrete walls. No windows that he could see. There was another large entrance, as if for cargo, down the wall about halfway and what might have been a personnel entrance at the far end. There was another building, purpose indeterminate, that started about halfway down the main building and was separated from it by a ten meter or so gap.

There was no moon and this side of the building was unlit.

But the starlight was bright and anyone coming out of the second building with adjusted night vision would see him.

Nonetheless, he started down the side of the building, crouched, keeping an eye out for hostiles. When he got about fifteen meters down the wall of the building he noticed a grate in the wall of the building. The floor of the building was, obviously, based on the loading dock, elevated. The grate, however, was at ground level. Mike stopped by it and leaned in when he heard faint mechanical sounds. There was air coming out, tinged even more strongly with sulfur, and various sounds, all indeterminate. Suddenly, he heard Arabic from the tunnel, quickly fading. Air shaft.

But it was *below* the level of the building. Which was . . . really odd. Unless there was an underground facility.

Some sort of facility on top as a cover, underground facility underneath. Chemical smell. It was a covert WMD facility, either research or production. And, now, a place to hold the girls.

The grate was fixed in place with large bolts. There was no way he could figure out to pull it off and he was in view of God and everybody here. For that matter, there was a faint tinge of dawn. He had to find someplace to hide, soon. Like a vampire, he needed to be out of sight by dawn.

He moved down the wall of the building, keeping an eye on the grates. Sooner or later, somebody would have to pull a grate for maintenance. And Arab mechanics were notoriously sloppy; they'd be just as likely to prop the grate back up as carefully bolt it back in place. Sure enough, as he reached the shadows of the smaller building, purpose unknown, he found a grate that only had two bolts on it. And they were only hand tight. He quickly unscrewed them and then pulled the grate out, quietly. His hand would fit through the bars so he slid into the narrow tunnel, lifted the grate back into place with only one faint ting of metal and put the screws back on hand tight. Now as long as nobody came along and tightened them down, he was golden.

The tunnel was large enough for him to twist around and point inward and he did so, then crawled deeper into the blackness. This tunnel was more or less silent, not even a sound of fans. He got well into it, then dropped his jump bag and weapon. He

extracted the sat phone and crawled back to the opening, keeping an ear out for movement.

He slid the sat phone forward until the antenna was sticking out of the bars and checked the readout. He had barely any signal but it would have to do. Carefully, he dialed the numbers that were still faintly visible on his forearm and hit send.

"Pierson. That you, Ghost?"

"Yes," Mike said. "Who's this?"

"My name's Bob Pierson. I'm an Army SF colonel in SOCOM. I'm going to be your control for the rest of the mission. You call the number you have; if it's you it automatically transfers to me. What's your status? Where are you?"

"I'm not sure," Mike admitted. "I'm in a base in a middle eastern country. Arabic spoken, not Farsi. There's some sort of large building but it's got facilities underneath it. Big air vents along the walls, down at the bottom of the building, and some chemical smell. I think it's a covert weapons lab. The girls were taken in the top facility. I don't know their current position. I'm in one of the air vents. East side. There's a smaller building on that side and an open area to the south. Fence and guard towers around the whole thing. Maybe three other buildings to the west but I didn't get a good look."

"Wait one," Pierson said. Then: "Right, NSA has a lock on your signal. You're in a facility called Aleppo Four. Suspected WMD site, supposed to be a military logistics base. You've got about a battalion of Syrian Army 'elite' on site, so don't get compromised. One point I want to cover: FBI pulled your prints so we can drop the Ghost between us two. Your ID is being closely held, though. And don't worry about charges: The President personally said he doesn't care about dead ragheads. I was in the briefing when he said it. You are *clear* of that."

"Tell the President 'thank you,'" Mike said, feeling an immense wave of relief.

"That's the good news. The bad news is that we *really* need to know the exact location of the girls. Guard force, the whole works. You need to find them for us and report back. Can do?"

"That's why they call me 'Ghost,'" Mike said, quietly.

"Hoowah. You know the mission. Watch your back. From now on, we'll be eyeballing from the sky but until we know where the girls are, more or less exactly, we can't do a blessed thing. Find out."

"Roger," Mike said.

"How's your physical condition?" Pierson said.

"Got a tad bent on the last flight," Mike admitted. "Joints are in bad shape. Dehydrated as hell, which doesn't help. Hungry. Tired. The usual. I'll survive."

"Okay," Pierson said. "Do what you can. Last item. If you don't report in for twenty-four hours, you will be considered compromised and any mission compromised. If there is a major alert at the base, you will be considered compromised. Don't get compromised."

"I won't," Mike said.

"Call us back when you've got a fix on the girls," Pierson said. "Good luck."

"Will do, out here," Mike replied, killing the call. He crawled back to his jump bag and stowed the phone, then considered his position. He really needed water. And he didn't want to go to sleep in this tunnel, where any sound he made might get carried who knew where.

The tunnel continued for about another five meters, then curved ninety degrees downward. Leaving his jump bag and weapon, he scooted forward and looked down. The tunnel continued, with the same width, beyond sight in the faint but growing light from the opening. He fished out his Surefire and checked it again. About ten meters down there was an unmoving fan. From the dust on it, it was nonfunctional and probably hadn't been worked on in some time. There were only two blades and more than enough room to work past. Furthermore, the width of the tunnel meant that he could "chimney" up and down, pressing his hands and feet against the walls to lower and raise himself. He still didn't hear anything from below, no mechanical sounds, no voices.

He went back and got his jump bag and weapon, then lowered himself down the chimney, his running shoes squeaking faintly on the smooth concrete walls. The construction was too good to be local and when he got to the fan and examined it he found

German names on it. Good old Germans, makers of fine underground lairs for dictators everywhere. It made you nostalgic for
the good old days when they were just Nazis and they only made
them for their own dictators.

He left his bag and weapon on the fan and shimmied past the
stuck blades, then lowered himself further into the gloom. He cut
his light as he descended in case it got spotted. But there still
wasn't any sound from below. Finally, he hit another ninety-degree
turn and crawled forward in stygian blackness until his questing
hand hit another grate. This one was lighter than the top-side
ones and slid out at pressure from his hands. He caught it before
it could drop and slid out of the airshaft onto a concrete floor.

He turned on his light and flashed it around. Plain concrete
corridor with some doors. Nobody in sight. No lights. Ran about
thirty meters to a large metal door on the south end. Concrete
wall on the north end.

He put the grate back on and went to the door at the south.
There was faint light coming from under it and he could hear
sounds, machinery in the distance, more of a rumble through his
feet than anything, and a sudden blat of a PA system announcing
something. Going out the door was clearly not an option.

He moved down the corridor, to one of the side doors on the
left and tried it. It was unlocked and he cautiously opened it.
Broom closet. With a sink. He considered that for a moment and
then tried the tap. The water ran brown at first but then cleared
up and he drank deeply, then washed his hands and face. The
water was probably lousy with pests and he knew he was court-
ing Montezuma's Revenge, but he had to have water and he had
drugs to counteract the trots. When he was done, he drank some
more then left. The door opposite on the right led to an empty
room, maybe some sort of unused office. The next one down on
the left was locked with a padlock and hasp. The opposite door
was another empty office. The last one on the left was unlocked
and had a variety of crates and cardboard boxes stacked in it as
well as a couple of toolboxes. He opened one of the toolboxes and
was happy as hell to find a big damned adjusting wrench. Getting
in the other grates just got easier. There was also a crowbar and
he started putting that to work on the crates.

Military uniforms, some of them gaudily ornate. Why in the *world* would anyone have a purple camouflage field uniform? One of the bottom crates turned out to be full of old Russian chemical uniforms, the horrible rubber kind. There was also a box of old gas masks. Both were an ominous sight, but the gas mask filters, at least, were sealed and might still be useable. There were some boxes of just junk from offices, pens that didn't work anymore, paper covered in Arabic writing. Forms. There was a box of railroad flares, though. His penlight was going to run out of light sooner or later; the flares might come in handy.

He gathered a few things he thought might be useful, including the whole box of railroad flares, and put them in a corner, then went out to the airshaft and retrieved his bag and weapon. He pulled stuff out of his bag, thoughtfully. He didn't need the laptop, that's for sure. It was just extra weight. He put that in one of the cardboard boxes. Most of the rest of the stuff he kept and he added some of the railroad flares.

When he was done sorting he took the crowbar and went to the locked room. What he wanted to do was open the lock, or pull the hasp, in such a way as it could be made to look as if it was still functional. He inserted the crowbar in the lock and pulled down, hard. The lock was apparently pretty flimsy and it popped open at the first pull without much sound.

When he opened the door, though, he had to whistle.

"Oh, baby," he muttered, looking around the room: it was an ammo bunker.

He could see boxes he recognized as holding 7.62x39, the common "AK" round. Lots of those. He hunted around and quickly found a case of a thousand rounds of 9mm. Standard 9mm was not as quiet as the subsonic rounds in the MP-5, but it was ammo. He took four hundred rounds out and stuffed them in his bag then kept hunting. There were cases of frag grenades and he took one. One was usually more than enough with frags. But towards the back he hit real pay dirt: cases of Czech Semtek plastic explosive and, in a clear safety violation that made his skin crawl, a case of Skoda detonators stacked on top.

Skoda weren't as good as NONEL, but beggars couldn't be choosers. He pulled open a case of Semtek and stuffed his bag with

about ten kilos of one of the best and most stable high explosives on earth, then carefully pulled out a handful of detonators in protective sleeves and, in another safety violation that made his skin, not to mention balls, crawl, put them in his pocket.

He knew that the mission was just to find the girls. But . . . having the capability to really blow the shit out of the place, not to mention plenty of ammo, finally, just made him happy-happy. At the last minute, he grabbed a few more blocks of Semtek, just to be sure. There was never such a thing as "too much demo" in his opinion.

He carefully covered up his pilfering and reset the lock so it looked as if it was locked, then moved back to his hide. Once there he thought about what he could do next. He hadn't gotten much of a look at the local workers, but his stubble was getting to proper Mideastern lengths and if he could just find some material he could tie a keffieh to cover his hair. Pants were still wrong.

One of the crates of uniforms, however, had been filled with khaki uniforms and he pulled that one back open and sorted through them until he found a pair of pants that were too big. That was better than too small so he pulled it out and rubbed it around on the dust of the floor. A little crawling would get it properly dirty so he'd look like a local. He put that on, using some string from one of the boxes of office supplies as a belt. He needed some cheap plastic shoes so he could stuff his feet in them and push the heel down like slippers. And a ratty polo shirt. *Then* he'd look like a local, he was pretty sure.

He was wearing a black T-shirt, unadorned, and that was sort of good and bad. Black was pretty common among muj but not among the workers, at least in T-shirts, and it showed his build. But. One of the khaki blouses worked to cover his build. He cut the bottom of the pants while he was at it and frayed the ends then worked some holes into it and frayed those. Now he looked like either a nineties teenager or an oppressed local worker. He hoped. All except his shoes, which were just too good. And his hair, which was too short and cut wrong.

He knew he had to leave the hide, but not yet. It would be daylight up top and no way to move around. Getting out the door to the corridor was problematic as well. So he had to wait and

he might as well use the time wisely. Sleep beckoned, but there were more things he could do. He lit one of the railroad flares, turned off his penlight and got to work.

He took out the Semtek and rolled it out on the ground into sheets about a half an inch thick using one of the railroad flares. Then he pulled out some more uniforms and cut them up for the cloth. Using the sewing kit from his bag, he sewed a sort of harness that would go over his shoulders and around his middle and then stuffed the rolled-out Semtek, with paper separating the sheets, into a sort of bag in the harness. This gave him about ten kilos of high explosive strapped to his stomach. It made him look fat but with some prodding and pressing to get it in place, it didn't really show otherwise. The detonators were then broken up and strapped to his calves with rigger tape. He always carried a small, half used, roll in his bag. Rigger tape had thousands of uses. Now all he needed was an appropriate target and some electrical current.

He refilled his empty magazines with regular 9mm and secured all of them, and the MP-5, under the khaki jacket along with a few of the flares. He had to break the 5 down for it not to really show, but he could work with that given the situation.

He went to the broom closet again and filled his bottle with water, then drank and drank and drank. Before he filled himself up totally he took some more Pepcid and ibuprofen along with three Imodium AD. Three Imodium would stop up an elephant, but he figured he was going to have worse problems than constipation and the *opposite* would be a nightmare.

No food but you could go a lot longer with no food than with no water. He needed to carry more with him, but there weren't any really good containers.

He took one more drink, then went back to his hide and gathered up all his gear. He was as set as he could imagine, given the situation. He carried the railroad flare back to the air shaft, opened the grate, crawled in, closed the grate and moved back to the vertical bend. Once there he set all his stuff in place, set the alarm on his watch for nine hours, put out the flare and lay back to consider the situation. He was reasonably secure, watered up, ammoed up and couldn't do anything until after dark. And

only maybe then. Tonight he'd find the girls and hope like hell that wasn't too late.

He'd had a busy two days and sleep hit him before he realized it was sneaking up.

CHAPTER
SEVEN

When Amy Townsend woke up, all she knew was that she didn't like the situation at all. She was seated on some sort of metal chair, there were bars across her thighs and butt, which she could tell were naked, rather than a solid bottom. It was a pretty uncomfortable seat but that wasn't the worst of the situation. There were metal restraints on her wrists and ankles. The room was echoey, like it had rock or concrete walls, and girls were crying. It also stank, shit and piss and a smell she could only define as "fear."

Amy was a twenty-year-old student at UGA from Bainbridge, Georgia, working on her nursing degree and letting ROTC pay for it. She was pretty in a square-jawed way with brown hair and pretty green eyes, but many of her friends considered her to be a bit "butch." She wore her hair fairly short, above the shoulders, and between being in shape from weight lifting instead of aerobics or cheerleading and her standard rolling walk which was anything but feminine, she tended to have a hard time finding guys that could look at her as a female rather than "just another one of the guys." This despite a rather large chest.

She kept her eyes shut, head down, and moved her ankles slightly. She could move them side to side pretty freely but only forward or back about four inches. When she moved her right

foot forward, something pulled on her left. And she felt a yank that wasn't from her after a moment.

She opened her eyes and looked down. She was fully naked and her ankles and wrists had metal bands on them. The bands each had a ring welded to them, shutting them closed. They weren't coming off short of a hacksaw. There was a chain, one for the feet, one for the wrists, that ran through metal rings on the seats, which turned out to be more of a long bench, then to the rings on the restraints. She looked to either side and saw she was part of a line of five girls, all similarly restrained. Some of them still appeared to be asleep or unconscious. There was a gap to her left, then another line of five girls. There was another line of girls in front of her as well and the girl directly in front of her was awake, crying, and had apparently relieved herself on the floor, explaining at least part of the smell.

She thought back, her brain getting more and more coherent as whatever drug had been used on her leached away. She remembered being royally pissed that she had been surprised. She usually had good situational awareness but the van had just come out of nowhere when she was crossing a student parking lot, headed home from a late class. She'd gotten one solid kick in when they got her in the van, struggling and screaming as loud as she could, then two men had gotten restraints on her and started stripping her. She'd refused to give in to hopelessness or despair, even when they took her to the warehouse and she saw the other girls and realized that the men were terrorists rather than just your generic serial rapists. She'd seen a couple of the girls stripped, loaded in what looked like coffins and then somebody had stuck a needle in her deltoid and that was the last she remembered.

"We are so totally screwed," the girl next to her whispered, fearfully. "We are so screwed."

"We're not screwed, they are," Amy said, quietly but definitely, keeping her head down. "I don't care where on earth we are, there are very violent guys who are gearing up right now to come rescue us."

"In your dreams," the girl said, bitterly. "Cliff won't care, he only cares about the oil."

"Oh, we *so* don't want to be having this conversation," Amy said. "I'll bet you a dollar, most of us get out of here. Alive. But you can give up if you want. Feel free. In the meantime, I'm Amy."

"Britney," the girl said. She was a short, fine-boned blonde with small breasts and a refined face that was twisted in fear. "God, I'm scared," she whispered, gritting her teeth. "You know what they're going to do to us, right?"

"Yeah," Amy said, slowly lifting her head. There was a single door at the far right end of the room. Two soldiers in *purple* camouflage guarding it. Who in the hell used *purple* camouflage? At the end of the room, in the center, was a dais and on the dais was the sort of table she'd only ever seen in nightmares. Metal, like a surgical table, with restraints on it. On the left was a camera, a regular TV news type camera, and lights. In the center of the end wall, directly behind the dais, was a large mirror that was obviously one-way glass. "This is truly going to suck."

"How can you be so . . ." Britney stopped and shook her head.

"Because unlike you, I trust the 'rough men' that Orwell talked about."

"What?" Britney said, confused.

"'People sleep soundly in their beds because rough men wait to do violence to those who would harm them,'" Amy replied, quietly. "Like I said, they *will* come for us."

"They didn't come for any of the other hostages in Iraq," Britney said, bitterly. "And how are they going to find us?"

"They will," Amy said. "If you can't hold tight to that thought, you're just going to break long before you make it to the table. And if you do, don't go crying on my shoulder."

"Start packing," Senior Chief Adams said, walking into the room where Charlie Platoon was getting ready for the evening's snatch mission. "We're locked down." Adams was the platoon's senior enlisted man, and usually passed the immediate "word" while the officers dealt with the rest of the "head shed."

"What the hell?" PO2 "Spooky" Vahn said, looking up. Vahn was a short little Vietnamese sniper that the rest of the team thought proved the truth that fighting the Vietnamese was a losing proposition. "What about the mission?"

"Scrubbed," the chief replied. "We're packing and taking a transport to Qatar. Everybody is scrambling in every direction."

"The girls," PO Third Sherman said, high-fiving his buddy PO Third Roman. "We're going to go rescue us some pussy from durance vile. If *that* don't get us laid, nothing will!"

"Navy SEALs," Roman shouted. "We're here to get you off! Errr . . . out!" They high-fived again as the new meats looked at them in amazement.

"Whatever," the chief said, shaking his head. "All I know is we need to be packed in one hour. So get with it."

"We're fully dialed in," the secretary of defense said. "We've got aerospace deconfliction and penetration planning going on, but it's not going to be easy."

"Don, if I've told you once . . ." the President said.

"We've got planning started on penetrating and taking their airspace, Mr. President," the secretary of defense said, smiling faintly.

"Now why couldn't you just say that?" the President asked, sighing. "I mean, we both *trained* in it, right? So why can't we just *call* it that? Never mind. Go on."

"Aleppo Four is right behind a major air-defense network that extends to Damascus. The airbase that the plane landed at is a fighter base. We're probably going to see air-to-air combat. And until we get that suppressed, we can't send in any sort of conventional force. Even if the helicopters or transports get through holes in the SAM belt, they'll still be cold meat to fighters."

"And as soon as we attack, Syria will know what we're going for," Secretary Powers said. "And if we cannot, in fact, prove that the girls are there, or if they are moved and Petty Officer Harmon doesn't detect that and we strike an empty base, the international and political repercussions are going to be enormous."

"We have them definitely tracked to Aleppo Four," the national security advisor pointed out. "The usual suspects will scream bloody murder. Other than that, I don't see the repercussions."

"It will seriously undermine the coalition if we cannot *prove* they were there," Powers said with relentless logic. "We need every bit of help we can get."

"Can we take down Syria?" President Cliff asked. "I mean, all the way down? Full regime change as in Iraq?"

"That would be . . . extremely hard," Brandeis said. "We don't have the forces to hold down both Syria and Iraq. We could probably ravage their army, but taking the cities and holding them would be problematic. We may send heavy forces in to support Operation Immediate Freedom, but I'd suggest a withdrawal immediately after the operation."

"That leaves us at Iraq, 1991," Cliff pointed out. "Which is one of the reasons my father lost his office. If we take territory, we hold it. If it's just a raid, fine. But if we take territory with heavy forces, we hold it and call for a regime change in Damascus. And then scrape up everything we can find to finish the job."

"Syria not only controls its own territory, but the Bekaa Valley and, effectively, Lebanon," Secretary Powers pointed out. "Even if we could take Aleppo and Damascus, we've discussed the problems with taking the Bekaa Valley and Lebanon. We simply don't have the troops."

"Then try to keep it to a very large-scale raid," the President said. "If we have to send in an armored division, we have to. But try to avoid it. I don't want to take ground and then give it back. That makes us look as if we lost. To the American people, and to the world. Don't give the RIFs an inch. And leave behind nothing but ruins. I want that whole facility trashed before we're gone. Smoking craters."

"That we can arrange," Secretary Brandeis said. "Once the air defenses are trashed, we'll fly C-17s over and drop MOABs on the whole thing. When they're in ground contact mode, they leave really nice craters."

"I wish I knew what was happening to the girls," the President said thoughtfully.

"I think we'll find out," Minuet replied. "And we won't like it."

Most of the girls had woken up when the first change occurred. Two men in regular camouflage pants and black T-shirts, with masks on their faces, carrying AK-47 variants, came in and relieved the more gaudy guards. They were followed by a couple

of unarmed men in similar garb who went to the video equipment and started setting up. They hooked into cables that went to the walls; power and a video feed as far as Amy could see from her position.

Last a group of soldiers, unarmed, with masks on their faces came in followed by two masked civilians and an unmasked man in a suit. He stepped up onto the dais and looked around the room, hands clasped in front of him and smiling.

"Good evening, ladies. My name is Hamid Halal and I'll be your host for what you're about to endure. Let me cover a few things before we get started. Some of you are, I'm sure, positive that you're going to be rescued. You're not. Not only does the United States government have *no* idea where you're being held, but even if they found out, this facility is guarded by over a battalion, that's six hundred, of the most elite commandos. Not to mention a large group of mujahideen such as these gentlemen," he added, gesturing to the guards by the door. "Furthermore, it is surrounded by heavy air defenses that will shoot down any approaching helicopters or such. And this country that you are in has an effective air force which is more than a match for the American Air Force. Last but not least, if they *do* try to rescue you, my friends here," he gestured at the guards, "will be more than happy to kill every one of you. And so will I. I will be *more* than happy to put a bullet through each of your heads." He looked around at the renewed crying and smiled, happily.

"Yes, please, cry. I like it. Soon you will find out just how *much* I like it," he added as the two men who had accompanied him opened up their bags and pulled out rubber aprons. "These gentlemen over here," he added, gesturing at the soldiers, "are from the elite commandos that guard this facility. There are, as I mentioned, six hundred of them. That works out to twelve apiece for each of you." He looked around and grinned, staring at crying faces, his smile getting wider and wider. "Oh, this is lovely. Such a sight. Please," he said, turning to the video technicians, "make sure you occasionally get a shot of the audience. They are such a wonderful sight. And," he added, turning back to the girls, "you'll, of course, get a clear view of the proceedings. At first those of you in the back may have trouble watching, but as time goes by,

you'll have a better view. We intend to take about two hours with each of you. That is one hundred hours or so. In one hundred hours, your ground forces defeated Saddam Hussein's forces in 1991. They called it the 'one hundred hour war.' This is our one hundred hour war. In one hundred hours, we intend to defeat the United States. For all time. We will break your country on its weakness," he finished, his eyes finally going cold as he looked at the front row of girls, each of whom was staring at him like a mouse in front of a snake. "I think," he said, slowly, looking back and forth at the row and then finally pointing to the girl on the left edge of the middle aisle, a short girl with light brown hair and shapely breasts. "I think we'll start with you."

"Noooo!" she screamed as the two men in aprons came forward along with a couple of the waiting soldiers. One of the aproned men pulled out a key and undid the lock for her hands while the other slid out the chain. The two soldiers grabbed her by the wrists and held her as her feet were undone, then she was lifted up, screaming, and dragged to the table. The soldiers secured her in place while the aproned men locked the chain back down. At no time had they lost control of the chain so that the other girls could snatch it away.

The camera was brought around so that it could focus in on her face and Hamid came around to her, holding out a microphone.

"What is your name, miss?" he asked in an interested tone, very much like a television interviewer.

"Clarissa," the girl said, her eyes screwed shut and face in a mask of terror. "Please don't do this to me," she sobbed. "Please!"

"Clarissa what?" Hamid asked.

"McCutcheon. Oh, God, you don't need to do this. Please!"

"And where are you from, Clarissa?"

Clarissa just shook her head, too panicked to answer.

Hamid looked nonplussed for a moment, then nodded at one of the men in aprons who reached under the table and came up with a pair of jumper cables. When the first one touched her Clarissa looked up with a muttered: "What's that?" then screamed and arched when the second touched her skin. She slumped back as the cable was withdrawn, sobbing.

"And you're from . . ."

"SNELLVILLE!" the girl screamed. "I'm from Snellville!"

"Well, Clarissa from Snellville," Hamid said, backing away from her and looking at the camera. "This is the last two hours of your life. We'll be capturing all of it in living color, and sound. Oh, most definitely sound. Bring over the boom mike, focus in on this lovely young example of American womanhood," he added, gesturing the camera to the side and then waving at the soldiers who reached for their belts with grins. "And let the fun begin."

Mike jerked up at the sound of helicopters and banged his head on the low ceiling.

"Fuck," he muttered, holding his forehead and scooching around in the tunnel. "Shit." He quickly slid into the chimney and shimmied up, interested to see who was coming in by helicopter. There hadn't been any explosions so it probably wasn't good guys.

By the time he made it to the opening, all he could see was a line of guards. But there was a tall figure descending from the now stopped helicopter and he was trying to place the face when he heard the crunching of footsteps approaching. He ducked back into the tunnel, quietly, and watched as two set of camouflage covered legs walked past. The butt of an AK was just visible with one of the men. So now there was a roving guard to contend with.

As he was beginning to draw back into the tunnel, a man came out of the side building and hurried towards the front of the main building. He was heavyset, somewhat fat looking, with brown hair like Mike's, wearing a white lab coat. But what caught Mike's attention was the gas mask on his hip and the fact that he didn't look like a local. If Mike ran into him on a city street, he'd have pegged him as a Serb or a Russian. He had that sallow complexion that the Russian men got from too much borscht and vodka. And he didn't move like a local. Middle Eastern men strolled, even when they were strolling fast. They walked with weight centered although sometimes with their head down, putting their legs out in front of them, almost a sashay but not as graceful. Europeans tended to walk with weight forward, legs and arms pumping, always looking up, as if to push through resistance. Arabs didn't swing their arms and kept close personal

space to the point of holding hands in public. Europeans tended to spread out more and it was one reason they tended to find Arabs and other Middle Easterners odd and uncomfortable. Middle Easterners would get right inside of what Europeans, and especially Americans, considered to be "personal space" and always appeared a bit effeminate. To American males, it always appeared as if Arab males were coming on to them.

Mike wasn't too sure what that said about the respective cultures, but that guy definitely was not local. And with the perimeter guards and all the activity, there was no way he could call in until the sun went down, which should be soon given the shadows.

He slid back down to the bottom of the air shaft and tried to be patient. But who knew what was happening to the girls. Nothing good, he was sure. He looked at his watch, willing the sun to go down, and worked some mental exercises. As he was doing that he heard noise from topside and chimneyed up to investigate.

A group of soldiers were carrying something towards a truck, with other soldiers gathering around for a look. As the group spread to lift the object into the truck, Mike got a flash of a limp white arm, a blood-covered torso and light brown hair. Then the body was lifted into the truck and it drove away.

"Oh, those motherfuckers," he said through gritted teeth. "I am going to *so* fuck them up." He didn't know how long they had worked on that poor girl, while he had been *sleeping*! But he knew he was on short time now. But they had to be ready to kill the girls at a moment's notice. And with all the guards and everything else around, whatever happened was going to need something to help it out, a distraction at least. But whatever it was, it had to happen *fast*.

He slid down to his hide again, gathered up his gear, slid on his "harness" and secreted everything he could around his body. Then he moved back up to the entrance and waited, wrench in hand. He timed the guards and they came around on a thirty-minute or so schedule. By the time they came around the next time, it was dark and he waited until their footsteps had dwindled, then undid the bolts and slipped out of the hole.

He nearly died of fright when he realized the large side entrance

now had sentries on it. He was in shadow but they had to be blind not to notice him. He stayed nonchalant, though, casually replacing the grate and using the wrench to apparently bolt it tight, then moving down the line of grates. He passed around the back of the building, aware that at any moment the perimeter guards might appear, until he hit one of the vents that had a smell of sulfur to it. Then he quickly undid the four bolts holding on the grate and slid into the darkness, pulling the grate shut and attaching only a single bolt. As his hand slid into the darkness of the air shaft he could hear the guards approaching.

As soon as he was sure they were clear he slid into the shaft and looked down the drop. This one had a functional fan and he considered how to handle that. However, the power leads were pretty plain, and on top. So he slid down and planted his feet above the spinning blades then carefully undid the power leads with his Leatherman tool. One of them sparked and shocked him as he was undoing it, but it was only a brief jolt and he even managed to hold onto the tool. He moved the leads to the wall, then put his foot on the blades to stop them spinning as quietly as possible.

He slid down the shaft, quietly, watching every move, then shimmied to the grate at the entrance. This one had a filter on it so he couldn't see through. But he also didn't hear anything from the other side. He lifted the filter out on his side then pushed out the grate and lowered it. The room on the far side appeared to be some sort of locker room. He slid out into the room, put the filter and grate back on and looked around.

He knew he was on borrowed time, that the girls were on borrowed time, but getting caught was still going to screw things up. Speaking of which, the time Pierson gave him was almost up; he should have called in. Too fucking bad: he was busy. Speaking of which, there was a telephone on the wall. He couldn't read Arabic, but he knew the numbers and it had an extension number on it. He picked it up and got a standard dial tone. Hmmm . . .

He checked the lockers, which were unlocked, and found a bunch of laundry that *really* needed washing. On the other hand, there were some shirts that made more sense, locally, than his black T-shirt and he found a perfect pair of shoes and a keffieh

rag. In a few moments, he was the perfect image of a modern major raghead. And what the hell, he had a wrench; a wrench was nearly as good as a clipboard. He balanced the wrench in his right hand, put on an expression of hopeless fatalism, and shuffled to the door.

The corridor beyond, as far as he could tell, headed out. But he didn't look around because there were guards at the far end. There was a double set of doors, obviously in frequent use from the dirt, almost across from the locker room. He stepped into them and looked around. Ahah. Even better. The room was filled with chemical suits and respirators. He quickly shucked his clothes and pulled on a chemical suit and mask, then picked the wrench back up and stepped through the far door.

He had never been in a chemical plant but this one looked pretty much as he'd envisioned. There was lots of piping on the ceiling and big tanks. There were some people crawling on the tanks and he kept an eye on them as he worked his way along one wall. Suddenly, he heard English and stopped to check a dial.

"Can you people not understand the words 'quality control'?" a man shouted in a thick eastern European accent. Mike ducked his head around the tank he was using for cover and saw his friend from before waving his arms at two other figures in suits. "The temperature has to be kept to *precisely* one hundred and fifteen degrees Celsius! Not one hundred. Not one fifty! One hundred and fifteen! The entire batch is *ruined*! Now we have only the original test batch to show! Am *I* to explain this to your president? He is depending on this to stop the Americans and you have put us back by *six months*."

Interesting, but not really getting him anywhere. Mike kept moving along the wall, trying to look like a worker who was trying not to work, and headed for the back of the facility. He'd noticed that most of the markings were in French, those wonderful people. Where the Germans just built the bunkers, the French built the chemical plants. And here they were, both of the finest lights of Europe, perfectly represented. The point, though, was that he could quite often decipher what was in the tanks. And when he came to one that was marked, quite clearly, H_2SO_4, he knew he'd hit pay dirt.

A pipe ran out of the bottom of the very large tank to a pump, then went across the high room. Mike followed the pipe, keeping behind tanks, until he found where it started to split up. He went around to the rear of the room and cautiously removed his chemical suit, hoping like hell that whatever mix they made in this place wasn't filling the air, then pulled out a bunch of the Semtek and some detonators. There was a phone conveniently situated near where the pipes branched and, after putting his suit back on, he spent a short time partially disassembling it, then finding some wire in a maintenance area. From time to time he'd look at a gauge or wave his wrench at a pipe, and twice people passed him but paid little or no attention to what he was doing. Finally, he found a ladder and climbed up to the branching, trailing wire behind him. He rigged the Semtek, most of this bunch, at the branch, then ran the wires from the detonator down behind some pipes to the phone. He also ran a wire across to the tank and fitted just about the last of the Semtek behind it.

When all the material was in place he carefully attached the last wire, wincing as he always did. But there was no immediate explosion. Now, as long as the phone didn't ring, the material wouldn't detonate. And he definitely wanted to be out of the room before it did.

Demo in place, he casually strolled towards the entrance, wrench in hand. As he was disrobing, the foreigner came into the room, carrying a sample case. He got undressed—his clothing clearly wasn't in the room—and more or less followed Mike into the locker room, muttering in what Mike took to be Russian.

The doctor went to one of the lockers, setting the sample case on the bench, and took out his clothes. As he was preparing to put his pants on, Mike swung the wrench into the back of his head.

It was a spur-of-the-moment decision but one that Mike didn't regret. Win or lose, he'd taken the primary intelligence out of the WMD effort. And the doctor clearly had more access than a worker. He might even be able to find the girls. Or be told where they were.

Mike stripped out of his clothes and donned the doctor's, stuffing the body in the locker. Then he looked in the sample case.

There were two things that looked like smoke grenades. One was labeled "Sarin" and the other "VX." There was a larger canister labeled "Sarin Area Weapon" and a can of what looked like wasp spray labeled "Mustard." Mike put that together with "test batch" and realized that he was, probably, holding live agents in his hands. That caused him to put the material back in the sample case and close it rapidly.

He picked up the doctor's glasses and looked in the mirror, trying for the proper expression of distracted and pissed off. The glasses made things a bit fuzzy but he could see well enough and he was pretty sure he'd gotten it right. The Herr Mad Scientist also had a pair of rubber gloves. Those went in the sample case. The last thing he did was pick up the belt with the gas mask and put it on.

He paused in thought, then shrugged, opening up the sample case and lifting out the rack with the samples in it. He still had about a kilo of Semtek left and he molded it into the bottom of the case. The nice thing about plastique was that it looked like plastic. Only a close examination would reveal it. He slid the detonators into his shoes, wincing. They *shouldn't* go off. He'd have been fine if they were NONEL; you couldn't get NONEL to go off without electrical current, period. But he wasn't positive with Skodas.

With that done, he hid the MP-5 and walked out of the locker room, practically running into a man in one of the purple camouflage uniforms.

"Doctor Chayanov?" the man said in passable English.

"Da?"

"You are *late*," the officer replied, grabbing his elbow. "Are those the samples?"

"Da," Mike answered in his best Russian accent. "Is terrible quality control. All of your people are shit, just shit."

"Well, you probably need to *try* not to say that to the president or the Great One," the officer replied tightly. "Be very polite."

"Da, I am polite," Mike replied as they hurried down the corridor. At the far end there was a door on the right guarded by two of the purple soldiers. That led to another corridor, with more soldiers, and the sound of the pumps from the facility on

the right-hand wall. Halfway down the corridor was a single-person door on the left. The only door along either wall. This led to another corridor. That one dead-ended in a wall. There were two doors halfway down, with two guards in front of either door. If Mike wasn't completely turned around, and he had pretty good spatial referencing ability, the door on the left led to his hidey-hole. They took the door on the right. The corridor was practically identical to the hidey-hole corridor, which added to the likelihood. The exception was that there was an exit at the far end and two guards were in front of one of the doors. If the design matched the other side, it was the "storage" room. He was taken to this room and stopped.

"You must be searched," the officer said. One of the guards handed his weapon to the other and then gave Mike a brief pat down, ignoring Mike's shoes. That was why the detonators were there; shoes and feet were untouchable to an Islamic. The guard looked at the locking blade knife and then gave it back. Then he gestured to the sample case.

Mike opened it up and pointed to the items in it. The guard looked at the officer and asked something in Arabic.

"He asks if these are bombs?" the officer said, glancing at the items uncomfortably.

"Nyet," Mike said. "Are not bomb. Are poison gas. Samples your leader asked to see."

"That's okay, then," the officer replied, waving at the case and not asking for the material to be removed for further search. "We are very careful of the life of our president."

"Da," Mike replied, trying not to roll his eyes. As he closed the sample case, he heard a muffled shriek and paused.

"We are entertaining some American young ladies," the officer said, looking at him carefully. "They are not enjoying the entertainment."

"Good, is all American bitches are for," Mike replied, closing the case.

"Glad you approve," the officer said, gesturing at the door. One of the guards opened it and Mike stepped into darkness.

CHAPTER EIGHT

"Mr. President, I think you should see this," Secretary Brandeis said, keying one of the overhead video screens. It was an oblique shot, probably from a satellite, of a line of soldiers and a helicopter. Two men were descending from the helicopter.

"We can't get resolution on faces, Mr. President," the secretary said. "But from the body shape and clothing, the man on the right is Basser Assad."

"So it's not a rogue Syrian operation," Minuet said. "That's good and bad to know. The tall one, though, is that who I think it is?"

"Probably," the secretary replied. "Given his height, movements and the way that he holds his right arm."

"Makes me tempted to nuke the facility right now," the President said, darkly. "I've heard about the first video tape. Have we gotten the demands, yet?"

"A group calling itself The Popular Front for the Islamic Jihad was the contact to Al Jazeera," the CIA director said. "They called for a withdrawal of all crusader forces from all areas of the Dar Al Islam. Now, that's an incredibly broad demand. Arguably, it includes not only all of the Balkans but Spain and Southern France as well. Certainly, they're referring to all European and American forces in the Middle East. Otherwise, they will do what they have

already done to one girl every two hours, until their demands are met. I had analysts go over the video, which is already on the Internet. Several of the girls who were kidnapping victims have been identified from 'audience shots.'"

"What's the download rate like?" Brandeis asked.

"High," the CIA director admitted. "It's flying around the net. And, of course, the news media is all over it like flies on shit. They're interviewing all the parents of the girls and various commentators are already talking about Stockholm syndrome."

"Unlikely in this situation," Minuet said. "Conditions are too extreme. And it takes some time to set in. Any word from Harmon?"

"Negative," the defense secretary said. "And he's overdue to check in. But security on the site has been increased. I'm not sure he can get out of his hidey-hole."

"We give him five more hours," the President said. "That is two and a half lives. Then we go whether we know where they are or not."

The room was dark with the only light coming from a sheet of one-way glass. It took Mike's eyes a moment to adjust.

"Come in, Doctor Chayanov," a voice said in Oxford-accented English. "You are very welcome. Come watch the show."

There was a desk set a meter or so from the window and Mike walked to it, setting the sample case on it, and glanced through the window. A girl with dark brown hair was being raped and had had part of the skin on her side peeled off. The man on her was rubbing his hands into the exposed flesh as he thrust into her. Even through the thick glass, the screams were clearly audible.

Mike turned away from the scene with apparent indifference. He was horrified and repulsed by what was happening. But, at the same time, hating himself, it turned him on. However, the sexual turn-on was close enough to rage that he could channel it and he was well prepped to explode.

He controlled his reaction and glanced at the group in the room. There were two guards by the door and a short-coupled man, the one who had spoken in English, that he vaguely recognized and

thought might be Basser Assad. His eyes widened, though, when he recognized the tall man at Assad's side.

"I am truly honored," he said, nodding. "It is a great pleasure to meet you, sir. You have done much damage to the American pig-bastards."

"As I did to the Russian pig-bastards," the tall man said darkly. "But as I worked with the Americans to defeat your kind, so I am happy to work with you to defeat them. Allah's ways are complex, but he gives his servants opportunities such as yourself. What did you bring to Allah's servants?"

As Mike opened the sample case, one of the guards stepped forward but all Mike pulled out at first was a pair of gloves. He tried to ignore the shrieks at his back as he pulled out the first of the gas grenades.

"Sarin," he said, setting it down. "Lethal in low concentrations but very short-lived. Which means you can move in the area no more than five hours after dispersal. This grenade will, well . . ." He turned around and gestured at the room full of naked women. "If I tossed it in that room, there would be no women to torture in less than five minutes. And that is just the time it would take to disperse fully." He turned back, set the grenade back inside and pulled out the next.

"VX. Lethal at the same level as Sarin, but persistent. Which means wherever it lands, it stays for from weeks to years. Decontamination after VX has been used widely is nearly impossible. For months after dispersal, people opening up a door will die from residue on the underside of the knob.

"This I particularly like," Mike said, putting the canister back in the case and lifting out the spray can. "It can be painted to resemble the sort of can that is used in wasp spray. Currently, we only have it in mustard gas, which is a very simple material, but we may have it in VX or Sarin soon. The problem is that VX and Sarin need to be mixed to function.

"It is very simple to use," he added, taking a subtle breath. "You simply point," he continued, pivoting towards the guards, "and spray," he added, depressing the tab.

The stream of yellow liquid hit the right guard square in the face then tracked across to the left guard. Assad was wearing a

sidearm in a fancy buckle-down holster and was trying to draw it as Mike pivoted to him and hit him in the face.

The tall terrorist had ducked to the side and was heading for the guards, who had fallen to the ground, clutching at their throats and gurgling as the gas reached their lungs and began burning them. Mike stepped around the desk and tripped him, then stamped on his lungs to get him to exhale and sprayed a puddle on the floor in front of his face. Then he stepped back, set the can on the desk and donned the gas mask. First he pressed it down to get a seal, then breathed out. Then he covered the inlet and inhaled, slightly. The mask pressed in indicating a good seal and he released the inlet and took a cautious breath. No scent of sulfur, no burning. Thank God.

As soon as he had it clear, he stepped over to check on the terrorist. The tall man was rolling back and forth, red froth bubbling out of his mouth, trying to scream, the frantic inhalations causing his lungs to melt faster.

"*Dulce et decorum est,*" Mike murmured, looking the man in the eye as he died, "*pro patria mori.* You motherfucker."

Two guards in the corridor, by the door. The door had been soundproofed and the nice thing about mustard was people couldn't really shout when they'd been hit by it. So the guards probably weren't even aware that anything had happened.

Mike picked up one of the dropped AKs and checked the magazine. Full. He visualized the two guards, aware of the screams that were continuing in the other room, flicked off the safety and opened the door.

The officer guide had, fortunately, left. And there were no additional guards. So he simply placed the barrel in the side of the left-hand guard, fired twice and then turned to the right-hand guard and did the same. Neither guard had time to do more than register surprise at the sight of a gas-mask-clad figure stepping out of the room.

Mike wasn't too sure at what level mustard was lethal. He had vague recollections of people talking about "a touch of mustard" from WWI, so apparently you could get some in your lungs and not automatically die. But he didn't want any of the girls dying from his mustard contamination. On the other hand . . . short time.

He hadn't gotten a *good* look in the torture room, but he was pretty sure he'd seen at least one guard and a group of unarmed soldiers. So he picked up a spare magazine and stuffed it in his back pocket. Then he stepped to the door to the torture room and opened it.

Amy was surprised that she'd almost gotten inured to the screams. Clarissa had taken two hours to die and, from what she could tell, Rachel was getting pretty close to the end. She'd learned to figure the time from the pattern of the torture. Clarissa had been raped by two of the soldiers, then tortured with electricity and had her skin stripped off in spots, then two more soldiers raped her in the mouth and ass, then she was tortured again and so on. Towards the end they had burned off her nipples with a blowtorch and after that they'd just beaten her with clubs to break her bones. Then they'd killed her by cutting her throat. Amy knew that Rachel was going to die, soon, in terrible agony, because while the soldiers were still raping her, one of the men in the aprons had started up the blowtorch.

She had her head down, just praying. She'd started off praying that somebody would come rescue them all. Now she was just praying that somebody would come before it was her turn. She'd done the math. Depending on what pattern they used, she had either forty-six or fifty-two hours to live. And the last two hours would be really bad. Bad enough she'd rather just die beforehand and get it over with. The one thing she had going for her was that the guards were pretty lax with the girls. When they got to her, assuming none of the others were any good at self defense, she'd have a trick or two for them. With any luck she'd be enough of a problem they'd just kill her. Assuming she could stay sane that long.

She looked up, though, at a scream from the front of the girls and the shot by the door.

"What's the situation with SpecOps, Don?" the President asked. He'd dropped just about everything to cover this situation and he was starting to get a little ragged at the edges. "Do we have a mission plan to get these girls out?"

"Yes, Mr. President," the secretary said. "We have the alert Ranger battalion at Fort Bragg rigged and in the air. Delta is on the way and performing mission planning enroute. However, it'll take time for Delta to get there. We're *going* to lose hostages if we wait. So. The best compromise between time to target and available forces is in theater SpecOps units. We've got a SEAL platoon staged out of Baghdad International looking at all the intel that we have. They're the closest, and best trained, team we have for this. Delta is as good as they come and I'd rather use them. But given the time constraints, I'd say go with the SEALs. It's going to be a high risk mission, though, even for the SEAL team."

"Why?" the President asked.

"I've brought in someone to brief on that," the secretary said, clearing his throat and gesturing at the major by his side. "Major Andreyev is an expert in advanced HALO, a special forces officer. It was his suggestion on insertion which is being implemented. It is . . . somewhat unusual . . ."

"It's insane, sir," the major said, in a soft-spoken voice. "But it's the only thing that might work."

"Go ahead, Major," the President said, leaning back.

"Sir," the major replied, getting up and going to the briefing stand. "The problem is that Syrian Integrated Air Defense System is as advanced as that of most first-world countries. They were defeated by the Israelis in 1978 but it took four days for the Israelis to fully suppress them. The Syrians have been playing against the varsity for a long time, and were positioned to learn all about our air operations during the previous fracas to the south. We don't have the time to roll back the air defense system prior to inserting the assault team. The need was to place a team on site, before the enemy was fully aware that they were under attack. There is only one way to do so: stealthily."

"You mean 'stealth,' don't you, major?" the NSA said, wonderingly. "As in inserting them by, what? Stealth bombers? We don't have enough B-2's to lift a large assault team! And where would you place the parachutists?"

"Yes, ma'am, I mean stealth," the major replied, bringing up a Top-Secret schematic of a bomb-bay rack. "Special Forces HALO did a very secret test with the Spirits last year at Nellis.

The bomb-rack ejector mechanisms were modified, and an O_2 distribution hookah was improvised. In addition, the B-2s are required to modify their climb profile for decompression. On the plus side, it is possible to eject a full SEAL platoon from a bomber, stealthily. Their insertion will be from forty thousand feet, twice normal height and about the maximum a person can handle without specialized equipment that can't be made available in time. We have already begun the necessary modification on a B-2 that was rotating through Prince Sultan Air Base in Saudi, and the SEALs will marry up with their transport there. The down side is that the bomber is visible to the enemy radar as long as the bomb bay is open, discharging the team. It has to offload the entire platoon in a hurry, which won't be pleasant for the SEALs, in order to avoid missile fire, which is more unpleasant. Given Syrian air defenses, we may lose a Spirit."

"Authorized," the President said, coldly. "How soon are they going to be on the ground?"

"The team is supposed to be being briefed about now, Mr. President."

"You have *got* to be shitting me!"

Petty Officer First Class Roy Simmons was the Leading Petty Officer of Charlie Platoon, SEAL Team Three. He had had been at Team Three his whole career. He'd gone through the predictable stages. The new meat that thought being a SEAL was just the coolest damned thing in the world but wasn't quite sure they were up to it. Then when he was "made" in the teams and promoted to PO Third he knew he could lick the whole world because he was a God Damned Frog. Then came the wife, then the kids, then the regular deployments and the advanced training, and now he knew it was just a job. One of the toughest jobs in the world, one that occasionally threw you a damned curve. But at the end of the deployment it was good to get back to the mamasan and forget the blood and the screams and just play with the kids. And he'd thought he'd heard it all until he heard this damned Air Force major lay out this shit in a calm and matter of fact voice.

"Oh, dude!" Roman snorted. "This is going to be *so* cool!"

"We're going to be SEAL legends!" Sherman said, raising his arms in victory. "Live or die, we're going to be fucking *legend*!"

"This ain't happening," Simmons said, looking over at the new meats. The poor guys' eyes were as round as saucers and they were looking at Roman and Sherman as if they were fucking insane. Which, of course, they were. That was the job of the PO3s on the teams and Roman and Sherman were *already* legends.

"We're inserting from a *B-2*?" Vahn asked. "I want to be clear about that. We're going to be loaded in the god damned *bomb bay*? Hooked in a rotating bomb release system and, what? *Automatically ejected?*"

"Yes," the Air Force officer replied. "It has been . . . successfully tested."

"How many *times*?" Simmons snapped. "And who in the fuck was crazy enough to try even once?"

"I'll go, daddy!" Roman said. "Me! Me!"

"Me, too!" Sherman said, grinning.

"Height?" Chief Adams asked, calmly.

"Forty thousand feet."

That shut Roman and Sherman up. Roman was left frozen with his mouth open and one hand raised in a "number one" sign. Sherman was just openmouthed.

"That's unsurvivable!" Vahn snapped. "Damn it, I was in Dev Group. You *don't* go over thirty thousand!"

"At thirty thousand the Spirit, especially with personnel and equipment in the bomb bay, is marginally detectable, given the radar signal strength that we are expecting over the target," the Air Force major said. "Again, forty thousand has been tested."

"Successfully?" Vahn snapped.

"Successfully," the major replied calmly.

"This ain't happening," Simmons said, his head in his hands and shaking back and forth. "This just ain't happening."

"In addition, it is anticipated that there may be significant aerial combat in the area of operations," the major continued with his briefing. "Your position will be noted and AWACs support will attempt to steer such combat into other areas of operation, however, the reason that the Spirit is being used is due to the conditions."

"You're talking about a dogfight going on," Vahn said, with the voice of calm terror. "*While* we're in the drop."

"Yes," the major said. "Time is of the essence, gentlemen. I would suggest you begin rigging up."

"Well, with all due respect, Major!" Simmons snapped. "Fu—"

"Wait," the chief said, holding up a finger. And everyone turned to look at him.

That's what Simmons remembered. The OIC had just been sitting there the whole time, trying to look frosty and doing a pretty good job even though Simmons knew he was probably on cloud nine with fear. The whacko E-5s were high-fiving. The new meats were terrified. Vahn and he were both *really* terrified because they'd done enough to know how just completely fucked they were. The mission was shit, no idea where the hostages were, maybe somebody on the inside but no name except "Ghost" and no idea who you're dealing with, no plan for the *building* for God's sake; ground penetrating radar hadn't been able to get anything more than ghost images. But everybody stopped and everybody turned to look at the chief, even the damned AF major.

"We're good," the chief said, nodding. "Let's get it on."

"Chief," Simmons said, quietly. "You *sure*?"

"Sure," the chief said, standing up. "I've done weirder things."

"Really?" the OIC asked, standing up as well as the chief headed for the door.

"Yeah," the chief said, pausing in the doorway. "I was in Class 201."

"No *shit*?" Roman asked, his eyes wide. "Jesus, Chief!"

"No shit," the chief said, his demeanor suddenly cracking slightly and a shiver shuddered through his body. "After that, being shot out of a B-2 at twice the recommended altitude into a dogfight and a mission with no damned plan or even a damned map . . . well . . . it ain't much."

"What in the hell is Class 201?" Meat Two whispered as the team quietly got up and started to file out.

"Meat, you're too young to know," Roman said, his head twitching in horror. "You're just too young. Maybe if you're drunk enough to take the horror. God. I knew Chief was *tough* but, God!" He shuddered again and walked out, shaking his head.

"Normally, Meat," Simmons said, gently putting his hand on the newbie's shoulder, "I'd tell you that Roman was as full of shit as a Christmas turkey. But . . . in this case, he's right. Sometimes, when you're a SEAL, you have to be harder than stone. When you're with a survivor of Class 201, well, you know that they're not going to quit unless they're dead."

CHAPTER NINE

Mike stepped through the door, kicked it closed and drove the barrel of his weapon into the guard on the left of the door. Then he turned and fired two rounds into the guard on the right, turned and fired two into the guard that was bent over and retching.

The group of soldiers lined up to rape the girl on the table stepped backwards, towards the wall, holding up their hands in placation but he didn't really care. He just started servicing them.

One of the men in aprons had pulled out a knife and held it to the girl's throat by the time Mike had killed all the soldiers.

"Put down the gun," the man said, calmly. He was wearing a suit under the apron and it had gotten spotted by blood. "Put it down or the girl dies."

Mike looked him in the eye and dropped the magazine out of the AK then reached into his back pocket to pull out the spare. Mike kept looking him in the eye as he raised the weapon to his shoulder and sighted on his forehead.

"Put down the knife, and I'll leave you the use of your upper body," Mike said mildly.

One of the other aproned torturers was shuffling around the one holding the girl hostage, knife in hand, clearly headed for another hostage. Mike kept the weapon on the one with the girl

97

until the other had almost reached the line of girls and then swung to the left, putting one round through the bastard's head and splattering the two girls on that end of the front rank in blood and brains.

He ignored the screams from the girls as he pivoted back and killed the two video technicians and the third torturer who was cowering behind the table, then pivoted back to target the hostage holder.

"I'll give you this. I won't put you on that table, I won't turn you over to the girls and I won't do more than break your back in the lumbar region. But you don't get the use of your dick. Take it or leave it."

"I *will* kill her," the man said, angrily. "You don't understand that?"

"You are one lousy negotiator," Mike said and put a round through his forehead. The knife nicked the girl's neck and that was about it. The body slumped backwards. "Never bluff if you're not even holding cards."

He walked over to the girl on the table, who even as fucked as she was looked pretty damned good, and looked her in the eye.

"You probably don't want to see guys at the moment or have them near you, so I'll get one of the girls to let you go," he said, nodding, then turned to the room. "Which one's got the keys?"

"The one that was holding Rachel hostage," one of the girls in the front rank said, gesturing with her chin. "Who are you?"

"A very bad man," Mike said, stooping down and going through the guy's pockets. "Who, in this one case, is willing to be a good guy for a while. But if I don't get at *least* a blowjob out of this, I'm going to be mighty pissed."

One of the girls in the front rank, dropped her head and shook it.

"How can you *say* something like that?" she shrieked. "You're as bad as them!"

"Yep, sure am," Mike said, standing up and holding the keys. "*I* was in Class 201, you weak-kneed pussies! But if you want to get out of this fucking place alive, and not end up back where you are right now, you'd all better get really damned frosty, really

damned quick. Quit fucking crying, quit bitching, quit quitting on me and get GOD DAMNED FROSTY. Because right now it's just *me*. And I'm not going to be able to hold this damned place by myself. I'm going to need help. Even nekkid female help will do. And I'm not going to use these damned keys until I get a big 'HOOWAH' out of y'all. Because if I can't get a big hoowah, then you're totally fucking useless to me, and I'll just god damned leave you to be raped. Am I *CLEAR* HERE? Now let me hear you give me a big HOOYAH!"

"What?" "What's hooyah?" "Who? Us?"

"HOO-YAH!"

"Ah, now there was one solid hooyah out there. You all heard it. Now, all of you, give me one great big fucking hooyah, or I'm walking out the door!"

"HOO-YAH!"

"There were some wimpy ones in there," Mike admitted. "But, overall, I'll give you a sixty, with the curve that comes up to eighty." He stepped off the dais and applied the key to the first rank on both sides and then stepped down the aisle.

"Where was that solid hooyah?" he asked, looking at the girls.

"Here," Amy said, lifting her chin. "What are you, Ranger?"

"Bite your tongue," Mike said. He unchained that rank and looked at the girl on the far end. "Pull it through, honey. I needs this girl. I wants her and I needs her.

"Okay," he said, stepping back up on the dais. "Get this girl loose, do what you can for her. I have some errands I need to run. I'd like most of you to stay in your seats or sitting down at least. Do *not* open that door until I tell you. Some of you bigger girls, drag the bodies over by the door, we might need them later. Waste not, want not."

"What are you going to need bodies for?" a short-coupled blonde who had sidled past him to get to the girl on the table asked.

"Barricades," Mike said. "Other than sandbags, there's not much better than a fresh dead body to use as cover."

"That is *gross*," another girl snapped. "Could you quit being so . . ."

"Mean?" Mike asked, angrily. "Hard? Macho? Male? Conservative?

Overbearing? I just tracked you god damned wenches from the States by getting the bends in the unpressurized nose wheel of an airplane, getting busted up holding onto the underside of a damned truck, getting stuck in holes and getting touched by mustard gas! Not to mention killing about twenty of the fuckers that kidnapped you and were torturing you! Do NOT give me any of your whining PC liberal bullshit! This is *why* guys like me hate you fucking whiners! We don't have *time* for you to go all weepy! Do you understand me?"

"Yes, sir," the girl said, meekly.

"You," Mike said, pointing at the solid hooyah. "Name."

"Amy," the girl said. "Private Amy Townsend, Army ROTC."

"Amy will do," Mike replied. "Call me Ghost. AKs," he said, turning and pointing to the weapons with two fingers. "Can you use one?"

"Yes, sir," Amy replied, crossing to the weapons and picking one up. Then she suddenly bent over and gagged. "Sorry."

"Dead bodies do that," Mike said, picking up some sort of big bone saw off the floor. "Cover the door."

He walked out and looked up and down the corridor. Still no sign of reaction. Good. He grabbed the second AK off the guard along with their web gear and slung one of the latter on. They not only had six magazines of ammo, the grenade pouches had fragmentation grenades in them. He shook his head at that. Frags were a good way to frag *yourself*; he hated the damned things.

He put his mask back on and went in the viewing room. The tall man had quit twitching as had the rest. He pulled the rest of the "samples" out of the bag, and the Semtek, then took the knife to the terrorist's neck, cutting off the head. It was still pretty drippy when he dropped it in the bag.

He left the two AKs in the room, but took the ammo and went down the corridor to the door that had been a broom closet in the other one. Sure enough, there was a sink. He rinsed off the outside of the sample case, the AK he'd been using, the gas weapons, his gloves, and finally unmasked. The air had a faint tinge of mustard that made him gag, as much from his clothes he suspected as anything, but it was survivable.

He walked back to the torture room and tried the room across

from it. It was being used as a storeroom as well. Not much useable except more railroad flares. He realized that they must be used for emergency lighting if there was a power outage in the building.

He put the case of them by the door, putting a few in his back pocket, and left it open. After that he walked back to the torture room. When he got back the room had, remarkably, organized itself. The girl had been taken off the table and was on the floor with two girls trying to staunch her wounds with more or less clean cloth taken from the bodies. The rest of the girls had mostly huddled by the walls, although a couple were puzzling over the video and computer equipment.

"I'm the only one with any firearms experience," Amy said. She'd put on one of the assault vests and Mike found the sight very fetching.

"That look really suits you," Mike said. "Really *really* suits you. Probably too well for my present lackanookie condition."

"Thanks," Amy said dryly. "I don't suppose there are any clothes around?"

"Nope. Okay, ladies, listen up," he continued, looking at the room. Most of the girls had seated themselves along the walls, as being more comfortable than the seats. "The good guys should be on their way soon. We have to hold this position for a few hours until they get here. We're just going to hang out here and wait for the good guys. Of course, the bad guys are closer, so we're going to have to engage them for a time. I need two girls who can run and one more that has guts and has played softball."

Some of the girls stood up and started forward but most sat down when there were other volunteers.

"Who's the runners?" Mike asked. "Amy, get the door open and cover down the corridor that way," he said pointing behind him.

"I can run, and I played softball," one of the girls said. She was a strongly built brunette with a nice set of hooters that even without a bra stood high and firm. "And my eyes are up here."

"I've made my decision," Mike said, continuing to stare at the tits for a second, then reaching into his harness and extracting a grenade. "Ever seen one of these?"

"Grenade?" the girl asked.

"Just like a baseball, with some differences," Mike replied. "Safety pin. Actuating spoon. Place the web of your right thumb over the spoon, maintaining a firm grip," he said, shoving the grenade into the girl's hand in the correct manner. "Keep squeezing the spoon. Straighten the pin. Pull pin. Throw grenade. Remember, once the pin is out of Mr. Grenade, Mr. Grenade is no longer your friend. Got it?"

"Got it," the girl said nervously.

"Runners?" Mike asked the other two.

"Yesss," a slim blonde said.

"Well, we're probably going to be killing a few bad guys," he said, pointing to the two dead guards on the floor. "And we're going to need ammo to do it. Your job will be, when I tell you, to run to the bodies and retrieve ammo."

"Okay," the brunette next to her said, looking at the bodies. "That's not going to be fun, is it?"

"Nope," Mike said, looking at the three. "You've all probably got names like Jenny or Ashley or Chelsea or something. But I can't keep track. So you're getting team nicknames." He looked at the thrower and nodded. "You're Babe. For Babe Ruth. Blondie is Bambi and brownie is Thumper."

"I don't like those nicknames," Bambi said. "My name's Britney."

"You're fucking joking," Mike said. "If you had better tits, you could be a dead ringer for her, too. But I don't really give a rat's ass if you don't like your handle, right now, you're nothing but meat, not even meat. Meat have at least been through BUDS. You're nobody. I should call you meat one two and three! You have to *do* something to get a better one. I was Ass-boy for a year after being in 201, so don't give me shit about handles."

"Ass-boy?" Amy asked from the door.

"Don't ask," Mike said with a sigh. "It's a *long* story. I kept trying for Winter born but nobody had a clue what I was talking about. Thumper," he continued, taking the flares out of his pocket. "If the lights go out, your first job is to light those. Got it?"

"Yes," Thumper said. "Can I at least be Flower?"

"No. You cannot be Flower. You are Thumper."

Mike walked out of the room and down the corridor to the doors he'd entered by. He could hold one end of the corridor, but not both. The door had a bolt on the inside but that was not going to hold against even a raghead assault. He knew what would, though, so he opened up the door and tossed the VX grenade through, quickly closing the door and bolting it. There was shouting from the far side, but it quit pretty quick. Then he trotted back to the torture room, cursing his aching knees, and went to the phone.

"Need to make a call?" Amy asked. "And what was that you tossed through the door?"

"You were supposed to be covering the other direction," Mike said, picking up the phone and dialing a combination. He smiled faintly at the distant explosion. "And it was a VX grenade."

"A *what*?" Amy snapped. "You're joking?"

"Nope, welcome to WMD central," Mike said, stepping out the door. "Now, the back way is pretty well blocked, what with the VX and the explosives I placed in the production area." As he said that there was another, louder but deeper explosion. "Secondaries are always nice. But that way," he said, pointing at the far end of the corridor, "leads, I think, to the surface. And we're about to get company," he finished as pounding footsteps were heard on the stairs. "Don't look at their faces and don't think of people. They're just targets. Service the targets."

"Yes, sir," Amy said.

"Ghost," Mike replied as the door opened and he serviced the first guy through the door. He was a muj like the two guards, black T-shirt and camouflage pants, and he dropped like a sack when hit in the chest. But there were more behind.

Mike engaged two tangos in the doorway, one of whom got off some shots, and tracked to service another but he was already down. He heard Amy gagging again and shot one on the landing to stop the first wave.

"Reload!" he snapped, covering the landing. He could hear Amy fumbling the reload but he wasn't worried about it. "You've got rounds left. Toss that one in the room. If it's dry it goes over your shoulder," he said, flipping his own out and setting it in the room he was using for cover. "When you've got a couple partials,

have some of the girls reload them for you. And lay out all your mags where you can reach them," he added, pulling his own out. "And *one* frag. No more. Give the rest to Babe."

"Okay," Amy said, setting out the magazines. "So, are the SEALs . . . what? How'd you find us?"

"Like I said, I tracked you," Mike responded. "I saw one of the snatches and tracked you the whole way. I'm not a current SEAL, I'm medically retired."

"For medically retired you're doing pretty well," Amy said, glancing over at him.

"You should have seen me in my prime," Mike said with a chuckle. "I would have worn you out."

"Well, let me get my head together about all this," she said, gesturing over her shoulder, "and I'll be the first in line to give you head so good it stops your poor old heart."

"You're on, Amy," Mike said, gesturing with his chin. "Company."

CHAPTER
TEN

Major Muhammed Tarzi had been looking forward to getting off work. The word had gotten around that American bitches were being held in the bunker and that soldiers would be chosen by lot to go down and rape them. As an officer, of course, he had first choice and as soon as he got off duty he was going to head down and get a taste of stuck-up American bitch pussy.

Major Tarzi had visited America several times and had even gone to the strip clubs that were everywhere. But he had never been able to get an American woman to fuck him. They seemed to fuck everyone else, flaunting and teasing in their short skirts and heavy makeup, but not him. He was planning on showing them what teasing got them and enjoying it immensely.

That was until the thud from underground followed by shrilling chemical alarms. His office was in the administrative building, but the sound and vibration carried clearly through the ground.

His first action was to panic as he realized he didn't know where his gas mask was. So he screamed for his orderly.

"Hasan! Where are you?"

"Major," the servant shouted, running in the room. "The alarms!"

"I can hear!" he yelled. "Where are the masks?"

"In your quarters, master," Hasan shrilled, nervously.

The quarters were all the way across the compound and the wind was usually from the northwest, which meant that gas might be drifting between him and the masks.

"Go get them," he ordered Hasan. "Then get back here with them. If I'm not here, find me."

"Yes, Major," the servant said nervously, backing out of the room as Lieutenant El Kheir pushed by him.

"The bunker," the lieutenant gasped, "the president . . ."

"What about the president?" the major asked. As the chief of security for the site, anything that happened to President Assad would fall on his shoulders.

"There is firing," the lieutenant said, finally getting his breath back. "The mujahideen tried to enter and were shot at. Someone is holding the passageway."

"Wake up the duty platoon," Tarzi snapped. "Get them over there." He reached for his phone and called the battalion orderly room. "Call out the battalion!" he screamed. "The president has been captured!"

The second wave was soldiers and Mike engaged them on the landing. The first one stuck his head out to see what was going on and left a red splash on the wall of the landing. This occasioned some shouting and then a group of at least a dozen charged down the stairs, firing as they came.

Mike and Amy engaged with single shots, filling the doorway with bodies, until the group broke and ran.

"Bambi, Thumper!" Mike called. "Ammo run." He flipped out his magazine, decided that a round or so wasn't worth it, and tossed it over his shoulder in the corridor as the two girls ran down the corridor to the bodies. Bambi stopped halfway and gagged, but then kept going.

"Stay to the left side of the corridor on the way down and back," Mike called. "And grab some of the grenades. Do *not* fuck with the pins or you will be two dead ammo grabbers." He paused, considering the view as Bambi bent over to pull out a magazine from a pouch, and sighed happily.

"You okay?" Amy asked nervously.

"Just admiring the view," Mike admitted. "Dead bad guys and

naked girls. It's like an op in a titty bar. All I need is beer and steak, maybe some heavy metal or Goth music, and this would be perfect."

Bambi pulled magazines out until her arms were full, then ran back, dumping them by Amy. Thumper, meanwhile, dragged some of the ammo vests off the bodies and carried those, and some loose magazines, back to the room, the vests dripping red as she ran.

"What, I don't get any ammo?" Mike asked, plaintively. "After all I've done for you girls? Nobody loves me."

"Here," Amy said, laughing and sliding some of the magazines across to him.

"I think they might try grenades or satchels next," Mike said as there was another distant thump. Suddenly, the lights went out to a series of screams from the girls in the room. "Thumper! Do you know where your flares are?"

"Got it, Ghost," Thumper called.

"I call you, Bringer of Fire," Mike yelled, triggering one of the flares and tossing it down the corridor. "But you'll always be Thumper to me. Anyway, if it's grenades, just flatten yourself into the doorway. If it's a satchel charge, I'll call 'satchel.' Roll all the way in the room, cover your ears and open your mouth, got it?"

"Yeah," Amy said. "Although my hearing's already going from this damned AK."

"Speaking of which, the next ammo run we need to get Bambi and Thumper to get us some more guns," Mike said. "There's going to come a time when we won't have time to reload." He watched the stairs for a second and then rolled back. "Grenades!"

The frags went off with sharp cracks and then feet could be heard on the stairs. He rolled back up and had to laugh. There were so many bodies on the steps, and so much blood, that the soldiers coming down the stairs, who were lit up by the flare but couldn't really see beyond it, were having to pick their way forward. It made them perfect targets and before Mike and Amy had to reload the newest wave of assailants had fled.

"Have the girls cross-load this one," Mike said, sliding his partially spent magazine across after he'd reloaded. "We'll wait until after the next attack to send out Bambi and Thumper."

Amy snickered and he looked over at her quizzically.

"Bambi," she half whispered, half mouthed, "real liberal."

"Good," Mike said. "But we'll make a conservative out of her, yet."

"CETCOM, General Bulder." General "Dutch" Bulder had been going nonstop for nearly thirty hours in the scramble to prepare for the upcoming mission. Rarely did the U.S. military snap-kick an operation, but this one was going to be a snap-kick and in any scramble, shit happened. It had been happening nonstop for thirty hours and he was afraid that when they finally did get a "go" on the target, it was only going to get worse.

"General, Major Rischard in Predator Central," the voice said. "Sorry to break chain, but you might want to look at the take from Drone Four, sir."

The general keyed his computer to bring up the take from the Predator that had been snuck into the mission area and blanched. Soldiers were running across the compound, heading towards the loading area. As he watched, a blast of smoke blew into the air and the south section, where the loading area was, collapsed into a smoking crater. The gas that washed over the soldiers was apparently toxic, or at least irritating, since they scattered away from it apparently blindly.

"Okay, I'm going to call the NCA," the general said. "Good call on the direct, Major, you're covered."

"Sir," the major answered, hanging up the phone.

Bulder turned and picked up a red phone.

"I need the President or the secretary, immediately."

"So is this an industrial accident, or did Harmon decide to start the game early?" the President asked, looking at the take from the Predator.

"Expert in demolitions," the defense secretary said, shrugging. "Whichever it is, I've started the pieces moving. The Spirit is in the air already. The Rangers are about two hours out, so they don't have an immediate play. The Alpha Strike is coming up and the combat elements of the Fourth ID are moving into jump-off positions near the Syrian border. Normally we set up

forward logistics systems but in this case we didn't to try not to tip our hands. We're taking an operational risk on that, but one I think is worth it. And we have airmobile and airborne forces standing by to assist, if the situation in the air becomes even mildly survivable."

"When will we know what is going on on the ground? With the girls I mean," the President said.

"The Spirit is up and the SEALs are depressurizing," the secretary said. "That will take nearly three hours, and that's pushing it to the point that some of the SEALs may get the bends anyway. An hour flight to the target. Some time on the ground. Say five hours. And it will be at least that long to get the full Alpha strike in place."

"Five hours for them to kill the girls," the President said, his face white. "Christ, I wish I knew what was going on in there." He paused, puzzled, and then his face cleared. "Look at that," he said, grinning.

On the video from the Predator, soldiers could be seen spilling out of one of the side entrances where they'd been gathering. The last two were carrying a body of a camouflage-clad figure.

"He could be a casualty from the damage in the facility," the National Security Advisor said. "But I'd suspect that he was dead from direct fire."

The Chairman of the Joint Chiefs had been called in to advise since most of the management of the operation was being handled at a lower level. His phone buzzed and he picked it up, speaking quietly for a moment and then hung up.

"Mr. President," he said, his face working. "That was a report from an analysis team. Their analysis is that there's a fight going on in reference to that door. Over sixty personnel have entered it in the last forty minutes, but only fifteen have emerged and some of them appeared to be wounded. Their analysis is that one or more persons are resisting, somewhere below ground level."

"Harmon found the girls," the national security advisor said. "And found out what was going on. And, somehow, sabotaged the facility as a signal to start the mission."

"How many troops?" the President asked.

"A battalion of Syrian commandos," the Chairman answered.

"And they're not, generally, the Keystone Kops you get with most Arab armies. They fought the Israelis to a standstill in the Golan Heights in '73. And an unknown number of mujahideen."

"They're forming up again," the national security advisor said. "They're getting ready to rush the door."

"I don't normally input at the tactical level," the President said, "but . . ."

"I'm making the call now, Mr. President," the Chairman said, picking up his phone. "More or less to *ensure* that everyone has the information and knows the target."

"Get them support," the secretary said. "Get them support as fast as we possibly can."

"Target," Mike said, firing at the first figure on the stairs.

The soldiers were not bothering to pick their way through the bodies and a couple of them, who hadn't been hit, tumbled down the stairs. But the rest kept coming, firing wildly but filling the air with lead nonetheless. Three of them paused on the landing, obviously picked marksmen, and tried to target the defenders in the gloom as the rest rushed Mike and Amy's position.

"I'm *out*," Amy said, rolling into the doorway.

"Babe!" Mike yelled. "Grenades!" He slowed his fire, dropping three in the front rank, and then felt the bolt lock back. He quickly grabbed another weapon, but by then two of the soldiers were nearly to the door and he had to fire up at them. One of them managed to get off a burst of "spray and pray" in his direction, and he felt a searing pain in his back and chest.

Amy shot the last of them off his back, but the stairway had filled with soldiers again and the marksmen were now firing at Mike and Amy's positions. He felt another round hit his leg, but he kept firing, willing the soldiers to break and run.

"Babe" had been playing ball since she was five years old. First two years of T-ball and then fast-pitch softball in a brutally Darwinian league. By high school she was considered one of the top pitchers in Georgia, an area that took its women's fast-pitch seriously, and was going to UGA on an athletic scholarship.

She pitched accurately enough, and hard enough, that she could

probably have taken down most of the front rank by simply *hitting* them with the grenades. However, that would have left the grenades rolling around on the floor to . . . "frag" Amy and Ghost. She considered the situation for just a moment, using pretty much the same thought process as if she was deciding to throw a grounder to first or second, then pulled the pin and spun her right arm in a whirlwind motion, slamming the grenade upward to ricochet off the roof and back down into the group. Before the first thud, and a cry of pain that could be heard even over the firing, she had spun another up and another . . .

Suddenly, there was an explosion in their midst and then another and bodies were tossed, screaming, to the floor. With the way clear he could spot the snipers on the landing and he engaged all three of them, hitting one simultaneously with shots from Amy.

The rush had fallen back but bodies littered the hallway, some of them simply wounded. He spotted one trying to crawl up the stairs and shot him, deliberately, in the head, then reloaded.

"More mags to cross-load," he said, sliding one across to Amy. "There any bandages in the room?"

"No," Amy said. "Why? Oh, crap!"

"Yeah," Mike said, sitting up and leaning back. When his back touched the wall he felt like screaming, but he was afraid he'd pass out if he stayed prone. "Fight until you die or drop time."

"Where have I heard that before?" Amy asked.

"*Axes flush, broadswords swing,*" Mike quietly sang. "*Shining armor's piercing ring. Horses run on a polished shield. Fight those bastards 'til they yield.*"

"*Midnight mare and blood red roan,*" Amy replied. "*Fight to keep this land your own.*"

"*Sound the horn and call the cry,*" they sang together. "*HOW MANY OF THEM CAN WE MAKE DIE!*"

"What is that?" Babe asked from the doorway.

"'March of Cambreadth,'" Amy replied. "Heather Alexander. Very cool song. That's the only verse I can ever remember. My dad used to play it."

"I think I'd like your dad," Mike said and coughed. His hand

came away dark in the flare light, but he was pretty sure it was blood. It wasn't a sucking chest wound but something had nicked his lung. "*Follow orders as you're told, make their yellow blood run cold. Fight until you die and drop. A force like ours is hard to stop. Close your mind to stress and pain, fight 'til you're no longer sane. Let not one damned cur pass by. How many of them can we make die.*"

"You know the whole song?" Amy asked.

"And lots of others," Mike said, weakly. "Right now I'm thinking of one by Crüxshadows."

"Who?" Amy asked.

"Great band," Mike whispered. "*I will not run, this is my sacrifice,*" he sang, softly then coughed. "*For I am Winter born . . .*"

"Bad song, Ghost," Amy said. "I really need you to hang in here."

"I will, Amy," Mike said. "I will. I hereby dub thee . . . Bo."

"Why *Bo* for God's Sake?" Amy asked, angrily. "It's better than Thumper, I suppose . . ."

"For Boadicea," Mike replied. "The Celtic warrior queen."

"Oh. In that case . . ."

"Of course, she lost," Mike added honestly. "And was dragged off to Rome in chains. But hopefully we'll do better."

"So, sing some better songs," Amy said. "If you can."

"How about poetry?" Mike asked.

"I hate poetry."

"What, your dad never told you about Kipling?"

"Only '*A woman is only a woman, but a good cigar is a smoke,*'" Amy said.

"Shame on him," Mike replied. "*This is the ballad of bo da thone, eerst the pretender to Theebaw's throne, who harried the district of Alalone. How he met with his fate and the VPP at the hands of Harandra Mukerji, senior Gomashta, GBT.*"

"What the hell is that?" Amy asked.

"The opening to the 'Ballad of Bo Da Thone,'" Mike said. "And, speaking of which, there's a bag in this room. A sample case. If I'm not . . . viable when support gets here, tell them the interior is contaminated and it's a *personal* present from me to the President."

"What's in the bag?" Amy asked.

"That's between me and the President," Mike said, chuckling and then coughing. "Crap that hurts. All these women around and not a pad or a tampon to be had."

"Mike," Amy said, quietly. "I know you're stressed and I know that things are tough, but we've really had a bad time, you know. Could you dial back on the . . ."

"Sexism?" Mike asked. "Yeah. Now I will. I needed to shock them before."

"I can tell that you're really a nice guy . . ." Amy started to say.

"Hah," Mike replied mirthlessly. "Don't be fooled. I'm a very bad man indeed."

"No, you're not," Amy said. "Quit trying to tell yourself you're . . ."

"Amy," Mike said quietly. "There are times when I don't know whether I'm going to slip all the way to the side of evil. There's bad in me you don't know. But I'll tell you this; if I didn't have . . . something that kept me on the very edge of good, I'd have happily lined up with those soldiers to rape you. And dug my fingers into your bleeding flesh to make you scream. I'm not just a little bit bad, I'm just about all the way bad. The sexist comments weren't all an act. That's how I *really* am when the stops are pulled out. The fake part is being a nice guy."

Amy was quiet for a time and then shook her head.

"I don't believe it," she said and then held up a hand to forestall the protest. "Yeah, okay, you have your demons. But . . . well . . . I'll get over what happened. I know I will. And, Mike, if you said you wanted to chain me to a table, just like the one in the room, and act like you were raping me, I'd do it. Because I *know* that I'd walk out alive and only harmed to the extent that I *let* you harm me. I trust you. I can just *look* at you and know I can trust you."

"I hate that," Mike said. "I really do. But . . . yeah, you're right."

"You've never raped a woman, have you?" Amy asked.

"Depends on the definition," Mike replied. "I don't think any

of the hookers in the third world are actual volunteers. I keep that in mind when I fuck 'em. It helps."

"I'll give you a pass on that," she said, shrugging. She looked down the hall. "They're holding back."

"Trying to figure out another way in," Mike replied. "They'll probably try the air shaft."

"That's behind us, right?" Amy asked, nervously.

"Yep," Mike said and grinned. "Let 'em."

Amy didn't ask why he was willing to let them try, but she didn't think the Syrians would like it much.

"*In the fury of this darkest hour,*" Mike whispered quietly, "*we will be your light. You ask me for my sacrifice and I am Winter born . . .*"

"You're right," Amy said. "Very appropriate. Is there more?"

"*Without denying a faith in God, that I have never known,*" Mike said, then coughed. "*I hear the angels call my name, and I am Winter born . . .*"

"Maybe you should back off," Amy said. "I'd love to hear all of it. But . . . when we're out of here."

"Okay," Mike said, leaning back and sighing.

"Okay, why tampons?" she asked after a while.

"Tampons and pads are some of the best bandages around," Mike replied. "If the hole is big, like from a bullet exit wound, you just stick a tampon in and you're good."

"That's sick!" Amy said, then giggled.

"Oh, it's better than that," Mike said, shifting around to find a convenient position. "You use tampons and pads for bandages. Before Lycra and Spandex, SEALs would use king-sized black pantyhose in place of wetsuits in extremely warm water. And there's an underwater demo firing device that's supposed to be waterproof, but usually isn't. The trigger of the device is a ring on the end. The way you waterproof it is to get a condom, an extra large, unlubricated condom with a receptacle tip, that's for the trigger, and put the firing device in that. With me?"

"Yeah," Amy said, grinning.

"So, sometimes, a team will be out in some third-world shithole and get a mission to, say, go into an enemy harbor and lay some

explosives," Mike said, grinning back. "So the supply guy, a SEAL mind you, has to go into some third-world pharmacy . . ."

"Oh, Christ," Amy said, laughing. "Stop! You're killing me . . ."

"And ask for a case of king-sized pantyhose, several cases of tampons and maxi pads. The ones with wings are best; you can just slap them right on . . ."

By this time, Amy was laughing uncontrollably, bent over her AK with tears running down her face while other girls were drifting to the door to know what in the world, especially given the conditions, could be so funny.

" . . . and a case of extra large, unlubricated . . ."

" . . . receptacle tip . . ." Amy managed to gasp, holding up a finger to make the point.

" . . . Receptacle tip, condoms," Mike finished, chuckling and coughing. "God, I got to quit cracking myself up."

"What in the *hell* was that all about?" Bambi asked. "It sounded . . ."

"Oh, oh . . ." Amy said, waving her hand. "Oh . . ." Then she collapsed again.

"Just trying to bring a little levity into the situation," Mike replied. "Everyone's going around with long faces like they're all gonna die or something."

"Amy?" one of the girls said. "Mr. Ghost?"

"Yeah?" Mike said and coughed again. "Crap that hurt. What?"

"Susie's on the Internet, she's on a chatboard trying to get the word out on what's going on. And Cassie's figured out the video feed. We can go live over the Internet. We're trying to get a link to one of the networks."

"Oh, Christ," Mike said. "Look, no video of the doorway, okay? Don't let them get a look at our defenses. Keep the camera pointed at the far wall. Al Jazeera will rebroadcast and somebody will see it up top and know there's only a couple of us. If you're going to do this, lie. Get some of the girls and give them guns, just to hold. And . . . get Fox. Not CNN, not ABC. Fox."

"You sure?" the girl asked.

"Yeah," Mike replied and coughed. "Tell 'em if they get anyone but Fox, I'll kick their fuzzy bunny-hugger ass."

CHAPTER ELEVEN

"Laurie," Tom Godwin said, sticking his head in the producer's cubicle. "You have got to see this!"

Laurie Weiner stood up and walked to his cubicle. Tom had an AIM chat up and she tried to make sense of it. Most of it seemed to be about the hostage crisis, which wasn't too surprising, especially given the name of the chat room: InsideThe-HostageRescue. But . . .

"What was that?" she said, scrolling up.

> HostageGirl: They haven't been back in about
>   ten minutes. Other than Rachel, so far we're
>   okay.
> DingBat111: That's good to hear. You hang in there,
>   Girl.
> HostageGirl: We're trying to get a feed out to one
>   of the networks. We've got their video gear.
>   Susie's figured out how to feed to the Internet.
>   She says she needs a server link point.

"Is this what I think it is?" Laurie whispered.

"Yeah, it looks real," Tom said, panting.

"GIVE 'EM OURS!" she shrieked. "How did they get free?"

"Some guy named Ghost broke them loose," Tom said, typing furiously and hitting Send.

> FoxieTom: THIS IS TOM GODWIN, A PRODUCER WITH FOX NEWS. EVERYONE GIVE ME A SECOND WITH HOSTAGEGIRL, PLEASE.
>
> FoxieTom: HostageGirl, first of all, glad to hear that everyone is okay so far except Clarissa. That's already in the news in case nobody told you. Tell Susie, the URL link for Internet vid is 126.10.05 and the password is GoFoxy. Everybody, you can't *link* to that, so stay away from the URL. HostageGirl, once you do the link, we should have two-way video and audio.
>
> HostageGirl: Thanks, Ghost said we could only link to Fox. I guess he's a fan.
>
> FoxieTom: Who is he?
>
> HostageGirl: I dunno, just a guy. Said he tracked us here. He killed the guards and now . . . I've got to think about what I can say and what I can't according to Thumper.
>
> FoxieTom: Thumper?
>
> HostageGirl: He hung nicknames on some of the girls who are helping him. Thumper's one of them. He also calls her "Bringer of Fire." He's . . . really weird. I don't care. He save my life, all of our lives. I'll forgive him everything for that. They're over by the door singing some song about "How many of them can we make die!" now.
>
> DingBat111: COOL. That's "March of Cambreadth"! Very good song for what's going on!

"I'll look up 'March of Cambreadth,'" Laurie said, "and tell video that there's a live feed coming in from the hostages. Jesus, I can't believe I just said that!"

"Power of the Internet," Tom said, and chuckled, going back to the chat session.

▲   ▲   ▲

"Welcome back to Fox and Friends, I'm Linda Braums filling in for E.D. Don . . . Gl . . . Hill!" the female anchor said. "The following is hard to believe but true. The hostages from Athens have been . . . partially rescued and are now using the terrorists' own video and Internet equipment to send out live pictures from the room where they were being tortured. We have a direct link to them over the Internet and are now going to be speaking to them, live. Be aware that . . . they were stripped as was seen on the horrible video the terrorists already released and they don't have access to clothing. And we cannot blur out in real time. So . . . I am speaking to Heather Carter, a journalism student at the University of Georgia. Heather, can you explain what happened?" The view changed to a shot of the face and upper chest of a young woman whose hair was horribly mussed and whose face was dirty but very pretty.

"Well, Linda, it was pretty confusing at first," the girl said, her face tight. "We'd . . . been present for Clarissa's . . ." She paused and shook her head for a second.

"Ordeal?" Linda prompted.

"I suppose that's a word to use," Heather replied, gulping and closing her eyes. "And then they took a break, a fairly long one. I think they'd decided to . . . take their time to let the word get around. Anyway, they started on Rachel . . ."

"It's probably better if we don't use names of victims, Heather," Linda said, tightly. "Not until their families can be informed."

"This is going to get tough," Heather said, grimacing. "They started on another girl. And they'd, well, they'd done most of the things they were going to do to her, short of some of the end stuff . . . when the door burst open and this guy just came in and started killing them. I mean, just killing them. One or two shots per person, almost like an execution. Mr. Halal, who was the guy leading them and doing a lot of the torturing, tried to take the girl on the table hostage and Ghost just . . . played with him. Shot all the other people, acted like he was negotiating, except he was really insulting, and then he shot him through the head. He released some of us and gave us the key and he and, well he's been organizing our defense ever since. He said this was a WMD

facility, by the way, and I trust his word because he also said he used some of their chemical weapons against them. 'Tossed a VX grenade through the door' is what got back to me. I don't know which door. And he blew up the plant or whatever, we heard the explosions, then got ready to defend us. According to Mr. Ghost, the U.S. government is aware of our location and on its way. But we have to hold on until they get here. So . . . tell them to hurry." The view cut back to the Fox crew, who were looking pretty stunned.

"Heather, Brian here," one of the male anchors said, being the first to recover. "Is 'Ghost' with the U.S. government?"

"I don't know," Heather admitted. "He said he tracked us here, not how or why. Just something about being on an airplane and a truck. Getting bent, whatever that means, in an airplane."

"Is he special operations?" Brian asked. "Ranger or SEAL?"

"Uhm, Brenda said she thought he was a Ranger," Heather replied. "She used to have a Ranger boyfriend and he was always saying 'hoowah'. Mr. Ghost made us all say 'hoowah' before he'd release us."

"He *what*?" Linda gasped.

"He made us all give him a big yell 'hoowah,'" Heather said, shrugging and bringing nipples almost in view. "He said he needed help and if he couldn't get a big hoowah, we weren't worth saving. I think . . ." She paused and frowned, then shrugged again. "It had been . . . really terrible. Really really terrible. And a lot of the girls had just gone, like, out of it. I think he was trying to shock us back to reality or something. It helped, in a way, and I'll never think of hoowah the same again, that's for sure."

"Okay," Linda said, frowning. "I guess I wasn't there and I won't judge."

"Oh, no, judge," Heather replied. "He's like some icon of everything girls hate about men. Sexist, overbearing, foulmouthed, insensitive to an amazing degree. And as soon as some of us get over what's happened in this room, to Clarissa and some of the rest of us, he's going to get screwed to death. If this is what it takes to keep this," she said, waving at the room, "from happening, then I'm all for it. Male-dominated society? Screw that, this room, *this* is male-dominated society. America's *heaven* compared to this

room, compared to these people. And if it takes guys like Ghost to keep us safe, then I'm all for it. When I get back I'm going to go to the ROTC department and kiss every single person in the building." She paused and grimaced. "I'm not going to have *sex* with any of them, because I don't want to see a dick for a long time, but I'm going to kiss them. Even the girls."

"Heather," Brian said, carefully. "It sounds like you've had, well, a life-changing experience in more than one way."

"If you mean politically," Heather said, frowning, "you bet your ass. I'm a journalism major and a card-carrying liberal. At least, I was. I spoke out against 'Cliff's War on Terror' and protested and all the rest. The *hell* with that. This is every decent person's war on terror, every American's war on terror, especially every *woman's* war on these Islamic motherfuckers. Nuke these fuckers. Nuke every god damned one of them. Fuck the 'religion of peace.' I won't shed a tear. And I'm going to vote Republican the rest of my life!"

"MR. SECRETARY! MR. SECRETARY!"

"Calm down!" Brandeis said, waving his hands. "Let me make my statement first. Yes, we were aware that there was an agent in place. We were aware that the girls were being held somewhere in a building we code named Aleppo Four, which was a suspected site of WMD design and possibly construction. We had been in contact with the agent, Codename Ghost. He was to find out *where* in the facility the girls were being held, because otherwise we suspected they'd be killed while the special operations team was looking for them. We lost contact with him and he apparently determined that the plight of the girls was so severe that he had to take action. He, apparently, sabotaged the WMD facility and somehow made his way into the section housing the girls and rescued them. This is from *your* news reports; we don't have contact with him at this time. There was a plan to retrieve the girls that was waiting on his report. When we noted the activity at the facility, we put the plan in operation. It is ongoing at this time. That concludes my statement. I will now take salient questions."

"Mr. Secretary!" one of the reporters shouted. "How long until—"

"I said *salient* questions," Brandeis snapped. "That means questions I can answer. I'm not going to give you a timetable because then the Syrians will have it."

"Mr. Secretary," a female reporter said, waving her hand. "The Syrians have denied responsibility and . . ."

"Lady, I've been looking at Predator drone footage for the past hour," the secretary said, shaking his head. "The Predator has been watching the whole incident. The call was tracked by technical means to Aleppo Four. NSA has traced the video link to Syria. The girls are in Syria. This is an act of war. We're going to treat it as such. Embeds are going to accompany the relief forces. You'll be able to see for yourself where the girls were being held. So, please, don't bother believing the Syrians, they lie about what they had for breakfast. I'm tired of the news media being enamored of the Baghdad Bobs of the world. When we tell you something, it's the truth or the best we can determine of the truth. Just about everything that you get from our enemies in the Middle East is lies. So would you *please* quit spreading the lies and *maybe* spend some time spreading the truth? The truth is, fifty girls were kidnapped by terrorists, not freedom fighters, not militants, *terrorists*. They were loaded on a plane in the Athens airport, flown to Algeria to refuel, in a section the government has spotty control of, by the way, then flown to an airbase in Syria, transported by truck to Aleppo Four and have been held in an underground room, stripped, tortured, raped and murdered. This is the *truth*. This is the face of our enemy. This is what the War on Terror seeks to end. And we are going to *end* this particular battle by pulling the girls out and turning Aleppo Four into a smoking crater. As a WMD facility, a secret one that has been used in an act of war, we could, under our guidelines, do that with nuclear weapons. It would not even count as 'first use.' A biological agent is WMD. Chemical weapons are WMD. Nukes are WMD. We consider all of them equal. Keep that in mind. Keep that in the *front* of your mind. Nukes equal gas equals germs. One single Sarin round used on our people or our troops means we can destroy *anything* in the supplying country with nuclear weapons and all our nuclear release procedures are satisfied. Just because we haven't done that in the War on Terror, doesn't mean we won't."

At that the room went silent until one of the reporters raised his hand.

"Does that mean the U.S. intends to use nuclear weapons on Syria?" the reporter asked quietly.

"That means that use of nuclear weapons is fully on the table at this time and is being discussed by such persons as are entrusted to their release by the American people," the secretary replied. "It does not mean the decision has been made. However, the American people are, justly, furious at this action, especially such an action by a member of the UN Security Council. And the President intends to place a war declaration before Congress. When it is passed, and I suspect it will pass with acclaim, our actions are free. We are, thereafter, free to make full war against Syria at a time and place of our choosing."

"Mr. Secretary, redirect," the same reporter asked. "Does that mean we intend to force a regime change in Syria?"

"It means that, at a time and place of our choosing, we can engage in any form of war we deem necessary," the secretary said. "The government of Syria had better think about that carefully. They not only supported this action, they maintain control of the Bekaa Valley, which is a hotbed of terrorism. We have solid evidence of links to Al Qaeda, not guesses, not rumors, solid evidence of links at the highest level. Syria is going to have a breather after this to consider what they want to be in the international community. And if they continue, in any way, shape or form, on the course they have laid in the past, then, yes, we will force regime change in Syria by *any* means we determine necessary. We will not ask the UN. We will not go begging the French and Germans to support us. *We* will wage war with every weapon, *every* weapon, in our arsenal. That is the determination of the National Command Authority. And we're not lying, bluffing, kidding or considering. That is the *decision* of the National Command Authority. They seriously screwed up when they thought they could kidnap young American girls and torture, rape and kill them to force us to withdraw. Nothing, *nothing* could have been more stupid."

"Mr. Secretary," the reporter said, frowning. "One of the tenets of fighting unconventional warfare is that the weaker side tries to

cause an overreaction from the stronger so as to get sympathy. And Al Qaeda has stated that they are trying to cause an over-reaction from the West in order to bring about the Great Jihad. Wouldn't the use of nuclear weapons be an overreaction?"

The secretary considered the reporter for a moment and then smiled, evilly.

"Tell that to the Mongols." There was a stirring amongst the group and he waved a hand and walked out.

"What did that mean?" a female reporter asked her more experienced colleague.

"When the Mongols invaded the Persian Empire," the guy said, frowning slightly, "which stretched through most of the Middle East, they killed four out of five inhabitants in the region. Laid waste to cities, destroyed wells and irrigation so that civilization could not exist. They killed every single resident of Baghdad, for example. The term was 'they made a desert and called it peace.' What he just said was that the President is furious enough to nuke the entire region."

The female reporter thought about that for a moment, thought about the few seconds, all she could watch, of the video of Clarissa McCutcheon being raped and tortured. She thought about beliefs she had held dear, of attitudes she felt were solid in her bones. She thought about what it would be like to be a woman in that room and nodded.

"Good." She paused and shrugged. "Do you think they can get them out?"

"It's going to be tough," the regular Pentagon reporter replied. "I was talking with some sources. Syria's got a tough air defense network so they can't just fly in by helicopter. And whatever they're doing to hold off the Syrians, sooner or later they'll get overrun. Trying to take down the defenses in a normal manner would be a several-day job. I don't know how they're going to get reinforcements into them although my source did say that there was a plan. He didn't know what it was, but he'd heard it was really crazy."

"Well, whoever's going in to help them," the female reporter said, "I wish I could give them a great big kiss. And I hope they're okay."

▲   ▲   ▲

"Dude," Roman said over the team link. "This totally sucks. I'm freezing to *death*. I can tell I'm getting frostbite on my toes. I can barely breathe from this damned ejector. My left arm has gone to sleep from being slammed into this fucking clamp. And I keep thinking what's going to happen if my hookah accidentally drops free."

The team was suited up in HALO gear, cold weather gear for high altitudes with an air bottle and mask somewhat like a fighter pilot's to provide them with oxygen. But the bottles were small and wouldn't last the entire time of decompression and flight. So to provide oxygen while they were in the bomb bay a large oxygen tank had been installed and tubes run to each of their masks. If the tube accidentally dropped loose, their oxygen bottle would start automatically. But it would only last so long. And there was no way to fix the problem since they were wrapped up like prey in a spider's web.

The B-2 Spirit bomber used a rotary bomb release system. Bombs were set in a rotary rack, something like a revolver type pistol, instead of being in a general release vertical rack. The beauty of the rotary system was that, instead of having to simply drop the whole stick, specific weapons could be rotated into position for dropping.

The problem was that the rotary system entirely filled the bomb bay. So the only way to carry the SEALs was *in* the rotary system. Bombs were raised into the system and then grabber clamps closed on them to hold them in place, until small explosive charges drove rams downwards, forcibly ejecting the payload of each position into the violent slipstream of the high-speed aircraft. In the case of the SEALS, a field expedient wrapper was improvised. After donning all their normal equipment, including a complete tactical loadout of weapons and ammunition, a belly slung payload carrying their ruck of demo, medical and commo and their parachute and reserve, the SEALs normally had all the grace of a pregnant hippo as they waddled to the door. Waddling wouldn't be required this time, since they had first been wrapped in foam rubber and taped to a metal backboard, then lifted into the bomb bay before the bomb clamp was closed on them. As each

SEAL was loaded, the rack was rotated and the next was loaded and so forth, just like bombs, but with more protests. So they were held in place, constricted by their equipment, wrapped in foam rubber, taped to a backboard and unable to move, watching their air lines dangling in front of their faces. In this wonderful condition they awaited the moment when the copilot would operate the weapons release, and the ejector mechanism would fire as the clamps released, launching each SEAL.

"Shut up, Roman," the chief said. "Focus on the mission."

"I'm trying, Chief," Roman said. "But I keep focusing on this hookah line. I mean, they could have rigger taped it or *something*."

"Charlie Platoon," the pilot said over the team net. "In-flight advisory. The agent in place, Codename Ghost, has released the girls and they are now holding a position on the lower level anticipating reinforcement. The enemy forces are attempting to force a door in the south wall, which is now your primary target. We're at altitude and are proceeding to the destination. The Alpha Strike has gone in and are in the process of suppressing defenses. There will be another Spirit up to give you JDAM support on call. They will be monitoring your platoon radio frequency."

"Thank you, sir," the OIC said. "This is a nice plane, but we'll be happy to get out."

"So I heard," the pilot said with a chuckle. "We're going EMCON at this time. Do *not* transmit on your team net again until you are released. There won't be a warning. The doors will open and you'll be launched automatically. I won't get back to you before the doors open, so good luck."

"You heard what the man said," the chief growled. "Not a word. Chimp down on the radios—full tactical emission control."

Roman shifted slightly, trying for a decent position, and looked over at the nearest jumper who was one of the new meats. The guy had his eyes closed and Roman suspected he was praying. That was all well and good, but since he couldn't bitch, there was only one thing to do. He hung his head down, closed his eyes and quickly went to sleep.

"Team," the pilot said a couple of minutes later. "There's an

intermittent sound. We need to maintain EMCON; we're entering detection range!"

"Roman!" the chief snapped. "Wake up! And stay awake! You're snoring!"

Fuck, Roman thought. *I hate being a SEAL.*

CHAPTER TWELVE

The last rush had included a satchel charge and Babe had had to demonstrate her throwing arm again. But Bambi and Thumper had gotten good at collecting magazines and there was plenty of ammo. Enough that Mike was pretty sure he wasn't going to be able to use it all. Not before he died.

"Amy," he gasped, slumping down. "Is there any riggers . . . duct tape in that room?"

"I think so," Amy said. "I think I saw a roll."

"Get Bambi over here with it," Mike replied, slowly lying down.

When Bambi crept across to him, Mike gestured with his chin at the dark room to his right.

"There's road flares by the door. Fire one. I saw some pieces of plasticlike folders in there." He inhaled with difficulty then paused to cough redly. "Get one. Hurry."

"Okay," Britney said, creeping in the room and fumbling a flare to light. She found the sheet and came back out.

"Knife in my pocket," Mike gasped. "Cut away my jacket and shirt."

Britney got it out and cut away the clothing, revealing two wounds in Mike's chest. One of them was bubbling air. She half gagged at the sight of the red wound and bone showing, but kept from completely puking.

"Sucking chest wound," Mike managed to gasp. "Nature's way of telling you to slow down. Caught it on the last attack. Put the plastic on it, tape it down, leave one edge untapped, so it can drain. You'll have to roll me over to do the back."

Britney pulled the cloth further away and laid the plastic on the wound. She was amazed to see it suck in automatically. Then she used the duct tape to strap it down. With all the blood, it was hard to find a place where it would hold but she finally got the plastic secure. She tried to roll Mike over, but he groaned so bad she stopped.

"Thumper," she called softly. "I need help."

"I thought I was Bringer of Fire," the girl said with a grin, then paused when she saw how bad off "Ghost" was. "Oh, no."

"Get the other one on," Mike gasped. "Quick."

Between the two of them they got him rolled over. Just as they did there was a shout from somewhere behind them and then an explosion. Most of the girls let out a shriek and Britney crouched down over Mike, covering his wounded chest as a wave of dust filled the air.

"I put a charge in the ventilation shaft," Mike gasped. "Get the plastic on."

The wound on his back was much larger than on his front and he was bleeding profusely, the blood making a large puddle on the floor that Britney's knee kept slipping in. She wiped some of the blood away with a cut off piece of shirt and slapped on the plastic, strapping it down as best she could.

"We need to get you in the room," she said, helping Thumper to gently roll him over.

"Fuck that," Mike said, coughing again. "This is my place to stand. Hand me my rifle and then get back in the room."

"Look, macho man," Britney snapped. "You're bleeding all over the place. There's only so much blood in the human body. You're going to die if we don't get some of it to stay in you."

"Got any tampons?" Amy asked. "We don't have bandages, we don't have medicine and we don't have anyone else who can shoot. Throw the flare to the far end and then leave him."

"No, I'm going into this room," Britney said. "That way I can hand him ammunition and stuff."

"Okay," Mike gasped. "Do it." He laid his head on the AK for a second and then coughed. "Britney?"

"Yeah?" she asked softly.

"You're good people," Mike said, coughing. "The reason I did this is I just fucking care too much, okay? I'm a bad guy, I know that, but I care, too. Too much. I'm sorry about what I said."

"It's okay," Britney replied, tears in her eyes. "I think we sort of knew that. You're going to make it, Ghost. Help's on the way. Fox said that Brandeis said they had forces on the way. I don't know how long, but you stay with us, okay? Please?"

"Yeah," Mike said, taking a breath. "*Hold your head up high, for there is no greater love . . .* God, I wish I had a Crüxshadows CD right now."

"Save your breath, Ghost," Britney said, rubbing him on the shoulder, lightly. There were more wounds there. There was blood pouring out of him . . . everywhere. "Save your strength, hero."

"Gotta fight the dark," Mike replied. "My way. *And in the fury of this darkest hour, we will be your light . . . we shall carry hope within our bloody hands . . .*" he continued to sing/whisper, coughing continuously.

"Movement," Amy snapped, triggering a round at the landing.

Mike could barely see the landing anymore, his vision was tunneling out. But he shot at the figures, like ghosts, that moved in the red light, as the pain from each recoil racked his broken body, kept firing and firing until he couldn't see anymore.

The bomb bay doors opened faster than the eye could follow. Without warning there was a blast of wind that filled the bomb bay.

"Tallyho!" the pilot said over the platoon net. "Good luck!"

The first jumper was Vahn, as the lightest of the group. As the clamps let go he felt the ram against his back thrust him out, and the foam rubber banging against him and then dropping away in the wind, and the wash from the B-2 tumbled him into the maelstrom.

He tucked into a fetal position until he was free, then opened out into a full spread, looking around with the Night Observation Device. With the NOD he could see that there was ground down

there but nothing else. There was a high bank of thin clouds they'd have to drop through to get a view of the target. Then he saw a flash of light, rising from the ground, that erupted from the clouds and tracked across the sky. He suddenly realized he was actually *seeing* a SAM missile targeting the B-2.

"SAM in the air!" he yelled on the tacnet, wondering just what good that would do.

He glanced over his shoulder and could see most of the team in the air behind him. He couldn't pick out who was who, but a quick check revealed seven members at least. Some of them were picking up to him pretty quick.

The ascending SAM was moving so quickly it was more like a laser than a missile, but suddenly it banked off to the right and went straight vertical before exploding like a firework.

"Lost track when the bomb bay closed," the OIC said over the net. "Glad it didn't track on one of us. Form up in a stack. We're angling southwest."

The jumpers started to form their stack, maintaining separation, when Roman suddenly broke the silence.

"What in the hell is . . ."

Vahn looked around and realized he could see something approaching at their altitude and at a high rate of speed. It looked like—

"INCOMING!" Chief Adams screamed.

"Bulldog Four, Bulldog Four, vector bogie, angle one seven five, Angels thirty," the AWACs technician said, then changed to intercom. "Sir, I've got a Mig-27 closing on Bulldog Four, but I'm getting a weird intermittent on my screen in the area."

The group commander in charge of the Aleppo patch brought up the screen and gave it a quick read. He was an experienced officer with hours of managing mock dogfights and this one was going more or less like training. The Syrian fighter pilots were generally chosen for their social position, rather than their skill. For all of that, they were probably the best the third world had to offer. Which simply meant that the F-15s and F-16s of the Combat Air Patrols were having a harder time killing them. So far, no American plane had been successfully engaged by

either the Syrian pilots or their much more dangerous SAMs. But anything could change that so he gave the screen a close study, noting the marker for the F-15 and the intermittent radar tracks. He puzzled over those, hooking one for closer scrutiny, then noted the altitude change on the nearly motionless tracks, and blanched.

"Bulldog Four! Bulldog Four! Break left and dive! Say again, *break left and dive!*"

Bulldog Four was an F-15C, the best damned fighter in the world in Major Mike Speare's opinion and he was the best damned pilot in the world. And he didn't have anything on his threat receptors. But he was an experienced fighter pilot and he'd learned to trust the AWACs people in the bones, so without a thought he broke left as hard as he could handle, pulling the Gs up to fifteen and turning his head right to see if he could spot the threat. What he saw, literally, made him piss his pants. Mostly it was just two very wide eyeballs above a pressure mask and a heavily rigged figure dropping through the air. The wing of his F-15 missed the descending HALO jumper by less than five meters.

"Holy shit!" he bellowed. "I almost hit a fucking jumper!"

"All aircraft, be aware," the AWACs mission officer said. "SEAL HALO team dropping near point 1148, currently Angels 32. All aircraft, avoid 1148 for five minutes and do not fire into region. Bulldog Four, turn right, descend to Angels Twenty and engage bandit point 1273 Angels Fourteen."

"Bandit locked," Speare said, calming. "Go Slammer."

Meat Two, the lowest jumper in the stick, had been nearly hit by the F-15 and the wash from it picked up him and Vahn and spun the two of them through the air like tops. The stick broke apart as it entered the wash, all of the jumpers going into out-of-control condition, which meant being whirled like leaves in a tornado.

"Ruck loose," Roman called as his rucksack bulging with ammunition and gear broke away from its rigging straps and dropped to the end of its descent line. Since he was spinning through the air at the time, the momentum of the heavy rucksack turned him

into something like a bolo, spinning horizontally in the air with blood rushing into his head with the building G forces.

"Holy shit!" Simmons shouted when he saw the ruck coming towards him. He desperately flopped into a position he'd never heard of, basically on his side and banking as well as he could, and saw the ruck flash past his face. He heard a grunt and looked over to see Meat One spinning off, limp and out of control, and the ruck dropping. It had apparently hit the Meat full force and lost most of its momentum.

"Meat One, you read?" The junior NCO got back into position and delta tracked towards the meat who was descending on his back.

"This is Vahn. Meat Two is either dead or unconscious from the miss."

"Ditto Meat One," Simmons said, catching up to the jumper and trying to get a look at him. His mask was still attached, which was all that he could say at the moment. "He got hit by Roman's ruck. Roman, you there?"

"Trying to catch my damned ruck," Roman gasped. "Okay, it's official. This job is just too fucking exciting sometimes."

"Vahn, Simmons, hold onto the Meats until we get to opening, then release. They'll drop towards the target and the chute will pop on its own at Angels Two. We'll try to find them and recover them after the mission. Team Check."

"Chief." "Simmons." "Vahn." "Roman, and I have to say that I take it back, this was a bad idea." "Sherman, ditto." "Meat Three, here. With all due respect, ditto."

They raced through the clouds, descending at nearly 150 mph, and Vahn finally got a look at the ground. They were following the OIC, who was tracking on GPS, but it didn't matter anymore. Below twenty thousand feet now, they could see the target and even see the smoke still billowing from the fires in the underground facility.

"Be advised, that smoke is hazardous to your health," the OIC said. "We're going to go in to the south, just inside the perimeter fence. Spirit in the Sky, I want a JDAMs at point North 23145 East 14315, now, now, now. Given forty seconds, we should be on the ground just after it lands."

"Sir, this is Meat Three."

"Go ahead, Johnson."

"I would like to state that I made a serious mistake when I didn't ring out in BUDS, sir, with all due respect."

There were chuckles on the team net and the OIC nodded his head.

"I think we're all with you there, son," the OIC said. "With the possible exception of the chief."

"Nope," the chief replied. "Gotta agree. This is even worse than 201." An air-to-air missile flashed by below them and they could see the silhouette of a Soviet style fighter, banking and climbing over the target. "Much worse."

"Mr. Ghost?"

Mike looked up into a fairly beatific face and a pair of really shapely breasts and smiled.

"Thank you," he muttered. "Valhalla is real."

"You passed out," Britney said. "They ran away again. What do we do?"

"Get in the room," Mike whispered, trying to move and realizing that he just didn't have the blood left. He was surprised he could think and his vision was going again. "I'm done. All of you, in the room. Get guns. Amy show. Hold the door. *I hear the angels call my name . . .*"

"He's out again," Britney said. "Thumper, help me drag him into the room."

Between the two of them they got him into the torture room and laid out by the dais. Then, with a great deal of trepidation, Britney picked up one of the rifles.

"How do you use this?" she asked Amy.

"First of all," Amy said carefully, "you put the safety on."

"What's a safety?"

"Coming up on pull," the OIC called. "Spread the stack."

The thickening air was noticeable as they descended and they had actually slowed. But they were still approaching the ground rapidly. The jumpers rotated away from each other and spread out, Vahn and Simmons moving to position and then more or less tossing the two dead or unconscious jumpers away.

"And . . . pull," the OIC called.

Almost simultaneously, seven chutes opened and began banking towards the darkened facility below.

"Oh, Spirit in the Sky," the OIC caroled. "Where's our JDAMs?"

As he asked the ground below was riven by a massive explosion and the shockwave slammed into their bodies.

"Thank you, Great Spirit," Roman said.

"Head for the impact point," the OIC called. "Ready personals. We're going straight in."

There were a series of screams as a massive explosion shook the room and concrete dust drifted down. Amy rolled into the room, her hands clamped over her ears and screaming in pain.

"Amy?" Britney yelled, grabbing her by the arms. "Are you okay?"

"Ow FUCK!" Amy shouted, shaking her head. "The blast must have gotten magnified by the corridor. That *really* hurt!" She rolled back into the doorway, shaking her head and clearly disoriented. "Babe! Flares!" she yelled, pointing down the corridor. "Flares, Babe!"

Babe picked up three of the flares and triggered them one by one, throwing them to land expertly right at the base of the stairs.

"Are you going to be okay?" Babe asked. When there wasn't any response she tapped Amy on the shoulder and got a rifle pointed at her. "Hey! Watch it! Are you going to be okay?"

"What?" Amy yelled, shaking her head.

"Can you hear me?" Babe shouted, pointing at her ear.

"Barely." Amy rolled back into the doorway and shook her head, leaning her chin on the rifle.

Britney's head came up at a series of popping noises. They sounded like guns, but not the ones that had been firing. Instead of the way the soldiers had been shooting, ripping off long bursts, this was short and sharp, more the way that Ghost fired.

"What's that?" she asked as one of the long rips started then stopped at a series of short bursts.

"I don't know," Babe said, then looked at Amy who was staring intently down the corridor. "AMY!"

The girl looked up and Babe squatted down by her.

"THERE'S FIRING," she shouted, pointing to the landing. "DIFFERENT FIRING. NOT THE SAME GUNS."

Amy looked confused for a second and then her face split in a grin.

"LIKE POPCORN?" she yelled.

"Yeah," Babe replied, nodding.

"STAY HERE," Amy said. "BE MY EARS."

"Okay," Babe said with a nod. But she picked up one of her grenades, just in case.

"Holy. Fucking. Shit," Roman said. The area outside the entrance was torn by the blast of the JDAMs, which had caught some of the Syrian commandos in its path. But it wasn't the torn bodies that got that expletive out of him. It was the sight inside the doorway. There was a landing and then a series of steps down to the left. Then another landing and a right angle turn. The second landing was, literally, covered with bodies. There was nowhere for a person to set a foot without stepping on at least one body and in some cases more than one. Some of them seemed to have been torn by blasts as well. The entire landing was drenched in blood, the floor covered in it, the walls splashed with it, even the ceiling. "This is *so* cool! It's like . . . Doom or something!"

"What?" the OIC called. The team had stacked on the door to the entrance, while two SEALs pulled rear security and Roman was *supposed* to be probing, not standing there gawking.

Roman actually paused, speechless, for a moment and then shrugged.

"It's just fucking bodies, sir," he replied. "I mean, lots and lots of bodies, piled up on each other. Like a Doom game scene, up to your knees in gore. It's so fucking cool."

"Are there stairs?" the OIC asked calmly.

"Uh, yeah," Roman replied, stepping into the landing. "That's covered in bodies too." The area was actually too brightly lit for his NODs, so he flipped them up onto his helmet. That, in a way, made the scene even cooler, since the light was red and made the stairs look like they went straight to hell. He walked down the steps until he got to the edge of the bodies, just above

the landing, and quickly peeked around the corner and ducked back. This came very close to getting his face shot off—a round actually hit his NODs, ripping them off his helmet.

"HEY!" he yelled. "NAVY SEALS. WE'RE HERE TO GET YOU O . . . OUT! SO PLEASE DON'T SHOOT US, OKAY?"

"SEALs," Babe said, pushing down on the barrel. "SEALs! Don't shoot, Amy!"

Amy laid the gun down on the floor and bent her head over it, nodding.

"SEALs!" Babe shouted. "Come ahead. We won't shoot."

CHAPTER THIRTEEN

Roman leaned around the corner again, then ducked back. When there wasn't another shot he stepped onto the bodies on the landing, watching his footing and trying to see who had been shooting at him. He realized that the attackers had been royally fucked in this engagement. There was no way to see beyond the flare light. They were sitting ducks to anybody in the darkness. He flicked on the tac light on his M-4 and flashed it down the corridor and stopped when it revealed an open door. A door with one naked girl lying on the floor in the prone position, her head bent over an AK lying on the floor, and another leaning out the door and waving him forward. He looked at the tableau for a moment and then quickly turned the light away along with his head.

"Sir," he said. "We have a problem."

"Say again, Roman?" the OIC replied. "You're broken."

"We have a problem," Roman said, stepping back up the stairs. "None of these girls have any clothes on."

"That was in the brief, Roman," the chief growled. "You should have been listening instead of high-fiving Sherman."

"Maybe I kinda caught that in the brief, Chief," Roman said. "But they Don't. Have. Any. Clothes. On."

"Roman," the chief said. "Get the fuck down there and . . . Oh, fuck it, I'm headed to your position."

The chief stumped down the steps, ignoring the bodies except to watch his footing and, at one point, catch a short sleigh ride as a pile slid downward, then flicked on his taclight and used it to negotiate his way down the body-strewn hallway.

"This your doing?" he asked the girl slumped over the AK.

"Hers and Ghost's," the other girl in the doorway said. "She can't hear, that blast got her pretty bad. I'm Babe, at least that's what Ghost called me, for Babe Ruth since I was throwing grenades."

Even the chief had to admit he was having a hard time not ogling Babe's well-formed breasts, but he mostly looked her in the eye.

"Did a good job," the chief said gruffly. "Where's this Ghost character?"

"He's . . . really badly shot up," Babe said, pulling on the chief's arm. "He's over here."

The chief negotiated his way past a couple of the girls who were around the doorway and bent down over the blood-covered figure. It took him a moment to place the face and then he laughed. A real, honest belly laugh. He leaned down and checked the pulse at the carotid, then took Ghost's chin in his hands and shook his head back and forth.

"Wake up, Ghost," the chief said loudly. "Quit fucking off on the job!"

"Wha . . ." Mike said, his eyelids fluttering open. "Adams?"

"Yeah, Ghost." The chief chuckled. "What the fuck are you doing here? Don't you know this is a job for professionals not Ass-boys?"

"Fuck you, Ass-boy Two," Mike muttered.

"You stay with us," the chief said, smiling. He dropped his assault ruck and pulled out an IV bag and catheter. With quick, sure, movements he inserted the IV and then handed the bag to Babe.

"Either hold this or get someone to hold it," Chief Adams said. Then he started digging deeper. And out came a box of tampons and another of maxipads. He heard a loud snort from behind him and saw the girl on the door, AK now at port, shaking her head.

"Where's the condoms?" she shouted slurrily. "Extra large, right? Unlubricated?"

"We're not doing underwater demo," the chief shouted back, grinning. He pulled out a pair of bandage scissors and started cutting away Ghost's clothes. As he'd come to a major hole, he'd either slap one of the maxipads on it or insert a tampon. From time to time Ghost would moan, but he kept working until most of the major external bleeding was stopped. By the time he was done with that, other members of the team had been deployed in and around the room and the OIC strode in, shaking his head.

"Ladies," the OIC said, looking around the room and trying to meet the girls' eyes by the light of the flares and some taclights that had been pointed at the ceiling, "the current plan is for us to hold this position until Syrian defenses are . . . banged up enough that we can get helicopters in. That shouldn't be more than a couple of hours. Let us do the fighting, you ladies just chill and try to stay calm. And, uhm . . ." He paused and shook his head again. "I know what you have been through, some of it anyway, and we're sorry. But, we're also men and SEALS aren't by any stretch of the imagination New Age guys or metromales, and with the exception of Petty Officer Roman we're not gay."

"Hey!"

"If any of my men give you a hard time, or are looking in an offensive way, tell me and I'll do something about it. Like kick his ass. But . . . there are going to be looks. There might even be comments. If any of them are offensive, tell me or the chief and we'll deal with it. I'm Lieutenant Reynolds, by the way, Charlie Platoon, SEAL Team Three."

"Lieutenant?" Babe said, handing the IV bag to Britney and walking over to him. "Can I say something?"

"Yes, miss?" the lieutenant replied.

"Thank you," she said, and wrapped her arms around him.

Before they knew it, all the SEALs were being hugged and kissed.

"Ladies," Reynolds said, after a bit. "We have a job to do and we can't do it if we're so distracted we don't know what day it is. So, thank you, too, and kindly let Roman and Meat go."

"Which one are you?" one of the girls asked, hanging on Roman's arm.

"Roman," he replied. "Petty Officer Third."

"Oh, the gay one?" the girl said and giggled. "Well, if you ever want to try the other way, I'm a Kappa Delta at UGA. We're right on Millege, you can't miss the house. Come on by any time."

"But, I'm not . . ." Roman said as the girl walked away.

Meat Three wrapped his arm around the confused petty officer's shoulder and led him out of the room.

"Face it," Meat said, giving his shoulder a hug-shake. "These girls have been traumatized. There's nothing that they'd like more than a gay rescuer, so they can feel safe. You lucky dog."

"I'm not *gay*," Roman protested.

"Pity," Meat Three replied.

"Meat, Roman, Sherman," the OIC said, coming out of the torture bunker. "Top-side. Watch for a counterattack. Simmons, Vahn, there's apparently a ventilation shaft back there," he said, pointing down the corridor. "Go check it out. Ghost had rigged an IED in it, but it got triggered already. See if you can rig another. Oh, and everybody give up your rations and spare canteens."

"Why?" Simmons asked, dropping his assault pack.

"Because the girls have had no food and no water for a while," Reynolds replied. "Share and share alike. Take a look around and see if you can find a sink. But watch your ass, there's apparently some chemical munitions spilled around here. Make sure the water's not contaminated, use your strips."

"How's Ghost?" Simmons said. "It's actually *Ghost*, isn't it?"

"Apparently," Reynolds replied. "You know him?"

"Knew him," Simmons said. "He was a senior team guy when I joined Charlie Three. He quit and went over to training. I heard he'd ETSed."

"Well, he's here, now," the OIC said. "Get to your jobs. We're not out of the woods, yet. Sherman," he added, reaching in his assault vest and handing the SEAL a satellite radio. "Call in. Tell them the girls are secure, Ghost is severely wounded, one of the girls is in a bad way. Ask that they control the JDAMs from satellite and Predator since we're going to be down here. And find out when we can expect extraction."

"Got it, sir," Sherman replied, turning for the entrance.

"Meat, Roman, cover him," the OIC finished, turning back into the room.

"Lieutenant?" one of the girls said. "I'm Bambi. Well, Britney, but . . ."

"I understand, miss," the lieutenant replied, trying to look her in the eye. She had perfect breasts, small but very well formed. And . . . blue eyes. Nice face. Shit, this was too much.

"Amy said that Ghost said that there's a bag over in the room across the hall," she said, pulling on his arm and ignoring the looks. "There's something in it for the President. She said it was contaminated; I don't know what that means."

"I do," the lieutenant said, allowing himself to be led. When they reached the door, Bambi . . . Britney bent down and pulled out a flare, sparking it to light, and gestured to the leather case.

"I thought I saw it before," she said. "He sent me in here to get plastic to put on one of the wounds on his chest."

The lieutenant walked to the sample case and touched it gingerly. It was wet, as if washed down.

"Any idea where he got the water?" the lieutenant asked. He pulled a strip of material out of a pouch and rubbed it on the outside of the case.

"No," Britney replied.

The test strip said that the outside of the bag was clean. He was sorely tempted to open it and find out what was inside.

"Bambi," he said, unthinkingly. "Could you leave the flare here and step out of the room?"

Britney nodded and set the flare on the floor, then backed out of the room.

Reynolds picked it up, pushed the door closed and then set it on the pile of boxes in the middle of the room. Then he set the sample case on the ground where the light would fall in it, took a breath and opened the case slowly. What he saw made him blow out his breath in an explosive: "HOLY FUCKING SHIT."

"Are you okay, Lieutenant?" Britney called, knocking on the door.

Reynolds closed the case gingerly, trying not to breathe and hoping he wasn't getting hit by neurotoxins, and then opened the

door back up. When he took a breath there was a faint whiff of sulfur and that actually made him happier. The contamination was probably mustard or maybe phosgene, which wasn't going to kill anyone at that level of concentration.

"I'm fine," Reynolds said, grinning and trying not to laugh. "Do you have any idea where the material in this case came from?"

"No," Britney said.

"Okay, we'll figure it out," Reynolds replied, dropping the case and hugging her. "Sorry, I'm just . . . tickled."

"What's in there?" Britney asked, surprised by the emotional response from the officer who had been so correct so far.

"A surprise," Reynolds said, grinning. "I've got to go."

He walked to the stairs and made his way up the pile of bodies to where Roman and Meat were covering Sherman, who was hooked into the satellite radio. The radio was smaller than a brick phone, with an internal directional antenna and a headset.

"Who's there?" Reynolds asked, squatting down and still grinning.

"Admiral Hayes," Sherman said, covering the mike. "Want to talk?"

"Got your camera?" Reynolds asked, pulling the mike away and jacking the earphone into his ear.

"Yes, sir," Sherman replied, shrugging off his assault pack and pulling out the small video recorder. "I got some shots of the bodies on the stairs but not of the girls."

"STARBASE, SIERRA ONE, OVER," Reynolds said. "Apparently, Agent Ghost wanted to give a present to the President. I totally agree. But I think you should see it, first. We're preparing for video uplink."

"Copy SIERRA. This is STARBASE Actual," the admiral said. "Be advised that the NCA may be monitoring this conversation and video linkage."

"Oh, I don't think he'll mind, sir," Reynolds said happily. "Sherman, back off. The inside of the case is contaminated. Mustard, I think, low concentration, but I'm going to hold my breath when I open it."

"Okay, sir," Sherman said, handing him the camera, which had been plugged into the satellite link, and backing away.

"Here goes," Reynolds said, taking a breath and then opening up the case with his left hand while shining the low-light camera with a very faint blue light at the case.

"HOLY SHIT!" the President shouted. "Yes! Yes! YES!"

"Oh, man," Brandeis said, shaking his head. "We have *got* to get this guy a medal. Barring that, one hell of a lot of money."

"Put me in contact with them," Cliff said, looking over at the communications technician.

"You're on, sir."

"SEAL Commander."

"SIERRA Six?" Reynolds asked.

"This is the President. I hate doing direct contacts, I don't want to be LBJ in Vietnam. But I have to ask. That *is* who I think it is, right?"

"As far as I can tell, sir," Reynolds replied, nervously. Knowing the President might be listening and actually *talking* to him were two different things. "We were told that Ghost wanted it to be a personal present to you."

"How is he?" the President asked.

"Very badly hit, sir," Reynolds said. "He's lost a lot of blood and he's probably got major internal bleeds. We don't have blood with us, just IV's. We're trying to keep him stabilized but . . ."

"Okay," the President said. "The girls?"

"Better than I expected, sir," the lieutenant admitted. "Some of them are nearly catatonic, but most of them seem to be holding it together pretty well. Ghost had a few of them helping him and they're particularly good. One of them took some hearing loss when we dropped a JDAM near the entrance, but she's otherwise okay. She was holding the door when we got here and nearly killed my point. Shot the NODs right off his helmet. Another one was apparently chucking grenades for him. I think, maybe, fighting back was kind of good therapy."

"I don't know about times, but somebody's on the way," the President said. "You just hang tough, SEAL. Damned good job. I want to see all of your team at the White House, or maybe Camp

David, as soon as you get back to the States. Camp David, that way you don't have to dress up."

"Yes, sir," Reynolds said.

"And *don't* lose that bag," the President added. "And try to find the rest of him."

"Will do, sir," Reynolds replied.

"Cut this and clear us, I've done enough damage . . ."

"I think he's clear," Admiral Hayes said. "I have to add, good job. How was the drop?"

"Not something I want to do again, sir," Reynolds admitted. "We nearly were mid-aired by an F-15, had a SAM fly by, an air-to-air, watched portions of the dogfight from the good seats, if you know what I mean. We lost two of our meats on the way down from effects from the F-15. Their chutes deployed, but I don't know where they are or if they're alive or dead."

"We'll get SAR in there, too," the admiral said. "And dial out the Predator to look for them. Security situation?"

"The JDAM must have convinced them we were serious, sir," Reynolds responded. "We had some contact on the way in, very light, brushed it aside, and no counterattacks. ETA on reinforcements?"

"According to the Air Force, we've dug a hole through their SAM belt and CAP is refueling. As soon as they're refueled, the 101 will move to your position by helo. Say an hour or so. Egress Ghost and the wounded girl first, then the women, then your team, then the 101 will pull out."

"Roger, sir," Reynolds said. "Sir, be advised. The ladies are completely unclothed. Respectfully request . . . well . . ."

"The 101 is supposed to be bringing spare clothes," the admiral said.

"Thank you, sir," Reynolds replied. "Anything else, sir?"

"Nope," the admiral said. "I'm looking at the take from the Predator and you're right, nobody seems to be sticking out their head. There was an armored column headed for your position, but the Air Force savaged it and it turned back. Fingers crossed, we're looking good."

"I'll go tell the ladies, sir," Reynolds replied. "SIERRA Six clear?"

"STARBASE out," the admiral said. "And make sure you bring the bag."

"Okay, ladies," Reynolds said, walking back into the room. "God willing and nothing goes particularly wrong, our reinforcements should be here in about an hour. When they get here, we leave. And they *are* bringing clothes."

That elicited applause from the girls and he smiled.

"I'd like to cover some details of the exit," he said. "We're going to put Ghost and Rachel on the first chopper. There are medics standing by. I'd like a couple of the ladies who have been with Rachel to accompany her, so figure out who they are. Then we'll get the rest of you out of here. The stairs, in case you haven't seen them, are covered in bodies and body parts. We're not going to have time to clear that; you'll have to walk on the bodies, so prepare yourselves. We'll station someone on the landing with clothes so you don't have to walk out in the open in your . . . current condition." He looked around and cleared his throat.

"This might be the wrong time to say this and the wrong thing to say, but please don't let what happened to you turn you into . . . something you don't want to be. We went through a lot to get here and secure the position. I won't get into the whole story except to say that we had to drop through the middle of a dogfight overhead and I lost two of my men when we were nearly hit by an F-15 fighter. We came here to rescue, Ghost fought to rescue, what you . . . were. Nice, decent, lovely young ladies who were just . . . getting on with your lives. This experience is, yeah, going to scar you. But when you get to thinking that all men are horrible assholes because of what you went through, or some friend tells you that, or some therapist tells you that, or some professor tells you that, or, hell, you run into some guy who *is* an asshole, think about us, too, and Ghost. If you turn your backs on the good guys . . . well . . . we'll still come for you whenever you need us, but it will take all of the joy out of what we do, what we've done. This is . . . what we live for. In the end, you ladies are what we fight and die for. Don't turn your backs on us, too."

He nodded at the group and then walked out of the room.

▲   ▲   ▲

"Sergeant Major Gunther, Third Batt, Rakasans," the NCO said as he neared the entrance followed by a group of soldiers carrying BDU tops in their arms. "We brought clothes."

"PO Roman," Roman said. "My L-T wants us to hand them out as the girls come up. We've been around them for a couple of hours now, they're used to us." His jaw flexed and he shook his head. "Try to get your guys to not ogle."

"Already covered," the NCO said tightly. "Where do you want them?"

"Meat," Roman said. "Grab an armful and station yourself on the landing. You're about to be very popular." Meat grabbed the first two armfuls and headed down the stairs.

"We've got enough choppers to lift all the girls and the team," Gunther said. "Then the choppers will turn around and pull us out."

"Have fun sitting on this patch," Roman said. "It's no fun. We need two stretchers."

"Incoming," Gunther said, looking over his shoulder. "Medics! Stretchers!"

"Okay, good stick whoever did it." Specialist Calvin Thomas was a pretty good medic in his opinion. He was an EMT in New York on September 11, 2001 and volunteered for the U.S. Army on October 1, as soon as they were sure there wasn't anything left to do at Ground Zero. He'd seen his share of shot-up bodies, both in New York and since. In his expert medical opinion, the guy on the floor should have already been dead. On the other hand, he'd seen people survive that should have died. And people die that should have lived. You just never knew. "Any idea what type he is?"

"O pos," Chief Adams said.

"You sure?"

"I'm sure," Adams said. "I know him like a brother."

"Good," Thomas replied. "Let's get him on the stretcher. Then I'll run some blood and intubate."

Ghost was lifted onto the stretcher as the medic pulled out a unit of O positive blood. Since almost anyone could take O pos, he had carried it down to the room just in case. He had other

types in a cooler in the chopper. He put a blood pressure cuff on the guy's arm and shook his head at the reading.

"Okay, easy with the stretcher," he said to the four infantrymen that had accompanied him into the bunker. "And keep your eyes on where you're going, not the view."

"The girl goes, too," Chief Adams said. "And the two girls with her. Her name is Rachel, I don't have a last. No idea of her medical. Call the two girls with her Bambi and Thumper."

"Ooo-kay," Thomas said, shaking his head. "Lift away, boys."

The stretchers were carried, carefully, up the stairs and then across the open area to the waiting choppers. Bambi and Thumper each gave Meat a quick kiss and then donned the BDU tops, buttoning them hurriedly. They barely had time to scramble into the chopper before the pilot revved the engines and lifted off the ground.

"Is he going to live?" Britney asked.

"Maybe," Thomas said. "His blood pressure is so low, though," he added, giving the liter of blood a squeeze. He had one more liter of O-pos and after that he'd be pumping in water where blood should go.

He slid an oxygen tube up Ghost's nose, then a breathing tube down his throat. He ran a cervical collar around his neck, for what good it would do, and checked the bandages.

"SEALs," he muttered, looking at the tampons and pads. He put pressure bandages on each of the wounds, right on top of the field expedient bandages. When he was done he checked for a pulse again and blanched.

"Crap," he muttered, pulling out a field defibrillator.

"Can I assist?" Bambi asked.

"You trained?" Thomas asked. "Not right now. Clear." He placed the pads on Ghost's body and set the sensor in place, hitting the on button of the defib kit then sitting back.

"Aren't you supposed to . . ." Thumper said.

"Wait."

"Checking for pulse," the machine said in a female voice. "No pulse. Charging, charging, stand clear, CLEAR." There was a sharp whine from the machine and Ghost's body jerked but didn't arch convulsively. "Checking for pulse. Pulse forty-five."

"It does it all," Bambi said. "I've never used one, but I've heard of them."

"I'm leaving it in place," Thomas said, going back to his bandaging. The liter was about out, so he changed it for a fresh one and ran another IV, after three sticks, to start a standard glucose drip. Anything to get the damned BP up. "Crew chief! How long?" he yelled.

"Twenty minutes," the crew chief yelled back over the thunder of the chopper. "There's a field station set up."

"He doesn't need a field station," Thomas snapped. "He needs a damned class one trauma center. If we can't get some more blood in him, his heart is going to *collapse*."

"No pulse," the machine said. "Charging . . ."

"Miss, we have to go now," Reynolds said as carefully as he could. He'd hardly noticed the girl in the back of the room, huddled in the corner, until the rest of the girls were filing out. She had a blank stare that he'd seen in seriously shell-shocked firefight survivors. He knew she wasn't seeing him, except, possibly, as a male shape.

"Chief," he called. "See if Babe is still around."

"I'm here, sir," Babe said. She was still stark naked but seemed to hardly notice anymore. The SEALs, despite the lieutenant's warning, had been solicitous to a fault. Yeah, they looked from time to time, but not in a bad way. Like Ghost, she felt she could trust them. But the girl in the back corner clearly could not. If she even noticed.

"Hi," Babe said, squatting down. "What's your name?"

The girl looked at her in fear, then shut her eyes and huddled into the corner.

"Okay," Babe said. "Wrong question. I know *why* it's the wrong question, even. It was stupid. But, listen to me, we're getting out of here. They're not going to hurt us anymore. We're safe. The Army's here and the SEALs and they're all good guys that aren't going to hurt us. But we need to *go*."

"Chief," Reynolds called. "Go get one of those BDU tops for Babe and this lady."

"Roger," Chief Adams said, striding out of the room.

"We can sedate her," Reynolds said.

"They gave us drugs to bring us over here," Babe responded tightly. "If you want her to totally panic, come at her with a needle. If you want *me* to totally panic, bring out a needle."

"Gotcha," Reynolds said, squatting down. "What can we do?"

"If we can get some clothes on her, maybe she'll calm down," Babe said.

"I was next," the girl whispered.

"What?" Reynolds said. "Honey, you're safe. The bad men are all dead. You're safe. Please, let us get you out of here."

"I was next," the girl said again, looking at the far wall. "I sat next to Rachel. She was my friend."

"Oh, crap," Babe said then swallowed. "When they were done with Rachel, she would have been next."

"I liked Clari," the girl said, tears forming in her eyes. "She was my friend, too. And they . . . they . . ."

"Clothes, boss," the chief said, shaking his head. "Miss, you're about the age of my daughter. Could you maybe put on some clothes? I know she started getting funny about being naked when she was ten. And I surely would like to get you out of here. There's a plane waiting to take you back to the United States. Your family is waiting. Could you please come back to us?"

The girl seemed to focus for a second and then shut her eyes, crying.

"Don't like to look at the room, do you?" the chief said, handing Babe a jacket and cradling the other one in his arms. "Can you let Babe put this on you?" he asked.

The girl nodded and Babe slid her arms in the sleeves, then buttoned up the front. Then she laughed.

"It's . . . a little big," Babe said, rolling up the sleeves so that the short female's hands would show.

"Miss," the chief said, gently. "I know you don't want a man touching you or even being near you. But getting out of this place with your eyes closed will be tough. Did your daddy ever carry you piggyback?"

"Yes," the girl said, quietly.

"No man can hurt a girl that's piggyback," the chief said. "If I turn around, will you climb on my back? I can carry you out of

here. I can carry you all the way home if that's what it takes. I can carry you around the world, if that's what it takes. You just say the word. I'll carry you anywhere, because you look a lot like my daughter and I'd want somebody to help her if she was hurt and scared like you are."

The girl nodded, her eyes closed.

"I'm going to turn around now," the chief said, suiting actions to words, "and Babe is going to help you up on my back. Can Babe do that? She's a girl, just like you."

"Okay," the girl said in a small voice.

"Come on," Babe said, taking one arm and lifting it up so it touched the chief's shoulder. As soon as the girl's hand touched, she leaned forward and swarmed onto the SEAL's back, wrapping her legs around his waist and grabbing his neck so hard it choked him.

"Maybe a little lighter?" the chief gasped. "I need to breathe a little."

The girl loosened up as the chief carefully climbed to his feet.

"Please take me home," the girl whispered in his ear, crying faintly and shaking. "Please? I don't want to be hurt. Please?"

"I will, sweetie," the chief said, walking carefully towards the front of the room and unconsciously moving his weapon to a tactical position. "And nobody, *nobody*, is going to hurt you anymore. Let me teach you a song as we go. It goes like this: *Out in the wood there's a band of small fairies if you walk unwary at night. They're laughing and drinking and soon you'll be thinking, that you'd like to join in their life . . .*"

CHAPTER FOURTEEN

"All of the surviving hostages have been extracted and are on their way to Germany on a medical evacuation flight," Secretary Brandeis told the packed audience. "They will be given a brief medical check in Germany, then returned to the States. Our first priority is getting them back to their families, although some of them are in poor psychological condition. On that score, they have bonded rather strongly with the SEAL team that was dropped in to hold the position and the team will be accompanying them all the way back to the States. This is at the rather pointed request of some of the young ladies who refused to board the evac plane unless the SEALs went too.

"The person known as Ghost is on the same evac plane and is in critical condition. Military doctors at the transfer point in Iraq stabilized him enough for movement but it's touch and go. Doctors have told me that we might not know for days, or even weeks, if he will live.

"As to Syria," the secretary continued, keying an overhead monitor that showed an oblique view of the set of buildings people had come to know, "this is Aleppo Four. A B-2 has been orbiting Aleppo Four continuously since the SEAL team was inserted. All of our personnel have been evacuated. And this is our answer to Aleppo Four."

There was a brief pause and then the screen flashed white and clicked out to a broader view that showed a boiling mushroom cloud.

"That is the lowest power nuclear weapon in our arsenal," Brandeis said, coldly. "Before anyone asks the question about 'won't that make people accelerate their WMD plans,' I'll make it simple. As our President once said: Bring it on. Every insane group of leaders in the world is trying to craft nuclear weapons, poison gas and biological agents. They have been for decades. Despite what the people in the press think, Saddam was working on it very hard. For today, we are not going into Syria. The state of war still holds. We can now confirm that Basser Assad was present at Aleppo Four, apparently watching the rapings and torture from behind a two-way mirror. He was killed by Ghost. And he was not the only person killed by Ghost." Brandeis keyed the screen again and a body was shown. It was twisted in death and someone in chemical protective clothing was holding the head more or less in place.

He waited until the shouts, from gleeful to horrified, died down and smiled.

"So for anyone who says there was 'no proven link to Al Qaeda,'" Brandeis snarled, "Agent Ghost *also* killed Osama Bin Laden, who was *also* watching the proceedings. He killed him, and Basser Assad, with the very mustard gas which was being produced in the facility. Aleppo Four is now a smoking hole. And let all of the terrorists of the world, all the governments of the world who support them, all the governments that are feverishly working on nukes and gas and germs, let all of them know that this is the end result. So, the question that you have to ask is: Exactly how far do I want to go to piss the United States off? Because now you know, that if you go far enough, what you're going to receive is a smoking hole and an increase in background radiation. If you push us far enough, our answer is simple: nuke them until they glow and shoot them in the dark. No questions."

Mike's throat was terribly sore. Then he forgot his throat as various bits of his body started informing his conscious mind just how very glad they were to have someone to complain to,

finally. He managed to drag his eyes open and got a glimpse of acoustic tile.

"I was hoping for Valhalla," he muttered. Or tried to, it was more of a mumble. "Ow."

"You're awake," a bright young female voice said. "Don't try to talk. Are you in any pain?"

"Uhhh!" he grunted.

"Let me get you some water for your throat," the voice said, "then I'll get the doctor and see if your medication needs to be adjusted."

A tube was inserted in his mouth and he got a brief flash of one of those unpleasant multicolored smocks nurses had taken to wearing. So much for Valkyries and feasting.

He closed his eyes as the nurse squeaked out in her rubber-soled shoes and wondered where he was. The U.S., probably: the nurse didn't have the "feel" of military nurses. Which meant he'd been out for a while.

"So you're finally awake," a female voice said.

The face that leaned into view wasn't bad, but it was terribly professional. Brown hair pulled back in a bun, more handsome than pretty. Nice eyes, but a trifle cold.

"How are you feeling?" the doctor asked. "There's going to be a high degree of soreness from the surgery, but is there any intense pain? Pain remediation at this point is important."

"If I don't move," he said slowly, wondering why he couldn't talk more clearly, "I'm okay."

"That's the idea," the doctor said. "Don't move. With the level of morphine in you right now, you'd have a hard time anyway."

"W'ere my?" Mike asked then worked his jaw. "Where am I?"

"You're in a . . . special hospital in Virginia," the doctor said. "And . . . we don't refer to our patients by name. You're Patient 1357. Sorry."

"S'okay," Mike replied. "CIA?"

"Somewhat, but primarily military, sort of," the doctor said, smiling in a way that cut off that avenue of conversation. "I'm Dr. Quinn." She looked at him for a moment and nodded. "Go ahead and get it out of your system, otherwise you'll be bothered until you do."

"Medicine woman?" Mike said, trying to grin.

"See, feel better?" the doctor said. "No relation. I'll send the nurse back in to take care of your needs. If the pain gets particularly bad, ring for the nurse and we'll make an adjustment. Let me be clear: Pain is *not* weakness leaving the body. You can play that game when you're operational, but when you're recovering, high-order pain reduces your ability to heal. We want to keep the pain *down*. Don't be a hero. If you're in a lot of pain, tell us. If you move and it hurts like hell and won't go away, tell us."

"Got it," Mike said. "I take it I'm going to live?"

"You're going to live," the doctor said, nodding. "There was some infection, but we got that under control days ago. You've been unconscious for nearly two weeks. Not in a coma, just unconscious. Not abnormal with injuries as severe as yours. But you're well on your way to recovery, now."

"Thanks," Mike said, working his head. His neck seemed, other than stiffness, to be the only thing that didn't hurt.

"You're welcome," Dr. Quinn said. "I spent nearly ten hours with my hands in various bits of you. I'm glad to see it was worth it."

The biggest problem was the tedium. In a civilian hospital, he'd probably have been discharged after a few days to a week, basically when the IV came out, which was three days after he woke up. Since this place was "sort of military," and he had nobody to help him at home, he had to stay. He watched TV and caught some of the replays of the return home of the girls. The government, thank God, had let them get together with their parents before the news media got a crack. President Cliff had waited until the day after the homecoming to go visit, and hadn't talked to the media on the way in or out, just turned up, spent some time and left. No grandstanding, no politicking. The scene of the girls getting off the plane in Dix was part of Fox's lead-in. Charlie Three had, apparently, been their escorts back and for some reason the chief had one of the girls stuck on his back like a limpet. That was a major shot in the lead-in.

Some general had taken over from Assad in Syria. He had promised that they were out of the WMD game and renounced

terrorism, then started playing the Saddam game of denying that there ever *was* any WMD and they *certainly* weren't sponsoring terrorism. All the while complaining largely of fallout from the remarkably clean burst over their soil. All America's fault, of course. The girls were never there. There was no proof. Show us the proof they were there.

Video footage by news media from the site certainly wasn't proof. Oh, no. And all the networks but Fox were eating it up and constantly asking "where's the proof?" Flipping idiots.

Some of the girls were on from time to time and he shook his head at the tenor of the questions. Bambi . . . Britney was interviewed on ABC. He'd made sure he stayed awake that evening, and the interviewer, some chick, was aghast that she would have actually tried to fight. That she wasn't viewing herself as a victim. Bambi just about tore her a new asshole. "I'm not a victim. I fought to help all of us stay alive and I refuse to be called or characterized as a victim. I'm a fighter and a survivor. Ghost taught me that."

The government had gone from giving updates on his health to refusing to speculate whether he was alive or dead. Since he was listening to that from inside a secure—he'd seen the guards outside—military hospital, it gave him a bit of a shiver. But he figured it was for his own safety. Various Islamic groups had pronounced jihad, personally, on the horrible person that would actually kill their Great Leader. Not, by the way, that the Great Leader was dead. Show us the proof. Pictures of a body are not proof. But the man called Ghost was going to be one when they got their hands on him.

He tracked his progress by the stuff that came out and what he could do. IV, drainage tubes, the day they let him walk to the bathroom and he found out how hard it was. He tried to play mental games, remember historical events; he got one of the nurses to get him some books and they all turned out to be romances. He read them anyway and came away wondering just how traumatic it really *was* for the girls in the bunker. If this was what women read for *fun* . . . ?

One day he was puzzling over a scene in one of the "historicals" that didn't match any "history" he knew, when a colonel in

undress greens walked in unannounced. One read of the nametag said it all.

"Good to finally meet you, Colonel Pierson," Mike said, holding out his hand.

"Glad to see you're going to make it," Pierson replied, grinning.

"Am I?" Mike asked with a raised eyebrow. "The government doesn't seem sure."

"That's why I'm here," Pierson admitted, pulling up a chair. "One of the reasons. You want to be alive or dead?"

"Can we stick with 'unsure'?" Mike asked.

"For the time being," Pierson said. "This administration will be more than happy to stay with 'unwilling to comment upon his mortality.' But . . . administrations change. Honestly, you-know-who is probably going to run in '08 and she's got a good chance of winning. We both know that."

"How hard would it be to classify it so the bitch can't get it?" Mike asked. "The teams won't talk."

"Hard but not impossible," Pierson admitted with a sigh. "Pretty hard to not say that you survived, but we can probably hide your identity."

"Works for me," Mike replied. "So what else do you have?"

"Well," Pierson said solemnly, clearing his throat and picking up his briefcase. "There are a number of forms that I need you to sign. We're handling the money through the Witness Protection Program . . ."

"Money?" Mike asked.

"Well, first there's Osama," Pierson said, his face cracking into a grin. "There was a Presidential Finding that the President's words to the news media, 'dead or alive' meant that the reward could be paid . . ."

"Dead or alive," Mike said and whistled. "How much?"

"Twenty-five million," Pierson said and grinned again. "It's being handled through the Witness Protection Program and they're pretty damned secure, even from presidents. It's split in various accounts so no one bank person sees a deposit of twenty-five million. But there's another five million for 'aid in disrupting a major terrorist operation.' So your grand total is thirty. There was

some quibbling about your medical expenses, which were size-able, and I'm told that when the discussion reached presidential level it descended to four-letter words. So you don't even have to pay the hospital bill."

"Damn," Mike said, his eyes wide. "What the hell am I going to do with twenty-five, thirty million dollars?"

"Uhm . . ." Pierson hummed. "Think, rather, what you *can't* do. But spend it wisely—most lottery winners go broke. Another reason to spend it wisely is that you don't want to become too visible."

"Boat," Mike said. "A yacht. That way I can move around. I'll come up with a cover story, but it will *look* like I'm a drug dealer or former drug dealer spending his ill-gotten gains."

"That works," Pierson said. "Now, we don't expect that you'll have actual trouble from the terrorists or any future adventures. But there may be repercussions. There is a special program for certain categories of protectees, and you're a good example, which gives them pseudo-police authority. Effectively, you're made a special version of the Reserve Federal Marshall. What that means is you can carry anywhere in the U.S., and in a good bit of the rest of the world. And it acts as a Class III permit, so you can carry *heavy* if you wish. Illegal use is illegal use, but if you can carry it, you can carry it."

"Good," Mike said. "I'd been somewhat worried about the tangos finding out who I was before I found out they found out. But if I'm *armed* in an ambush, that's a different story."

"Don't go Rambo," Pierson said sternly.

"Don't intend to," Mike replied. "But it's a comfort."

"Also, in the same vein," Pierson continued. "You don't exactly have a 'get-out-of-jail-free' card. But some things may come up relating to your . . . special status. Part of this," he said, holding up the briefcase, "besides instructions on what you can do with your status and what you can't and how to handle it, is a number of the Office of Special Operations Liaison. Or, as we call it, Oh-so-SOL. It's where I work. The phone is manned twenty-four hours a day. If you have problems or questions, call it. You're also going to be on the military database as a 'special contractor.' That could mean anything from a contract weapons instructor to . . . well,

you. However, if anyone brings up your record, all the salient information is Code Word classified, so they'll probably put two and two together and get something near four. At the very least, if it's a military or police situation, they'll recognize you're not just one of the narod. Don't use it if you don't have to."

"Understood," Mike said, sighing. "I don't just get to be myself the rest of my life, do I?"

"Nope," Pierson said. "When I retire, I'll be nobody. You'll *always* be, at least until the terrorists get worked down to a regional nuisance, the guy who killed Osama. Sprayed him with poison gas then cut his head off. Arguably, you should be surrounded by bodyguards the rest of your life. Knowing you, though..."

"Ain't gonna happen," Mike said. "I'm a good enough body-guard, thanks. That it?"

"Except for the paperwork," Pierson said with a nod. "And running you over the instructions. Yes."

"When can I get discharged?" Mike asked. "I have a bunch of money to spend."

"As soon as this gets cleared up," the colonel replied. "And we'd really like a written after-action report..."

"Don't hold your breath," Mike replied, grunting. "What happens on the mission, stays on the mission. Let's get started on the rest of it, though. I have people to see...."

It was a shitty day in Athens. A weak cold front was coming through and the light, misty, rain was soaking into Brenda McCarthy's sweatshirt as she walked up College Street. The conditions fit her mood, which was crappy. The girls had been given A averages for the semester that had been "disrupted" as the administration put it. But since the beginning of this new semester she'd had to contend with being "One of the Syria Girls." The whispers and looks in class were bad enough. But the experience tended to attract... the wrong kind of guys. Guys that she really didn't want calling her "Babe." Guys that, frankly, set off her creep meter.

So it was just adding insult to a screwed up day when some loser sitting at the Starbucks called out to her.

"Hey, Babe, it is *Babe*, isn't it?"

She spun around to deliver an angry reply and stopped as the man stood up and took off his sunglasses. She stood still as he approached to where he could speak quietly.

"I don't like it when most people call me that," she said, her face working, trying not to cry.

"Well, I don't know your real name," the man said. "But some people call me Ghost."

BOOK TWO
Thunder Island

CHAPTER
ONE

"Hey, Mike, how was the fishing?" Sol Shatalin called from the dock.

"Pretty good," Mike yelled, as he backed the forty-five-foot Bertram up to the pier. "Grab my lines, will ya?"

He'd spent the first month or so pretty much out of sight of land, working on his tan and fishing, using various products to get the scars to look older than they were. By the time he started taking his shirt off in public, they didn't look fresh except to a very trained eye. Now he fished and SCUBAed in the area of Islamorada, and his "address" was Slip 19-C, Islamorada Yacht Club.

Spending that much time offshore had had another benefit; he caught a lot of fish and learned *how* to catch them and how to fillet them, which brought more money than whole. Now, he rarely went out without at least making gas money. In fact, since he really lived a pretty Spartan existence, he was living pretty much on money from fishing. Of course, it wouldn't have covered the payments on the Bertram, but he'd paid for that in cash. All three-quarters of a mil.

He'd recently, though, been considering a developing lackanookie condition. He could fix that easy enough by a run up to Athens, but he'd started to think he might be using the girls, and that

was the last thing he wanted to do. He hadn't been in contact with all of them, just a core of about twelve. And of those twelve, he'd only had sex with three. It had been healing for both sides. And with a few of the others, he'd just slept, and that had been healing, too.

But he didn't want to get into a habit of just turning up for nookie. He wasn't planning on spending his life with any of them, for various reasons. And they needed to get on with their lives. For that matter, every trip to Athens meant a possibility of somebody who recognized him from a class putting Mike Harmon, former SEAL and jerk in class, together with one of the "Syria Girls" and getting four. So letting the girls go, slowly, was a good idea.

But it wasn't helping his lackanookie.

There were, as around any major yacht club, various "boat bunnies." But they didn't appeal, either, even the good-looking ones, and they were in short supply. It was a philosophical thing. He didn't mind paying for sex; he'd done it often enough in various third-world countries. And he didn't mind having a girlfriend who was "a little hard up." Christy, his ex, had been a live-in aspiring actress who didn't make her share of the rent most of the time before they'd gotten married. But boat bunnies lived "on the kindness of strangers" as Mae West would say. It *was* prostitution, but even hint at that fact and you got one hell of a telling-off and generally a cleared boat. Then there was the issue of "Bluebeard's Stateroom."

The boat had five cabins: the "master" cabin forward (with a really nice bathroom, the nicest he'd ever owned) and four "regular" cabins, two with bunk beds and two with doubles. He'd converted one of the doubles cabins into his "team locker." Besides using his "special" status to buy various interesting weapons, he'd contacted a company that sold gear to the teams and ordered, well, one of everything. He now was as well equipped as anyone on a team: body armor, ammo vest, everything down to boots and wetsuits. He didn't figure he'd ever need it, but he also hadn't figured he'd end up in Syria shot to shit.

But he'd really rather not have to explain to a boat bunny why one of his cabins had a weapons' locker, weight set and various

military equipment. The cabin was locked, but some of the boat bunnies wouldn't have cared. More than one owner had come back to find their boat stripped of everything valuable and their "girlfriend" gone. Which was why he called it "Bluebeard's Stateroom." And another reason not to pick up boat bunnies.

He considered what he wanted to do for the evening while running the lackanookie in the background. Fixing dinner and eating alone was getting tiresome but so was going out alone. Finally, he decided to just bite the bullet and go over to Rumrunners II and get dinner. They didn't cook mahi as well as he did, but he also didn't have to do the dishes.

As he pulled out of the club in the truck, the air conditioning going at full blast, he considered, again, whether he should get a pussy-mobile. He'd kept the truck even though he could buy any car in the world for some of the same reasons that he didn't like boat bunnies. If he met a girl, he wanted her to like him for him, not for his money. So far that hadn't worked very well, so he was considering getting a car that would reflect his . . . how did Pierson put it that one time . . . "comfortable" status. A Ferrari would do that but he really liked the look of the Jaguar XK-8. It was just a sweet-looking car. Not as hot as the Ferrari or the Bentley Continental, but . . . great lines. Like a woman's body. And much more of an eye magnet than a five-year-old pickup truck.

There were people sitting outside of Rumrunners, some of them quite pleasantly female. But it meant the place was probably packed. He wandered into the open air front and got in line for the hostess anyway.

"How many in your party?" the cute little blonde asked. Quite shapely, she reminded him of Bambi, same pretty face and curly blonde hair. As he thought that he got hit with a nasty flashback of the blonde bending over to scavenge ammo from the dead, arms and legs covered in blood and lovely blonde bush reflecting in the red flare light. "Are you okay?" the girl asked hurriedly.

"Yeah," he answered after a second, closing his eyes and telling himself that he was in Islamorada and at Rumrunners. Not back in the bunker. "Sorry, sort of a headache thing," he continued, taking off his sunglasses to dangle on their lanyard. "One, non-smoking."

"We're pretty busy this afternoon," the girl said nervously. "It will be about an hour."

"I'll wait in the bar," Mike replied, taking the flashy buzzy pager thing and dropping it in his pocket.

The bar was even more crowded than the front, all the tables taken and no room to even move up to the bar and get a beer. Finally he spotted an open seat next to a curvy brunette and pushed his way through the crowd to it.

"This seat taken?" he asked, groaning to himself. He'd be more than happy to hit on the brunette, who was wearing a light sundress and looked even better from the front than the back, but mostly he was just trying to get to the bar.

"Yes, as a matter of fact it is," the girl said coldly. "My friend will be back in a minute."

"Not hitting on you," Mike said, trying to get the barmaid's attention. "I was just trying to find a seat."

The girl turned away and he shrugged. Finally, the barmaid got free and came over to him.

"I'll take a Fosters," Mike said. "And please give the young lady and her 'friend' a refill so she won't think I'm a jerk."

The barmaid glanced at the brunette, who shrugged and nodded.

"I'm sorry I snapped," the girl said, not turning her head.

"It's okay," Mike replied. "You probably *do* get hit on all the time. I think it would be different for a guy, but for young ladies it probably gets to being a pain in the butt."

"It is," she said as a short, well-set-up blonde with short hair and lovely green eyes walked up and looked at Mike. He realized he was enough in the space that she couldn't sit down.

"Sorry," Mike said, backing away. "Just trying to get a drink."

"And buying us one," the brunette said, with a slight grin. "I'm Pam Shover."

"Mike Jenkins," Mike said, holding out his hand over the blonde's back. "Boat bum."

"What's a boat bum?" the blonde asked, interested despite herself.

"Somebody who lives full time on a boat and has no visible means of income," Mike replied, taking out a card and handing

it to "Pam." "If you ever want to go fishing or cruising or whatever, give me a call. Again, not a hit. I just like to show off my boat."

"Probably not," Pam said, tucking the card away. "We're only down here for a week."

"Summer break?" Mike asked.

"Yes," Pam said. "And even with all the other girls in town, I feel like the main character in the song 'Fins.'"

" *'Got fins to the left,'* " Mike sang, chuckling. "Gotcha." He glanced at his watch and shrugged. "I've got about fifty minutes until my table's ready. So can we talk or should I just crawl under a rock?"

"We can talk," Pam said, grinning again and looking over the blonde's shoulder. "So, what does a professional boat bum do?"

"Mostly fish," Mike admitted.

"I'd wondered what the smell was," the blonde said, then flinched. "Jesus, I'm sorry, that came out as a real cut and it wasn't intended."

"I was catching dolphin this morning and spent a couple of hours filleting them all out," Mike said. "I showered and scrubbed before I landed. But getting all the smell off is tough."

"You were catching *dolphin*?" the blonde said angrily, looking up at him with flashing green eyes.

"Uh, dolphin *fish*," Mike said. "You'd probably call it mahi-mahi."

"People call it dolphin?" the blonde asked, confused.

"Yeah," Mike replied. "Don't worry about it, though, everybody gets it confused. But if somebody is talking about fishing for a run of dolphin, they're talking about mahi-mahi, not Flipper."

"Okay," the blonde said, chuckling. "Sorry about that."

"Like I said, common," Mike replied. "Anyway, that's pretty much what I do."

"And that pays the bills?" Pam said, raising an eyebrow.

"Oh, no," Mike replied. "Well, not all of them. I'm sort of retired."

"You're young to retire," Pam said, leaning back and looking at him with real interest for the first time.

"Short story or long?" Mike asked, trotting out his standard

cover. "I used to run a very small company that sold communications widgets to the military. Classified, very low use, very niche market. Decent income but not rich or anything. Then, well, then 9/11 happened and my particular widget got really popular. The third buyout offer from a major defense contractor was too good to pass up. Now I'm semi-retired. The fishing pays for gas and food and sometimes docking charges. The *company* paid for the boat," he finished, grinning.

"Nice," the blonde said, glancing at him. "What'd you walk away with?"

"Uhmmm ..." Mike said, shrugging. "That's ... not classified because it's business, the term is proprietary. The IRS was really happy, though," he added sourly.

"So now you just ... fish?" the blonde asked.

"Pretty much," Mike said, shrugging again. "Sometimes I do a little consulting."

"Classified?" Pam asked.

"Yep," Mike replied with a grin. "In general it falls into military communications and operational analysis. From my boat I tell guys who are out on the sharp end what they did wrong."

"The sharp end?" the blonde asked.

"Guys who do fighting," Pam said. "Like special forces and stuff."

"And do you know much about that?" the blonde asked, disbelievingly.

"I used commo gadgets before I sold them," Mike said with a shrug. "Now, I am just a retired widget maker."

"That's our table," Pam said, as their pager started to buzz. "Nice talking to you ... Mike?"

"Jenkins," Mike said, nodding as the two got up. "And, hey, I get a seat!"

"Still warm," the blonde said, smiling.

"I've hot bunked with smelly guys," Mike replied. "This is much better. Don't forget your drinks."

He sipped his Fosters until his pager went off and then had dinner. He wondered why he hadn't made more of a play for the girls. He *could* have played the hero card, that's for damned sure. Lift up his shirt just a bit and the blonde's disbelief would have

gone away like a light. And there was still a certain amount of newly modified patriotic fervor after Aleppo. Young ladies who hadn't previously were suddenly finding military guys interesting. But . . . he'd just been willing to pass for some reason. And there was zero chance that they'd want to go fishing; they weren't the type.

Three days later he was upside down under his starboard engine and cursing the idiot Swede who had thought putting an oil pump in the *bottom* of an engine was a good idea. To reach the oil pump required a trained gymnast and he was just glad he'd been doing some limbering exercises along with the working out. To get to the pump, he had to lie down on top of the engine and then slide down the side and underneath. Getting back out was on the near order of impossible, but he'd rigged a line that he could pull, over his back, to give him some leverage.

But he'd managed it, finally, and was just cranking down the last of the bolts when he heard a female voice hailing from the pier.

"Hang on!" he yelled, sliding the wrench back where he'd be able to retrieve it and then slipping out from under the engine. He clambered, awkwardly, up onto the top of the engine and then stuck his head out of the hatch to see who it was; he was surprised as hell to see the blonde and brunette from the bar carrying small bags.

"Hey," he called. "Come aboard. I'd shake your hand, but you don't want to get within ten feet of me right now."

"Nice *boat*," Pam said, walking across the gangway. "I thought you meant some sort of sailboat or something. What is this?"

"Bertram 45," Mike replied. "With a God damned Volvo engine designed by an idiot. But it's fixed now."

"Rich *and* a mechanic," the blonde said wonderingly. "Will wonders never cease?"

"And I cook," Mike said, grinning and standing up.

"Holy SHIT," the blonde said, obviously staring even with sunglasses in the way. "You weren't *kidding* about having some experience, were you?"

"No," Mike said, wiping his hands and then slipping on a shirt over his oil-covered torso.

"Sorry," the blonde said, shaking her head. "What was all that?"

"Bullets and shrapnel," Mike replied, picking up his tools and cleaning them off. "Shrapnel is little pieces of metal. Those were from a grenade, I think. Must have been; there wasn't any artillery or mortars incoming."

"Where'd it happen?" Pam asked, softly. "Or is that . . ."

"Classified, yeah," Mike said simply.

"What were you?" the blonde asked. "Or is that . . ."

"No, I was a SEAL," Mike replied. "That's not classified. And I can tell some great training stories that will have you laughing your ass off. But I can't talk, won't talk, about missions."

"Okay," Pam said. "But . . . were you in Syria?"

"That was after I was out," Mike said, not exactly lying. "The team is open source, it was Charlie Three. It was actually the same team and platoon I was in when I was operational. I know a couple of the guys who are still in it, were on the mission. But I wasn't in the team for that." He set the cleaned tools in their box and climbed out of the hatch. "Let me show you the boat. I'm really proud of her."

He led them up to the flying bridge and then down the companionway to the closed bridge and into the lounge.

"Lots of electronics," the blonde said.

"Yeah, when you're by yourself you need them," Mike said. "By the way, your friend is Pam and you are . . . ?"

"Sorry, we didn't get introduced, did we?" the blonde said. "Courtney Trays."

"Mike," he said. "Let me go get cleaned up and I'll shake your hand. Drinks in the fridge, two bathrooms down the companionway on either side, liquor cabinet if you're of a mind."

"It's a little early," Pam said.

"You're on vacation," Mike said, grinning. "And the sun's over the yardarm somewhere."

He walked down the companionway to the main cabin and into the bathroom. He wasn't about to scatter oil over the marble countertop, so he pulled off his shirt and bundled it and the shorts he'd been

wearing together, then pulled out a can of Go-Jo and worked off most of the grime. After a very quick shower he was mostly clean, as a glance in the mirror proved. He slipped on a pair of swimming trunks and another T-shirt, then went back to the lounge.

"Hi, I'm Mike Jenkins," he said, holding out his hand to the blonde, who was perched at the bar sipping a Coke.

"Nice to meet you, Mike," the girl said, grinning.

"I hadn't, frankly, expected you two to show up," Mike said, getting out a Gatorade.

"Well, coming down to Islamorada sounded like a great idea after last semester," Pam said, sipping her drink. "We're from the University of Missouri in Springfield and it had not only been a bitch of a winter, it had been a bitch of a semester. Courtney said: 'Let's go to the Keys,' so we dropped our stuff at the parents' and got in the car."

"Little did we know how much staying here was going to cost," Courtney said sourly. "We're not moving in on you, but we're, frankly, getting tapped except for the money we need to get home. So, since you'd offered to go fishing or something, we decided, what the heck?"

"Did you make a safe call?" Mike asked neutrally.

"Uhm . . . a what?" Pam asked.

"Oh, Christ," Mike said, shaking his head. "You must be freshmen or something."

"And your point?" Courtney asked sharply.

"Safe call," Mike said. "You don't know diddly about some guy you've met in a bar. So you have somebody you know is home that you call and say: 'Hey, I met this guy named George Winson, his address is 52 Bonny Lane. If you don't hear from me by tomorrow morning, call the police.'"

"That's a little . . ." Courtney said.

"Cold-blooded?" Mike asked. "It's better than the alternative. And get ID."

"Okay," Pam replied. "Uh . . ."

"Hang on," Mike said, grinning. He found his wallet and handed over his, entirely fictitious, Florida driver's license. "I wish I still had my *Kinky Single Girl's Guide to Sex and Dating,* but my ex took off with it."

"Your *what*?" Courtney asked, aghast.

"One of the funniest books you'll ever read," Mike said, taking the ID back from Pam. "Great tips about dating, even if you're not kinky. Including a great section on safe calls. Got a cell phone?"

"Yes," Pam said, shaking her head. "Who should I call?"

"Well, your parents might be a bit much," Mike said. "But you're sure to have somebody on your speed dial list. Tell them we're going out and you'll call them back around a specified time, even to leave a message. Depending on how far out we go and how long we stay out, you might not have cell coverage. But you decide the time and we'll work around it. If nothing else, I've got a satellite phone."

"You do?" Courtney said. "Why?"

"Because I'm not always where there's cell coverage when I need to make a call," Mike said, shrugging.

"Like on the 'sharp end'?" Courtney asked, curiously.

"No," Mike said, shaking his head. "Like in the Bahamas Deeps and I just caught a really nice marlin and I want to call a friend and rub it in."

"Oh," Courtney said, grinning.

"I'll call Stacey," Pam said, smiling. "She'll get green with envy."

"I'll go topside," Mike said after a moment's thought. "Get the bollards in and the gangway up. Come on up when you're ready to go."

CHAPTER
TWO

He had gotten all the lines in but the stern and was on the flying bridge lifting the gangway when Courtney came up, carrying her Coke and his Gatorade.

"You forgot this," she said, sitting down on the bench and looking out. "This is so cool."

"I sometimes forget that," Mike said, nodding. "It's better than . . . some stuff in my life. Lots. I'll get tired of it after a while and have to go find something interesting to do. But right now . . . I need the downtime."

"What are we going to do?" Courtney asked, looking at the instruments. "And how do you read all that stuff?"

"It takes practice," Mike admitted. "There's radar, GPS with charts, depth-finder, anchor, winch and gangway controls and various stuff about the boat," Mike said, pointing to each of the screens and buttons. "The closed bridge below has duplicate instruments and controls as well as more and larger. There's a tuna tower up there," he said, pointing overhead. "It's got most of the same stuff, but in miniature and harder to read. It's also only got a Bimini top, so I mostly stay here. Except in storms, then I go in the closed bridge."

"I was right," Pam said, climbing up onto the flying bridge. "Stacey was just green. Where are we going?"

"I'd say 'up to you,'" Mike replied thoughtfully. "But you don't know what's around. The snorkeling in Islamorada is only so-so, but there are a few shallow reefs. Go for that, first?"

"Fine by me," Pam said, looking at Courtney.

"I've never been," Courtney said.

"It's not hard," Mike said, grinning. "And, well, SEALs make Number One life guards."

"Okay, we'll try that I guess," Courtney said, shrugging. "I was just planning on, well, boating and sunning."

"That too," Mike said, opening up a glove box and pulling out a foil packet. "You guys know if you're susceptible to seasickness?"

"No," Pam said. "I don't. Courtney?"

"No," she said, warily, eying the packet.

"Bonine," Mike said, showing her the printing. "Better than Dramamine, lasts longer, very little in the way of side effects. Not perfect. If you turn out to have real problems, I've got scopolamine tablets. They're prescription in the U.S., but I get mine from Canada where they're over-the-counter. You probably won't have any problems, but I recommend taking one before we go out." He paused and flicked the packet to Courtney. "Sealed."

"You take this safety stuff seriously, don't you?" Pam asked, taking the packet from Courtney and pulling out a tablet.

"They're chewable," Mike said, starting both engines. "And, yes, I do."

He climbed down and walked to the stern, throwing the docking lines onto the pier, then scrambling back into position.

"If we do this much, I'll probably have you guys do that the next time," he said, engaging the engines and pulling out of the slip, turning hard left with a bit of bow thruster.

"That's not bad," Courtney said, washing down a Bonine with her Coke. "You're strange, Mike. Most guys wouldn't talk about safe calls and whether a drug is in a sealed packet."

"Most of the guys you date, maybe," Mike said, shrugging. "They're your age and wouldn't know about it, most of them. Or they'd take it as an insult. 'What, don't you trust me?' 'Don't you trust me?' translates as 'The check is in the mail' and 'I won't come in your mouth.'"

Pam nearly snorted Coke out of her nose at that. "I can't believe you said that!"

"Why?" Mike said, maneuvering into the narrow channel out of the marina. "You don't know the list of great lies in history? 'The DZ is wide enough' is one that we loved in the teams. Yeah, for one guy to land on at a time," he added, chuckling. "By the way, you guys want classes in what I'm doing?"

"I'm interested," Pam said. "But those controls are beyond me."

"Now," Mike said, "but I was talking about general navigation. See those posts with signs on them?" he said, pointing to the channel markers.

"Yeah," Courtney said, frowning. "They've got numbers."

"Thing to remember is color," Mike said. "Red, Right, Returning. That is, the red one is on your right when you are coming back to port. Which side is it on right now?"

"Left," Pam said. "We're going out."

"Yep," Mike replied. "But when you're in some channels, especially in turns, all you'll have is one channel marker to figure out where the channel is." He leaned forward and dialed in the GPS to maximum. "See these contour lines? They say what the depth is to either side. This thing draws nearly six feet. See that two? That's how shallow it can get to either side of the channel. If we drift out of the channel, we're going aground. That's why you have to know which side of the channel marker to follow."

He waved at a passing jet ski and turned to watch as the man jumped his wake.

"That's what I'd like to do," Courtney said, watching it recede.

"Hate those things," Mike replied. "Most of the people who ride them are just fine, but you'll get some drunk idiot going eighty miles an hour and not realizing he can't turn in time, and then you've got blood on the side of your boat and a hole and a big investigation. But yeah, they're fun."

"Well, I'd like to try one," Courtney said. "Carefully."

"I shall, as Bill Slim's logistics chief said, arrange," Mike replied, grinning.

"I'm going to go up front and sun," Pam said. "Do you mind?"

"Oh, jeeze," Mike said. "Break my heart. Beautiful college coed laid out forward. I don't think I can handle that."

"You are a tease," Pam said, getting up and going below.

"Okay, what's that?" Courtney said, pointing to a screen. "I know that one's a map or something. But what's that one?"

"Radar," Mike said, pointing. "See the red dot?"

"Yes."

He pointed off to starboard at a boat nearing the end of the channel.

"That's that dot," he said, then pointed to a moving blue dot. "That's an aircraft," he continued, looking over his shoulder. "Yeah, Coast Guard helicopter."

"Do you use it much?" Courtney asked, looking around. "I mean, you can see . . ."

"It's more useful at night or in storms," Mike said. "Boats are supposed to have running lights and most do. But this radar is on a computer that can be set to beep if there's something coming up that looks as if there might be a collision. So, say I'm off coast and I want to go below and get something to eat? I set it for a close point approach of, say, a mile. So when I'm eating and some idiot in a cigarette boat comes barreling in, I have time to get to the bridge and maneuver."

"Oh."

"Or, say I'm in a storm, which I have been. I can see what's around even through the storm. I can see the land forms, the way the islands are laid out," he added, pointing to the land that was visible on the screen. "Sometimes that gives me a better feel for where I am than the GPS. But mostly I use the GPS to navigate."

"What's that one with the fish symbols?" she asked. "Oh, a fish-finder. Stupid."

"Not stupid, good guess," Mike said. "It's that, but it also tells me the depth. I would like to take you guys offshore, if you have time. The water out there . . ." He paused and shook his head. "Pelagic water has to be seen to be believed. This stuff is what's called brown water, then you hit green and finally the real blue of the ocean. It's beautiful."

"You really like the water," Courtney said musingly.

"Love it," Mike replied. "But when I was a SEAL it was almost like it was the enemy. When we trained it was always at night and half the time it was in the northern Pacific, which is mostly zero viz and cold as hell. But this stuff?" he said, waving around. "This is great, brown, green and blue. This is as close as I've come to heaven. Great water, good reefs, good fishing and pretty girls," he finished, grinning at her.

"Have you had a lot of pretty girls on your boat?" Courtney asked archly.

"You're the first ones," Mike admitted. "There are ladies who make something of a profession of moving from boat to boat. I prefer not to deal with them, even the pretty ones." He paused and shook his head. "Crap."

"What?" Courtney asked as he leaned across her.

"Pam? Can you hear me?"

"Yes," the girl called from forward.

"There's a cabin on the right, forward, that's locked," he yelled. "Kindly don't try to find out why. Remember the story of Blue-beard."

"Now you've got me nervous," Courtney said as he straightened back up and made the next turn in the channel.

"Not like that," Mike said. "Like I said, sometimes I do classified stuff. That room has some of that stuff in it. That's why I keep it locked. Also has my weight gear. Do you mind if I take off my shirt?"

"Changing the subject?" Courtney asked, smiling. "Go ahead."

"The scars make people comment, so I generally keep it on when I'm in dock," he said, setting the autosteer for a second and stripping out of the T-shirt. "But I like to keep it off when I'm out."

"Nice bathroom," Pam said, coming topside. "Wow, you really are scarred up, aren't you?"

"See?" Mike said, shaking his head. "Yeah."

"That's some major damage," Courtney said, running her finger over a suture mark in his side. "Like, I'm surprised you lived."

"Nursing student?" Mike asked.

"Pre-med," Courtney said shortly.

"Well, the doctors told me they spent about ten hours with their hands in various parts of me," Mike admitted. "And about half of my insides are now plastic. Wonder of modern medicine, that's me."

"You want to go sun?" Pam asked Courtney.

"I'm going to sit and talk with Mike. Maybe later."

"We can actually do both," Mike said as Pam made her way forward. "Up on the tuna tower. And you can see more."

"Uh, it's kind of high," Courtney said.

"You'll hardly notice," Mike replied. "Let me get out of the channel, first, though. And there's more motion up there."

"It's pretty smooth so far," Courtney said.

"Well," Mike said, spinning the wheel and engaging the bow thrusters to make the final turn, "that's because the bar we're about to go through is breaking the waves. It's pretty calm today; inshore, which is where we're going to be most of the time, it's only a foot. Offshore it's two feet and glassy. That's good conditions. Very good. We'll rock up there," he said, gesturing up. "But it's fun."

They passed through the final turn and he powered up, the nose of the cruiser rising and riding easily across the small swells.

"Now this is more like it," Courtney said, grinning.

"Look," Mike said, pointing off to the left. "Dolphin."

"Where?" Courtney asked, standing up and shading her eyes.

"Look for a fin at about ten o'clock," Mike said, keeping his eye in the direction and on close boats. "There."

"Oh, cool," Courtney said. "Pam! There's a dolphin off on the left!"

"Port," Mike automatically corrected.

"What is it with sailors and all this port and starboard stuff?" Courtney asked, watching the dolphins. "There's three of them."

"Two females and a juvenile," Mike said, nodding. "You can tell the young one because its fin is smaller."

"Can we swim with them?" Courtney asked. "They're going away."

"Most dolphins won't swim with people," Mike said. "Sometimes you can slide over the side and get them to look you over. But there are very few that actively enjoy swimming with humans.

Come on up on the tuna tower," he said, setting the autosteer. "You'll enjoy it."

"I need a bathing suit," Courtney said, temporizing.

"And sunscreen," Mike said.

"I've got a pretty good tan," Courtney replied.

"Trust me," Mike replied. "Up there you'll want at least fifteen SPF. Twenty-five would be better."

"Somebody will have to do my back," she said coyly.

"Twist my arm and we'll discuss it," Mike said, grinning.

He made his way up to the tuna tower and checked the controls. The autosteer had been set to run towards a break in the outer reefs, He leaned back and propped up his feet, reclining the chair and trying not to grin from ear to ear. After a second, though, he leaned forward and looked down at Pam.

"Pam!"

The girl sat up and looked around, confused.

"Up here," Mike said, smiling. "Did you put on sunscreen?"

"I put on tanning oil," she said, turning around and looking up at him. "Like the view?"

"Love it," Mike said, grinning. She had an exceptionally nice chest and the legs were outstanding. "I'd strongly advise more than tanning oil. But it's up to you."

"I want a *tan* when I get back," Pam said, shrugging.

"Okay," Mike said, sitting down. "Don't say I didn't warn you," he muttered.

"This is cool," Courtney said, coming up the ladder. "But a bit . . ."

Mike helped her up the last few feet and into the chair next to his.

"I love it up here," he said, sitting up. "More dolphins, way off to port, forward. And you see those," he said, pointing to some circles to the right. "That's bait fish feeding on the surface."

"Wow!" Courtney said, pointing forward as a small finny shape jumped out of the water and tail walked off to the left. "Flying fish!"

"They're pretty rare inshore," Mike said. "But you see a lot of them out in the Stream."

"The Gulf Stream," Courtney said, nodding. "That I've heard of."

"That's where you get the pelagics," he said, pointing down to port. "There, you see that flashing. Those are the bait fish."

"Something just jumped over there," Courtney said, pointing off to port.

"Probably mullet," Mike said, shrugging. "They jump a lot. Nobody knows why."

"Where are we going?" Courtney asked, looking around.

"There's a shallow reef," Mike said, pointing at the GPS. "You can't see it very well on this little bitty screen. It's not all *that* shallow, unfortunately, with the current tide you're talking six or seven feet. But it's pretty and you can dance to it . . ."

"What?" Courtney asked.

"What was that show?" Mike asked. "*Soul Train*? One of the judges was always saying 'it has a nice beat and you can dance to it.' I guess it's a generational thing."

"Okay," Courtney said with a laugh. "Whatever."

"Anyway, we'll hook up there," Mike said, "and you can try your hand at snorkeling."

"Hook up?" Courtney said, raising an eyebrow.

"Yeah, there's a buoy you hook up to rather than anchor," Mike said, looking at her. "Why?"

"Uh . . ." Courtney paused and shrugged. "It's a generational thing. Hook up is . . . well it's one way of saying you're sort of . . . dating . . ."

"Or having sex?" Mike asked, grinning.

"Maybe," Courtney said, shrugging. "Hooking up just means you're . . . together for a while. Maybe sex, maybe just making out, maybe just dating and none of the above. Generally at *least* making out is involved."

"Like going steady?" Mike asked.

"Not exactly," Courtney said, shrugging again. "God, I haven't heard anyone use *that* term since high school."

"Last time I heard it, too," Mike admitted. "But hooking up is a new one on me. Except for buoys."

"I wouldn't have picked you for going both ways," Courtney said, blank faced. "But, then again, you were a sailor, right?"

"Did you just make a *joke*?" Mike asked, grinning.

"What? I can't joke?" Courtney asked, smiling.

"Joke all you want," Mike said. "As long as they're not farmer's-daughter jokes."

The reef only had one other boat on it, a snorkel trip boat that was already starting to recover its group of dentists from Cleveland or whatever. Mike turned downwind, then lined up on the buoy and leaned over the tuna tower.

"Pam, I need some help," he called. "On the starboard . . . the right side, in a holder is a boat hook, could you grab it?"

"Sure," she called, getting up off her towel and getting the boat hook.

"Okay," Mike yelled. "There's a knurled grip in the middle. If you twist it loose, you can extend the boat hook."

"Got it," Pam said after a few moments. She extended the hook and clamped it back down.

"Okay, I'm going to pull up to the buoy. You'll need to pull it up to the boat." He looked at Courtney and shrugged. "I think two people."

"Going," Courtney said, heading for the ladder.

"Courtney's coming down. If you can pull the buoy up a bit, there's a rope down there with a clip on it. Clip that to the line on the bottom of the buoy and we're good."

"How heavy is it?" Pam asked.

"Pretty heavy," Mike admitted. "But I don't think you want to do this end, do you?"

"No," she said, walking forward.

When Courtney got to the bow, he pulled forward, slowly, until he lost sight of the buoy.

"Missed it," Pam called. She was bent over the front rail and it was an entirely pleasant sight.

"Coming up again," Mike called, giving the engine a nudge.

"Got it!" Pam called. She wriggled out from under the rail and hauled on the line. Mike pulled forward a bit more and Courtney got down on the deck with the bowline.

"I got it on!" she yelled. "I got it."

"Get out of the way and let Pam drop the buoy," Mike called, putting the engine in neutral.

"There, that wasn't that bad," he said when he reached the main deck.

"Not bad," Pam said. "Good steering."

"Thanks," he said, getting out the snorkeling gear. He defogged the masks with baby shampoo, fitted the masks for the girls, then found foot fins that fit them.

"You've got a lot of this gear," Courtney said.

"I'd hoped to have visitors, frankly," Mike replied. "So I laid in a lot of stuff I don't have use for. I even . . . well . . ." He paused and grinned sheepishly. "I even laid in stuff in case I had female visitors."

"Tampons and pads?" Pam asked, raising an eyebrow.

"Well, yeah, but they're for something else," Mike said. "No, I bought some other stuff. Don't think I'm a perv or anything. But . . . well . . . if a young lady ends up unexpectedly spending time on the boat, she'll probably be able to find panties and a bra that fit."

"Really?" Courtney said, laughing. "You're serious."

"Really," Mike said. "Look, I dated a lot when I was younger. A young lady spends time at a gentleman's apartment or whatever and she gets up in the morning and the one thing you can tell she's thinking about is: 'Damn, I've got to put on my underwear from yesterday.' So I laid in supplies."

"That's . . ." Courtney stopped and shrugged. "I guess that makes a lot of sense. If you're incredibly sensitive and forward thinking."

"Forward thinking, yes," Mike said. "Very few people have *ever* accused me of being sensitive."

"Okay," Courtney said, laughing. "It wasn't intended as an insult."

"What's the other thing that tampons and pads are for?" Pam asked, curiously.

"Let's just say I like being prepared," Mike answered. "And in that vein," he said, pulling out a bottle of Bullfrog 45, "I don't care *how* much you want a tan when you get home. We go snorkeling for a few hours with your current tan and you're going to burn to a crisp and not even know it until you're back onboard."

"Fine," Pam sighed, turning around and flipping her hair forward. "Do me."

"In a heartbeat," Mike said.

When all three of them were lathered, he swung out the dive ladder. The yacht had a water-level deck for bringing in large fish that the ladder hung down from. He got the girls in their gear then got his own on.

"Just keep the snorkel in your mouth and your body level," he said, slipping over the side. "Pam first. I'll support you at first so you get used to it."

Pam slipped into the water and he held her by the midsection, getting a world-class erection in the process. After a second she pulled her head out of the water and spit out the snorkel.

"That is *so* cool," she said, grinning.

"To swim around just kick with your fins," Mike said, releasing her. "You okay?"

"Great," she said, putting the snorkel back in and kicking off.

"Me next," Courtney said. "But I think I can do it myself."

"Works," Mike said, kicking backwards and putting on his mask. "After you."

He followed the two girls towards the reef, listening to their snorkel-muffled oaths and *amahs* and just enjoying himself immensely. Suddenly there was a muffled shriek and Courtney turned around and made a beeline for the boat. Mike beat her back easily and was in the transom by the time she spit out her snorkel and climbed on board.

"There was this *big*, nasty-looking fish," she said nervously.

"Barracuda," Mike said, nodding. "Not a big deal. They don't attack snorkelers. Well, to be honest I should say hardly ever. Not if you don't have any necklaces or shiny stuff; I checked for that. You're okay."

"You're sure?" she asked.

"I'll go with you," Mike said, sliding into the water and holding out his hand as Pam closed on the boat, too.

"Did you see it?" Pam asked after she spit out her snorkel.

"It's okay," Mike said, shaking his head and trying not to grin. "Three things to remember about barracuda. They're curious, so they follow you around. Don't wave your fingers at them, they

might think they're fish. Don't wear shiny necklaces, they look like lures. Oh, and they're fun to catch, but don't eat the big ones."

"Why?" Courtney said, slipping into the water and checking under her with her mask.

"They build up a toxin in their flesh as they get older," Mike said when she'd surfaced. "Makes them poisonous. Come on."

He led both of them by the hand back to the reef and started pointing out particular fish and coral. When the 'cuda cruised back in, he just ignored it, and after a while the 'cuda ignored them.

They snorkeled on the reef for a good hour before Courtney surfaced and spat out her snorkel.

"My shins are killing me," she admitted. "I'm about done."

"Me, too," Pam said.

"Suits," Mike said, glancing at his watch. "Let's do lunch."

CHAPTER
THREE

They had sandwiches, sitting at the bar with their suits on.

"Mike, thanks," Pam said, washing down the sandwich with a swallow of Coke. "This is just loads of fun. But I feel like I'm . . . I'm eating your food and using your gas and stuff. This should be costing us money. How much would it cost to rent a boat like this to do this? I mean, I just don't feel right."

"Look, it's just enormous fun having you both here, okay?" Mike said, shrugging. "I feel like I ought to be paying *you* money it's so much fun."

"How much?" Courtney said, grinning. "And, admit it, you're just hoping to get laid."

"I wouldn't kick you out of bed," Mike said, shrugging and grinning back. "Maybe if you were messy eating crackers. But, no, I'm just having fun watching you guys have fun. It's a real high for a guy to get a girl to smile, and that's a fact. So don't sweat what it would cost. Trust me, I can afford it. I'd take you two to the Bahamas if you asked. Hell, I'd cruise you down to the Virgin Islands if you wanted. You're both very nice young ladies, both in personality and in looks. Consider this boat yours until you have to go home."

"Well, we'll have to leave in a couple of days," Pam said, frowning. "We can't afford to stay in the hotel beyond then."

"Uh, I did say the boat is yours," Mike pointed out diffidently. "There are three open cabins. They're small, but comfortable. If hotel costs are the only thing making you go home, move in. You can still go back whenever you'd like, in two days if you want. But it's stupid to pay for the hotel when you can stay on the boat."

Courtney raised an eyebrow at that and cocked her head.

"No strings?" she asked incredulously.

"I'm not using them," Mike said, shrugging. "I already said I wouldn't kick you out of bed, but I'm not going to drag you there, either. Or attach strings. No strings. Okay, a couple. Leave the cabins in the same shape they were when you got here, which is neat. Help with cooking and the dishes. Help wash down the boat."

"Those aren't what I'd call strings," Pam said, frowning. "That's just being polite."

"There are lots of people in the world who are extremely impolite," Mike said, picking up the paper plates and putting them in the trash. "Are you still checked into the hotel?"

"No, we were going to try to find a cheaper one," Pam said.

"Okay, you decide," Mike said. "But the cabins are yours if you want them."

"What do you plan on doing this afternoon?" Courtney asked.

"I'd like to go fishing, frankly," Mike said.

"I'm not that into fishing," Courtney replied. "But I can catch a tan."

"If you hook into a sailfish you'll never look back," Mike said, grinning. "But I don't think we will this time of day. If we run out to the Stream we might be able to find some dolphin. Dolphin fish," he added. "They're fun to catch on light tackle. Or we could go after grouper."

"Is this like big-game fishing?" Pam asked. "In a chair with a big rod? I saw those kind of chairs in the back."

"Would be with sailfish," Mike said. "But, like I said, I don't think we'll get any of those today. Maybe tomorrow if we start early. Maybe this evening we might scare some up. Or we can snorkel some more."

"I'm game for fishing," Courtney said, shrugging.

"Let's go, then," Mike said. "We can run out to the Stream and see what we can scare up." He stopped and touched a control, bringing up a text screen.

"What's that?" Pam asked.

"Text version of the national weather reports," Mike said, nodding. "I can read the weather around here pretty well and it didn't look as if anything was coming up. But I didn't want you to find out how crazy it can get on the Stream on your first day out."

"Thanks," Courtney said dryly.

Mike unhooked, then started up and spun the boat to point out to sea. As soon as they were away from the reef, he pushed the throttles forward to maximum and set the autosteer, climbing up onto the tuna tower.

"This is great," Courtney said, climbing up the ladder, followed by Pam.

"This is a great view," Pam said, clutching at the railing as the tower swayed from side to side.

"Sure is," Mike said, gesturing to the seats to either side of the captain's chair. "You can see for miles." He pulled a pair of binoculars out of a case and tracked around the horizon.

"Okay, what are you looking for, now?" Courtney asked.

"Hmmm . . ." Mike said. "Various things. Certain types of birds, splashes at the surface would be nice, debris, weed lines. Stuff."

"Okay," Pam said, then gasped at the sight in the water below. "There's a big . . ."

"Hammerhead," Mike said, lowering the binoculars and looking over her side. "About twelve feet. That's why I like it up here; you can see all sorts of stuff in the water."

"This is so *cool*," Courtney said, then threw her arms around Mike.

"You're welcome," Mike said uncomfortably. "What was that for?"

"'Cause it's so *cool*," Courtney said, letting him go. "I was worried you were a jerk when we met in the bar. But you're . . . this is so *great*!"

"Good," Mike said, smiling. "All that I ask is that you have fun. If there's something that's bugging you, or you've got a problem, just tell me, okay? And I'll see what I can do to fix it. But if you

want to thank me, have the maximum amount of fun you can have. That's all the thanks I need."

"Why?" Pam asked, frowning. "That's so weird."

"Because I'm a guy," Mike said, shrugging. "You want the simple answer that's been the answer for centuries? Or do you want the modern answer."

"Both," Pam said, her brow crinkling.

"Okay," Mike said, picking up the binoculars again. "The old, short, answer is that when you're happy, it makes me really happy. There's some sort of quote about a man will give a kingdom to make a woman smile. The face that launched a thousand ships. The whole bit."

"So what's the modern answer?" Courtney asked.

"It takes all the fun, all the soul out of it," Mike said, lowering the binoculars. "But . . . males that see any of several expressions on a female face have an endorphin rush from the sight. It's a form of drug, a high. For that matter, males have an average of forty percent fall-off in long-term decision-making at the sight of a pretty female face. Those are both clinical studies. I could extrapolate from them, but I won't. However, it's definitely the reason that there are topless bars all over the place while things like Chippendales are rare. Women don't have the same reactions. They can be somewhat visual, but they don't have the same chemical reaction. It's called 'thinking with the other head' but it's not. It's just a chemical reaction in the brain. It's real for all that," Mike said. "So if you want to pay me back, just smile. It's worth every moment, every penny."

"So we're a drug?" Courtney asked quizzically.

"A strong one," Mike said, shrugging.

"I can live with that," Pam said. "But I want to help, too."

"I can live with that," Mike replied, and got the expected laugh. "I hereby promote you to deck wench! Your first duty is to see if you can maneuver a beer up here."

"Aye, aye, Captain!" Pam said, grinning. "Courtney, you want anything?"

"I'll take a beer," Courtney said. "If that's okay?"

"Let me check," Mike said, leaning forward and shading the GPS. "By the time she gets back it will be."

"Huh?" Courtney asked.

"Twelve mile limit," Mike replied, grinning. "Technically, this being an American flagged ship, there's still some sort of law. But past the twelve mile limit, nobody cares if I let a minor drink. But don't get hammered."

"Trust me, I won't on one beer," Courtney said.

"Three beers, coming up," Pam said, sliding down the ladder.

"What's the deal with the twelve mile limit?" Courtney asked, curiously.

"Past the twelve-mile limit, we're no longer in U.S. jurisdiction," Mike said. "The reality is that the U.S. *owns* these waters. They'll stop anyone they want in this region. But the law gets really tricky beyond the limit. And the reality is that things like drinking ages, and gambling, go out the window. Past the twelve mile limit, you're beyond the law. Doesn't matter for you guys, really, but I don't have to worry about getting hassled for contributing."

"Oh," Courtney said, turning around and looking behind them. "Hey, I can just barely see land!"

"Yep," Mike said. "And see how the water is changing?" he added, pointing over the side.

"Getting pretty blue," she said, nodding.

"Not real blue, yet," Mike said. "You'll see."

"Beers," Pam said. "But getting them up there . . ."

Courtney retrieved the Fosters and put them in holders.

"All I could find," Pam said.

"If you're stuck on something else, we'll get it when we get back," Mike said.

"We can at least buy our own beers," Pam said, frowning.

"Ah, ah," Mike said. "And take all my fun away?"

"This is good," Courtney said, taking a swig of the Fosters and rolling the cap in her hand. "Trash?"

Mike took it from her and flicked it over the side.

"Don't look so shocked," he said, grinning. "It'll sink to the bottom and decompose. Little fish will use it for shelter in the meantime. You don't want to deprive them, do you?"

"I'm just so kneejerk about littering," Pam said, then tossed hers over the side. "But that felt really fun."

"Simple guilty pleasures are the most fun," Mike said, flicking his over the side. "Better than complicated guilty pleasures."

"What are complicated guilty pleasures?" Courtney asked.

"Think about it," Mike replied, grinning. "What, you don't have any complicated guilty pleasures?"

"I'm lost here," Pam admitted. "Could you explain?"

"Not without getting more graphic than I'd like to," Mike said. "But I'll ask a rhetorical question: What do you fantasize about when you masturbate?" He looked from side to side and nodded. "The light dawns. Those can be *very* complicated guilty pleasures. And don't ask me, nonrhetorically, please."

"I won't," Courtney said, blushing. "But, you know, complicated guilty pleasures can be fun, too," she added, wiggling from side to side.

"Don't tease an old dog," Mike said. "He might have one bite left."

"So what *are* your complicated guilty pleasures, Mike?" Courtney asked coquettishly.

"I told you not to tease," Mike said, frowning. "Some of my guilty pleasures are really complicated. And really dark. I don't think we know each other well enough to get into them. But I'll tell you one: I've serviced a few targets in my day, and if I've got a regret, it's that I probably won't be able to service any more."

"Serviced targets?" Pam asked carefully.

"Killed bad guys," Mike answered. "I don't get any nightmares from serviced targets, even the ones that I've had to look at for some time. Screwed-up ops, I flashback on those. I had a bad one in Rumrunners the night I met you two. But targets? No problem."

That provoked a rather long silence.

"Okay, now I'm having some problems," Courtney said finally. "I hadn't really internalized that I was out in a boat with a guy who used to kill people for a living. Has actually killed people, is what I mean."

"Bad guys," Mike said. "But, yeah, I told you not to tease an old dog. If you want to turn around I will," he said, reaching for the wheel.

"No," Courtney said, leaning forward and touching his hand. "Don't. It just takes some getting used to. But I'd guess that with

what happened to you," she said, gesturing at the scars, "some of the same things happened to . . . targets."

"Quite a few," Mike said, having a clear image of the stairway. "But there are some very bad people in the world that desperately need servicing."

"Syria," Pam said, darkly.

"That was one of those good missions," Mike admitted. "Very clear cut. But those aren't the only bad people in the world, ladies."

Courtney leaned over and laid her hand on his shoulder, then leaned further over to kiss his cheek.

"Thank you for servicing targets," she said, rubbing his shoulder. "And I won't tease you about your complicated guilty pleasures. Much."

"If you do I'll tease you right back," Mike said, grinning. "I spent a lot of time in the body and fender shop. And the only thing to read was what the nurses had, which were very *very* trashy romances. Based on those . . ."

"Don't go there," Courtney said, leaning back and laughing. "I'll definitely stop teasing."

"Birds," Mike said, picking up the binoculars and focusing them in. "Yeah, they're feeding on a surface shoal." He put his feet down and touched the wheel, turning the boat to starboard slowly. Even with his care, the tuna tower still leaned to the side.

"Whoa!" Pam said, grasping the rail. "That's a little . . ."

"Exciting?" Mike asked, straightening out. "Courtney, think you can take the wheel?"

"Maybe," she said as he stood up.

"I'll back off on the speed," he said, throttling down. "It won't sway so much. You see those birds," he added, pointing.

"Yeah?"

"Steer for them," he said, picking up his beer and going to the ladder.

"Where are you going?" she asked.

"To get out the rods."

"I'm steering this boat," Courtney said nervously.

"I know," Pam replied just as nervously.

"I don't know what I'm doing."

"I know," Pam said, trying to sound supportive. "Just . . . steer for the birds."

"They've moved," Courtney said, turning the wheel slightly. The boat turned, and she had to turn back and forth a couple of times to get lined up, the tuna tower swaying, to her, dangerously.

"You're doing great!" Mike yelled from the deck.

"He's . . ." Courtney said and stopped.

"Yeah," Pam replied. "Is it just me . . ."

"No," Courtney said. "And did you see those *pecs*?"

"Yeah," Pam said. "And he said women aren't visual. God, what does he do, work out all day?"

"I know," Courtney said, steering a touch to port. "It was all I could do to not run my finger over them just to see if they were real."

"Oh, they're real, all right," Pam said. "And you know what gets me?"

"Not a single come-on," Courtney said. "He's not gay, I can tell that. But he's not . . ."

"I know. It's like he's waiting for us to make the first move."

"I know. It's weird. And that thing about . . . servicing targets."

"He's actually killed people," Pam said. "I mean, not just maybe. Has. No muss, no bragging, no bullshit."

"Which just makes it worse," Courtney admitted. "When he mentioned romance novels I just about wet my pants."

"You too?" Pam said, shaking her head. "He said he stocked up for female visitors. I wonder if there's a vibrator on board."

"You mean other than the seats?" Courtney said. "Besides, who needs a vibrator. I've just been crossing my legs and rocking!"

"Courtney, you are such a slut," Pam said, closing her eyes and leaning back in the chair. "And he wants to go *fishing*!"

CHAPTER
FOUR

"Courtney," Mike called. "You did great, but I've got it from down here. You want to come on down?"

"What's up?" Courtney asked, sliding down to the flying bridge and looking around. Two heavy rods had been rigged aft, and two more that she pegged as "regular" rods with normal reels were set to one side.

"There's a school of bait fish under the birds," Mike said, throttling down. "What I'm going to do is point the boat at them and let out the lines. When we go through we should hook on to whatever is feeding on them, probably dolphin. I've got to get you rigged, though."

He set the throttles to a fast cruise and led the two of them back to the aft.

"This is a fighting rig," he said, putting a harness on Courtney. "You won't really need it for dolphin, but it should help. You put the butt of the rod in the holder on your stomach. What happens is that a fish will get hooked. You take the rod out of the holder, set the butt in place and hit the drag. That should hook the fish for sure. These should be chicken tuna, little ones, and that rod is way oversized for them. But what we'll do is bring one up to the boat and let it stay on the line. That will bring others around. Then we'll fish for them with the lighter tackle."

"Okay," Courtney said, totally confused.

"I'll walk you through it when we hook on," Mike said, putting another harness on Pam. After he'd done that he let out the lines, already rigged with ballyhoo. He probably could have just used lures, but the hoo made it more likely they'd get a fish hooked and he wanted the girls to get some fish.

"Courtney, your rod," Mike said, pointing to starboard. "Pam, that's yours," he added, pointing to the port rod. "I'm going up to the bridge."

He'd set the autosteer to go past the bait pod, but he touched the controls and turned to port, coming around into the Stream to drag the lines past the edge of the pod. He could see the flash of hunting fish at the surface and even some leaping, dolphin for sure. The dolphin school was huge. This was going to be good.

"*Mike! Mike!*" Courtney suddenly yelled as the reel began to scream.

He went to reverse for a second to take the way off and turned around. "Pick up the rod and put the butt in the holder," he called, calmly.

By the time Courtney had the rod in place he was next to her. The dolphin had stopped its initial run, and he leaned over and hit the drag just as Pam's line started to run. When the line went taut the dolphin shook hard against it and Courtney nearly dropped the rod.

"That's a *big* fish!" she yelled happily.

"Not all that big," Mike said, smiling. "Just reel it in; that line's way strong enough," he said, going over to Pam.

Pam had gotten the rod in place without asking and was holding on tight when he hit the drag. She, too, grinned as she felt the fish on the end.

"Just reel them up to the boat," Mike said, going over to the bait well. He had a mess of sardines, most of them still alive, and he scooped out a big netful and tossed them over the side, live chum to bring the dolphin up to the boat. He could see some breaking away from the main school and heading over to the largesse, their bodies flashing silver in the sunlight.

"Mike," Courtney said, holding her rod up. "It's nearly up to the boat."

"That's fine," Mike said, taking the rod and looking over the side. He reeled in a bit more and set the rod in a rocket launcher, the line tracking back and forth as the dolphin tried to escape. "The other dolphin will be attracted to it, since it's excited and they can't tell the difference between being on a line and feeding. So now we really fish."

He took one of the open-face rods and hooked a sardine on it by the tail.

"You ever cast before?" Mike asked.

"Yes," Courtney said, looking at the rod. "Nothing this big, but I can do it."

"Right out there," Mike said, pointing towards the bait pod. "When it's in the water, close the face and then hit this switch," he said, pointing to the trolling control. "That way when the fish hits it can run with the line at first. Give it three seconds, then flick the switch back and hang *on*," he added with a grin.

He went over and more or less repeated the performance with Pam, but he had hardly gotten to the stage of explaining the open-face reel when Courtney shrieked and he looked over to see the rod bending nearly in half.

"Now *that's* fighting a fish," he yelled.

"What do I do?" Courtney asked as the dolphin tracked back and forth.

"Bow to the rod," Mike said, coming over and readjusting the drag. "When it gives you line, reel in. When it runs, just let the drag handle it. It will tire out."

He went over and finished explaining the mysteries to Pam, then went back to Courtney, who was reeling in from time to time.

"I think it's tiring out," Courtney said. "I know I am."

"You can use the leaning board," Mike said. "But you're going to be doing this a lot. Keep your right arm straight and let your back pull. Bow to the fish, reel in as you do, then lean back and pull it in."

"That works," Courtney said, trying it. "I was trying to pull in with my arm. You say these are little fish?"

"Tiny," Mike said. "Maybe tomorrow we'll go after sailfish. I'd love to see you pull in a sail."

He headed back over to Pam who, having watched Courtney, was solidly pulling in her dolphin.

"Doing great," Mike said.

"You were right," Pam said. "This is fun."

"We were lucky," Mike replied. "You don't usually get this surface action. It's very fun when you do."

"Mike!" Courtney called. "What do I do now?"

"Bring it around to the transom," he said, pointing to the flush deck. He climbed down there, and when the fish came around he grabbed the leader and flipped it onto the boat, then up onto the fishing deck.

"That's so pretty," Courtney said, shaking her head.

"They are," Mike said. "But they're awfully plentiful, too." He went forward and got out a digital camera. "Want a picture?" he asked.

"How?" Courtney asked, looking at the flopping fish.

"Grab the leader, the line, down by its mouth," Mike said. "Wrap it around your hand—it's thick mono, it won't cut—and lift it up."

Courtney got it up in the air and grinned, cheesily, for the camera.

"Vacation pictures," Mike said, grabbing the fish and pulling the hook out. Then he grabbed it by the gill and tossed it in the cooler.

"I'll need to throw some ice in there soon," he said, rerigging Courtney's line, then climbing down to the flush deck to land Pam's fish.

He got ice, moved the boat, landed fish, took pictures, rerigged lines, untangled lines, baited lines, until the *girls* got tired.

"I'm beat," Courtney said, rubbing her arm. "Can we quit soon?"

"Have to," Mike admitted. "There's a limit on dolphin and we're getting close to it."

"I'm done," Pam said. "But that was lots of fun."

"That's the punchline to a really old joke," Mike said, taking their rods. He took the rigs off, then took them forward to the rod locker and stowed them.

"What about these two?" Courtney asked.

"Just reel them over the side," Mike said. "We'll toss them in the cooler, too."

"What time is it?" Courtney asked, yawning as Mike spun the boat around and headed inshore. "I'm *beat*. Did you slip something in my beer?" she asked, mock suspiciously.

"No," Mike said, smiling. "Being out on a small boat tends to wear you out at first. You get used to it after a couple of days."

"And I'm *hungry*," Pam said, coming up to the bridge with three beers.

"That we can assuage," Mike said. "I can either cook or we can pull into Rumrunners."

"We were just there the other night," Pam said, smiling. "Remember?"

"Not that one," Mike said, shaking his head. "That's Rumrunners II. The *original* Rumrunners is by itself on a small key; it was originally a speakeasy where the rumrunners actually brought in their loads. You can only get there by boat. Sometimes I sell my fish there. I think, in deference to you ladies and your fatigue and hunger, I'll just sell them whole. But I know the cook, and that means we can get his orange mahi for free, fresh from the fish we land."

"That sounds good," Pam said. "But I need to wash up."

"We'll go park at Rumrunners," Mike said. "I'll go dicker for dinner and you two can wash up and get more beautiful, if that's possible. Then I'll wash up and we three can go to dinner. They also generally have a great band."

"I don't know if I can stay *awake* to party," Courtney said, yawning again. "But . . . you're on."

"Hey, Louise," Mike said, walking in the back door of Rumrunners.

"Hey, Mike," the cook said, wiping his hands on his apron. "What you got?"

"Mahi," Mike said. "Fresh and quivering. Whole, though."

"I take," the cook said. "You see the docks? Tree boats already bring in dorado, we're still nearly out."

"It's why I parked around back," Mike admitted. "Get Jose to give me a hand with the cooler?"

When the fish had been weighed Mike held up his hand.

"Louise, got two young ladies with me," he said. "Can we get three of your delectable orange mahi? From those?" he asked, gesturing at the fish.

"Pick," Louise said, grinning. "Finally get some girlfriend, huh? 'Bout time."

"Just friends," Mike replied, shrugging. "A couple of nice tourist girls who enjoy fishing. And any of them will do."

"This one really is still twitching," Louise said, pulling out his fillet knife and prodding one of the mahi. "Tree orange mahi coming up. I'll get you table."

"Gimme time to wash up," Mike said. "And thanks."

"You have fun," Louise said, grinning evilly. "Two girls? You tink you're man enough?"

"They're just friends," Mike said, shaking his head on the way out.

"How'd you get us past the line?" Pam asked.

"I have friends in low places," Mike answered, pulling out her chair. "The cook was really happy to get more mahi; the tourists are eating him out."

"This is great," Courtney said, bending her head down. "But I'm still beat. And sunburned all over but my back. You were right."

"We'll aloe up when we get to the boat," Mike said, and waved at the menus. "I already ordered for us; you really need to try Louise's orange mahi. But if you want an appetizer . . ."

"God, that was great," Courtney said, polishing off the last of the mahi with a bite of rice. "And this rice . . ."

"Fragrant rice," Mike said. "Not on the usual menu. Like I said, the cook was really glad to have the fish. And we're friends. He used to be a Navy steward, so we keep an eye on each other."

"Can I get the check?" Pam asked. "I feel like . . ."

"We landed over sixty pounds of fish, Pam," Mike said. "The meal was more or less on the house. Even with the drinks' cost, there's a net that will go on the account I run here. Actually, I think I owe you girls some money."

"Don't," Pam said, definitely. "You wouldn't if you figured gas. Let's just call it even."

"I can live with that," Mike said. "You want some of the key lime pie?"

"I was starved and now I'm stuffed," Courtney said. "I think I just want to chill. Can we really stay on the boat tonight?"

"You can stay for weeks if you want," Mike said, getting up. "No dancing?"

"Not tonight," Courtney said, standing up and then swaying. "Definitely not tonight. Among other things, I feel like a french fry."

"Then may I take your arm?" Mike asked, offering his to both girls.

"A beautiful lady on either arm?" Pam asked. "Yes, you may."

"Every man's dream," Mike said, leading them out and around the restaurant to the boat. "Aloe first, then we'll head over to the slip. You ladies can rack out as soon as you're aloed. I need to move slightly offshore, though; they need the dock space."

"That's fine," Courtney said, yawning as she stepped on board. "Where's the aloe?"

"All three bathrooms," Mike said. "Could I suggest that you put your suits back on for aloe? Getting it on past shirts and bras . . ."

"Will do, Captain," Pam said, smiling.

"I'll meet you in the front cabin as soon as I get this thing anchored," he said, casting off.

By the time Mike got the anchors down, one forward and two aft, and he got to the cabin, only Pam was there.

"Courtney is O-U-T, out," Pam said, shaking her head. "She got aloe on the worst of it and collapsed." She had changed back into her bathing suit, a blue-and-red string bikini, and was rubbing aloe on her stomach when he came in.

"Well, your back is okay," Mike said, sitting next to her on the bed. "But the backs of your legs, I think I should have gotten them."

"Give me a hand?" Pam asked, diffidently, holding out the bottle of aloe and rolling sideways.

"I know you want a tan," Mike said, gently smoothing on the thick green after-sun gel. "But you need to take it easy. It took me a month to get this tan after I got down here."

"That feels good," Pam said, sighing. "I really am burned."

"Not too badly," Mike said, turning her to check her other leg. "Side of the thigh," he said, leaning across her long, shapely, legs and smoothing on some more of the gel. "Probably reflection from the boat or the water when you were fishing." He straightened up, looked her in the eye, then leaned forward and kissed her.

Pam had felt ready to explode as he gently rubbed on the aloe and she did explode when he kissed her, a totally unexpected wave of emotion that approached an orgasm and made her moan. She found herself running her hands over his pecs and across his shoulders, humming in pleasure.

"Whoa," Mike said, pulling back and chuckling throatily. "Let's make this last awhile," he continued, lowering her down and sliding his tongue across her throat and then up to her ear, tickling the earlobe. His hands slid up and undid her bikini top, gently sliding it out and away. Then he brought his tongue down to the juncture of her neck and shoulder, probing hard, while one hand played with her nipple.

"Oh, God," Pam moaned, running her hands over his back and shoulders. "I've wanted you to touch me all *day*."

"I know." Mike chuckled. "Well, I knew after a while. That's why I didn't. Anticipation and all that."

"You evil bastard," she whispered, her eyes closed. "Be evil to me. Please."

"Do you know what you're asking?" Mike asked, his face hovering over hers.

"I don't . . . I . . ." Pam said, opening her eyes and looking at him with pleading in them.

"Softly tonight, love," Mike said, gently brushing one finger up her neck. "Softly. Perhaps another night we'll talk about what you're asking."

"How do you *do* that?" Pam asked, shuddering. "How do you know *just* where to stroke?"

"Experience," Mike said, lowering his mouth to her neck again. He played with her nipples, then slid his mouth down to them, his right hand on her left arm, reading the goosebumps. When the goosebumps were up above her elbow, he knew she was having a good time. It was a trick he'd learned years before, and it stood him in good stead as he slid down from her beautiful breasts, nibbling at her aloe-covered stomach, down lower, the bikini bottom coming off . . .

Pam bit back a scream when she came, her legs clamping down hard. Mike had both his hands on them, though, holding them open. As soon as she came, he lifted himself up and entered her, filling her and resonating with the orgasm in a way she'd never experienced. She was shouting, but she realized that his hand was over her mouth, muffling her shrieks, his other hand on the back of her head, totally controlling her, and that just made it better, so much better that she went into a continuous stream of orgasms, shaking and moaning, scratching at his back in desperation to escape and so out of her mind she couldn't begin to think beyond the waves of pleasure . . .

CHAPTER
FIVE

When Courtney woke up, her first considered action was to brush her teeth and go to the bathroom. She figured she'd passed out about nine and it was after six. She tended to be an early riser and didn't usually sleep that much and she really needed to pee.

After that she slipped on her shorts and T-shirt, sans bra and panties. She knew Mike had some around somewhere, but she could survive without either for a bit.

She brushed her hair but didn't bother with makeup, instead creeping out of her room and trying the door of the cabin Pam had planned on using. Which was empty, the bed unused. Pam's bag was on the floor, so she didn't have the wrong room.

She raised an eyebrow and looked at the door to the main cabin, then crept to it and tried the door handle. Unlocked. She slowly twisted it down and slid the door open soundlessly . . .

Mike had woken up when Courtney opened the door to the bathroom. It wasn't that he was a particularly light sleeper. He could sleep through a firefight if he wasn't on duty, but he had a very acute security switch, so when someone started moving around he had to ID it. And he was curious what Courtney would do, so he stayed awake. When she headed for his door, he pulled the sheet up to cover most of Pam and simply waited.

Courtney's expression was . . . crestfallen when she looked in the room. Mike wanted to laugh, but instead he shook his head and made a motion for silence and for her to wait. Then he carefully slid his arm out from under Pam's head, gently replacing it with a pillow, and carefully, grimacing, rolled to the side of the bed. He was totally naked, but he figured Courtney could either hide her eyes or get a good look.

Getting out of bed was, as always, a trial. But he finally managed to snag his shorts and get them on, then crept to the door and past Courtney, quietly closing it behind them.

"Are you okay?" Courtney asked as he limped down the companionway.

"I will be," he said, straightening slowly until he was fully erect. "God, mornings are bad."

"You're in worse shape than it looks," Courtney said, following him into the lounge.

"Lots," Mike said, slowly bending and stretching. "I didn't get medically discharged because of this," he said, waving at the scars. "I got medically discharged because I've got major joint damage, well, all over." He got out the makings of coffee, as well as an apple, taking a bite. "Apple?"

"So you and Pam . . . ?" Courtney asked, taking a bite of the apple and then finally getting a good look at his back. "Jesus! You're bleeding in places," she muttered around the bite.

"Yes, me and Pam," Mike said, walking over to take a bite as well. He crunched it up for a bit, then leaned down and kissed her.

The apple fell on the floor as her hand went up behind his head and pulled him in, hard. Suddenly they were on the floor, her hands running over his ruined back.

"What will Pam think?" she asked as they came up for air.

"I dunno," Mike said, his tongue sliding into the juncture between her neck and shoulder. "Let's go in and ask her."

"Oh, God," she moaned as his hand slid down into her shorts and over her ass. "I wanted you to do that," she moaned.

"I've been wanting to do it," Mike admitted, pushing her shorts down her legs. He pushed her shirt up and over her head and then down, trapping her arms. "And I've been wanting to do that, too," he said, roughly.

"Oh, God," she moaned, her head falling back.

Mike ripped the shorts off her legs then balled them up, stuffing them in her mouth. Her eyes flew open but then shut again as his mouth closed on her nipple and his hand went between her legs. She bit down on the cloth, smelling her own scent and getting even more excited as Mike expertly manipulated her, slowly stroking at her pleasure center, his mouth working on her nipple, sucking and blowing and occasionally nipping lightly until she shook her head from side to side and came so hard she thought she was going to stroke out.

Suddenly he was in her, taking her, one hand clamped over her mouth and the other kneading her breast, hard, pulling at the nipples. She was beyond pleasure, beyond thought, totally in the moment and almost unable to breathe for the strength of the ongoing climax until she thought she would just die right there.

Finally it was over, and as he slipped out of her, she made a little moan of sadness and longing.

Mike pulled the shorts from her mouth and kissed her, tenderly.

"Thank you," he said, laying his forehead on hers. "Thank you, very much. I'm sorry about that."

"Thank *you*," Courtney said, slipping an arm out of her entrapping shirt and her hand over the back of his neck. "How are you feeling?"

"You mean the joints?" Mike asked, backing away from her gently and smiling. "Exercise helps." He stood up and held out his hand.

"I think I need a Kleenex or something," Courtney said.

"Your wish, milady," Mike said, getting a Kleenex and handing it to her.

"I'll be right back," Courtney said, taking his hand to stand up, the other hand between her legs. "This is always embarrassing."

"I don't think so," Mike said, running his hand over her back. "I'll be right here. There is cuddle time I'm missing."

When she came out he was on the couch in the lounge, nursing a cup of coffee and another by his side. He had slipped on a pair of shorts, but she was still naked.

"I didn't know how you took it," Mike said, waving at the coffee.

"Cream and sugar," she said, picking up her shirt and shorts and shaking her head. "I'm running out of clothes."

"And you don't have any short of your car, which is far far away," Mike said, waggling his eyebrows and leering. "You are so at my mercy!"

"Oh, be merciful kind sir!" Courtney said, dropping to her knees and grasping at his legs in mock horror. "Please don't force me to be naked and at your mercy!"

"Don't tease an old dog," Mike said, holding out the cup. "I have cream and sugar, but how much?"

"Much," she said. "Where is it?"

"I'll get," Mike said. "You rest your lovely bones."

"I do need to get some clothes," Courtney said, looking out the window. "Where are we?"

"Still about five hundred yards from Rumrunners," Mike said, bringing over cream and sugar and a spoon.

"We *are* going to be allowed to go back to get clothes, right?" Courtney said, coquettishly.

"Do you play those games?" Mike asked. "From some signs, I'd guess you'd enjoy them."

"What games?" Courtney asked, taking a sip of coffee. It was strong but not bitter, very smooth. "You make good coffee."

"Thanks," Mike said. "Bondage and dominance games was what I was talking about."

"Uhm, no," Courtney said, her eyes flying wide. "Are you talking about whips?"

"No," Mike said, taking his own sip. "We really just played one, right there," he said, pointing to the spot where they'd made love. "I pinned your arms and gagged you. You seemed to enjoy it."

Courtney closed her eyes and her nipples sprung erect at his words.

"Whoa," she whispered after a moment. "Uhm, I guess so."

"It's a form of bondage," Mike said, shrugging. "Bondage and discipline are about dominance and submission. There are various ways to play it, master-slave, rapist-rapee, but the thing to keep in mind is that it's all play. The point is for both parties to have fun."

"Complicated guilty pleasures," Courtney said quietly. "That's what you were talking about."

"Yep," Mike said.

"So . . . what is your complicated guilty pleasure?" Courtney asked, still quietly.

"Shorts stuffed in your mouth?" Mike said, reaching out to stroke one nipple lightly. "Arms pinned? Hand on mouth? Guess. So what *do* you fantasize about when you're masturbating, Courtney?"

"God," she whispered. "Is it obvious? *Is* there some sort of mark on my forehead?"

"Not particularly," Mike said. "And at this point I need to be careful . . ." He looked up and smiled faintly. "This should be interesting."

Pam appeared in the opening to the companionway and looked at both of them blearily.

"How come you're still *alive*?" she asked, shaking her head. "Much less up? Much less . . ." She looked at Courtney, still sitting on the couch naked, her head down. "Much less . . . God!"

"Morning, Pam," Mike said, smiling. "Coffee?"

"How many times last night?" Pam asked, sitting at the table shakily.

"Orgasms?" Mike asked. "You have to keep count. Engagements? Three, I think."

"What was I?" Courtney snapped. "A quick breakfast snack?"

"No," Mike said, leaning over and kissing her on the head. "You, my dear, were a truly great wake-up. My joints aren't even stiff anymore."

"I need some clothes," Courtney said, hugging her breasts.

"I'll arrange," Mike said, getting up and going to the cabins. He came back with a towel. "Here."

"Is that all I get?" Courtney asked. "All that you'll . . . permit me?"

"For now," Mike said with a grin. "Pam, when you walked in, we were discussing . . . guilty pleasures."

"Like two at a time?" Pam asked, shaking her head. "I'm not sure I'm ready for that."

"No, actually we were discussing dominance and submission," Mike answered. "Coffee?"

"Coffee?" Pam said, screwing up her face in confusion. "You just trot that out and ask if I want *coffee*?"

"Cream and sugar?" Mike asked. "Black?"

"Cream and sugar," Pam said, shaking her head.

"Dominance and submission is the last love that dare not speak its name," Mike said, getting her a cup of coffee and carrying the cream and sugar over. "Say when."

"When."

"Despite the fact that most studies put it as the most common fantasy," Mike continued, sitting down by Courtney. "Something like fifty percent of women are willing to admit to submission fantasies. The total is probably higher."

"I know girls who . . ." Courtney said, adjusting her towel. "Well, they're definitely not submissive."

"I think of it as a bell curve," Mike said. "Some women are towards the dominance end all the way to full mistresses. Some are so submissive that they're full masochists. The 'do anything to me, Master' types."

"Do you know any of those?" Pam asked.

"I've known a few," Mike admitted. "Not many. I don't really travel in the circles, what's referred to as the 'scene' among those that really get into it. But many females, I'd say most, fall somewhere in the middle. They enjoy being dominated, and I'm talking about in agreed to scenes here, not in day-to-day life, but they're not full-scale masochists. They may even like to be spanked and told they're bad girls or whatever, but they don't want to be whipped until they bleed."

"Pass," Courtney said hastily.

"But . . . well . . ." he said, pausing. "What went on between Pam and me last night was not that far from what went on between Courtney and me."

The two girls looked at each other for a second and then, almost simultaneously, dropped their heads and shook them.

"Girls," Mike said, trying not to laugh, "there's nothing to be ashamed about. You're both very nice young ladies who have an . . . interest. Apparently, I might add. You certainly each seemed to have a good time."

"I did," Pam admitted, looking up. "But . . . it's pretty hard to just talk about it."

"Talking about it is important," Mike said. "For a few reasons. One of them is that, well . . . do you want to continue to play? I mean for more than just today and tomorrow? That's one thing to talk about. Another is the details of what you're interested in exploring and, more importantly, what you're not willing to explore. The term for it is 'negotiation.' "

"I don't want to be one of those weirdos who goes around town being led on a leash," Courtney said definitely.

"Agreed," Mike said. "And now we work out the details. Would you be willing to wear a collar here on the boat? Inside? Outside when we're out of sight of other boats?"

Courtney writhed for a minute on the couch and took a deep breath.

"I don't know," she said, looking at Pam.

"Well," Pam said, "I don't know about you, Courtney, but I just got horny again *thinking* about it."

"Thank you," Mike said, nodding at her. "Let me lay some pretty boring groundwork. Dominance and submission, and bondage and discipline, first have to involve trust. You have to trust that the dom, in this case me, will use his intelligence and skill to not push you past the point that you're comfortable. A scene is something like a scary movie. You go see a scary movie and there's a bad guy chasing some girl around and killing her. That's scary, but you *know* it's not real. D and S is the same thing. It's setting up something that in real life would be terrible. Rape. Being owned as a slave. Being forced to submit to a stranger, like a cop, for some reason. All of them, effectively, revolve around rape. But the difference is, the sub is *in control.* The sub can, at any time, say 'I'm done' or 'time out, we need to talk.' You can't say that in real rape."

"How do you do that?" Pam asked. "I don't think I could have talked most of last night. I was too . . ."

"In the moment," Mike filled in. "When a sub is fully in the moment, they often describe it as flying, like an out-of-body experience. But that moment can get broken very easily. Trust me, you could have if I'd pushed past your boundaries. Do you like anal sex?"

"No," Pam said definitely.

"Then if I'd rolled you over and gotten out the butter?" Mike asked, grinning.

"You would have had a fight on your hands," Pam said.

"You definitely would have been out of the moment," Mike said. "I didn't push at any real boundaries last night. It was far too soon, for one thing. What you do is you say 'yellow' if you need a time out and discussion. You say 'red' if you're done, take me back to shore you asshole! If you're gagged, and if we do this you're going to be gagged a lot, you grunt in the gag. What you don't do is say 'stop' or 'no' or 'please.' Those mean 'more and harder, master.'"

Pam grinned at that and dropped her head, shaking it from side to side.

"I have a hard time with the way that you just trot stuff like that out," Courtney said, shaking her own head. "I kind of like it, but it's hard for me to accept how ... open you are about it."

"I'm open in here," Mike said. "With you two, between us. But I don't go around in leather bondage gear in public ..."

"Do you *have* leather bondage gear?" Courtney said, involuntarily wriggling again.

"Some," Mike said, frowning. "Not enough if we're going to get ... complicated. I can fix that in a day or so. The point is, this is 'behind the bedroom door.' Even out on the boat, in the middle of the Stream with nobody around to see, would be behind the bedroom door. And you can push it further, a bit, but you have to know when to stop, both as the dom and as the sub. Otherwise you really do get *Nine and a Half Weeks.*"

"Lost me again," Pam said, frowning.

"It's about the only major movie ever made about dom sub games and it was horrible," Mike said, shrugging. "Basically a dom finds a newbie sub and completely takes over her life. You can do it. I could do it to you two, probably. Slowly take away your will to resist, break every barrier, turn you into submissive sluts ..."

"Are you *trying* to get me horny again?" Courtney said.

"A bit," Mike admitted with a grin. "But ... I sort of did that, accidentally, once. In the movie, the sub finally ran away from the relationship, broke the mental bond, which is way more important

than the physical ones, and ran. That . . . rarely happens in real life when something like that occurs, and it does. And it didn't happen in my relationship. I was young and just wanted to get laid and . . . be able to say 'bend over' whenever I wanted. And she . . . wasn't quite right when I met her and she fell, well, not in love but into total submission. And I used her. I knew I was using her, liked it and didn't like it at the same time, she knew she was being used, liked it and didn't like it at the same time. Finally, I broke up with her and told her to hold onto her soul. I couldn't just . . . back away. It was too easy to just use her. My resistance, then, wasn't that high. Young, dumb and full of cum. I had to simply . . . leave."

"That must have been tough," Pam said, frowning. "I mean a guy walking away from . . . you could do pretty much anything you wanted?"

"Anything," Mike said, clicking his teeth. "Anytime, any-where."

"And you walked away," Pam said.

"Had to," Mike said with a shrug. "For her. I won't say she took it well. But the point is, I can manage that, now. But, if you get into this . . . scene, it's something that you have to look out for. There are other guys, like me, who won't back away. Who won't . . . let you go. There are predators in this subsec-tion of the sex world, guys who will gladly hold onto you and break you, knowing what they're doing and using you instead of . . ." He shrugged. "Instead of caring for you and wanting to simply have you enjoy yourselves and get their enjoyment as well. The 'bedroom door' is tricky. If you stay in the scene, get deeper in it, you might do full scenes, with other people watching . . ."

"Not on your life," Courtney said, shaking her head.

"You'd be surprised," Mike said. "Think about what you fantasize about when you masturbate."

"Uh . . ." Courtney said, then paused.

"Yeah," Mike said, nodding and working his jaw. "Or . . . hmm . . . going to a club in a miniskirt and no panties and sort of . . . sitting on your master's lap, with his dick out through his zipper and . . . moving to the beat . . ."

"Okay," Pam said, holding up her hand. "I can see what you mean by the bedroom door being tricky."

"You also have to know when the scene ends," Mike continued. "Firmly know when you're . . . yourself again and the scene is over. Submissive means in sex play, not in 'real life.' That's part of the dom's job, to make it plain when the scene is over. In a way, I've made a mistake by leaving Courtney in nothing but a towel. It's continuing the scene when we should really be out of scene. But I thought she'd sort of like it. Just a guess."

"No comment," Courtney said, pulling at the top of the towel.

"Here's the question: When do you *have* to go back to Missouri?"

"That's a big question," Pam said carefully. "Not until classes start, I guess."

"I've said it before, you can stay as long as you'd like," Mike said, just as carefully. "If you'd like, we can just fish and dive—I'm a qualified SCUBA instructor by the way, so I can get you qualified on that if you want. Or we can fish and dive and . . . play. For as long as you'd like. Or, rather, until it's time to go back to Missouri. Not forever."

"Why not forever?" Courtney asked sharply. "Commitment issues?"

"Really complicated ones," Mike answered, nodding. "Let's put it this way, for reasons I won't get into it would be a really bad idea for me to ever get married. Really bad. Having kids is out of the question."

"Well, I wasn't talking *marriage*," Courtney said, shaking her head.

"Just leave it, if we can," Mike said, shrugging. "But you can stay for a couple of days, or a week, or until it's time to go back to Missouri. No strings at all. But. If we're going to do scenes, we're going to do it right. Full contract."

"Contract?" Pam said, raising an eyebrow.

"Contract," Mike answered, grinning.

"That sounds ominous," Courtney muttered, pulling at her towel again.

"Not nearly as ominous as the actual contract," Mike replied,

grinning again. "Trust me, you'll love it. Just *doing* the contract is a scene."

Pam looked at Courtney, who shrugged and waggled her head.

"Okay," Pam said carefully. "We'll stay for . . . a bit longer."

"Works," Mike said, nodding. "Okay, we are very much out of scene at this point. Courtney, I've got a bunch of T-shirts that are going to be long enough to be a dress for you. Why don't you grab one of those for the time being, or your suit. Maybe your suit under the shirt if you want. I'll get the anchors in, we'll head back to the marina and get your gear. Maybe do a little shopping unless you have more suits."

"I've got one more," Pam said.

"I don't," Courtney said. "I never used them for anything except sunning, really. I don't swim much at home."

"We'll be swimming, and sunning, a lot," Mike said, standing up. "And let me pay for the suits, okay? The proprietary amount I got in the buyout? Just say it was in excess of ten mil. I can afford bathing suits. Even very pretty, very expensive ones."

"And anything else you'd want!" Courtney said, her eyes wide.

"No," Mike said, pausing at the opening to the companionway and not turning around. "I can't buy the very real pleasure I'm getting from your company. I don't even mean the sex, which, by the way, was incredible in case I didn't mention it. I mean the real honest pleasure I'm getting from just having the two of you around."

CHAPTER
SIX

"Are we insane?" Pam said quietly, when the cabin door closed.

"If I am," Courtney said, lying back on the couch and closing her eyes, "I don't ever want to go back to sanity."

"I think that's the trap he was talking about," Pam said, shaking her head. "I think I know what he means. I think if he told me to do . . . just about anything, I'd do it."

"Yeah," Courtney said, sitting up. "But . . . I trust him not to really hurt me. Except, maybe, break my heart," she added sadly.

"He really hit the nail on the head with that one," Pam admitted. "The M word."

"I'd marry him in a heartbeat," Courtney agreed, nodding. "And he says he can cook."

"I'm a great cook," Mike said, tossing her a brown T-shirt. "Sorry, I need to do laundry. It was all I had left clean."

"What is it?" Courtney asked, holding up the light tan shirt with "Alpha Five" stenciled on the front.

"One of my team shirts," Mike said, shrugging. "It will cover your lovely nakedness, which is a pity. Your gorgeous blonde bush is showing under the towel."

Courtney stood up and dropped the towel, posing.

"Does this make you think of anything?" she asked coyly.

"Nope," Mike said, shrugging. "Can't think of a thing."

"Take your pants off and prove it," Courtney said, stretching and arching. "Nothing?"

"You really want me to prove it?" Mike said, raising an eyebrow.

"You're serious?" Courtney asked, looking at his crotch. "God, you're serious."

"One of the requirements of being a good dom is control," Mike said. "Okay, I'll prove it," he added, backing towards the companionway. "Pam, could you take off your suit, please?"

"Uhm . . ." Pam said, looking from one to the other and then shrugging. "God, I can't believe I'm doing this," she muttered, reaching up to untie her top.

When she was naked, Mike shrugged off his shorts and raised an eyebrow.

"You're not even a *little* hard," Courtney said accusingly.

"Nope," Mike said calmly.

"How 'bout this?" Courtney said, writhing towards him, hands behind her head, hips working.

"Nope," Mike said, looking over her body disinterestedly.

"He's serious," Pam said, shaking her head and looking away.

"That's . . . sick," Courtney said, stopping and looking at him angrily. "It's *insulting*! I *know* you like us!"

"Very much," Mike said in the same calm tone. "Would you like to see *how* much?"

"Yes," Pam said, looking back, her eyes widening as he thickened and lengthened before her eyes. "Jesus!"

Mike reached out quickly and took Courtney's jaw in a hard one-handed grip.

"So do you really want to challenge me?" he growled, looking her hard in the eye.

"No," Courtney whispered, panting.

" 'No, *master*,' " Mike growled.

"No . . ." Courtney closed her eyes and panted for a second. "No . . . master."

"Very good," Mike said, smiling at her, his eyes hard. He released her and pulled up his shorts, then looked over at her. "Are you okay?" he asked gently.

She just looked at him in confusion and raised a hand that fluttered in the air like a bird.

Mike gently took it and pulled her into his arms, his face in her neck, holding her naked body gently.

"It's a strange feeling, isn't it?" he asked quietly. "But it's okay. I really do care. But if you tease or challenge, well," he said, pulling back and looking her in the eye, grinning, "this old dog has way more than *one* bite."

"Okay," Courtney said, smiling and rubbing at his chest, still obviously agitated. "I won't tease."

"Unless you *want* to get bit," Mike said, rubbing at her hair. "That's part of the play, too."

"Uh, I'm sort of . . ."

"Later, unfortunately," Mike replied. "We have real life to contend with for a while. You probably should get dressed and catch a breather; this is a lot to deal with all of a sudden."

"Yes," Pam said, softly, "it is."

He pulled Courtney back into his arms, then moved to Pam, bringing her into a group hug.

"We'll have fun," Mike said gently. "And any time, *any* time, that you want to stop or just take a breather, you can tell me that and we'll stop for as long as you want. Permanently, if that's what you want. I'm *not* a rapist. I'm *not* a slave owner. We're, all three, friends. And we need to stay that way. Okay?"

"Okay," Pam said, smiling, her face working. "This is just . . ."

"Scary like a scary movie?" Mike asked, loosening up his hold. "Or scary like . . . Syria?"

"Truth?" Pam said. "Somewhere in between."

"Probably about right," Mike said, shrugging. "The analogy isn't perfect. There's no physical touch in a movie. Speaking of which, did you call your friend back?"

"No!" Pam said, her eyes wide.

"Do that while I go get the anchors in and head back to the marina."

When he was gone on deck, Pam looked down, realized she was naked, and blushed scarlet.

"I think we're going insane," she repeated, putting on her suit and heading to her cabin to dig out her cell phone.

"I'm all for it," Courtney said, picking up the T-shirt and sniffing it. No smell of Mike, more's the pity.

"You're a slut, Courtney," Pam said from the cabin. "Oh, crap."

"What?" Courtney said, walking to her door.

"There are six messages," Pam said. "Probably all from Stacey. I hope she didn't freak out too bad." She hit the speed dial.

"Pam!" Stacey said, desperately. "Are you okay?"

"Yeah," Pam said, giggling. "More than okay. Really, really *insanely* okay, okay?"

"You didn't call!" Stacey said. "And you didn't answer your phone. I was going out of my mind! I almost called the police."

"Sorry, sorry," Pam said. "Don't, it's okay. It's really, really okay. It's not just okay, it's great."

"Me!" Courtney said, grabbing at the phone. "Me!"

"Courtney wants to talk," Pam said, handing over the phone.

"Stacey!" Courtney squealed. "You know the tall, dark, and handsome stranger? How about tall, dark, rich, dangerous, handsome stranger?"

"You're kidding," Stacey said enviously.

"Did I mention great in bed?" Courtney said, flopping down in the lower bunk and kicking at the top one happily. "Did I?"

"Just you or . . . ?" Stacey asked incredulously.

"Both!" Courtney squealed. "Pam . . . well, a bunch of times. Me once. Came twice!"

"Courtney!" Pam said, gritting her teeth.

"I think Pam came . . ." She looked over and shook her head. "How many?"

"Some." Pam sighed, shaking her head.

"Like, six?" Courtney asked, raising an eyebrow.

"*Six?*" Stacey shouted. "You're joking!"

"More like . . ." Pam said, shaking her head. "Give me the phone, Courtney."

"Come on," Courtney replied. "You can count that high, right? Three, four? Five?"

"Give me the phone," Pam said, holding out her hand.

"Stacey," she said carefully, "we're having a lot of fun. We're probably going to stay down here for a few more days . . ."

"Weeks you mean!" Courtney yelled. "Months!"

"Mike's invited us to stay," Pam said calmly. "He'd invited us to stay before last night and I think we'll take him up on his kind invitation."

"We're slaves!" Courtney yelled. "Slaves to his desire!"

"Is she out of her mind?" Stacey asked.

"Yes," Pam replied calmly. "And so am I. Completely round the bend. Head over heels in . . . lust, I guess." She shook her head and sighed. "But Courtney's right. This guy is nice, he's . . . pretty handsome, he's got a body like . . . Christ you just want to spend your *life* running your hands over his pecs. Great boat, we went fishing for dolphin fish, that's mahi-mahi, and we caught a bunch and then took them to this great restaurant he knows and the cook fixed them up great. Then when we got back to the boat Courtney kind of passed out . . ."

"He didn't drug her, did he?" Stacey asked, suspiciously.

"No, she was just worn out," Pam said.

"Exhausted from looking at him," Courtney said, humming happily.

"It wasn't drugs," Pam said. "She went to bed while Mike was reparking the boat, then he was helping me put on aloe and . . ." She paused and sighed. "Whooo. Great hands. Did I mention great hands? And you know the bondage thing?"

"He didn't tie you up!" Stacey said.

"Not yet," Pam sighed. "But he totally took charge. I could barely think. It's like he reads your mind, it's just insane. I think we did it about four times last night and I came at least three times, but a couple of them were like one continuous . . ."

"Me, too!" Courtney caroled.

"Hush," Pam hissed. "Anyway, we're going to stay for awhile. We'll call our parents. And I'll call you, too. He was the one who *told* me to call you last night, and he reminded me that I hadn't called back this morning."

"Courtney said something about 'dangerous,'" Stacey said cautiously. "I'm still worried about the 'dangerous.'"

"He's a former SEAL," Pam said. "And just about covered in

scars; he got really shot up somewhere. But ... he's a nice guy. He can be *really* dominant in a *good* way, then turn caring in the next second. It's ..."

"It's making me cum just thinking about it," Courtney said, her legs in the air, crossed, and rubbing back and forth.

"Courtney, would you *quit* that?" Pam said, looking away. "Courtney is just ... gone. She's turning into a total whore, I swear."

"As long as I'm Mike's ho," Courtney said, laughing and sitting up. "Me."

"Here's Courtney."

"I really was tired last night," Courtney said. "It wasn't drugs, it was being out on the boat and being *amazingly* horny for hours. It really took it out of me."

"He's that great?" Stacey said, disbelieving.

"He's got a body like a ruined Adonis," Courtney said. "Great legs, huge thighs, nice calves, stomach's a bit big, but I think that's age because it's strong too. Arms, shoulders, great tan, and these massive scars on his chest and stomach. Like Pam said, he got really shot up; I don't know how he lived, you know? When I got up I checked Pam's cabin ..."

"You were on the boat last night?" Stacey asked.

"Oh, yeah, it's a big boat," Courtney said. "A yacht, I guess. Did I mention he's rich? Anyway, I checked Pam's room and she wasn't therrre ..." she caroled, grinning evilly.

"Oh, shut up," Pam said, shaking her head.

"So I crept up to the main cabin and peeked in and he was awake and Pam was just out like a light. I guess she was worn out," she added, winking at Pam.

"It *had* been a long day," Pam said.

"Long night more like it," Courtney said. "When he got out of bed it was like watching a Cro-Magnon or something. He's apparently got a lot of joint damage. And he *still* looked good. Well, except for the new scars on his *back*," she said with a grin, winking at Pam.

"And he started making coffee, moving better by then, and then ..." Courtney paused and shook her head. "It got sort of confused. There was this apple and then we were on the

floor and he pinned my arms down with my shirt and stuffed my . . . anyway, he just . . . took me. He played with me, I mean *really* played, not just 'let's get her wet enough to get it in,' but just worked me all the way 'til I came and then just . . . took me." She stopped, panting.

"Courtney," Stacey said, a bit breathlessly. "I don't have a boyfriend right now. Could we cut back a little on the description?"

"Well, let's just say I know what Pam meant by one continuous cum," Courtney said, shaking her head. "Mindblowing doesn't begin to describe it. When Pam came out I was still stark naked and I *liked* it. He's into bondage and all that, by the way. We talked about it this morning. But he's . . . he keeps talking about safety and making sure we're clear when we're *not* in what he calls 'scene.' He's . . . just so *blunt* about some things. But in a good way. It's almost like taking a class. A really *fun* class!" she finished.

"I wish I was there," Stacey sighed. "But I've got to work."

"Come on down," Courtney said. "Plenty of room. And I'm sure he could wear all three of us out!"

"Won't fly," Stacey said. "But I'm glad you're having fun."

"We are," Courtney said. "Lots of fun. Fun fishing, fun snorkeling, fun partying, and *lots* of fun screwing. God, I want to screw him again. I want him to screw *me* again. I'm getting wet just thinking about it."

"I'm getting wet just hearing about it," Stacey sighed. "Look, call me, okay? Every day you can."

"Okay," Courtney said. "Talk later."

"Girls," Mike said when Pam and Courtney came up on the flying bridge. "Do either of you have a passport? Barring that, how about a birth certificate?"

"I've got a birth certificate," Pam said, frowning. "But not with me."

"Me, too," Courtney said. "But, why?"

"I want to take you to the Bahamas," Mike said. "It's just over the Stream. The diving's better, for one thing. And less boats, for another, once you get away from Bimini. Some good clubs on the islands, too. I was thinking about just going . . . cruising.

Fish some, dive some, play around, do a little clubbing. I don't dance, but I'd love to watch you two. But you need birth certificates. Getting into the Bahamas is no big deal, but you need one to get back in the States. Technically. Probably we could slip you in to Islamorada, but it would get sticky if we got stopped or if customs found out."

"Mine's at home," Pam said, shrugging. "So's Courtney's."

Mike nodded and sighed. "You'd have to ask your parents to send it down, right?"

"Oh, that would be a great call," Courtney said, grimacing in panic. "'Hi, Dad, I've met this guy who's into bondage who wants to take me to a foreign country so he can work his will on me.' Not."

"Well, we've got a couple of days to decide," Mike said, shrugging. "I need to call a friend to send me some gear, and that will take a day or so to get here."

"Bondage gear?" Pam asked nervously.

"Very," Mike replied. "I've got a FedEx number. If you can work up the courage, all you have to do is give it to your parents and they can send the paperwork. You're both eighteen or older, right? I should have asked before, my bad that I didn't."

"Yes," Courtney said. "I'm eighteen, Pam's nineteen."

"Well, I'd really like you to call your parents and get the paperwork," Mike said. "If we can't, we can't, and I might just go ahead and go anyway. Like I said, we probably wouldn't get caught coming back in. And even if we did, well . . ." He shrugged. "I've got some strings I can pull to get it cleared up." He suddenly stopped and blanched as he imagined the report getting to the President. It probably wouldn't go higher than Pierson, which would be funny rather than embarrassing. But if it got to the President, or even the NSA . . .

"What's wrong?" Pam asked worriedly.

"I was just imagining if the conversation got . . . as high as it might," Mike said, shaking his head. "Embarrassing doesn't begin to cover it. Much as you don't want your parents getting in on the conversation, you *really* don't want it going where it might go otherwise."

"What do you mean?" Courtney said uncertainly.

"Well . . ." Mike said, wanting to explain but not knowing how to do so. "Let's put it this way. From what I did with the Navy, I've got some pretty high contacts who would be willing to pull strings to let my two coed . . . girlfriends, who obviously *are* American citizens, back into the country. But do you *really* want your names going across the desk of, say, an undersecretary of defense?" *Not to mention Donald Brandeis's*, he thought.

"Oh," Pam said, blanching.

"So, if you can screw up your courage, call your parents," Mike said. "The sooner the better. If they can get the certificates out today, it would be best."

CHAPTER
SEVEN

"Hi, Mom?" Courtney said brightly.

"Hi, Courtney," Abigail Trays said. "How are you enjoying the Keys?"

"Uhm . . . really enjoying them," Courtney said. "In fact, Pam and I are going to stay down here for a while longer. If that's okay."

"You're an adult now, Courtney," her mother said sadly. "You can do whatever you want. Are you okay for money?"

"Yeah, we're . . . fine," Courtney said.

"What's wrong?" Abigail asked. "And don't say 'nothing.'"

"I need a favor," Courtney admitted. "And I don't want you to freak. Or Dad. And I can really see Dad freaking."

"What's wrong?" her mother asked. "You are okay?"

"I'm fine," Courtney said, shaking her head from side to side. "It's just . . . I need a favor. Uhm . . . Pam and I met this really nice guy down here. And . . . we want to go to the Bahamas with him on his boat . . ." she said, pausing and wincing. "He really is a nice guy, Mom. And he's really into making sure we feel safe about it. We went out fishing yesterday for dolphin, the fish not the other, mahi-mahi . . ."

"I know what dolphin is, dear," her mother said tightly. "I'm just having a problem with my little baby meeting some guy with a boat . . . what kind of boat?"

"Well, more of a yacht," Courtney said. "He's a SEAL who's retired and made money selling what he calls widgets to the military. Now he lives down on the boat. Honestly, Mom, he hardly even tried to pick us up. Just asked if we wanted to go fishing and said to give him a call. But . . . it's a really nice boat and he's a nice guy and I've never been to the Bahamas . . ."

"Courtney," her mother said, sighing. "Yes, okay. But . . . yes, you're a grown-up young lady and can make your own decisions but . . . how old is he?"

"Thirty something," Courtney said tightly. "I know that's kind of old, but he's in . . ." She paused and sighed. "Really *incredible* shape, even with all his . . . anyway, he's a really nice guy, Mom. And he told us we could stay as long as we liked, as long as we left on time to go back to school."

"Sounds like he's got the best of both worlds," Abigail said. "He gets fun and then when the summer's over . . ."

"I guess, maybe," Courtney said. "But it doesn't feel like that. I think he really cares, but he said he has some, complicated commitment issues, too. And I've learned that when he uses the word 'complicated' to be very careful where I tread."

"That sounds ominous," Abigail said. "Honey, are you sure about this?"

"Yes," Courtney said definitely. "It's not going to interfere with school and I'm having . . . lots of fun. I really want to do this. Some kids get to go to Europe for the summer. You know I couldn't do that. I'd like to *at least* get to the Bahamas. Please, Mom?"

"I think you don't know what you're getting yourself into," Abigail said carefully. "But you *are* an adult. But, honey . . . be careful, okay?" She paused for a time and Courtney wasn't sure what she wanted to say.

"Mom," Courtney said. "Mike's all over about safety with us. He's . . . he really wants to make sure we're not only safe, we feel safe. And he's . . ." She stopped and sighed. "There's things I'd like to talk about, but you're my mother. I don't think you'd understand."

"You might be surprised, dear," Abigail said gently.

"If you *do* understand, I don't want to know," Courtney said,

sighing, then paused. "Mom, have you ever heard the . . . term I guess: scene."

There was a very long pause.

"Yes," Abigail said calmly.

"Oh," Courtney replied, her eyes widening.

"Is he a top or a bottom?" Abigail asked.

"A *what*?" Courtney asked.

"Is he a dominant or a submissive, then?" her mother asked.

"Mom!"

"Dear, do you know what a spreader bar is?"

"Mom!" Courtney gasped. "No. And I don't want to know if you do!"

"You know those rosewood planter hangers in your father's and my bedroom?"

"*Mother!*"

"Now I'm particularly worried, Courtney," Abigail said firmly. "Because I know *exactly* how badly this can go. I don't think you have any idea . . ."

"Mike . . . talked about that a little," Courtney said. "About . . . only doing . . . that behind the bedroom door. But he also said something about . . . sometimes it's a bit hard to figure out where the bedroom door is."

"That's simple," Abigail said. "You simply don't do anything in such a way as mundanes are aware. But he sounds like he kind of has his head on his shoulders. However, safety *is* important, I don't think you realize how important. I've had a good friend die because her dom didn't get a gag off in time. And . . . many people who get far into the scene *never* have a normal life. It's a form of arrested development and I'm not sure if it's a chicken or egg situation, whether they weren't ever going to get beyond that stage or if getting too far into the scene caused it. I don't want that happening to you, Courtney, you have too much potential. And what you're doing, really, is called boat bunnying. Buying your way to a vacation on your back—"

"Mike invited us before we'd . . . done anything," Courtney said. "He said he wouldn't kick us out of bed but there were no strings. I don't think there are any even now. I think I could say 'I'd like

to just go along for the ride' and it would be fine. But . . . I can't believe I'm having this conversation with my *mother!*"

"I don't think you know what truly good is, dear," Abigail said, trying to get through to her.

"I know Pam came at least three times last night," Courtney said. "And I don't know whether to count this morning as one, two or one continuous amazing climax, Mother, if you want me to be blunt."

"Oh," Abigail said. "Uhm . . . What was his name again?"

"Mother!"

"Well, your father and I do swing," Abigail said.

"Mother!"

"And, I suppose I'm probably too old for him, but some guys do enjoy mother-daughter action . . ."

"*Mother!*"

"Sorry, dear, just teasing," Abigail said, laughing. "You started this."

"There are things you don't want to *know* about your parents!" Courtney said, closing her eyes, tightly. "God!"

"This is a conversation, frankly, that I've both wanted to have and dreaded," Abigail said sadly, "because things like this, I've noticed, tend to run in families. Now you know why I've tried to get you to act more like a lady. A woman should be a perfect lady in public and a whore when the bedroom door closes. And the bedroom door, dear, is anything that prevents the mundanes from knowing what is going on. I won't tell you some of the things that I've done that would shock you. But they *would* shock you. And there is a group here, friends of ours. All the times your father and I went out to 'dinner and a movie' and left you with a sitter, we weren't going out to a movie."

"Do I *know* any of these people?" Courtney said, her eyes wide.

"Yes," her mother said. "And I won't name names. I strongly doubt that you'd guess who most of them are."

"Mrs. Mathers," Courtney said definitely. "But . . ."

"She wouldn't mind," Abigail said humorously. "Good guess. But call her *Mistress* Mathers, if you would. But not in public."

"God," Courtney said. "I can't believe I'm having this conversation."

"I'm telling you this so you understand that I'm not just some old fogy of your mother," Abigail said. "I *know* what you are getting into. And it can be . . . yes, wonderful. It also has a real element of danger. And I don't *know* your master. I would have much preferred that you become involved with a master I knew I could trust. One who wouldn't . . . warp you and who will be cautious about . . . various things. Are you a mas, dear?"

"Mom, you're getting beyond me, here," Courtney said, her head reeling.

"Are you a masochist?" Abigail said tightly. "Has he whipped you?"

"*No!*" Courtney said. "God, Mother."

"Okay." Abigail sighed. "We'll talk about that later."

"Mom?" Courtney said, her eyes wide. "Are you a . . . mas?"

"No comment," Abigail said.

"Mom?"

"Well," her mother said, "you know how sometimes we'd go to the pool and I'd wear a shirt and long pants?"

"Mom?"

"Choose your own limits, dear," her mother said tightly. "And allow me to choose mine."

"What are your limits?" Courtney asked.

"That is for me, and your father, to know," Abigail said primly. "But I will say that . . . there is a terrible glory in a good whipping."

"*Mother!*"

"Don't let him strike you on the breasts or across the kidneys. He should know that. I don't suppose I could speak to this young man?"

Courtney's eyes flew wide in horror at the thought and she shook her head.

"I don't think . . ."

"If you're going out of the country with him, surely I should speak to him," Abigail said with remorseless logic. "And much more so if you're going to enter a master-slave relationship."

"Mother!"

"Clear communication is *vital* in a relationship like that, dear," her mother said.

"I'm an *adult*, mother," Courtney said, shaking her head.

"And do you *want* your birth certificate?" Abigail said. "How am I going to get it to you?"

"He gave me his FedEx number," Courtney said. "He still does some consulting for the military."

"You're sure this person isn't simply . . ." Abigail said and paused. "There are many people who . . . talk about having experiences they didn't have. Up to pathological liars, who are very dangerous people, dear."

"Well, from his scars, I'd say not," Courtney answered. "He's been shot, that's for sure."

"Oh," Abigail said uncertainly. "I really do need to talk to this young man."

"He's not exactly *young*," Courtney said.

"He's in his thirties, dear," her mother said. "I am forty-two. He's a young man to me."

"Okay," Courtney said, sighing. "Hang on."

She went up on deck where Mike was backing the boat into the dock.

"Courtney, could you grab those . . ." He started to say, then saw she had the phone clutched to her chest.

"My mom would like to talk to you," she said desperately.

"I half-expected that," Mike said. "But I need to get the lines on, first."

Mike got the boat secured to the rear and decided the rest could wait. He walked over to Courtney and took the phone.

"Mike Jenkins," he said. "This is Courtney's mother?"

"Yes," Abigail said pleasantly. "How do you do, Mr. Jenkins?"

"Fine," Mike replied, going into the closed bridge and then down to the lounge. He could faintly hear Pam doggedly arguing with someone in her cabin.

"I understand you'd like to go to the Bahamas with my daughter?" Abigail asked.

"If it can be arranged," Mike answered. "Getting over there is easy, you just point the boat east and go. Getting back, however, requires getting past American customs and immigration. They

want to ensure that even your daughter is, in fact, an American citizen. Thus the birth certificate."

"It's the going on the trip that interests me," Abigail said sweetly. "I understand you're a top?"

Mike paused and his eyebrow raised.

"Have an interesting conversation with Courtney?" Mike asked. "I heard the occasional shouts of 'Mother!' from the flying bridge. Yes, I am."

"Are you a member of the Society?" Abigail asked evenly.

"No," Mike said. "I've never been in the Black Rose. It's . . . a bit further out than I care to go. I don't suppose you were at Disclave?"

"No," Abigail said tartly. "But I've heard the story. I'm very worried about safety."

"And I know what safety you're worried about," Mike said, shrugging. "I was in a monogamous dom-sub relationship for seven years with no problems. The girls are . . . inexperienced. That is, of course, fun. But I'm being very careful and intend to be very careful with their boundaries and with all standard safety issues, especially gags. I generally prefer ring gags, anyway, which are about as safe as you can get. I order from JR and Discrete in Boston."

"Oh, do you know Bob Thorson at Discrete?" Abigail asked.

Mike opened his mouth to reply and froze. He did, but not as Mike "Jenkins." Bob was a former Force Recon Marine and had a Ph.D. in Abnormal Psychology. He was a world expert in B&D and S&M and had been an adjunct professor at Harvard before quitting to become, in his words, "a professional pervert," and opening a bondage shop. His favorite part was that he didn't have to pay for workers; all his assistants were volunteers who got "paid" in testing out the gear he ordered.

"Mr. Jenkins?"

"Mike, please," he replied. "Ma'am, I do, but not as Mike Jenkins. Due to the work that I do with the government, I have more than one, fully legal, identity. That is not bullshitting and I'd prefer that you not tell the girls." He closed his eyes and shook his head. "If you want a reference, ask him about Mike Harmon." Shit, he even knew his damned *team* name! "But I'd really prefer that you just say some guy named 'Mike' who used to be a SEAL."

"Okay," Abigail said uncertainly. "That bothers me, but I'll call Bob and ask him. Did you know him when he was a Marine?"

"No," Mike said. "That was before my time and the teams and Recon don't mix much, anyway. I called him to order some stuff and we got to talking, you know how he is. I was pretty inexperienced at the time. I'd been doing B and D and didn't know what I was doing and I got his book . . ."

"*Roses* is a great book," Abigail said, the grin clear in her voice.

"That it is," Mike said, grinning right back. "Anyway, we got to talking. I was a SEAL instructor at the time, married. He gave me a great lecture on safety . . ."

"He's big on safety," Abigail said. "I'd hate to say 'too' big on safety, but . . ."

"He's a pro," Mike said, shrugging. "Anyway, I know him. But he doesn't know me as Mike Jenkins. He doesn't even know that I'm in the Keys, or for that matter out of the teams. I don't think I've talked to him in three or four years. He might not remember me."

"Well, I think I'll take you on your word," Abigail said. "What are you planning on doing for scene with the girls?"

Mike rolled his eyes and shrugged.

"We've got the time and luxury to . . . take our time," Mike said. "I'd, frankly, planned a rather drawn-out slave-training scene. Captured girls, being taken on a boat to be sold, et cetera. Pseudo Gorian, I suppose."

"Sounds heavenly," Abigail said, sighing. "But . . ."

"I don't intend to break them," Mike said. "I want them to be clear about the bedroom door. If they want to expand, later, fine. But . . . I don't want the scene to become their life."

"You're pretty smart for a SEAL," Abigail said.

"We're smarter than you think," Mike said. "But . . . I'm a bit unusual even for a team guy, yeah."

"Well, give me the FedEx number and I'll get the birth certificate out today," Abigail said, then sniffed theatrically. "My little girl is growing up and getting her own master. It's so sad."

"Mrs. Tray?" Mike said. "And is it Mrs. Tray or Mistress Tray?"

"Oh, it's Mrs.," Abigail said.

"Mrs. Tray? You are a nut."

"Takes one to know one," Abigail said, laughing. "Be careful with my daughter, please, Mike whoever you are."

"Harmon," Mike said quietly.

"You're not DEA or something, are you?" Abigail asked.

"No," Mike said, chuckling. "I don't do the drug thing. I do the other war."

"Oh. Well, it was good talking to you Mr. . . . Jenkins," Abigail said after a moment's thought. "And, well, if you're ever in Steelville and are interested in training a forty-two-year-old slave, give me a call," she said with a laugh.

"Hmmm . . ." Mike said, smiling. "Do you look anything like your daughter?"

"Somewhat older," Abigail said. "I keep in pretty good shape, though.'"

"You tempt me, madam," Mike said, smiling.

"I'll let you go to tempt my daughter now," Abigail said. "Good talking to you."

"And you," Mike replied, hitting the disconnect and going up on the flying bridge.

"I need a beer," Courtney said. "I can't believe the conversation I just had with my mother."

"I can't believe the conversation *I* just had with your mother," Mike said, sighing and sitting down next to her. "But I don't suppose there's any possibility of mother-daughter . . ."

"Don't even *go* there!" Courtney said, dropping her face into her hands. "Oh, God!"

"Well, she did suggest if I was ever in Steelville I should give her a call," he said teasingly.

"Oh, God!" Courtney replied, shaking her head. "There are things you *don't* want to know about your parents!"

"Well, *that* wasn't fun," Pam said, coming up on deck. "They're going to 'think' about it. My mom's calling *Courtney's* mom to talk to her."

"Oh," Courtney said, shaking her head. "That could be bad."

"Why?" Pam said. "Did she go off on you?"

"No," Courtney said. "But . . ."

"Courtney just found out far more about her parents' love life than she ever wanted to," Mike said. "So did I."

"My *mom* came on to him!" Courtney wailed.

"What?" Pam gasped.

"Her parents are, apparently, in the 'scene,'" Mike said, chuckling. "We had a long talk about bondage safety."

"Dad *whips* her," Courtney gasped. "My mom has *always* been the boss in the family. This is getting a little hard to take."

Pam's phone rang and she looked at it as if it was a snake, then hit Connect.

"Yeah, Mom?" she said, then blinked. "Really? Great. Okaaay." She held it out to Mike. "She wants to talk to you."

"Hello?" Mike said, trying not to sigh. This was turning into one hell of a lot of work for a couple of . . . no, it wasn't. What in the hell was he *thinking*?

"Yes, ma'am," Mike said, taking a breath and definitely *not* sighing. There was a pause as he listened to Pam's mother.

"Go ahead," Mike said, his eyebrows raising.

"Probably ring," Mike said. "Some ball but only monitored. Possibly cock." . . .

"I will be." . . .

"I'm still making up my order in my mind," Mike said. "But leather. Probably locking." . . .

"Can't get it off if there's a panic attack," Mike said. "You can cut leather." He looked over at Pam, who was staring at him, wide-eyed, and shrugged.

"Possibly," Mike said. "I'm a trained bosun, we are trained to raise multihundred-ton boats. In a storm. If I do, it will probably be my own rig; I don't like most of the suspension rigs out there." . . .

"I'm going to contract and do the best negotiation I can," Mike said. "I was going to go over that sometime today or tomorrow and no major scene until we do." . . .

"Yes," Mike said. "I was. I'm still scripting the details." . . .

"Fine," he said, nodding. "Good talking to you, too, ma'am. No, I won't say that in front of the girls. Yes I will. Goodbye."

"Was that conversation about what I *think* it was about?" Pam said, staring in horror.

"Yep," Mike said, shaking his head. "You two have got a couple of *kinky* moms. I guess the acorn doesn't fall far from the tree."

"Oh, God!" Pam wailed. "I did *so* not want to know that!"

"It was better than having the conversation with her *yourself*," Courtney said. "Trust me." She paused and her brow furrowed. "Oh, God, your parents and my parents have been friends since . . ."

"We were in *grade* school," Pam said, closing her eyes. "I don't want to think about this!"

"At least *your* mom didn't describe to you the pleasure of being *whipped*," Courtney said.

"Really?" Mike asked.

"No!" Pam said.

"Yes! It was a . . . terribly weird conversation," Courtney said. "She ended up telling Mike to come by if he was ever in Steelville! And don't you *dare* say anything about . . ."

"Mother-daughter action?" Mike asked, grinning. "Never crossed my mind."

"I *so* don't want to think about . . ." Courtney said, closing her eyes. "You. My mom. Me. Oh, God, I need some brain floss!"

Pam was simply staring, wide-eyed, at the horizon.

"Hello?" Mike said, somewhat seriously. "Earth to Pam."

"Us," she whispered. "In a scene. With our parents."

"Aaaah!" Courtney wailed. "You *had* to say that! I've *seen* some bondage pictures. I *so* don't want to think about that!"

"Your dad's . . . kinda cute," Pam said, still staring at the horizon.

"Noooo!" Courtney said. "Don't *say* these things!"

CHAPTER
EIGHT

There were quite a few things, besides bondage gear, to pick up before they were ready to head out. Most of the food and drinks for the trip they picked up in the Islamorada Wal-Mart, but Mike took them to specialty shops to get bathing suits. He had them pick up some light-weight "sun" shirts as well as broad-brimmed hats. He also had them each get a pair of high-heeled shoes but didn't shop for any other clothing. He, meanwhile, shopped the tools and hardware section, picking up various items he felt might be useful.

They didn't sleep together, at Mike's insistence, while they got ready for the trip. And they didn't spend all their time on land; he took them out after sailfish, unsuccessfully, the next morning.

The birth certificates arrived, as did several large boxes from "Fourth Level Equipment Company." Mike stored those in the "Bluebeard" room.

Finally, everything was prepared and they cast off as the sun was setting over the Key, making their way out through the channel with Pam at the wheel and Mike taking control when the going got particularly tricky. He'd asked Courtney to prep some chicken and vegetables while they were headed out.

As soon as they were beyond the last reefs and well away

from land, Mike checked the radar and set the autosteer for the Bahamas with the boat moving just fast enough to get it up on plane.

"Okay," he said, joining the girls in the lounge. "First, I cook dinner."

"You said you can cook," Courtney said, waving at the chunked-up chicken breasts. "But so far it's all talk."

"O, ye of little faith," Mike said.

He made chicken paprikash—chicken in paprika and sour cream sauce—and fettuccine Alfredo with fresh parmesan, asparagus on the side. It was a bit of hit.

"God," Courtney said, sitting down to the table. "I take it back. You *can* cook. Marry me!"

"No," Mike said seriously. "Look, there are reasons, okay? But I won't, can't, get into them. But we can have a very good time together and then . . . part as friends, okay? It's important to me that you understand. We can't be more than friends and, maybe, occasional lovers. If we can't work on that basis, we need to just . . . go have fun in the islands and forget all the rest."

"I can, Mike," Courtney said, shrugging. "I think . . . I think I'll always remember you. Heck, I *know* I will. But . . ." She shrugged again.

"Pam, are you going to be okay with that?" Mike asked.

"Yeah," she said. "I think so."

"Let's talk a bit about what we're trying to accomplish here," Mike said. "Like I explained before, when a person gets fully into submission, it's basically a transcendental state. But some things will push you right out of scene or, sometimes, they'll push you to an even higher level."

"Example?" Pam asked, rolling up a string of fettuccine.

"You said you didn't like anal sex?" Mike asked.

"Not a lot," Pam said. "It's . . ."

"Icky or humiliating or both?" Mike asked.

"Both," Pam said carefully, then wriggled.

"But the humiliation aspect actually has some attraction from the point of view of submission, right?" Mike asked.

"Yes," Pam admitted. "But it also hurts." Then she thought about it and wriggled again.

"Do you want Courtney to be forced to see you taken?" Mike asked.

"God," Pam said nervously. "I'm not sure. It's . . . sort of exciting. I think."

"Courtney," Mike said. "Tell me what you think is absolutely not permissible."

"I don't want to be whipped," Courtney said. "And . . . there's all that stuff with scat and golden showers. Don't go there. I don't want anal sex or for you to cum in my mouth. I don't like the taste."

"How about being fitted with a butt plug?" Mike asked.

"Uh . . ." She paused and thought about that. "Maybe."

"Exciting?" Mike asked. "Humiliating? Both?"

"Both," she admitted.

"I will tell you, both, that there will be dual scenes," Mike said. "Where one of you will be toyed with and the other forced to watch. You will be forced to touch each other, to play with tits at least, and to kiss in places, possibly on the lips but I'll have to read that. For one thing, with two of you, I can't do it all myself."

"I can . . . live with that," Courtney said.

"I'm planning on setting up a scene which will be longer than normal," Mike said. "We have nothing but time. I'm thinking that it will go for a day at least, maybe a couple of days, with you in continuous submission. I'll try to make sure I read you right, and I'll call time-outs from time to time to check on your state. If you feel that it's pushing your limits, edge play, beyond where you want to go, simply call yellow. If you're gagged, then grunt and I'll remove the gag. Especially do so if you feel panicked or trapped. I will be in complete control, but you can be free at any time and the play will *end* if you wish it. I don't want to drive you away from your current interest by pushing you too hard and too fast. But . . . the scene will be intense. Can you handle that?"

"I hope so," Pam said. "I'm getting squirmy just thinking about it."

"Well, let's wash up," Mike said, glancing at the radar and blinking. "Pam, could you go up forward and see if there are any ships out there? There's an odd blip on the radar."

"Sure," she said, walking up to the bridge as Mike and Courtney cleared the dishes.

As soon as she was up on deck, Mike picked up the knife he had been doing the dishes with and clamped his hand over her mouth.

"One *sound*," he said, keeping the knife well clear of her throat, "and I'll cut your throat and throw you to the sharks."

He dragged her, panting, into her cabin and pulled out a pair of handcuffs he'd slipped under her pillow. He used those to secure her and used her pillowcase to gag her.

"I'll come get you as soon as I grab the other idiot who thought she was safe," he said, walking out.

"Where's Courtney?" Pam asked when she came back in. "And when are we going to start?" she added, smiling.

"We already did," Mike said, grabbing her wrist and twisting her arm up behind her back then clamping his hand over her mouth. "Now I'm going to go explain the facts of life to you."

He dragged her into Courtney's cabin and cuffed her on the floor, gagging her with another pillowcase. Then he went and got the serious gear.

He carefully put a collar on Courtney's neck, locking it in place, then wrist and ankle restraints, using snap-locks to hold them together and taking off the handcuffs without permitting her any chance to escape. Last he replaced the pillowcase with a ring gag that kept her mouth open in an O but made it impossible to speak. It did, however, give access to the mouth, and he stuck his finger and ran it around, laughing at her.

"You two are so gullible," Mike said. "And so, I might add, are your parents. Bunch of bondage freaks. I'm not a bondage freak, I'm a damned slaver. Two pretty bitches like you are going to make me a bunch of money."

"Aaaah ooooh," Courtney groaned. "Aaah."

"But you have to be well trained," he said as he secured the last lock on Pam. She'd struggled to get away when he explained what was going to happen, but it hadn't mattered. "And I'm going to train you. But first you're going to be stripped. You won't need clothes anymore on this trip. Oh, and we're not going to the

Bahamas, we're going to Morocco. Good slave market in Morocco. I should get, oh, thirty grand for you as a pair. They like pairs in Morocco, so much sweeter." He paused and pulled Pam's gag out. "Time out, Pam, you okay?"

"I am now!" Pam said. "God! I thought you were serious!"

"That is half of the point," Mike said, reinserting the gag. "You will learn to be in total submission to your master. I will train you well. And then, I will sell you two bitches and head back to pick up more."

Courtney had been stripped and now lay on her bed, spread-eagled, looking at the overhead bunk and flinching at each crack of the whip. Mike had dragged Pam out of the room and now, to tell from the sounds, was whipping her. She wasn't sure anymore, what was real and what was fantasy. All she knew was that she didn't want to be whipped and would do anything to avoid it.

"You will learn to like me cuming in your mouth, bitch," Mike said, cracking the whip just above Pam's butt and eliciting another moan of fear. He'd touched her, the first time, just with the tip on the ass so she'd know how it felt. Now each time the whip cracked above her butt, she couldn't be sure it wasn't real. He knew she was on another plane and was getting worried he was pushing her too far.

He grabbed her hair and pulled her head back, taking out the gag and replacing it with the whip.

"Do you taste that leather, bitch?" Mike growled. "That leather is going to be covered in your blood if you don't suck me, and suck me hard, do you understand?"

"Yes," she said around the gag of the whip. "Please . . ."

"That's right," Mike said. "Beg me, bitch. I like begging. Good slaves beg."

He tied the whip in place, then undid her bonds and shackled her hands behind her back and her feet together.

"Down on your knees, bitch," Mike said, dragging her off the bed. "You're going to suck me and suck me well or you're going to be whipped. And then I'll cum in your mouth and you're going

to *swallow* my cum. If you let one drop spill, you'll be tortured until you beg me to kill you."

He took her in the mouth, grabbing her hair in his right hand, his left hand wrapped with the whip so he had a short lash.

"Suck it, bitch," Mike said, pushing her head back and forth, careful not to penetrate too deeply. "Suck it harder," he growled, popping the lash behind her back.

"Please . . ." Pam said, pulling back.

"Please . . . who?" Mike said, whipping her lightly.

"Please, master," Pam moaned. "Don't come in my mouth."

"I'll do whatever I like to you," Mike said, stuffing his dick back in her mouth and whipping her again. "You are my slave. You *will* do my bidding."

"Base, this is 315, go crypt, over."

"Base on crypt, go ahead, 315."

"Be aware, Yacht *Winter Born* has left territorial waters and appears to be headed for Bahamas waters, over."

"Roger, 315."

"315, out."

Courtney flinched when the door opened, and she turned away when she saw Mike leading Pam in and carrying a black bag in his hand. Pam's hands were bound behind her and her legs hobbled with a chain so she could only take small steps. Mike smacked her on the ass with the whip to get her to move faster, and she hobbled over to Courtney's bed, standing with her head bowed.

"I think it's time for me to take this little bitch," Mike said. "She can't give head worth a damn, so I guess I'm going to have to get mine in her pussy. But I didn't think you should be left out, Blondie, so I brought her over so you could join in the good time."

Courtney moaned and turned her head away, shaking it.

"First, I think Courtney needs to be properly fitted," Mike said, laughing harshly and forcing Pam to her knees, then pointed at the bunk. "Stay there, bitch. Try to run and you'll be whipped until you bleed."

He reached into the bag and extracted two lengths of chain

that he secured to the overhead bunk, then unclipped each of Courtney's ankles and reclipped them to the chain. When she was restrained, her butt was lifted slightly off the bunk and her legs spread.

"Now for the fun part," Mike said, reaching into the bag and pulling out a harness that looked something like a leather chastity belt with attachments.

Courtney craned her head around to see it, then closed her eyes and let out a yell.

"Yes, you're going to have these jammed in your pussy and ass," Mike said, chuckling evilly. "And it's going to happen with your stupid little friend watching you be humiliated. But it's okay; she's going to get raped right in front of your eyes. You avoid that, for now."

Mike took out a tube of KY jelly and rubbed it into Courtney's pussy and ass, liberally covered the plugs on the harness. He gently inserted the butt plug, then the vaginal plug, then buckled the belt in place.

"You like that, bitch?" Mike shouted, grabbing Courtney's hair and shaking her head back and forth. "You like the feel of that, bitch? Having a plug shoved up your ass? I bet you like it."

"Now for you, bitch," Mike said, pulling Pam up by her arm and hair. He pushed her onto the bed then got her kneeling between Courtney's legs. He unbound Pam's arms and connected each of the wristbands to the D-rings on either side of Courtney's collar so that she was supporting her weight on her hands and forced to look right into Courtney's face. Last, he got a longer length of chain and spread her legs to either side of Courtney's, running the chain under Courtney's thighs so that there was no way for Pam to get away. She was left, wide spread, doggy position.

"Ooooo," Pam moaned, shaking her head.

"Yes, bitch," Mike said, picking up the whip and flicking it to barely touch her butt. The crack as much as the touch elicited a yelp of pain and she started crying.

"I'm going to take you, now," Mike said, pulling a box out of the bag and setting it to the side. "I'm going to shove my dick right up your pussy and cum in it. I'm going to fucking rape you, bitch. You're nothing but my little slave, now, and a slave is

all you'll ever be." He opened up the box and took out a vibrator, dropping his shorts and lining up on Pam's opening. "You're going to be raped, bitch, and raped hard. But I don't want the other little bitch to feel left out, so . . ." He reached down to the harness and threw a small switch, engaging the vibrator that was built into Courtney's vaginal plug.

Courtney let out a moan and her head went back, then shook from side to side as her wrists pulled at the restraints.

As she began to thrash, Mike thrust his fingers into Pam's opening, twisting them around and making sure she was wet.

"You like that, bitch?" Mike asked to a shaken head. "I'll give you something you like," he added, shoving his dick into her pussy. She moaned and shook her head, crying.

"That's right, bitch, cry," Mike said. "That's a good little crying bitch. I'm going to break you, bitch, and make you into a good slave for men to take over and over again." As he said it, he slid the vibrator up and onto her clit, turning it on. "Men are going to do nothing but fuck you for the rest of your life. You're both nothing but receptacles for men's cum, for the rest of your lives."

Courtney came first, arching against the restraints, and he reached down and shut off the vibrator on the harness, then shut off the other as Pam came only moments later. He pounded her hard for a few seconds, really slamming her and imagining it as real rape, then came himself. All three of them had come in less than thirty seconds.

Pam was barely able to support herself, and he quickly released her and rolled her to the side, picking up a tissue from the box and gently sliding it between her legs, then took the harness off Courtney and released her hands.

"Christ," Courtney gasped, when she got the gag out of her mouth. "That was . . ."

"I don't know how much more of this I can take," Pam said, still quivering.

"Come into the main cabin," Mike said. "I think this needs a solid snuggle to complete it."

When Pam had cleaned up and come into the cabin, her head down and looking ashamed, Mike pulled her and Courtney into his arms and hugged both of them to his chest.

"Do you remember when I told you I got a high just having you around?" Mike asked.

"Yes," Pam said quietly, ducking her head down.

"That time when we were first going out," Mike said, "and you were both up on the tuna tower and just . . . grooving on the experience and having a blast, that was like the biggest high I could ever have. It was almost like being out of body. That is what I'm supposed to try to create in you girls, when we do those scenes. The job of the dom is to engage a series of emotions to cause some sort of a disconnect. You're almost insane, so into the moment you're no longer really in your body. That's what we're trying to achieve."

"Got it with me," Courtney said. "I was half that way before you got in the room from hearing you torturing Pam. I couldn't believe you were whipping her like that. Still can't."

"He wasn't, really," Pam said, quietly. "He popped me once, at first, and then slightly a couple of other times. But that first one was so . . . something, that every time the whip cracked after that I had to scream."

"I was trying to build the mood," Mike said. "Big question, did I push anyone out of scene? No, were you in scene?"

"I sure was," Pam said, shaking her head against his chest. "I couldn't keep track of reality and fantasy. I just stopped trying. You could have made me do anything and I would have obeyed. It was . . . scary. I didn't know there was that much . . ."

"Submission," Mike said, nodding.

"Submission in me," Pam said. "I'm not sure I like it."

"We'll work on that," Mike promised. "Courtney."

"The harness was . . ." She shook her head. "It was . . . fun and it really made me feel submissive, but the butt plug was . . . that sort of threw me out of scene and into a near panic for a second or two. Then I just sort of . . . floated. I totally lost it when you put Pam over me. She was drooling . . ."

"That was so . . ." Pam said and stopped. "God . . ."

"Too much?" Mike asked.

"No, it was . . . so humiliating," Pam said, nearly crying. "And it felt so *good*! I just . . ."

"Okay," Mike said, pulling her into his arms tighter. "It's okay.

You're not a bad person for feeling this way. It's really, really *normal*; it's just something that people don't talk about. We'll talk about it over the next couple of days. I was going to stay in scene, but I think you guys need some distance to work through the emotions. Remember, it's all friends. And it's all about getting that mystic high that comes from really good sex, really mind-blowing sex. If it's no fun, if there's no bonding and no . . . love, then it's no good."

"Part of my problem," Pam said, shaking her head against his chest, "is I feel like such a . . . a . . . slut. I got used and abused and I really *liked* it."

"It's okay," Mike said, stroking her hair. "That's the point. It's just that you're finding out, for the first time, what really good sex, for you, is all about, and finding out how far into zone you can fall and what puts you there. You're still a good person, a lovely young lady, with emphasis on lady. What goes on beyond the bedroom door doesn't change that."

"You've got a nice voice, Mike," Courtney said, snuggling into his chest and yawning. "Aren't you the one who's supposed to go to sleep?"

"I will," Mike said, "in a bit. Coast into the arms of Morpheus," he said softly, holding them both. "Good dreams."

"Are you my lover or my father?" Pam asked sleepily.

"I'm your master," Mike said gently. "Nothing more nor less."

CHAPTER NINE

When both of them were well asleep he slipped carefully out of the bed and out of the cabin. He'd been watching a blip on the radar for some time and was worried about it; it looked like a freighter coming up the Stream and they were going to pass close to each other.

He slipped on shorts and a shirt against the cool of the night and headed up to the flying bridge, getting some coffee going as he passed through the lounge. He *was* tired, from both the exercise and the day, and it was going to be a long night. He couldn't really assume that there wasn't anything on his course; he'd been keeping an eye on the radar during the entire scene. And he much preferred to be able to head up to the bridge without worrying about the girls' safety if he had to maneuver.

He checked all the instruments when he reached the bridge and everything was in the green, so he sped up, pushing the boat to its maximum cruising speed. The freighter was still on course to a close approach and he considered changing to pass astern. He probably would have to soon. But he got a cup of coffee first and considered the approaches. There was a way to calculate it, but he'd pretty much forgotten that particular equation over the years.

As it turned out, he only had to change course slightly to pass

astern of the freighter. The wash was pretty heavy, but the yacht rode over it easily enough.

It was a couple of hours before dawn when he pulled into the protected harbor at Palm Key and dropped anchor. He'd considered continuing up the coast to Bimini and the Bahamas Customs Station where he could get his customs flag. That was going to be interesting. The Bahamas had an agreement about American officials carrying arms in the area, but they were generally death on firearms on ships. It was going to be interesting seeing how they reacted to his arms locker.

He got the anchors down, locked the doors against random pilfering, made his way to the cabin, got undressed, and snuggled up to Pam, wrapping an arm around her before falling fast asleep.

"God," Courtney said over a bowl of cereal, "I am sore in some of the oddest places."

"Me, too," Pam said, craning to look at her back. Both of the girls were wearing bikinis. "Are there marks?"

"Not as many as the ones that are still fading on Mike," Courtney said, grinning.

"They should fade pretty quick," Mike said. "We need to run up to Bimini to the Customs Station and get our flag."

"Flag?" Courtney asked.

"When you clear customs you fly a special flag," Mike said. "After that you can cruise anywhere in the Bahamas and not get stopped. But until we get the flag, if a customs or Coast Guard boat sees us, they'll stop us. I'll go weigh anchor and we'll get under way."

They cruised fast up the coastline of low-lying keys and shallow shoals, the girls oooing and aaahing in the tuna tower, until they reached Bimini and Mike slowed as they came to the entrance.

"Bimini's entrance really sucks," he said. "The Stream and storms can shift it a lot. And the Bahamas government hasn't dredged it in years."

"The channel markers are over there," Pam said, pointing to port.

"Yeah," Mike said, glancing over. "Only one problem, you can

tell that's a shoal," he said. "Look at the sand. There it is," he said, pointing closer to starboard. "See where it's deeper?"

"Are we going to go aground?" Courtney asked, grabbing the railing.

"Hopefully not," Mike said, shrugging. The entrance channel had to be entered perpendicular to the Stream, which was a little tricky, and then the deeper water—it couldn't be characterized as "deep"—turned hard to port. He made the turn with a touch of bow thruster and continued up the channel, which was more or less straight, into the deeper water of the dredged harbor.

When they got to the customs dock, he had the girls help him with the lines and told them to stay on the boat.

"Why?" Pam asked, looking around the harbor.

"Technically, until you're checked in, you're illegal in the Bahamas," Mike said. "I have to go get us checked in."

He carried his scanty log, well aware that there should be more entries—exited Islamorada harbor, took two slave-girls . . . no—and headed for the customs shed. There was a small Bahamas Coast Guard cutter tied by the shed and he noticed that the crew seemed unusually alert and sharp for Bahamas troops.

The shed was a small building broken up into a couple of rooms with a counter at the front manned by a bored clerk.

"Yacht *Winter Born*, U.S., out of Islamorada," Mike said, handing over his log and passenger list. "Myself and two passengers." Then he started pulling out credentials.

The clerk took the passenger list and made an entry, then glanced at the log in disinterest and picked up the credentials. When he saw the Federal Marshal certification and weapons cert, his eyes widened.

"Hold on, mon," he said, getting up. "I gotta get an officer."

"That's fine," Mike said.

Two officers came out of the back with the clerk, one that was clearly the station chief and another, a colonel of the constabulary if Mike remembered his insignia, who was a big, broad man in stiffly starched khakis.

"Mr. . . . Jenkins," the colonel said, shaking his hand. "Colonel Horatio Montcrief, Constabulary. Glad to have you in Bimini. Business or pleasure?"

"Pleasure," Mike said. "I have a couple of college coeds with me who have never been to the Bahamas. I hope to show them a very good time."

"Yes, I'm sure," the colonel said, grinning as he came around the counter. "May we, perhaps, step outside?"

"Much prefer it," Mike said, following him out.

The colonel waited until he was outside and then lit a cigar. "Even here in the Islands, the stupid antismoking people reign," he said, sticking the stogie in his teeth. "Those are interesting credentials. You are not here on business?"

"Not at all," Mike said. "I'm effectively retired. The materials I carry are purely for reasons of . . . past experience. I hope to *have* no future similar experiences."

"You were DEA?" the colonel asked, tilting his head to the side.

"Bite your tongue," Mike said. "I don't do the War on Drugs."

"There is another war, however, that you don't mention," the colonel said, waving his cigar. "No matter. We have no problem with terrorism in the islands."

"As I said," Mike repeated doggedly, "I'm here for pleasure, purely."

"And can I enquire as to the nature of the material?" the colonel asked delicately.

"I could show you a manifest," Mike said. "But you'd shit a brick. I carry heavy."

"For defensive purposes?" the colonel asked, one eyebrow raised.

"Sometimes the best defense is a good offense," Mike said. "Colonel, I'm not planning on using anything here in the islands. They're in a locker. I'm not planning on opening the locker in the islands. And if I have to, you'll be the third to know."

"The third?" the colonel said, interestedly.

"The first will be whoever I use them on," Mike said. "The second . . . well, I'm sorry, you don't have the need to know," he added with a chuckle.

"Very well," the colonel said dryly. "Try not to open your locker. Two college coeds, eh? Pretty?"

"Fricking gorgeous."

"Have a very good time in the islands, then," the colonel said, smiling. "I do ask one thing. We occasionally have situations which . . . are difficult to deal with alone. Frequently, we ask the U.S. government, quietly, to assist us in such things. Are you . . . ?"

"Not at this time," Mike said. "But if you ask me, and I get an okay, anything for a friend."

"And are you . . . formidable?"

"I'm pretty good," Mike said. "I've got a 'still alive' track record. My enemies don't."

"Very good," the colonel said, nodding. "I hope to meet you again some time. Hopefully, under equally good circumstances."

"Agreed," Mike said, smiling. "Have a good day."

"All days are good days in the islands," the colonel said, waving his cigar. "Hadn't you heard?"

Pam was cleaning up in the lounge when she heard a faint beeping and followed it to something that looked like a small laptop on the closed bridge. It had a phone on it, though, so she picked it up.

"Hello?" she asked.

"Hello," a man's voice said. "Who is this?"

"Pam," she said. "Are you looking for Mike?"

"Yes," the man answered dryly. "I was a little worried I'd dialed the wrong number."

"He's over at the customs shed," Pam said.

"Okay," the man said. "When he gets back, ask him to give Bob Pierson a call, would you?"

"Sure," Pam said.

"I take it you're a . . . friend of Mike's?" the man asked.

"Yeah," she said, sighing. "I think the term would be 'very good friend.'"

"Ah," the man said and paused. "Where are you from?"

"Can I ask why you're asking?" Pam said curiously.

"You sound Midwestern," the man answered.

"I'm from Missouri," Pam said. "Why?"

"Just curious," the man replied. "Please ask Mike to give me a call right away when he gets back."

"Will do," Pam said. "Bye."

▲   ▲   ▲

"Mike," Pam said when he got on board. "You're supposed to call somebody named Person or something like that. I forgot to write it down and he didn't leave a number."

"Oh, great," Mike said, shaking his head.

"Problem?"

"One of my former customers," Mike said, shrugging. "The sort of people I do contracting for. But I am most definitely on vacation at the moment."

Mike went down to the sat phone and found Pierson's number on the speed dial.

"Pierson."

"Jenkins, what's up, Bob?"

"Mike, clear the room please and go scramble," Pierson replied.

Mike frowned and hit the scrambler combination.

"There's nobody in here at the moment," he said.

"I guess I should have mentioned that you're under very casual surveillance," Pierson said. "And if you go out of the country you need to check in."

"I wasn't aware I was under surveillance at all," Mike said angrily.

"The Coast Guard just has a general 'keep an eye on' on you," Pierson said. "Half protection for you and half because if you go out of the country you're treading in waters you're not really familiar with, legally. The Caribbean is no big deal; we own it. But if you go to Europe or something, give me a call first, okay?"

"Sure," Mike said, sighing. "Just another example of change of life, I guess."

"That's what it is," Pierson said. "The young lady who answered the phone. She's not from . . ."

"Nope," Mike said. "Missouri, University of. And, lord, she's good looking."

"Glad to hear it," Pierson said honestly. "I'd been getting a little worried about you down there doing your Travis McGee imitation."

"Travis who?" Mike asked, confused.

"Oh," Pierson said, chuckling. "I'd assumed it was intentional.

Look up the Travis McGee books, some time. And have fun in the Bahamas."

"I will," Mike replied.

They stayed in Bimini that day and into the night, the girls dancing at one of the clubs, then made their way back to the boat. Mike had reciprocal rights at the Bimini Big Game Club and was docked there. The Game Club had good enough security that he didn't feel he had to leave an anchor watch. Not that there was much theft in Bimini. The island was so small that if anything turned up missing, everyone knew who had stolen it.

That night they had a pleasant and casual ménage with only occasional, joking, references to master and slave. At one point the girls tried to pin him down and he proved that he could take one of them, more or less against her will, while simultaneously controlling the other. It wasn't easy, but he could do it. They all were pleasantly exhausted, as well as a little drunk, when they went to sleep.

Mike had the boat moving before dawn, though, slight hangover and all. At the Game Club he'd heard that the sail were moving and he really wanted to have the girls hook into a sailfish. By dawn he was floating in the Stream and rigging the kites.

Courtney came up on deck, and her eyes widened when she saw what he was doing.

"We're flying kites today?" she asked, looking at the bird-shaped, collapsible, kite he was rigging to fly in the wind.

"It's a fishing rig," Mike said. "The shadow of the kite looks like a bird and that attracts game fish. And you can get your bait well away from the boat."

He rigged a live ballyhoo on each of four lines and floated them out on kites, then went downstairs to get breakfast.

"I'm hunting for sail today," Mike said. "We might get wahoo or dolphin, but I'm hoping for sail. The lines are rigged for sail. If we get dolphin, just muscle it in. But we should get up on deck pretty soon to watch the lines."

When the two girls joined him on deck, he looked at them for a moment, the bottle of sunscreen in his hand, and waved.

"Take off the suits," he ordered.

"Uh," Pam said, looking at Courtney. Then they both stripped off their bikinis.

"Pam, do my back while I do Courtney's," Mike said, getting a handful of Bullfrog on his palm. "Courtney, kneel down, knees together, wrists crossed in front of you and on your thighs."

Courtney breathed hard for a moment and then complied, turning around so her back was to him.

Mike got down on his knees and spread the sunscreen across her back, liberally. There was, as he intended, plenty left over and he reached around, rubbing it on her breasts and stomach.

"Head up," Mike ordered. "Chin up. Back straight, little slave."

"Yes, master," Courtney said.

Pam was rubbing down his arms, her breasts pressing into his back, as he reached down and spread Courtney's legs, rubbing the last of the sunscreen onto her inner thighs and then sliding his finger up against her clit. He pulled her arms around her back and crossed her wrists there, then reached back around and gently pulled on one nipple while massaging her clit, running his finger in and out of her opening.

"Stay still, slave," he ordered, roughly, as she began to squirm and moan. "If you move from that position, you will be punished."

He continued to stroke her until with a gasp and a clench she came. Then he grabbed Pam and pulled her around, simultaneously twisting Courtney to the deck. He pulled his bathing suit down and then entered Courtney, hard, pulling Pam's head down to her breast.

"Lick it, bitch," he ordered Pam, pressing her lips against Courtney's nipple. "Lick her tit!"

Pam resisted for a moment, then her pink tongue flickered out to touch Courtney's nipple, eliciting a moan of despair and pleasure from her friend.

"Play with her tits," Mike ordered, pinning Courtney down and holding himself up, then thrusting into her again, hard.

Courtney came, again, as he pounded her, moaning and crying at the waves of pleasure from his taking her and having Pam play with her at the same time. As her shudders eased, Mike pulled out, to a moan of sadness, and pulled Pam around, roughly, to where her tits were in Courtney's face.

"Now it's your turn, little slave," he said, pushing her back down so that her nipple dangled above Courtney's lips. "Pleasure this bitch," he said, grabbing Courtney's hand and lifting it up to Pam's pussy.

"Wait," Courtney said, as Pam flinched.

"You can do it," Mike said, much more gently. "You know what feels good for you. Do it to her," he added, pulling her hand into position and manipulating her finger against Pam's clit. At that Pam whimpered and bucked, but didn't back away. He rolled Pam down onto her back, keeping Courtney's hand in place, then put Courtney in position to play with her nipples and pussy.

"Stay together," he added, sliding his finger into Courtney's opening and his own mouth to her lovely breast. The position left him with his head on Pam's stomach, Courtney lying on Pam's arm and Pam on her back, spread-eagled, pinned by his body and totally in the moment.

They stayed like that until Pam came and then he rolled over to her, entering her and thrusting hard; Courtney backed away, but he pulled her back to continue sucking on Pam's breasts. He reached over and slid his hand back into Courtney's vagina, playing with her clitoris as Pam moaned and shrieked into a hard climax. Courtney came at the same time and he followed shortly after.

"Okay," Courtney said, rolling over to lie on her back, panting. "I'm not too sure about that one. It was fun, but . . ."

"You don't want to become a lesbian," Mike said.

"No," Pam replied tightly. "And that felt a little . . ."

"You're not a lesbian from having a touch of fun with each other," Mike replied, pulling them both to their feet and setting them in the bridge couch. He sat down between them and gently rested his arms across their shoulders.

"Kleee-*nex*," Pam said, desperately, flipping open one of the glove boxes and diving for a tissue.

"You both prefer guys, in general, right?" Mike continued when Pam had the flood under control. He hugged them both to him and then let them up so they could be comfortable.

"Yeah," Courtney said, looking over at Pam a bit shamefacedly.

"But I . . . sort of enjoyed it. I *don't* want to lick Pam, though. Ever."

"You won't have to, then," Mike said, nodding. "A bit of sex play with the same sex is not the same thing as being homosexual, especially when you're in a threesome like we are. Now, if there were two guys and one girl, it would be different. The sexual wiring is a bit different, for one thing. While women are sensual in various places, most guys are just sensual in their penis. Two guys and one female, it's the two males, generally, working on the woman . . ."

"Now that has a certain . . . something," Pam said, grinning.

"In a way that was what was going on," Mike pointed out. "You were, each, helping me to bring pleasure to the other. Maybe you'll take it further, between you two. I know several girls who take the position of 'girls for comfort, boys for pleasure.' It doesn't make you a lesbian." He paused and grinned. "Okay, maybe a touch bi."

"You are *evil*," Pam said.

"The very devil," Mike admitted. "And the one who has to keep his head about him, despite your lovely nipple staring me in the face. We need to finish *really* putting on sunscreen and then get ready to fish. We're just lucky we didn't get a hit while we were in play; it would have really ruined the mood."

Courtney was sitting on the port fighting chair, sipping a Fosters, when the nearest line unclipped from the kite and began screaming out.

"That's not sail," Mike said, hooking the harness on her naked body. "Probably wahoo."

"Why's it called wahoo?" Courtney asked, picking up the line and settling it in her holder.

"When I hit the drag, give it a good yank," Mike said. "Then hang the hell on."

When the hook hit the wahoo, it took off like a rocket in a three-hundred-yard run, the line screaming out of the reel.

"Waaaaaahoo!" Courtney screamed, fighting the bucking rod.

"Now you know," Mike said, grinning ear to ear.

Wahoo weren't sustained fighters, and lighter than most sail,

so in twenty minutes it was onboard and pictures taken. They were, however, good eating, and it went in the cooler. The fight hadn't even disturbed the other kites, so Mike got the whole line rerigged pretty quick.

"Mike, I gotta know," Courtney said. "What's in the Bluebeard Room?"

"Get used to disappointment," Mike said, chuckling. "Okay, I'll tell you. I have locks of hair from each of my conquests, with date and time, up on the walls. It's a little bizarre, so I stopped showing them off and now I keep it locked."

"That I can almost believe," Pam said. "Are we going to do a scene tonight?"

"How do you feel about it?" Mike asked.

"Nervous as a virgin," Pam admitted. "Eager as one, too. I'll admit, I really, *really* enjoyed the scene the other night. And, okay, what we did this morning."

"I've got one problem with it," Courtney said, frowning. "I hate to be petty, but you've had more . . . *in* time with Mike than I have."

"Pam, do you mind if we adjust that a bit, tonight?" he asked. "It might mean you get a bit shortchanged."

"I can handle that," Pam said.

Mike turned to a control and hit a series of keys, and steel guitar started to ring from the speakers.

"What is that?" Courtney asked.

"A one-hit wonder from the '70s," Mike said. "It's off an MP3 collection from my CDs. This piece is called 'Thunder Island' by Jay Ferguson. There's probably a bunch of stuff you won't recognize. Generational thing, and I'm also into Goth and industrial. On the other hand, there's also Pink, Enya, Evanescence, stuff like that. I like a lot of modern music." He looked up as one of the lines dropped loose then nodded. "Fish on. Pam's side."

Pam got up and put on the harness and lifted the rod, stepping back and then hitting the drag.

"Holy cow!" she shouted as the fish began its initial run. Suddenly the sail burst out of the water and tail-walked from port to starboard, shaking its head.

"Keep pressure on it," Mike warned. "Otherwise it will throw the hook."

"It's *strong*," Pam yelled.

"That's what the harness is for," Mike said. "Let your back do the work."

He got the other lines reeling in with electric motors and halfway back one of them hit.

"Damn," he said. "Courtney, get it. Try not to cross the lines."

Fortunately, the two sails stayed well apart and both girls had one hell of a fight on their hands. Pam got hers in in about thirty minutes, bringing it into the transom where Mike pulled it up onto the deck.

"I'd like to make sure we can release it," Mike said. "Can you get the camera and get down here?"

They took pictures of Pam with her sail in the flooded flush deck and then Mike fed it some raw wash and a ballyhoo and got it back running with a tap on the tail.

By that time Courtney had brought hers alongside and he landed that one and got pictures. All in all it took about an hour to get the two sails to the boat and off, and by that time both girls were elated and exhausted.

Mike got the lines back up and soon after there was a dolphin on board. He climbed up to the tuna tower and noticed that, by luck as much as anything, the kites were dropping by a weed line. Shortly after the dolphin, Courtney hooked up to another tail walker—her first one hadn't left the water—and she fought it for about three minutes after its first run and then the line went, mostly, slack.

"Probably threw the hook," Mike said, letting the kites back out. "Put it on the winch and let that reel the line in."

When the line came alongside it was clear the fish hadn't thrown the hook. The sail was gone from just behind the head with a big, crescent, bite mark just past its gills.

"Oh, wow," Courtney said, looking at the head as Mike pulled it over the side.

"Want a picture of this?" Mike asked, grinning and unhooking the head.

"Yeah," Courtney said. "And you want us to go *swimming* in this water?"

"Any time you enter the water you're in the food chain," Mike said. "But snorkelers and divers hardly ever get unprovoked attacks. It's safer than driving in Springfield."

"Maybe," Courtney said. "But if you're in a wreck, they don't eat you."

They landed a couple more sail and dolphin by noon, then the run pretty much ended.

"Let's get lunch," Mike said, reeling in the lines. "They probably won't start hitting again until this evening."

CHAPTER
TEN

Mike pulled the wahoo out of the cooler, skinned and gutted it, and cut it into steaks with a machete. Three of those went on the deck grill in a light olive oil marinade. Along with leftover rice and some cut fruit, it made a great lunch.

"If we keep eating this light," Courtney said, "and getting all this . . . exercise, I'm liable to lose weight."

"You don't have any weight to lose," Mike said, laughing.

"I could lose some on the hips," Courtney said, shaking her head.

"You could stand to *gain* some on the hips," Mike said. "But, yeah, eating like this is as natural a way to lose weight as you can ask. I actually have to be careful or I start losing muscle mass. I need to do more swimming."

"How far can you swim?" Pam asked curiously.

"I've done twenty miles," Mike said, shrugging. "But that was when I was younger and in shape for it. Five miles is about right these days. That's just swimming with goggles. With fins I'm good for ten to fifteen."

"Damn," Courtney said. "That's a long ways."

"And staying able to do it takes doing it," Mike said, smiling. "I haven't been keeping in shape since you girls have been here."

"Don't let us stop you," Pam said. "I'd love to have *something* wear you out."

"You wear me out, Pam," Mike said, grinning. "But, yeah, I think I'll go swim."

"Out here?" Courtney said. "What about that sailfish?"

"If I worried about sharks I never would have joined the SEALs," Mike said. He walked up on deck, picking up a pair of swimming goggles, and went over the side with a splash.

The boat was well out to sea and moving with the different vectors of wind and current. Mike decided that keeping no more than a hundred yards away was prudent. He generally stayed within no more than fifty meters, letting the Stream be his opponent and swimming into it. He was used to swimming in deep water, having done so all over the world. Sometimes fleets would just stop at sea for some down time; it was called "Steel Beach." SEALs attached to the fleets would generally spend the time doing races from ship to ship, sometimes swimming as much as ten miles.

He got into the rhythm, riding the swells, keeping half an eye on the shadow of the boat, just looking into the deeps. One time he saw a pod of sailfish riding the current northwards to cooler, more productive, waters. They turned to check him out, their sides flashing in bands of color, then turned away, hurrying north. Another time it was a turtle, uninterested in the marine mammal paddling overhead, being carried in the current and headed to wherever turtles head thinking whatever turtles thought. A small bait pod came past, chased by a tiny pod of dolphin. A string of sargassum weed came past and he ducked under it, turning over to look at the small fish on the underside. The weed lines were the only cover in the blue waters and the small fish huddled in their shade, hoping to escape the predators that roamed the big blue. The predators, however, knew that and thus homed in on the weeds, or human trash, or floating tree trunks, whatever floated at the surface. It was the reason to fish along the weed lines.

He noticed that the boat was drifting faster and quickly swam to the side, climbing up onto the flush deck and shaking water out of his hair.

"That was just amazing," Pam said from the fishing deck. "I'd have run out of energy half an hour ago, max."

"I didn't swim long enough," Mike said, walking up the stairs to the deck. "The wind is picking up a bit."

"Mike, do we have to fish this afternoon?" Courtney said, coming down from the bridge and handing him a beer in a koozie.

"No," Mike admitted.

"Good," she replied, tossing a cushion on the deck and dropping to her knees, head bowed. "Master, can this slave service you on her knees?"

"Over here," Mike said, walking to the fighting chair and sitting down. It was adjustable vertically and he dropped it to the lowest setting then pointed at Pam.

"Slave, take off your clothes, grab another cushion, and come over here."

He put Courtney in front of him and Pam to his side, facing Courtney, carefully resting the beer bottle on Pam's back.

"Stay very still," he said roughly, "and it won't fall over. If you spill my beer you will be punished. And watch this training; you will be next."

He looked at Courtney and pointed to his crotch. "Show me what you can do. I doubt that you know how to truly give a blowjob."

Courtney's eyes widened in anger and he held up a finger.

"I checked the repeater," he said, waving at the small group of instruments on the fishing deck. "There aren't any boats around. Consider this in scene."

"I'm still not too sure about being told how to 'truly give a blowjob,'" Courtney said exasperatedly. "Most guys are just glad to get them at all."

"Well, we can play a different game," Mike admitted, "or we can find out if you know how to give a *really good* blowjob. And, if not, I can give you some tips. Your call."

"If she's not game, I am," Pam said, desperately trying to keep the bottle upright. "And she can be the table."

Mike picked up the bottle and set it on the deck.

"Your call," Mike repeated.

"What's involved in a really *good* blowjob, then?" Courtney asked.

"Well, I haven't found out if you already know, yet," Mike admitted, grinning. "Care to test the waters?"

Courtney raised one eyebrow, then pulled his shorts down, trailing her hair over his crotch and using her hand to take him in her mouth. She started fellating him, slowly, sucking moderately hard.

"Okay," Mike said, "question: Are you trying to make it last or get it over with, quick?"

"Huh?" Courtney said, straightening up.

"Because if you're trying to get it over with quick, we need to talk," Mike said, shrugging.

"I was . . . just doing it," Courtney said, confused.

"All right, first item to know," Mike said. "If you go slow, you're drawing it out. By that I mean head motion. If you want to give a long, slow blow, that's cool. If you're trying to drive the guy crazy, it's very cool. If you're trying to get it over with, you'd better speed *way* up and suck harder."

"I'm always afraid to suck too hard," Courtney admitted. "I bothered a guy that way one time. He said it hurt."

"There's sucking and sucking," Mike said. "But the way to get a guy off, quick, is to suck very hard, move your head fast and use your hands at the same time. For that matter," he added, shrugging, "if you want to get him off *really* quick, you can stick a finger up his rectum and tickle his prostate."

"That's *gross*," Pam said. "Yick!"

"I'm not saying you *should* do it," Mike said. "I, personally, don't like it. But it's how to get a guy off really fast."

Courtney had found herself lightly stroking him and she suddenly stopped, blushing.

"I can't believe . . . sometimes I sort of catch myself . . ." she said, half laughing.

"Same here," Pam said, moving from her knees to sit cross legged on the deck. "So slow and light for a long blow and hard and fast for a short one?"

"In general," Mike said. "Some guys get off really fast on them. Some don't. Some guys, and I think they're either lying or nuts, say they don't like them. Me, I love them, good, bad, or indifferent."

"Hand and head will be tricky," Courtney said, grasping his member with her hand and lowering her head.

"Try just the forefinger and thumb," Mike said as she started to get in rhythm. "It's easier. And you won't keep slamming the heel of your hand into my balls."

"Mmmm," Courtney said, her head starting to move faster.

"Try sucking harder," Mike said hoarsely. "Like you're trying to give a hickey . . . *that's* it." He lay back and groaned. "Yeah . . . like that."

"Don't cum in my mouth," Courtney said, leaning back for a moment but continuing to stroke.

"Won't," Mike promised, his eyes closed.

"This is hard on the neck," Courtney said, coming up for air again and pulling out a hair.

"Practice makes perfect," Mike admitted, pulling her hand away. "Pam's turn."

"Yes, O master," Pam said, chuckling. But she scooched over to where Courtney had been as Courtney took her pad.

"You didn't cum," Courtney said, frowning.

"I was holding back," Mike admitted. "Otherwise you would have tasted the fruit of knowledge."

"That's one I haven't heard," Pam said, taking his member in forefinger and thumb and going down on him.

"You're going slow on purpose," Mike said accusingly.

"Yep," Pam said, coming up with a grin. "I figure it's payback time."

"Can I cum in your mouth?" Mike asked.

"Sure," Pam said, going down on him again. No more than a minute later she felt his member start to pulse and then her mouth was filled with cum.

"That was quick," she said, swallowing and then picking up his beer to wash the taste out.

"Let's just say that I was ready," Mike admitted, grinning. "And I wasn't about to let you tease me *too* long."

"But now the lesson is all over," Pam said, mock sadly.

"Oh, we haven't even started," Mike promised.

Afterwards he led them through the five major positions of dominance, then shackled them together on the lounge floor,

forcing them to play with each other while he moved the boat to a protected harbor and got supper ready. When it was prepared, he tied them, facing him, on their knees, and fed them bites from his plate, forcing them to ask for each morsel and each sip of wine. They played on into the night and only stopped near dawn, tumbling into the main cabin bed in an exhausted, happy pile.

Late the next morning, when Mike woke up, he could feel by the rocking of the boat that the weather had changed. Sure enough, when he looked outside, there were high alto-cumulus clouds and a thunderhead building. Crap.

He limped into the lounge and checked the weather radar, which showed that things were definitely building, then went back to the cabin to wake the girls.

"I think we need to cancel the day's fishing," he said. "Looks like weather's coming in."

"What should I do?" Pam asked nervously.

"Not much," Mike said. "Maybe rinse down the rods with fresh water, then put them away; we should have done that yesterday, but I got sort of caught up. Then fold the kites and put them away. They go in the locker forward of the rod locker." He grabbed a shirt and bathing suit, heading for the closed bridge. He first checked the text message system and shook his head.

"What's going on?" Courtney asked, coming up from below.

"There's a tropical depression forming," Mike said, pointing to a weather map. "It's over in the Gulf, but the storm track is for it to cross the peninsula and come this way."

"Is it a hurricane?" she asked as Pam came onto the bridge.

"No," Mike said. "It's a storm, but a small one." He thought about the different waters around and shrugged. "We can dodge it. But we'll have to dodge south. We might try to run the Gap over to the Deeps and the Tongue of the Ocean. But I'm not sure about that because the storm might catch us in the Gap and that would be bad. Or we can just run straight south to hook around Andros. I'd rather do that, but we're still probably going to get some effects."

"Define effects," Pam said.

"Rain," Mike said. "Maybe lots. Some winds. Like a thunderstorm,

but going on for a day or so. Nastier in a small boat, and this is a small boat make no mistake, than in a house. You might want to take some scop; we're liable to pitch a good bit."

"You want to go south, go south," Courtney said.

"I'm game," Pam said. "I could use some help with the rods."

They headed south at max speed, but Mike pulled into a protected, and empty, harbor just after dusk. After dinner he set up a scene where Pam was tied watching as he played with Courtney and "taught" her. He finally took Courtney after he'd brought her to orgasm and he held back, continuing to screw her much longer than she'd expected. She had gone into a continuous quiver when he entered her, but as he continued to take her she orgasmed again.

Still, he'd held back, and when he left her he started on Pam, spread-eagling her alongside Courtney and playing with both of them until Pam orgasmed and he took her as well, then went back to Courtney.

The storm had caught them at anchor, and as it built up the boat began to rock and the two girls seemed to climb to some other plane. They were blindfolded and gagged and the rocking motion left them both quivering uncontrollably by the time Mike, finally, came into Courtney and called the scene.

They spent the night cuddled up in a ball in the main cabin as the storm raged outside. He got up from time to time to ensure the anchors were holding, then went back to the warm bundle in the bed.

"It's wild outside," Courtney said at breakfast, looking out at the sheets of rain running down the windows.

"It is that," Mike said, looking at the weather instruments. The wind was blowing about thirty knots, steady, with gusts to forty. "This is going to get interesting."

"Up to you, Mike," Courtney said. "I trust that you're not going to drown us."

"No," Mike said calmly. "But you might get seasick. *Strongly* recommend the scop."

"Where is it?" Pam asked.

▲   ▲   ▲

"This is cool," Courtney said, staggering onto the closed bridge and looking out the windows. The rain was so solid there really wasn't anything to see even with the wipers going full blast. "What are you doing? Driving on GPS?"

"Mostly," Mike said, gesturing at the instruments. There were even more than on the flying bridge, and larger, giving the closed bridge something of the look of flying a plane. "Keeping an eye on the radar and the sonar, too. Watching the weather map update. I think we'll probably be out of this by the time we get to Andros."

"It's rough," Courtney said, holding on to a stanchion and then making her way to one of the seats.

"It is that," Mike said. "Seas are about nine, ten feet. I'm staying to the outside of the islands, rather than trying to run the Gap. We'll just hook around the south of Andros and head over in the direction of Long Island. I'll keep going tonight and we'll be clear by tomorrow morning. But there's not really anywhere to dock down there, a few outlying keys, but no really good harbors." He frowned and shrugged. "It's a bit . . . lawless in that area. Lots of drug running goes through there. And there are . . . well, I'd hate to dignify them with the description 'pirates,' but there are people that occasionally attack boats."

"And you'll do what about that?" Courtney said, her eyes wide. "Throw a whip at them?"

"There is far more than a whip on this boat, Courtney," Mike said, glancing at the radar. "But I think I'll be on watch for a couple of days."

By the next morning they were clear of the wind and rain, but the storm to the north was still kicking up the seas to nearly six feet.

"I managed to make coffee," Pam said, coming up to the bridge with a travel mug. "I didn't make a *huge* mess."

"Not much fun being battened down, is it?" Mike said, smiling as he took it from her and set it in a holder.

"It's cleared up at least," she said, looking around. "Except for the clouds."

"They'll clear off by, oh, tomorrow," Mike replied, shrugging. "I won't be happy until we're down to the south of Andros, though."

"The pirates Courtney was asking about?" Pam said, looking off to port. "There's clear water over there," she said, pointing.

"Yep," Mike said. "And see the breakers between us and that clear water? That's the great Bahama Banks. You can't get a cabin cruiser in there. You can't even get a cigarette boat in most of it. It's an area where conditions are just right to form calcium carbonate from sea water and carbon dioxide. Major carbon dioxide sink. There's an old land-form that supports it. And it's mostly extremely shallow. There are a few channels in it, but they move and nobody tries to chart them. Also a *few* very small keys. They're technically uninhabited, but some of them are used as layovers by drug runners and some have the 'pirates' on them. Really just criminals with small boats that try to sneak out and pick up . . . well, the occasional passing yacht like us. They've generally got *very* small boats, though. What you'd probably call a john boat. I doubt even they would try in these conditions. But I'm keeping a close eye on the radar. And an eye out in general—sometimes they don't show very well on radar."

"That's scary," Pam said.

"I have various methods to convince them we're not a good target," Mike said. "Just going up on deck with a fake rifle will usually make them veer off."

"And do you have a fake rifle?" Pam asked nervously.

"Yes," Mike replied.

"What about a real one?" Pam asked. "In case they don't scare off?"

"No comment," Mike said. "The Bahamas is very down on guns. One of the reasons that criminals find local yachts easy pickings since plenty of guns come in with the drugs."

"I noticed that the customs guys didn't actually search the boat," Pam said.

"They generally don't," Mike said. "But they're very down on guns, nonetheless. Using one to defend yourself is nearly as bad as getting picked off by pirates. Nearly."

"What do the pirates do with the boat?" she asked, gulping. "And, uhm, the people on board?"

"You don't want to know," Mike answered.

"Thought so," Pam said with a sigh.

CHAPTER
ELEVEN

Mike allowed Pam and Courtney to spell him in the late morning, as the waves moderated, and caught a few hours of sleep. By the time he got up in the afternoon, things had really started to calm down, but there was still solid overcast. He looked at the tropical satellite update and the general storm tracks. There was another depression forming off Africa, but other than that it looked pretty clear.

He was munching a sandwich for supper, watching the sun go down in the west with Pam sitting next to him, when the sat phone rang. He'd called in to the OSOL last night, giving his location and destination to the duty officer. It was a pain in the ass, but if it was the price of being armed, he was willing to pay it.

"Jenkins," he said after putting in the optional headset. Nobody but OSOL had the number, so it had to be them.

"Pierson," the colonel said. "Go scramble."

Mike punched in the code, watched by a puzzled Pam.

"Go scramble," he said.

"Mike, what is your position, exactly?"

Mike frowned and glanced at the GPS.

"24, 33, 93 by 78, 46, 21, more or less," Mike said. "Why?"

"Hang on," Pierson said, then sighed. "Mike, you have a presidential request to go operational."

"*What?*" Mike shouted. "Pam, could you go below?" he said, more calmly. "Hang on, Bob." When she was gone he said: "*What?*"

"Mike, we have a fixed location on WMD in movement," Pierson said tightly. "Specifically a nuke, probably refurbished Russian in origin. It's located at a key in the outer Great Banks, but it's going to move by tomorrow morning about four-thirty. We'd forward punched all our teams, trying to intercept it in Europe or the Mideast. We've got *no* spec ops that can deploy to the Bahamas before about 0600 tomorrow. If it moves, we'll lose it and have to reacquire. You're in position. It's less than forty miles from your current position."

"What's the threat level?" Mike asked.

"Low," Pierson said. "Okay, not great for one guy. Seven currently sitting on the device. At four-thirty, more or less, there's a cigarette boat coming in for it and there should be five more on the cig. But you should be able to get in position and take down the two groups separately."

"Thanks for the morale boost, buddy," Mike snorted. "And *where* is it, by the way?"

Pierson gave him the coordinates and Mike blanched. "That's *inside* the Banks, Bob! How the hell am I supposed to get there? Wade?"

"Mike, work the problem," Pierson said. "They've got a way in and out; find it."

"You're not Navy, Bob, that's for sure," Mike snorted, dialing up his charts, for what they were worth. "Okay, I think I can see what they're using. There's a narrow channel that leads up to a cluster of keys. Crap, they're not even named. And that channel is *not* very deep or wide. And who knows when this chart was last updated. I could end up stuck on a mud bank in pirate central."

"I'm looking at the satellite image," Pierson said. "There are five keys, more or less in a star pattern. On the center one is a small block building. The key is shaped sort of like a kidney, the inside pointed south. The block building is on the southwest side. Our information is that the device is on that key."

"I see 'em on the chart," Mike said, shaking his head and

spinning the wheel to port to turn the boat northwards. "I'm already past the Gap. And they'll be able to see me from the horizon if I close inside of ten miles or so." He thought about it and shrugged. "I've got the Zod. It's marginally doable."

"You'll do it?" Pierson asked.

"I'll do it," Mike said. "WMD in motion? Of course I'll do it. I just didn't think I could actually get there in time."

"The President also noted that the reward for stopping a WMD attack is five million," Pierson pointed out.

"I've got plenty of money, Bob," Mike snorted. "But tell the President thank you."

"Hurry," Pierson said.

"I already turned around," Mike said. "Call me if there's an intel update."

"Will do," Pierson said. "The reinforcements are FAST Three, coming out of Rota. I'll give you a contact frequency. What's your call sign? I think your usual would be a bad idea."

Mike thought about that then shrugged. "Use 'Winter born,'" he replied.

Mike looked up at the sky and frowned. Crescent moon tonight. "Please, clouds, hold," he muttered, then set the autosteer and went below.

"Mike, what's going on?" Pam asked.

"Something's come up," Mike said, thinking about what to do about the girls. This really was pirate central. Be a hell of a thing to go grab the nuke and lose the girls. "Either one of you know how to use a pistol?"

"I do," Courtney said. "My dad taught me."

"What kind?" Mike asked.

"Some kind of automatic," Courtney said.

"Semiautomatic I hope," Mike said. "Ladies, there's some sort of U.S. Code that covers what you're about to see," he said, pulling out a pair of pantyhose.

"You're a cross-dresser and it's covered by U.S. Code?" Courtney giggled.

"No," Mike said. "I'm about to open Bluebeard's Stateroom," he said, humming a tune. "That is what is covered by U.S. Code."

He got the key and opened up the room and waved for them to look.

"Uniforms?" Courtney asked, stepping inside and sitting on the bed. "You're still a SEAL?"

"Not exactly," Mike said, unlocking the weapons locker. While it wasn't exactly packed full with weapons, it was close, and the gleam of lethal black was a sight to see.

"Holy shit," Pam whispered.

"There's something going on nearby," Mike said. "What it is I can't specify. I was asked, as a favor, to look into it," he said, squatting down and pulling out a pair of team shorts, which he laid down beside the panty-hose. "We're going to have to actually run into the Banks, and then I'll have to leave for a while. I'll be back in the morning. But you guys will be sitting ducks while I'm gone," he added, pulling out a silenced .22-caliber pistol and a .40-caliber Sig. "Which one do you want?"

"I don't want either one," Courtney said, her eyes wide. "I don't want you to go."

"That's ... not an option," Mike said.

"Why don't they send ..."

"Real SEALs?" Mike said, slipping a magazine into the Sig and setting it on the floor. "Better the .40. Never get in a gunfight with a weapon that doesn't start with at least point four. Very good rule. They're all running around Bosnia and the Middle East kicking doors. The terrorists got inside of our net. I'm in position. I took the contract."

"You said you were a contractor," Pam said. "You didn't exactly say that you were still selling widgets."

"Well, I lied about selling widgets, frankly," Mike said, shrugging. "I never sold widgets. The boat, the rest, all came from contracting."

"That's a lot of money for a contractor," Courtney said, her eyes wide.

"You get paid a lot of money for what I do," Mike said, shrugging and starting to assemble his gear. "If I manage this mission, the vig is five mil. Again, this is all secret. The only reason I'm telling you is that you're going to have to see some of it and I've been wanting to really impress you. This is my big chance. When

I get back all shot up, you'll be less impressed," he added, looking up. "Pam, could you go get that big case of maxipads and the case of tampons, please?"

"What do you need these for—padding?" Pam asked when she came back in.

"No," Mike said, taking a handful of each and putting them in gallon Ziploc bags. He sealed them with as little air as possible and set them to the side. "Could you ladies go topside and watch our position? When we get to N24 40.656 W78 46.228—it's marked on the GPS—come down and tell me. And, of course, keep an eye out for unfriendly locals."

Mike continued to assemble what he considered essential gear for the mission until Courtney came down. He'd been pretty sure they were at the entrance to the channel when the boat slowed.

"We're pretty close," Courtney said. "There's breakers off to the east. Close."

"The edge of the Banks." Mike sighed, getting up and stretching; his joints ached from the weather change and sitting on the floor. "Now comes the fun part."

The wind was still blowing pretty steadily from the northeast and it was fairly cool up on the tuna tower. But it was the only place he might be able to see if the channel marked on the map was imaginary or not.

"There it is," Mike said, pointing to a break in the surf line. He eased the boat over and blanched at the narrowness and depth of the channel. "We're going to go aground, I just know it." He pulled up the tide tables for the area and nodded. "Tide's making, so if we do go aground, we'll be able to float off. But I'll need to find a deep hole to set this thing or we'll be screwed when the tide goes out." He flipped a switch and the speakers started to boom with heavy bass.

"More Goth?" Courtney asked, sighing.

"I'm going to take you to a Goth concert, someday," Mike said, grinning. "You'll have a blast. And I need to get my head into mission mode. And in this debt, a better world is made . . ." he whispered. "*In the fury of this darkest hour, we will be your light. You ask me for this sacrifice and I am Winter born . . . I hear the angels call my name . . .*"

Mike carefully negotiated his way into the channel, which widened out a bit beyond the entrance, and then began the process of trying to find his way through the maze.

Much of the channel marked on the maps was gone, storms and currents having torn down the walls of the channel and created shoals where clear water had been. But by luck as much as anything he was able to make his way through. He realized after a bit that it must have been dredged once upon a time and wondered why. Possibly for a salt extraction plant, long defunct. Now it was a ruined remnant of civilization in an uncivilized area.

Finally, well after dark, he reached the crop of keys that he'd spotted on the chart. There was a small open area on the northeast side of the islands, well out of sight of the target, and he dropped anchor while watching the area carefully for signs of life. This seemed like a natural spot for the local criminals to use for a base, but when he swept the islands with a thermal imager there weren't any hot spots. He still intended to circle the keys before he went in.

He'd kept navigational lights off as he approached and had the girls turn off all the interior lights, both so they wouldn't betray their presence and to let his eyes adjust to the darkness.

Now he slipped below, using a blue lens flashlight to make his way to the weapons room. Pam and Courtney were in the darkness of the lounge and, having run out of things to talk about, were now sitting on the couch and looking nervous.

"When I'm gone," Mike said, "lock the doors and hunker down. If anyone but me comes to the boat, just tell them to go away. If they don't, just put a round through the door. If that doesn't work, get in the Bluebeard Room; it's got reinforcing that's not exactly noticeable and the door is armored. They won't be able to take the boat anywhere, so just let them take whatever they want to take. I can replace anything except you two," he added with a smile.

"Okay," Courtney said unhappily. "I don't suppose going with you would be better."

"Not hardly." Mike grinned. He handed the light to Pam, then made his way to the weapons room, turned on the bluelight in there, then picked up his packs, going back out to the fishing deck.

The boat had had a nice center console inflatable for a dinghy when he got it. He'd replaced it with a black Zodiac for reasons that had never been clearly articulated in his mind. Now he knew why and why he'd also gotten an engine silencer installed. He undid the Zodiac, then swung it over the side, bringing it around to the fishing deck to load.

There was another bluelight on the fishing deck and he turned it on, then stripped and put on pantyhose. Over that went a black 3mm wetsuit. He wouldn't need it for the water, but it was better, he thought, than using fatigues for a combat swim, and the pressure of the neoprene tended to reduce bleeding in minor wounds. Once he had the suit on he camouflaged his face, then loaded all the gear he'd assembled from the weapons room into the Zodiac. Last he got out a Kryton rebreather and dropped that in the Zod. Rebreathers, which were underwater breathing apparatuses that didn't release bubbles, instead "rebreathing" the diver's exhalations, were generally considered to be military gear. However, modern rebreathers not only gave very long endurance underwater, up to twenty-four hours, but because there were no bubbles they also made spearfishing much easier. Fish tended to run from the sound of the bubbles with normal SCUBA. He'd picked up the rebreather for sport diving, but it would work just as well for a combat swim.

Once the Zod was fully loaded he climbed in and put on a set of NODs. The night was clearly lit with the goggles on and he started up the Zod, first circling the small string of keys and making sure that there was no sign of life, occasionally switching to a small thermal viewer to look for heat signatures. There didn't appear to be anything there, so he picked up his GPS, keyed it on, and headed south.

"This really sucks," Pam said as she heard the tiny sound of the motor fade into the distance. They were sitting in the near darkness of the lounge with only the small bluelight filtering out of the Bluebeard Room.

"I know," Courtney replied, fingering the pistol. "I really don't want to think about trying to defend this boat. I'm scared and bored at the same time."

"And horny," Pam said. "Is that crazy?"

"I dunno," Courtney said. "But so am I."

"I don't want to stay here," Pam said, looking around the room. "It's too spooky. But I don't want to put on a light, either."

"There aren't any windows in the Bluebeard Room," Courtney pointed out. "And it's got that reinforcing he was talking about."

"Right," Pam said, standing up and making her way into the room.

"Well, now I'm really bored," Courtney admitted after a minute, setting the pistol on a locker. "And still horny. I wonder when he'll be back."

"I wonder *if* he'll be back," Pam said, leaning into her. She paused as she did it and cleared her throat. "Uh, Courtney . . . ?"

"I was wondering what you were waiting for," Courtney said, putting her arms around the girl and lying back on the bed.

CHAPTER
TWELVE

There was still a wind from the north kicking up a light chop and he used the chop to look for shoals. Small breakers could be seen on the upwind side and the shoals were also marked by flatter water. He steered clear of these while keeping one eye on the GPS and checking around for signs of life.

He saw nothing on the transit to the target area. The water was clear of boats as well as islands. When he neared the target area he bore southeast, swinging in from the east towards the target and using the cover of the small islands northeast of the target, hopefully unsentineled, for cover.

He drove the Zod onto a slip of open beach and donned his gear. He'd loaded most of his weaponry in a waterproof bag, but he donned his armor and combat harness, with a USP .45 for a sidearm and MP-5 SPD on a friction strap. Then he put on his swim gear, including the rebreather, and slipped over the side, dragging the bag behind him.

The water was shallow around the keys but deep enough that, with the weights loaded into the rebreather harness, he could keep below water level. He crab-walked along the bottom, using the contour of the bottom and his compass, to move towards the northeast end of the island. He hit a couple of shoals and had

to maneuver around them. He tried to stay eastward, where the map indicated thick mangrove cover.

The Kryton rebreather was good for nearly twenty-four hours and he could have made a much longer swim approach, but getting the yacht into position and all the rest had pushed him for time. It was nearly two AM by the time he started his swim and if the intel was correct—that the pickup was to be at around four—he barely had time to make the short swim from the Zod to the target, recon and do his raid. So he pushed his movement faster than he'd have liked, occasionally surfacing and using the waterproof NODs to check his position.

Finally he got to within a few dozen meters of the mangroves on the northeast side of the island and found a fairly deep channel in which to rerig. He dropped the rebreather, attaching his fins to it, and slowly surfaced, MP-5 in one hand, dive bag in the other, checking his position and looking for threats.

No one was in sight so he kicked towards the mangroves until his dive booties found soft ground. In moments he'd made his way into the outer rank of the mangroves and started making his way deeper into the thicket.

Mangroves were the major nurseries of tropical waters, small trees with complex root systems that acted to form cover for small fish and invertebrates. The roots curved downwards from the trunk and often were covered in oysters. In addition to being a nursery, they captured soil and held it in place, slowly building up land around their roots; many keys in the Caribbean were nothing more than the build-up from mangroves. They dropped their leaves regularly and the decaying leaves both supplied food and added to the material trapped in the roots. The roots prevented erosion from wind and wave, often being the only thing that survived hurricanes and kept the land from being completely swept away. All in all they were something of a miracle plant.

They also were a pain in the ass. The tangled roots constantly tried to trap him as he made his way through the thicket. The microclimates formed in the roots mostly consisted of hot, almost boiling hot it seemed, water that stank to high heaven from decay. Each step raised bubbles of foul-smelling hydrogen sulfide gas,

and the oysters and barnacles on the roots tore at his wetsuit, shredding it before he could even get shot.

But they gave him cover as he made his way onto the land, finally passing into a narrow strip of sand where the mangroves ended and the sea grape still hadn't started. He paused before he entered that strip, sticking his head out of the mangroves and looking around carefully as well as using his ears and nose to check for signs of threats. Since nothing was in sight, he slid out into the open area and considered the situation.

There was a small gap in the mangroves on the north side, a strip of dirty beach about three meters wide. On the south side of the island there was a strip of real beach. The charts indicated truly shallow water near the north opening, so it was unlikely the relief boat would come in that way. However, it was a natural place to put a sentry.

The small island was covered in scattered palms with a heavy undergrowth of sea grape. Sea grape wasn't thorny or particularly unpleasant, but it *was* thick, too thick to walk through. However, it had open area under it. He paused and opened up his bag, pulling out equipment and checking it. The main thing he needed from it was the thermal imager. Nobody had ever made a thermal imager that could handle a dive approach, unlike standard NODs. He flipped up the NODs and swept the imager around, looking for hot spots. The immediate area seemed to be clear, so he slid the imager into a pouch on his combat harness, stored the bag in the mangroves and started crawling northeast under the grapes, cautiously probing for sentries.

He found the first one more or less where he expected, sitting on the sand of the north beach, looking out at the water and smoking a cigarette. The wind had shifted around to the south and Mike moved cautiously so as not to give away his position, choosing each placement of his hands and knees with care.

There was a narrow path running generally southeast to northwest and terminating at the water. He slid out into this open area carefully, checking to see that the sentry wasn't in sight of any of his friends, then slid the MP-5 to burst and put three rounds in his head. The sentry flopped backwards so that he looked like he had simply fallen asleep, except for the twitching of his legs

and arms. Mike wasn't sure exactly why one guy in four was a twitcher, but it was pretty consistent. Make for a great doctoral dissertation some day.

He used the path, cautiously, probing southwest towards the target building, stopping from time to time to check with the thermal for heat. Finally, after a move of about fifty meters, he spotted a heat image and dropped down to crawl cautiously forward.

There was an open area running up from the beach. It was about seventy meters long and about fifty deep, in an irregular oval. The target building, which was lit, was on the north side, the beach on the south, and otherwise it was surrounded by sea grape. There were a few palm trees scattered around, but not many. The ground was sand covered liberally with palm fronds.

There was another sentry standing outside the main door of the small shack. He was looking pretty bored, but reasonably alert. He also was close enough that simply shooting him was likely to trigger the group on the interior.

Mike crawled backwards and into the sea grape, cautiously and silently making his way to the building under cover of the grapes. When he reached the building he found that the thicket came right up to the walls and moving through the thick portion at the edge was hard to do silently. He slowly slid up through the plants, though, until he could get an optical viewer over the edge of an open window and get a look inside the target building.

There were five Middle Eastern males in the room, lounging on cots or seated. At the far end of the room was a large bomb-looking thing on a rolling cart. It didn't have the shape of a MIRV and his last class in Soviet nuclear weapons was a very faint memory. It more or less had to be the target, though. The light came from a Coleman lantern on a table.

He made his way back down through the sea grape, silently, then low crawled to the front edge of the thicket. He slid slowly out, keeping the MP-5 centered on the chest of the sentry, who was totally oblivious. The wind was from the south, filling the area with the sound of rustling palm trees and sea grape, and that rustling hid the faint noises he was making. It was dark by the sea grape, with shadows cast by the light from the windows;

it was unlikely that the sentry would have seen him if he'd looked right at Mike's position. Which he wasn't doing, simply looking down towards the sea, clearly hoping that the boat would get here soon.

When Mike was clear of the entangling vegetation he slowly stood up, keeping the sentry targeted, and stepped forward, one step, two, then triggered a burst into the sentry.

The sound of the weapon was masked by the sound of the wind and trees, but the thump of the sentry hitting the ground was noticed by those inside as Mike could tell by the questioning tones in Arabic. He didn't give them much time to react, though, stepping to the nearest window and tossing a frag through, then up to the door. The building was cast concrete and he stood to the side of the thin wooden door until the frag went off, extinguishing the light, then flipped down his NODs, opened up the door and stepped into the room.

Three of the terrorists were on the ground, screaming in pain from the fragments tossed around the room by the grenade. Another had apparently been right by it when it detonated and he wasn't going to ever scream again. The fifth was wounded, but trying to get his AK operational. Mike triggered a burst into him and then into each of the surviving terrorists, filling the already blood-soaked room with more spray.

The bomb had apparently been undamaged by the grenade. He hadn't been worried about it sympathetically detonating. Nukes were hard enough to get to go off at all; it wasn't going to be detonated by a grenade.

However, he didn't want the reinforcements snatching it away from him, so he needed to do something with it. He rolled it out the door and to the east, driving it up a small path in the grape until he was well away from the building. Then he carefully lifted the heavy device off the cart, knowing he was probably getting radiation exposure, and rolled it under the sea grape.

After that he rolled the cart back into the building and followed the path to the beach. From there he made his way through the entangling grape to where he'd dropped his swim bag. With that in hand, he made his way back to the edge of the open area and set up.

Mike was more than capable of fighting at close range, but if he could take out the enemy at a distance he much preferred it. And while the MP-5 was great for close, silent work, he preferred something with a bit more range and punch if he had to engage an enemy in open field. Thus he'd packed along both a Mannlicher 7mm sniper rifle and a silenced M-4. The silencer on the M-4 didn't really make it silent, but it did reduce and modify the sound. It also made it harder to pinpoint.

He put the MP-5 in the bag, switched out magazines and rolled the bag back under the sea grape. Then he set up a good sniper position, including dragging a couple of the cooling bodies over for cover. He got some of the palm fronds for minor camouflage. He was only expecting five, but it never hurt to be safe.

That done he took a pull of water from his camelbak and got out a power bar. The whole mission had been more exercise than he'd been getting lately and he was pretty tired. He also ached, probably due to the weather change, and if he had to sit still for long he was going to lock up.

He'd hydrated and gotten down a couple of power bars when he spotted a faint white mark on the sea a few hundred meters out. He flipped down the NODs and spotted the cigarette boat immediately, moving in slowly, making its way through the shoals. He glanced at his watch and it was right on time. The only problem being that it was followed by four more.

"You said five," he muttered. "Five targets. Not five boats!"

As the boats got closer he saw that they were also filled with targets. Each seemed to have about four or five. Crap.

He snugged the Mannlicher into his shoulder and tracked them with the thermal scope as they got closer. As the first boat came in sight of the building it slid to a stop, working back and forth at steerage and apparently unsure if it should come in. Mike suddenly realized they were either waiting for a signal or bothered by the building being unlit. He probably should have replaced the broken Coleman with something, although he couldn't think off the top of his head what.

Finally the boat came forward, cautiously, followed by the other four. They spread out as they approached the beach. When they'd beached, armed men came forward and jumped to the sand,

running out anchors, looking around at the darkness under the trees and calling out softly.

Mike scanned the sniper rifle over the target-rich environment until one of the men on the boat climbed onto the bow and started ordering the terrorists on the beach to head for the building and waving at others to land.

Mike laid the crosshairs on the man's head and gently squeezed the trigger. The target's head exploded like a melon and he started tracking other targets.

The men on the ground had spread out and gone to ground, most of them firing wildly into the darkness. Mike slid the Mannlicher from one to the next, pumping rounds into them and silencing the panicked fire.

One of the cigarette boats suddenly sprung to life, backing away, dragging its anchor. Mike tried to target the pilot, but the man was hunched down, so he put three rounds into the engine compartment and the boat gave a cough and stopped.

By this time most of the terrorists on the boats had unloaded and were firing in his general direction, some of them coming forward at a run. The area was getting a bit hot, so he dropped the Mannlicher and picked up the M-4. The Mannlicher only had a five-round magazine compared to the thirty-round mag on the assault rifle. He targeted three of the terrorists, spinning them into the sand, then rolled backward into the sea grape.

He wasn't sure how many terrorists were left, but his main concern was the cigarette boats. He didn't want them either getting away or, worse, being used to move terrorists around to the sides of the island. So he made his way quickly through the sea grape, pausing only to connect the MP-5's friction strap, until he was at the edge of the open area by the sea.

The open area was swarming with terrorists by this point so he couldn't go in there. He made his way southward, then into the mangroves on that side, cautiously making his way down to the waterline. He found a small channel, stinking with rot, and sunk down into the putrid water, cautiously sliding out into the open water and submerging.

It was a short swim to the boats and one that he could make entirely on a lungful of air. He was mainly worried about

phosphorescence. Any movement in tropical waters caused flashes of luminescent light from small planktonic creatures in the water. But the terrorists apparently were focusing on the land and ignoring the water. Stupid terrorists, water is for SEALs.

He reached the hull of the nearest cigarette boat and slowly surfaced, letting out his breath silently and getting another lungful. He was shielded from view by the hull of the boat and he paused a moment to consider his next move. Then he lifted his left hand up to the bulwark of the boat and gently lifted himself from the water.

There were two terrorists in the boat, watching the goings-on on the land. He could see more on the other boats. He quietly lifted himself, one-handed, up to the bulwark, lowering his barrel to clear it of water, sliding over on his belly as quietly as he could. When he was in the boat, he triggered a burst into each of the terrorists.

The faint sound of the M-4 apparently didn't carry to the other boats, or the terrorists couldn't place it, since they continued to pay more attention to the land than the boat he'd boarded. Mike carefully corrected for the rocking of the boat and targeted the terrorist on the next boat, taking him down as well.

That was noticed by the next boat, but before the terrorists on that one could react, he had hit one. The other dove out of sight with a scream and he took that as indication that his position was compromised. He took a breath and rolled backwards off the boat and into the water.

He swam down the line of boats, keeping his eyes open in the salt water, until he was up to the third boat, again letting himself surface by the hull. Suddenly the boat burst into life and he lifted himself quickly over the side, targeting the terrorist in the boat, who was hunkered down by the controls and yelling to his fellows on the shore.

Fire started to come from the land and Mike dove over the side, chased by fire from the land and boats. He felt a searing pain in his right leg when he hit the water and realized that he must have taken a round on the way out.

He used the boats for cover, breathing in their shadow, and made his way back to the mangroves. Once there he passed through them

fast, ignoring the pain in his leg and reloading. The entire engagement on the boats hadn't used up a full magazine.

He heard shouting from the east end of the island and realized that the terrorists must have found the nuke. That simply wasn't on, so he made his way back to the edge of the open area and scanned around with the NOD on the M-4.

Three terrorists had gotten the cart from the building and were manhandling it towards the path. He got two, but the third dove into the concealment of the sea grape. However, the bomb was on the other side of the open area and to get to the boats they'd have to pass his line of fire.

Mike suddenly heard a rustle behind him and rolled over, triggering a burst into the terrorist that had been trying to sneak up on him. The guy had a buddy, though, and even on spray and pray at less than five yards it was hard to entirely miss. He felt a familiar punch in his side, like being hit by a baseball bat, and another in his chest. He was pretty sure the one in his chest had been stopped by the armor, but the other one started to sting like hell from the salt water even before he put another burst in the remaining terrorist.

The brief firefight had attracted attention, though, and more were moving across the open area towards his position. He serviced two of those but had to roll deeper into the grape as the scrub around him started to be flailed by bullets. He took another round in the back of his armor, knocking him forward, before he got out of the beaten area.

He circled to the right, crawling under the sea grape as fast as he could, and got another look at the open area. The cart was gone, probably up the path to pick up the bomb, and he decided it was time for serious action. However, he was bleeding like a pig and the pain in his leg was starting to slow him down.

He pulled out the packet of tampons and pads and explored the wound in his leg. That was a through-and-through in the calf that was bleeding freely, but it wasn't pumping, so no major vessels had been hit. First he pulled out a small foil packet and tore it open, dumping the contents in the wound. The material was a combination of antibiotics and a new blood coagulant made from shrimp shells, of all things. It was supposed to be the cat's

pajamas in stopping hemorrhaging and he could use that at the moment. When he'd gotten the stuff in the wound he plugged it with a tampon, then injected the area with novocaine. The one on his side was a through-and-through as well, basically through his love-handles, as if he didn't have enough reasons to go on a diet. More shrimp, another tampon, and a shot of novocaine and it was good to go.

He checked the open area and nothing was moving. But he could hear Arabic voices on the far side, presumably wrestling with the bomb. He wasn't sure how many were left on the boats, but they could wait.

He continued circling right, getting all the way up to the building before he heard the group struggling with the bomb. From the sound of it they were right by where the path reached the open area. Mike decided that bold was the only course open to him and simply stepped out of the sea grape and headed for the path.

There were four of the terrorists in the group manhandling the cart down the path. Two were actually handling the cart with another giving orders while the fourth was sweeping his AK around nervously.

The night was dark, still overcast, and the terrorists didn't have night-vision devices. They were as plain as day to Mike, but apparently they hadn't seen him. Oh, well. He shot the one with the AK, then the two manhandling the bomb. By the time he'd taken them down, the one giving the orders had fled down the path. The fucker had been armed; Mike had anticipated taking rounds. But usually "martyrdom" meant for the lowly and not the guys giving orders. Nine times out of ten with muj, the leadership ran like rabbits and let the brainwashed teenage muj take the heat.

He suddenly started taking fire from the direction of the boats and cursed. He was getting really tired of those guys. He moved down the path, out of sight of the boats, then crawled under the sea grape to a position where he could keep an eye on the bomb and still be out of sight.

He didn't know how many terrorists were still on the island. He'd never gotten an accurate count and hadn't been able to keep

up with how many he'd taken down. He figured it was somewhere between three and seven with about three on the boats.

One of the boat drivers called out in a questioning tone. At first there was no answer, then a voice yelled from somewhere nearby, high and fast in Arabic. Mike stayed still, anticipating that the leader would move after yelling. Three men got off of one of the boats and started moving towards the bomb, cautiously, their weapons swinging back and forth. Suddenly, one of them ripped off a whole magazine towards the building and there was a shout of pain in that direction, followed by cursing in Arabic.

Mike took the opportunity to move back into the sea grape, shifting his position towards where the leader had been. It put him out of sight of the bomb, but he wanted to take the leader out while he could.

The sea grape gave way to a narrow path and he figured the leader type had used that. There were no apparent footprints, so he didn't know if the guy had gone left or right. He slid out of the sea grape cautiously and stepped carefully down the path to the east.

The path terminated behind the building and he paused at the edge, his spidey-sense tingling. There was somebody nearby. He could hear the target getting to the bomb and cursed to himself. Keeping the bomb secure was his primary mission and he needed to get back to it.

He stepped to the side of the building, then paused and threw himself flat as he heard a hissing sound passing through the air. Frickin' grenade.

CHAPTER THIRTEEN

Bakr Majali had been a street child in Jordan until he joined the madrassa. There he was fed and trained in the Word of God. The madrassas were supposed to teach things other than just the Koran, but for most that was enough. He had been filled with the words of Mohammed, living on the sufferance of the good Islamics who contributed to the support of the madrassa, and growing day by day in his hatred of the infidel. He was a Palestinian, one of the millions that made up the bulk of the population of Jordan. And besides the Word of God he was filled with the stories of the suffering of his people, both at the hands of the Jews and at the hands of the Hashemites who ruled Jordan.

He had planted his first bomb when he was barely twelve and had lived his life as a mujahideen, first as a street fighter, then as a leader. Over the years his fervor had died, but he still fought for the only cause he had ever known. He had no other skills than those of a terrorist.

He had been sent on this mission because of his knowledge of English and his loyalty to the cause. And he intended to both survive and succeed, despite this infidel who stood in their way.

The man was very good, as good as an Israeli commando, but he was but one man. And he had never fought the likes of Bakr Majali. Bakr had learned long ago that standing in the

middle of the street and firing off a whole magazine, like Rambo in some action movie, was never going to kill the enemies of Allah. Silence was required, and aiming and hiding. But a good grenade never hurt.

He heard the faint movement as the commando neared the house. It was so faint it was nearly lost on the night wind, but it was there, the soft compression of the sand, a crackle of leaf. He quietly pulled the pin on the grenade and then threw it around the corner.

Mike lay flat, taking the impact of the grenade as much as he could on his armor and helmet. Most grenade fragments tended to fly upwards when the device hit the ground, and they did this time. But he could feel some of them ripping into his legs and arms.

It was the latter that caused him to be slow as the figure leaned around the corner, quickly spotting him in the faint star-light and opening fire at the figure on the ground. Mike felt the aimed rounds track across his back, most of them stopped by the armor, and then into his legs. But he stayed in the prone, targeting the figure in return and put a burst into his chest. The figure, though, stayed upright, continuing to fire, and he felt more rounds flail into his legs and a sharp, stabbing, pain in his left arm that caused him to flinch and let go of the weapon with that hand. He pointed the weapon like a pistol and threw three more bursts of 5.56 into the target, sending him staggering backwards to fall on his back.

Allah's curse on all Westerners and their damned body armor, Bakr thought as he lay on the ground looking at the stars. The bullets had slammed into him like so many punches and while he'd continued to fire, he could feel his life seeping away. Now he could no longer move. He looked at the fading stars and thought of the words of the mullahs in that faraway madrassa. Allah, the Kind, the Beneficent, the Merciful. *Allahu Akbar.* Allah is Great. There is no God besides Allah. To die in battle . . .

His left arm was useless; the bullet seemed to have broken the ulnar bone. Mike used his right arm to pull himself forward,

trying to get to the open area where he could cover the retreating mujahideen and stop them from departing with the bomb. He couldn't get to his feet, either, and he was worried that one or more of the bullets might have punched an artery. If so, he might bleed out before he could get back to the battle.

He crawled forward, the pain so great that it was causing an endorphin rush high, dragging his useless legs and arm, each bump making him nearly scream in agony. But he kept his mouth shut until he was at the edge of the sea grape that cloaked the west side of the building.

The remaining mujahideen were wheeling the bomb down to the waterline. He propped himself against a palm tree, compensating for the faint sway, and lined up the one who was doing the most pushing.

Haroun Arif was terrified and elated. Although the apparently lone commando had nearly stopped them from securing the bomb, they were almost to the boats. A few more meters and they would have it in the boat and be gone. Let the Americans try to stop them then. With all the losses the cells had taken, it would be hard to smuggle the weapon all the way into America, but they would persevere. Allah was with them and . . .

He felt the punch in his back before he processed the faint cracks behind him. Suddenly, his legs were not working as well and his vision was going black. His hands slipped from the handle of the bomb carrier and he slipped to his knees.

"Allah is Merciful," he whispered. "Great is Allah . . ."

Mike started to target the other two, but one of them pushed the bomb carrier over on its side and the two crouched behind it. He couldn't get a clear shot at them from where he was, so he painfully started crawling to the side, keeping one eye on them and the other on the boats.

Assadolah Shaath had been a physics student at Princeton University when he was recruited to the jihad. He had traveled first to Syria and then to the camps in Afghanistan before the invasion by the infidel. There he had tried to use his skills to create such

a bomb as he now touched, but it was beyond his ability given the conditions and what he had to work with. But he knew how they worked. As had Jalal Azhiri, one of the Brethren who had waited in the darkness until the American cowboy came and sent him into Allah's arms.

But, as he had been told, the bomb had already been rigged for destruction. Setting it off in America would be better than here, but just having it go off *near* America was surely better than losing it entirely. And with only he and Halim Shahid left, it was more than likely that the American would soon recapture it.

However, while he believed in the Great Jihad, he had no interest in martyrdom. He had many skills the jihad needed. So he opened up the arming panel and keyed in a sequence.

"What are you doing?" Halim asked, nervously.

"Setting the bomb to blow," Assadolah answered. "When I am done, we will run to the boats and drive away. There will be enough time for us to escape, but not enough for the American to disarm it. This will send a message to the world that Allah is Great."

Mike could see one of the targets crouched behind the weapon but the other was still covered. He lined him up and fired carefully.

Halim let out a grunt and reared up as something thudded into his body. As he lifted himself, there were more thuds, like thunking a melon, and he collapsed. Assadolah reached up and wiped at a wetness on his cheek, the hand coming away black in the faint light.

"Allah is Great," Assadolah said, keying the last sequence and closing the box. "Let Allah be Merciful."

The second terrorist suddenly leapt to his feet and ran for the boats. Mike tracked him but couldn't quite hit the moving target despite two bursts in his direction. The tango darted behind one of the cigarette boats and then Mike could faintly see him tumbling over the side. Suddenly, the engine coughed to life and the boat started backing up, like the first one dragging its anchor.

This time, though, the terr backed straight up, engine at max, the anchor leaping out of the sand and bounding into the water. Mike tried to target the driver, but with only one arm he could barely keep the boat in his sights. He fired some shots but then the bolt locked back on an empty mag.

Changing out the magazine with only one arm, on his stomach, was a pain not only in the ass but in every wound. And his vision was going funny again. He realized he was bleeding out, but he wanted to get this last damned terrorist. However, before he could even get the magazine changed, the terrorist darted forward, cut the anchor rope, spun the boat around and was moving out of range.

Mike crawled towards the bomb painfully, wondering if there were any remaining tangos and not really caring anymore. He was going to do the same thing as the target, set up by the bomb and use it for cover until he either bled out or the FAST guys showed up.

It took him nearly three minutes to crawl across the sand to the bomb and slide around behind it. When he got there, he pulled out his bag of field-expedient bandages and tried to give himself first aid. Most of the rounds, however, were in places he couldn't reach anymore. He got a tampon in his arm, nearly screaming at the pain, and another in a big hole in his leg. The holes in his legs were filled with sand, as well, and the tampon wasn't particularly fun to put in.

By the end of getting the bleeding reduced—and he knew it was only reduced, not stopped—he was panting and his vision was going in and out. But he noticed a blue glow from a panel on what would be the top of the bomb. Cautiously, he lifted the panel and then blanched. There was a countdown clock and it was just passing twenty minutes.

He thought about that for a second and then did the only thing he could think of, crawling towards the nearest remaining cigarette boat. He could sort of use his legs, especially the right one, and he used his right arm and that leg to pull himself up with the anchor rope and onto the bow.

He cut the anchor rope and then slid across the front of the boat, around the windscreen and then more or less fell into the

driver's seat, finally crying out at the pain of the impact. There was a dead body on the floor of the cockpit, but he ignored it, taking his weapon off and setting it on the seat beside him.

There was a glowing GPS on the dash with a track on it. Clearly that was the way the boats had taken in and it was, hopefully, a way out.

He started the boat, reversed it, spun it around much more expertly than the muj, and got the hell out of Dodge.

"What is he doing?" Colonel Pierson said, watching the take from the satellite. "I'm pretty sure that's Winter Born."

"I don't know," the guy in civilian clothes said. He was pretty clearly CIA, but one of the "field" hands, a big, burly, bearded guy who looked out of place in the suit he was wearing. "He's leaving the device."

"Is he after the remaining terrorist?" Captain Polumbo wondered. The captain was a SEAL currently working in OSOL like Pierson and had been called in for consultation on the waterborne aspects of the op.

"He looked at the device and then immediately went to the boat," Pierson said. "We don't have commo with him, yet, do we?"

"Negative," the technician manning the console replied. "The FAST team is inbound by helicopter," he added, pointing to an overhead map. "They're seven minutes out. The range on those radios is only about ten klicks, though. I'm not sure they're ever going to be in range."

Pierson thought about Mike's actions, then blanched. He picked up a phone at his place at the table and punched a button.

"General," he said. "Request that the FAST divert to close with Agent Winter Born. The nuke *may* repeat *may* be armed at this time."

Mike could barely keep conscious. He was driving in a pool of blood and his vision kept creeping in and out. But he kept his eye on the GPS and kept driving, going as fast as he could given his condition.

The track was not constant, since it wove in and out of the shoals in the banks. But he was reaching the edge of the Banks

now, and as soon as he hit open water he was going to push this thing up to full speed and put his ass to the blast.

He was just reaching the edge of the Banks when his radio crackled to life.

"Winter Born, Winter Born," the voice said. "FAST Three. What is your situation?"

Mike slowed the boat for a moment and propped the wheel with his still mostly functional right leg.

"The nuke is *armed*," Mike said. "Get clear. I read it as about five minutes to detonation." With that he dropped the radio, put the boat back up to power and headed for the edge of the Banks.

"Holy crap," the pilot of Seahawk 412 said, turning the helicopter to the side and going to max power, nose down and hauling.

"FAST, this is SOCOM Six," the sat radio said. "Copy weapon armed. Abort, abort, abort. Move towards Agent Winter Born's position. After detonation, recover if possible. Navy surface support is inbound. If you have to ditch, they have your location."

"Roger," Captain Talbot said, keying his mike and nodding. "We need to get clear, ASAP." He turned to the team and waved. "Mission is *ay*-bort! Weapon is armed. Say, again, weapon is *armed*. Prepare for ditching maneuvers!"

Mike had strapped himself into the seat and the boat was now on autopilot, slamming southeast as fast as it could go. He couldn't really see anymore, his vision going gray and red at the impacts of the speedboat over the waves that remained from the storm. He wasn't sure if the thing was going to go airborne first or if he was going to bleed out or the bomb was going to detonate. When it did, it would send a tsunami in every direction. The girls were probably going to be fine. The Banks weren't going to allow for a major wave and they were not only ten miles away but shielded by the small islands. He, however, was still less than five, with nothing between him and the bomb but open water.

The boat hit a particularly bad wave, going airborne, its engine screaming, as the world suddenly went white. He saw that, but it was really the last thing he remembered.

▲   ▲   ▲

"Oh shit," the Seahawk's pilot said, quietly, as a new sun erupted to her northeast. Captain Kacey Bathlick was a short-coupled brunette with moderate breasts and shapely legs who had wanted to be a pilot since she had read her first Dragonriders of Pern book. She had considered all three services before opting for the Marines. She'd joined the Marines because she considered herself just as much of a warrior as the "cargo" in the back, and over the years she had handled more than a few midair emergencies. But, as her stick and all her instruments went dead from the nearby EMP, she admitted to herself that she'd much rather have been fighting Thread on Pern. "BRACE! BRACE! BRACE!" she shouted in a throaty contralto as she prepared to autorotate.

"EVAC!" Captain Talbot yelled, yanking open the troop door. He grabbed the FAST Marine next to him as the trooper dropped his armor, and tossed him out the door, then followed, yanking the quick releases on his armor in midair.

The technique the Marines used was called helocast. It was a fast water-entry method that could also be used for just such emergencies. Talbot rotated his body in midair to turn his back into the motion of the helicopter. By holding his nose and putting the body in a "half-pike" position it was possible to enter the water from rather high and rather fast.

But normally not quite as high as they were, and not as fast. And then there was the fact that the helicopter was falling *towards* them. The last thing Talbot saw before his feet hit the water was the rotating blades of the chopper above him coming *down*.

As his feet hit, his body was tumbled backwards so that it hit on the legs and then butt, breaking into the water in a V formation with a tremendous splash, the speed of the impact actually causing him to tumble in the water. The impact drove the air out of his lungs, but he automatically hit the inflator on his buoyancy vest and bobbed back to the surface just as the chopper hit, with a tremendous splash, less than thirty meters from his position, one of the still-rotating blades slapping the water not far from his nose and then sinking out of sight as the helicopter rolled over ...

▲   ▲   ▲

Autorotation was, conceptually, simple. As a helicopter fell, its blades tended to pick up the spin of the air running across them. By occasionally reversing the pitch of the blades, it was possible to use their momentum to get momentary lift.

However, it worked much better at, say, a thousand feet, than at two hundred. The props continued to spin for a moment, giving her a smidgeon of lift, then stopped and reversed. She was an expert pilot and had practiced autorotation hundreds of times. And she knew damned well there was not nearly enough rotation going to slow them as she reversed. But they were going in, no question, and *any* lift was better than no lift as the helicopter plunged towards the tossing sea.

"Oh, well," her left seat said. "At least the water will be warm."

"I'm just hoping to survive the *impact*," Kacey snapped, reversing the blades at the last moment possible. There was a smidgeon of lift again and then they hit the water's surface. Hard.

Mike came to lolling on the sea, boat engine dead. There was a new sun just dying to the northeast and in the light of it he could see a helicopter pinwheeling into the ocean to his northwest. It hit with one hell of a splash, then immediately turned over and began to sink, fast.

The engine had cut, but he managed to nurse it to life and turned the boat northwest, breathing ragged and the pain getting to be unimaginable. Spray had covered him, the salt like fire in his wounds.

As he was running northwest he glanced towards the direction of the dying fireball and, in the luminance of lightning crackling across its surface, saw one hell of a wave headed for his position. He turned into it, the boat lifting into the air again, and crashed to the water on the far side. He nearly passed out from the wave of pain and let out a shriek.

"Crap, that hurt," he muttered. "This had better be worth it."

The impact had been bad, but Kacey had gotten enough lift at the last moment that the water had only come up to cover the windows for a second. Then the Seahawk rolled over and started

to sink. Choppers have, effectively, no buoyancy so the multiton aircraft went under like a stone.

"Everybody out!" she shouted, taking a last gulp of breath as the water in the cabin rose up to her chest level.

The water was already over the fast-sinking chopper, but she'd trained for this eventuality. She found her chest and waist and removed her harness. Then she moved her right knee to the door and used it to find the door handle. She opened the door handle, grabbed the edges of the door, and headed out into open water. Her side was *down* so she had to pull herself around the chopper into the open water. She had her eyes open so she could vaguely see the rotor of the chopper going past, windmilling, and it was a sight she hoped she'd never see again in her life. Assuming her life lasted more than a few seconds.

As lack of air got to her, causing a sudden panic reaction, she remembered the *other* thing she was supposed to be doing and reached for her Helicopter Emergency Egress Device. This was a small tank of air, generally kept on one or the other leg, that could be used for just such a situation. She yanked the HEEDs off her right leg, put it in her mouth and blew out, clearing the regulator, then sucked in a glorious lungful of air. That problem covered, she started kicking for the surface, breathing in and out as trained.

When she got there she did a quick head count. The wind was blowing like a son-of-a-bitch and it was hard to count bobbing heads. But she got a glimpse of her co and crew chief and that was all she really cared about. Her responsibility for cargo ended when she got them on the ground, or in the water as the case might be. She hit the release on her Personal Flotation Device, called a Mae West by all and sundry, and rolled up to the surface of the water.

"Hey," her co called. "Nice landing. Any one you can walk away from . . . or float as it may be . . ."

"Oh, shut up, Tammy," Kacey snapped.

"Form up!" Captain Talbot yelled, grabbing Private Gowey as he passed. "Get in a group! Don't get separated!"

Gunny Hilton came crawling over dragging Sergeant Goweda,

who seemed to have taken a hit on the head and was mildly incoherent. They'd managed to hang onto their Mae Wests on the exit, at least.

"Where's Pawlick?" the Gunny said, looking around the group.

"I think we lost him, Gunny," Sergeant Klip said. "I don't think he made it out of the bird."

"Fuck," Hilton muttered. "Sir, all of the team is present and accounted for except Lance Corporal Pawlick."

"Thank you, Gunny," the captain said. Everybody had their Mae Wests inflated and he could see the pilots and their crew chief moving towards the group. "The good news is that we were being watched as we went down. The bad news is that our locator beacons probably took a hit from the EMP just like the chopper. So I hope they find us fast."

"I hope they find us, period, sir," Klip said, looking around. "There's lots of sharks in these waters."

"Hey," Captain Bathlick said as she backstroked over and hooked into the group. "Sorry about that. The EMP took out all my controls."

"Figured as much," Captain Talbot replied.

"Anybody got any shark repellent?" Klip said. "I got followed by one of those bastards on an op and I don't care for them at all."

"Got it," the crew chief said, lifting out a canister and dumping it in the water. It quickly spread and dyed the waters bright yellow. "There's supposed to be a frigate out there somewhere. Hopefully they'll find us soon."

"I dunno," Talbot said, looking towards the dwindling mushroom cloud. "We're drifting pretty fast. And there's going to be worries about fallout. We'd better be prepared to spend some time in the drink."

"Great," Bathlick said, grinning. "Know any good dirty jokes? I've got a million of 'em."

"Sir," Private Gowey said, kicking upwards. "I think I just saw a boat." He pointed southwards and kicked up again.

"Sure is," Gunny Hilton said. The sun was starting to rise and it was just possible to glimpse a cigarette boat inbound on a

snaking course. "But I'm not sure if that's good or bad. There's lots of cigarette boats in these waters we don't want to meet."

"And whoever is driving that doesn't look as if he knows what he's doing," Captain Bathlick observed.

The cigarette boat seemed to spot them and came forward, occasionally crabbing on the waves. It stopped just short of their position and started drifting to the south in the north wind.

"Gowey," Talbot snapped. "Dump your Mae West and try like hell to catch that thing."

Gowey slid out of his vest and down under the group, surfacing to the south and crawling fast towards the boat. He'd dropped his boots earlier and was a very strong swimmer, but by the time he got to the boat it was nearly a hundred meters away.

It was drifting away nose forward and he managed to snag the dive platform at the rear, dragging himself into the boat. The first thing he saw was a body on the floor of the cockpit, but he ignored it. There was another person, in armor, behind the wheel, slumped to one side and only held up by the four-point restraints for the driver.

He wasn't sure if the guy was alive or dead, but he had other things on his mind. He undid the restraints, dumping the driver unceremoniously to the side, and keyed the boat to life. Then, inexpertly, he turned it towards the group.

"There's a guy on here I think's the agent we were supposed to reinforce," he shouted, as he neared the gaggle of drifting Marines. "He's in pretty bad shape."

CHAPTER
FOURTEEN

"I'm getting really tired of waking up in this same damned hospital," Mike said as Pierson walked through the door.

"Be glad you woke up at all," Pierson replied. "Exsanguinated doesn't begin to cover it. And it took FAST quite a while to find the frigate that was in support. All they could do was plug the holes with the stuff you had on you. Good tip on the tampons, by the way. FAST's carrying them, now. They ran out, but one of the pilots from the helicopter had some spares with her."

"I hope they kept my damned cigarette boat," Mike said.

"Your cigarette boat?" Pierson said, grinning. "You were practically dead when they got to it. I think that counts as salvage. Surely it's the FAST's boat."

"I wasn't all dead," Mike replied. "Salvage only counts if you're all dead. And you'd better not have lost it. I captured it fair and square."

"We kept the cigarette boat," Pierson said, relenting. "I take it you want to keep it?"

"Yep," Mike said. "Gonna paint it silver and black. Call it the *Too Late*."

"Well, you stopped the nuke from getting to the U.S. or any other major populated area," Pierson pointed out. "And the fallout

fell in open ocean. It was pretty nasty, too. That's what ground-level nukes do with water: very, very nasty fallout. The fishing in the area will be somewhat hazardous for a while."

"I'm not planning on going fishing anytime soon," Mike said, leaning back and closing his eyes. "I hope somebody remembered my girls."

"That we did," Pierson said. "FAST and a Navy team dropped on your boat and picked it up. One of the FASTs nearly got shot, but everything's kosher. I'm sorry to tell you the girls decided that, all things considered, they wanted to go home. So . . . nobody waiting for you on your little Caribbean idyll."

"I think the Caribbean is getting a bit too hot for me, anyway," Mike replied, shrugging with his one good shoulder. "I think I'll go down for a while, just to rest up. But then I'm going traveling."

"Well, you're entitled to a rest," Pierson said. "And the Finding decided that you still were owed for the mission. So you'll have plenty of money to rest with."

"Money, shmoney," Mike said, closing his eyes. "I'm going to miss Pam and Courtney, though. They were good for an old soldier's soul."

Mike slid the Maker's Mark around in a puddle of condensation as he waited for his table.

He'd been in the body and fender shop for over a month, long enough to be fully capable of getting around on his own, and then headed back to Islamorada. When he got there there was a cigarette boat tied up next to the *Winter Born*. It was black and silver with the legend "Too Late" already painted on the rear.

He'd taken it out a time or two, but mostly he'd stayed on the yacht. The explosion in the Andros was the talk of the town but nobody seemed to connect him to it, which was fine by him.

So he'd been doing his usual, hanging out, fishing, generally getting his head back together, working on his tan and new set of scars. But that meant he was back in the same lackanookie situation he'd been in before the girls showed up in his life. And he was pretty sure it was almost time to travel. It had been a while since he'd seen Europe and he'd never been to Eastern Europe. He was looking forward to traveling—among other things the

hookers in Eastern Europe were supposed to be the finest on earth—but something had kept him around. A nagging sense of something left unfinished.

He'd just glanced at his pager, wondering when his table was going to be ready, when a soft voice spoke behind him.

"Excuse me," the familiar voice said, "is this seat taken?"

Mike looked over his shoulder at Pam and Courtney and shrugged, grinning slightly.

"I dunno," he said. "I was waiting for some friends to show up. But it looks like they just did."

BOOK THREE
On the Dark Side

CHAPTER
ONE

"Come 'ere, lovely," Mike said, pulling a blonde into his lap as she walked past. The girl—she was probably no more than sixteen but nobody cared in a place like this—was wearing a thong and a garter stuffed with bills. She had very nice tits, large with small pink nipples and fricking gorgeous blue eyes, true cornflower blue, with that sexy Tartar lift that so many of the Russian girls sported. Great cheekbones. Gorgeous tits.

"You gonna show me a good time?" he asked, sliding a five euro note into the garter and playing with her nipple.

Mike had decided that he purely loved Eastern Europe. The living was cheap, not that that mattered much, and the women were *gorgeous*. It was more than the fact that they dressed to the nines to go to the grocery store and didn't tend to run to obesity. It must be pure breeding or something. Just gorgeous, one and all.

He'd started in Amsterdam, where he found out that most of the really good-looking hookers were Polish. Which had taken him to Poland, one damned beautiful country, where quite a few of the hookers were Lithuanian. This had led him to Lithuania, which he still felt had the best overall quality in Europe. But a bunch of the best-looking whores were from Russia, so he wandered that way. It was like that Beach Boys' song, but with lots

more screwing and some damned fine head. No training these girls; they were teaching him a thing or two.

"I show you very good time," the girl said, wriggling in his lap and leaning forward to breathe in his ear, her nipples rubbing on his chest. "I be very good to you and you give me much money."

Even in Russia he hadn't stayed in one place, generally moving further eastward. He'd been fascinated by Siberia since he was a kid and wanted to get a look at it. He'd made it as far as Perm, moving slow and taking his time with the girls. This place, though, was the back of beyond. But the girls were fantastic and the price was sure right. He figured this one would be less than fifty euros for the whole night. And he intended to have one hell of a time.

"Just another rich American," Mike snorted, starting to lift the girl up as another hooker sat down at the table.

"She has the pox," the woman said. She wasn't nearly as young, or pretty, as the girl on his lap. The term "rode hard and put up wet" came to mind. But she fixed him with her eye and shook her head. "Besides, you need to talk to me, not her. My name is Tanya."

"About what?" Mike asked, tickling the girl's nipple again.

The girl on his lap spat something in Russian at the newcomer and stuck out her tongue. Mike was picking up some of the local languages, but this was too fast for him to catch. He did catch the word for "old," though.

"Go away," the newcomer said. "He'll be around for you later. We need to talk."

"I'm not particularly interested in talking to you," Mike said, standing up and taking the girl's hand.

"You will be," the woman said, standing up and coming over to whisper in his ear. "You want a nuclear weapon?" she asked quietly.

Mike froze and leaned back, looking her in the eye. She regarded him calmly, then raised an eyebrow.

"Take off, honey," Mike said, pulling out another note without looking at it and handing it to the girl. "Me and Tanya gotta talk."

The girl looked at the money, then rolled her hand over it and walked away quickly.

"You're joking, right?" Mike said, sitting down and leaning back in his chair. The nearest patron in the dive was ten feet away, so they could talk without being overheard. He hoped. This was not something that you talked about in public. Or private. Hell, outside of a secure facility. "And why me?"

"I have been watching you," "Tanya" said. "Not only here. I have seen you in other places. You don't move like most of the Americans who come to places like this. They are fearful, afraid of being attacked. You move like . . . a panther. Everyone sees it. You are a player, as they say. And you are rich."

"And how would you know that?" Mike asked.

"You realized you just handed Lydia a hundred-euro note, right?" Tanya said, laughing.

"Shit," Mike snorted. "Is that what I did?"

"Yes," "Tanya" said dryly. "And a man who can hand a cheap whore a hundred euros without noticing it, might have the money to buy . . . what we have to sell. And . . . Americans, even 'player' Americans, are more trustworthy than Russians."

"And a man who had that much money might smell a rat," Mike said. "For that matter, the American government would buy it. Why don't you go to the embassy? Even a consulate?"

"Then there would be questions and problems . . ." the woman said, drawing the words out and shrugging. "That was talked about. As was simply pointing out their . . . misstep to the Russian government or selling it to an oligarch. I convinced them that I could find . . . a better buyer. One who would ask fewer questions."

"I'm going to ask a damned sight of questions," Mike said. "Because I smell what we call in America a con job."

"No con job," the woman said. "I can take you to a man who can explain where it came from. I can show you the . . . thing. You can test it as you wish."

"And if I agree to buy this item?" Mike said. "What in the hell do I do with it, then?"

"You are a player," the woman said, shrugging. "I can see that in your face, in your moves, in your eyes. You will already have an idea of what to do with it."

▲   ▲   ▲

If it wasn't a con job, it might be a roll. That was looking more and more likely as "Tanya" got out of the cab and waved him towards an alleyway.

Mike stepped out, though, walking carefully and following the old whore. He had his senses dialed up to code orange, expecting at any moment to hear a stealthy movement as someone tried to mug him, or a group of thugs to appear and tell him to give them all his money. He could give them everything he had on him—even the money in his jump bag—and it wouldn't make a dent in his bank account. But he was planning on shooting first and asking questions *much* later. Because Russian thugs tended to believe in the axiom that "dead men tell no tales."

But there were no thugs, no stealthy movements. The woman led him to a set of steps to a basement club, a dive to make his previous haunts look serene. The door was guarded by a bouncer, a big guy who looked as if he used to be on the Russian wrestling team. And he had a telltale bulge on his hip that said he was packed. Hell, from the looks of the room, most of the patrons were as packed as they were drunk.

The room stank of spilled vodka, body odor and cheap tobacco smoke with a faint underlay of puke and piss. The whores were nowhere near as pretty as at the club he had come from and the patrons were not much better: low-class factory workers, bums and pensioners. He saw a few uniforms in the place and the Red Army pay was notoriously low. If the hookers in this place cost more than *ten* euros a night, it was because they were farming out their daughters as well. Five-ruble stand-ups were probably the order of the day.

The woman led him to a table at the back where a Russian lieutenant was slumped, staring at a shot of vodka like it was the Holy Grail. He picked it up and downed it as they reached the table and shook his head.

"I have found someone who is interested in the item," Tanya said, sitting down with her back to the room, thus giving Mike the choice of a chair against the wall.

"It is too late," the Russian said, shrugging. "Those idiots..."

"What do you mean 'too late'?" the woman said, then broke into Russian.

The babble went back and forth and started to rise in volume as Mike surveyed the room.

"Uh, folks," Mike said, waving a hand between them. "I don't know what you are saying, but keep it the fuck down, okay?"

"He said that his men that were guarding the item have already sold it," Tanya snapped. "He thinks it was to Chechens."

"Okay, now this is bad," Mike said angrily. "And this is no place to be discussing it. First things first," he continued, digging in his pocket. "Tanya, go get a bottle of the most decent vodka they have in this place. When you do, we are getting the fuck out and taking this conversation to a hotel room, pronto."

"Okay," Mike said when they were in his hotel room. It was the best hotel in town, but it still would be a low-end Best Western in the U.S. It dated from the Soviet era and the construction showed: cheap carpets, horrible beds, lousy plumbing and walls of cast concrete that were flaking onto the cheap carpet. "Start at the beginning, go through the middle and get to now." He placed the vodka on the table and waved at it. "You can have as much of that as you need, as long as you can keep talking."

The lieutenant looked at the bottle for a moment and then shrugged.

"We are guards on an old nuclear facility," he said, picking up the bottle, tearing off the thin metal cap and putting a splash of vodka in a glass. "Was accident in it, long ago. Is contaminated. But still stores some nuclear material, what they call isotopes."

"I know what an isotope is," Mike said, pouring himself some vodka and downing it. It was very, very bad. "Go on," he gasped.

"Americans cannot handle their liquor," "Tanya" said, pouring her own shot.

"There's liquor and then there's ant piss," Mike said, waving at the bottle. "You can have all that ant piss you want. Keep going."

"Is very boring," the lieutenant said. "We are not to go in facility, but we get bored. We have radiation detectors. Is not so bad in most places. One of my men, Yuri, is very bored. He goes in facility. Is much of it underground. Is flooded, yes?"

"Yeah," Mike said, thinking about groundwater contamination. But the whole of Eastern Europe was still such a cesspool from "enlightened Communism" and its approach to environmentalism that a nuclear facility leaking radioactive isotopes into the groundwater was barely a blip on the screen.

"So he finds part where flooding is not so bad," the lieutenant continued. "And goes back up. There he finds . . . item."

"Let's get specific," Mike said. "Are we talking a gravity bomb or a warhead or what?"

"Is very old warhead," the lieutenant said, shrugging. "We cannot get manuals but Yuri is interested in these things. Thinks it was warhead from old missile. Is shaped like warhead," he said, making a cone shape in the air, "and is very radioactive."

"So Yuri ran and told you?" Mike asked.

"No," the lieutenant admitted. "Tells others. Is . . . big fight. Yuri is wanting to tell government. Others, Oleg especially, want to sell to anyone. I am told by platoon sergeant. We all agree that I will find a *good* buyer. I sign myself on pass, yes? Know Tanya from . . . before. She knows people, so I tell her. We think, is much money, enough we can share. But . . . while I wait, Oleg is found buyer. They come and bring money. Platoon sells while I am gone. I find out tonight." He stopped and poured another, large, shot and downed it. "Is gone. So is Oleg, went with buyer. Others have deserted, are afraid of what will happen when government finds out."

"How much money did they get?" Tanya asked, angrily.

"Ten thousand euros," the lieutenant said, shrugging. "Is not much, split up among platoon. Oleg takes nothing, goes with buyers."

"Ten grand?" Mike snapped. "That's *it*?"

"The buyers, they say that it is training weapon," the lieutenant said, shrugging. "Is not real weapon. And they offer money *now*. Have it in hand. Is gone," he repeated, shrugging again.

"Like hell," Mike said, shaking his head. "Look, we *have* to find this nuke. I don't think for a second it was a 'training round.' Why in the hell would they *buy* a training round? And why was it radioactive?"

"They say is for training," the lieutenant said. "I don't believe either. But they have money."

"Well, we're in a right pickle," Mike said, thinking hard. "We're going to have to come clean, tell the American government and then tell the *Russian* government. The *American* government will cover you as best they can *if* you get us all the information you have on the buyers. Because we're going to have to track this mother down before it gets refurbished and used."

"What is it with you, Mike?" Colonel Pierson yelled over the wash from the helicopter. "Can't stay away?" The colonel was wearing an Extreme Cold Weather Gortex suit over BDUs, a necessity for the day.

It was early fall but the weather was more like winter, a cold wind blowing from the north and a light dusting of snow already on the ground. The hard-looking clouds overhead presaged more bad weather to come.

The helicopter had landed in a brush-grown field right outside the gates to the facility. The facility was mostly crumbling Soviet-era buildings with one fixed up to house the "guard" platoon. All of it was overrun with weeds with the exception of a small area around the barracks and the gravel road leading in and out. Beyond the fence, with the exception of the clearing where the helicopter had landed, fir and pine trees stretched for miles into the almost limitless Siberian taiga.

"Bad luck," Mike answered, shaking his hand and looking at the Russian colonel who was following him.

"This is Colonel Erkin Chechnik," Pierson said, waving at the Red Army colonel. "Russian Intelligence. Sort of my opposite number; he works in an office that briefs Putin."

"Pleased to meet you, Colonel," Mike said, taking the Russian's hand.

"Am wishing I could say the same," the colonel said. "Is very embarrassing for my country."

"Shit happens," Mike replied. "Look, we're not going to get diddly, short of harsh interrogation methods, from these guys if . . ."

"Is covered as you Americans say," the colonel said, shaking his head. "As long as are giving answers, is not a problem. And the American government is going to be . . . how you say? Supplementing their salary," he added, glancing at Pierson.

"As soon as we have all the answers we can get," Pierson said, "the platoon, and the hooker, have a one-way trip to the Land of the Free and an entrée into the Witness Protection Program. If they come clean."

"Okay," Mike said, blowing out. "Most of the platoon had already deserted when we got here. Sergeant Oleg Zazulya was the ringleader of the sale. He left with the buyers. The rest ran off on their own, taking the platoon truck. The only remaining witnesses are Sergeant Ivar Fadzaev, the platoon sergeant, and Private Yuri Khabelov. They're in the barracks, hoping like hell that I can work a miracle on their behalf."

"What about the hooker?" Pierson asked. "We want to cover this up entirely."

"She's here, too," Mike said. "And by cover up, I assume we're not talking graves. These guys seem to be . . . sort of patriots. As close as you get among the narod in Russia."

"No graves," Colonel Chechnik said, shaking his head. "Just questions, yes?"

"Yes," Mike said. "Well, let's get to it."

"Hello, Private Khabelov," Colonel Chechnik said. The interrogation was taking place in the lieutenant's old office with the Russian colonel behind the desk and Mike and Pierson on a ratty couch. The room was sparsely decorated with a single picture of Putin on the wall and a small representation of the Russian flag behind the desk. The private was standing at attention, sweating in the cold room, clearly wishing he'd cut and run.

"The American colonel is Robert Pierson, a man who speaks directly to their president and I speak to President Putin. The colonel speaks Russian but his fellow does not. I understand you have good English so please use it. As you were told, you have been promised emigration to America, if you wish, if you give us all the information you have about the weapon and those who took it. Alternatively, you will be given money and, if you wish, an honorable discharge from the Russian military and can remain in Russia. But you *must* give us all the information you have. Do you understand?"

"Yes, Colonel," the private replied. "I will give you all the information I have, freely. And if I may remain in the Motherland I would prefer it."

"This is good," the colonel said, sighing. "Your lieutenant has opted to go to America, but your sergeant also wishes to remain. I am glad for this. So, tell me what you know about the weapon. And take a position of at-ease, if you will."

"It was on the second level below ground," the private said, dropping to something that was more like parade rest. "In a room marked C-142. It was conical shaped, about a meter and a half long and perhaps two thirds of a meter wide at the base. There were no markings on the exterior, but on the base there was a plate, perhaps steel, with a number inscribed. It was corroded," he reached in his breast pocket and pulled out a sheet of paper, "but I could make out the numbers 7493. We moved it up to the upper levels and secured it in a top-side weapons locker. After it was determined to . . ." He paused and swallowed. "Colonel, I argued to turn the weapon over to the government . . ."

"So I have been told," the colonel said, nodding in understanding. "This reflects well upon you. But . . ." he added, shrugging, "there is great corruption in Russia. And the Red Army is not well paid. This I know and have argued against, for this sort of reason if no other. Do not worry about the decision, just give us the facts."

"Very well, Colonel," the boy replied, swallowing again. "The lieutenant went to town to try to find a buyer for the weapon. While he was gone, two men arrived in a white van, a nine-passenger Mercedes van with tinted windows. The license plate had been removed. Oleg met them at the gate, as if the meeting had been prearranged, and let them in the compound. Sergeant Fadzaev ordered us to prepare our weapons, but Oleg said that they were potential buyers. They appeared to be unarmed. They were not Russian; they spoke with an accent that . . . well, if I was to guess I'd say Chechen, and Sergeant Fadzaev agreed. They were dark-skinned and had black hair: real black-asses. They looked at the weapon and told us it was a practice system, that the radiation was from isotopes that were in it to make it seem like a real bomb. They said that they wanted it

for the isotopes, since they could be resold, but that it was not worth much.

"We discussed it a long time, everyone was involved. They had brought vodka and we drank, although they did not. They had ten thousand euros with them and most of the platoon thought that since the lieutenant had been gone for almost a week, we should take the money and be done with it. There was . . . great fear that the government would find out and take it from us, and that we would get in trouble for not having reported it and trying to sell it. Finally, most of the platoon decided that they should sell it for the ten thousand. I and Sergeant Fadzaev disagreed but . . . everyone was armed and we could tell that if we didn't agree to selling it . . . we might be killed. When it was agreed, the weapon was loaded in the back of the van, the men gave us the money and then they left. Oleg went with them. The rest of the platoon became frightened about what might happen if the government found out. I stayed with Sergeant Fadzaev in his quarters, with both of us keeping watch. In the middle of the night, we heard the platoon truck start up and then drive out of the compound. We went to investigate and found the rest of the platoon gone. It was then that Sergeant Fadzaev called the lieutenant and told him what had happened."

"Two dark-skinned, black-haired, possibly Chechen males in a white, nine-passenger Mercedes van with tinted windows," Colonel Pierson said, sighing. "Same from both witnesses. And not much to go on."

"Why a *passenger* van?" Mike asked, puzzled. "Why not a panel van if they knew what they were buying?"

"I dunno," Pierson said. "But we've got the information; it's up to others to analyze it. Colonel," he said, turning to Chechnik, "we need to get the FSB involved as soon as possible. And I'd like to turn all this over to our intel people, start seeing if the weapon is going out of Russia."

"I am thinking it is headed for Chechnya," the colonel said. "Or for a Russian city."

"That's an internal Russian matter," Pierson said. "Although, if we develop any leads, we'll turn them over to you of course.

But we need to get moving on the basis that it's going to go in play *outside* of Russia."

"*Da*," the Russian said, nodding. "The helicopter will take you to Perm and there is a jet waiting to take you to Moscow."

"Colonel," Mike said, standing up, "no unmarked graves."

"Not for these," the colonel said, waving at the still nervous private. "But if I find this Oleg fellow . . ."

"I'll hand you the shovel," Mike replied.

CHAPTER
TWO

"Chatham Aviation, Gloria speaking, how may I help you?"

"Hi, the name's Mike Jenkins," Mike shouted over the racket from the Russian Hip helicopter. He knew diddly about Chatham Aviation, but they came up high on Google for "charter aircraft business jet" and their website promised on-call service. "I need a jet in Moscow. I don't know where I'm going to be going from there, but I need it there as soon as it can get there. I'll pay layabout fees or whatever. Something small and fast."

"Layover," the receptionist corrected. "I don't seem to find an account for you, Mr. . . . Jenkins."

"I've never used you," Mike said. "I got your name from the Internet. I figured an English company would have English-speaking pilots and I don't have time to wait on one from the States. I really need a jet, quick."

"Mike," Pierson said, "we can get you transport."

"Hold one," Mike said into the phone, hitting the mute. "I don't want to be begging for transport, Bob," he said, shrugging at the colonel. "And I figure I can afford a charter." He unmuted to the sound of the receptionist talking to someone in the background. "Is there a problem?"

"No problem, Mr. Jenkins," Gloria said. "Chartering a jet is . . ."

"Expensive, I know," Mike said sharply. "I take it you take American Express?"

"We *do*," the receptionist said cautiously. "However . . ."

"It's got a hundred-thousand-dollar line," Mike said. "And it's paid up. Or I can hand your pilots a sack of cash. I need a jet and I need one *now*. Or do I call the next charter company on the list?"

"Not a problem, Mr. Jenkins," Gloria said. "Hold on while I take your information . . ."

"Everybody's running around like a chicken with its head cut off, Colonel."

Tech Sergeant Walter Johnson was career Air Force. He'd started off in satellite imagery and had slowly migrated to general intel and analysis. He was the only analyst currently assigned to the American embassy in Moscow and, as such, he was very busy. But he'd seen the directive for Colonel Pierson and the civilian he'd mentally pegged as CIA spec ops, Mike Jenkins. So when Pierson had come in with his latest intel dump, he'd dropped everything else on his desk. They were meeting in a secure room and Johnson had brought in a disc with his current analysis to use on the room's computer.

"Normal in the early stages of the game," Pierson said, sighing, "all the intel groups will be going ape-shit and the spec-ops boys will be running scenarios. What's the current playboard look like?"

"Well, you didn't give us much to go on," Johnson admitted. "Right now, the current thinking is that it's a Chechen operation. The Chechens, though, don't have anyone we know of who can do work with a nuke. So they'll probably sell it to someone or do a combined op. Whatever they do, whoever uses it, they'll have to call in an expert."

Johnson brought up an image on the screen of a "Middle Eastern Male."

"Assadolah Shaath," Johnson said. "The most likely 'expert.' Thirty-seven. Born in Islamabad, Pakistan. Dad is a minor official in the government. Educated at boarding schools in Pakistan and England, took a BS in Physics at Reading University and was

working on his masters at Princeton when he was recruited by the Popular Front for the Islamic Jihad. Also picked up a BA in English literature, of all things, while at Princeton, centering on nineteenth- and twentieth-century American poets. Wrote a very nice paper on Longfellow, according to his analyst, and was a big fan of Poe. Went to Poe's grave and such like. Sexual tastes run to long, slim blondes. Reported to be rather heavy handed with them. Also likes rock and roll, heavy metal and Goth music."

"Great," Mike grumped. "A mujahideen poet-engineer with my same sexual and musical interests. Just what we need."

"Trained in Afghanistan in mujahideen techniques," Johnson continued, frowning slightly at the input. "Appears on several captured Al Qaeda lists as an 'engineer,' what we would call a demolitions expert. Appeared to be working on nuclear assembly with the Al Qaeda, unsuccessfully. Possibly worked with the Pakistani nuclear program for up to a year. Possibly connected to the Shoe Bomber, Richard Reid. Tagged as one of the mujahideen involved in the Andros Incident, but that might be false info since there's a high probability he was spotted by a Mossad informant in Lebanon three months ago."

"One of them got away," Mike pointed out. "The one that armed the nuke."

"Really?" Johnson said, looking at his notes. "I don't have that."

"Trust me," Mike said. "Your intel is wrong. The one that got away probably set the timer."

"You're sure?" Johnson asked, quizzically.

"He's sure," Pierson said dryly. "Go on."

"Ooo-kay," Johnson said, reevaluating the civilian. "He's the top guy for potential weapons refiguring that we know of. There are two others that have almost his training and background. We've got a call in to Mossad to see if they can track him down."

"Preferably followed by a nine millimeter to the medulla," Mike said. "What about the van?"

"Lots of Mercedes vans running around," Johnson said. "The FSB has an all points out for it, but don't get your hopes up. It's probably in Chechnya or Georgia already."

"I'm bugged by one thing," Mike said. "It was a passenger van. Why a passenger van?"

"I'd thought about the same thing," Johnson admitted. "And I've got an idea, but it's a long-shot." He brought up a picture of a similar van. This one was apparently filled with people, and unless Mike was mistaken, they were all female except the driver. "The Chechens are into everything you can think of in the way of illegal moneymaking. Money laundering, drugs, gun running, what have you. All of them aren't funding the resistance in Chechnya, but a good bit of the money flows that way. But one of the things they're into is the sex trade."

"Slaving," Mike said.

"Bingo," Johnson replied. "It's not exactly the way that it's portrayed in the news media, though. Yeah, some of the girls *are* snatched off the street. But most of them are *sold* by people that have authority over them. Parents, orphanages, what have you. The Chechens go on regular rounds and gather up girls, then sell them to various buyers."

"There's a main market," Pierson said. "Eagle Market in Bosnia."

"Agreed," Johnson said. "I ran that idea past the analysts and Langley and they put it as a low-order probability. The max prob is the device is going through Georgia or St. Petersburg to be shipped elsewhere, or down to Chechnya, possibly into Georgia, to be refurbished and used against the Russians."

"Yeah," Mike said. "But if it's internal to Russia, it's not our ballgame. And all of that more or less ignores the passenger van anomaly."

"You want to try to track it?" Pierson asked.

"That's why I'm here," Mike replied. "And why I put that jet on standby. Do we have anyone in Bosnia that's a kind of expert in the slave trade?"

"I don't have that info right here," Johnson said. "But I can round it up."

"Call me," Mike replied, standing up. "Pierson will give you my scrambler code."

"You're going to Bosnia?" Pierson asked. "Now?"

"Better now than later," Mike said, shrugging. "We're five

days behind them. I don't know how long it takes to refurbish a nuke . . ."

"Depending upon their equipment," Johnson interjected, "as little as ten hours. I checked. If they're planning on planting it somewhere, they'll probably trap it. Longer for that."

"But we don't have all the time in the world," Mike finished, looking at the face of the terrorist "engineer" and burning it into his brain. "When I get there, I'm going to need a radiation detector. Preferably something I can secret on my person and use covertly."

"We can do that," Pierson said, standing up as well. "I'll get you a contact in IFOR to get the stuff and the name of a person to guide you around."

"Johnson, thanks for the brief," Mike said, walking to the door. "And you need to update your intel. At the island—one got away."

"Yes, sir," Johnson said as Mike left the room. "Although, I'd love to know where he gets *his* intel. As far as I knew, just about everybody on that island got vaporized. And I didn't know that the guy who armed the nuke escaped."

"Let's just say that some people are tough to get an after-actions report out of," Pierson replied with a sigh.

The Gulfstream V was sitting at an out-of-the-way hangar at Moscow International when Mike arrived. He paid off the taxi driver and strode over, his jump bag on his shoulder. It was all the luggage he was carrying. It held the usual toiletries, a couple of pairs of socks and underpants and two shirts. Between that and the jacket and jeans he was wearing, he figured it would do. It also held his "walking-around money," about sixty thousand dollars in mixed euros and dollars, mostly hundreds. The door of the plane was open and the steps down, but nobody seemed to be around.

"Hello, the plane," he called, stepping up to the door.

"Mr. Jenkins?" the pilot asked, stepping out of the cockpit. He had a strong southern British accent and a military bearing. Mike pegged him immediately for former Royal Air Force.

"The same," Mike replied, handing over his entirely fictitious passport.

"John Hardesty, sir," the pilot said handing back the passport after a searching study. "I'm pleased to be piloting you to wherever your destination might be."

"Former military?" Mike asked, stepping past him and tossing his jump bag on one of the front seats.

"Astute of you to guess, sir," the pilot replied neutrally.

"Okay," Mike said, shrugging. "RAF . . . Tornadoes. Close?"

"Bang on, sir," the pilot replied, frowning.

"And you got out as . . . oh, a major I'd say," Mike continued, grinning. "Because you could see from there on out it was going to be, at best, squadron command and much more likely a coalition staff position. Flying was going to go away."

"Did you read my bio or something?" Hardesty asked, going from somewhat annoyed to amused.

"No," Mike replied, shrugging. "Just a very 'astute' judge of character. Bit of a hobby figuring out plane drivers' backgrounds."

"And may I ask what your profession is, sir?" Hardesty queried carefully.

"I do odd jobs," Mike replied, sitting in one of the forward seats.

"If you'll pardon me, sir," the pilot said, still curious. "You don't get the money to charter a jet, much less have it sit around on call, by digging ditches with a shovel."

"I've used a shovel in my time," Mike said, smiling broadly. "But I usually prefer to find the local guy with a backhoe. Quicker and easier to hide the bodies. You ready to go?"

"Of course, sir," the pilot said, reevaluating his passenger. "We're refueled. I need to do a preflight."

"Make it snappy, please," Mike said, pulling out his satellite phone. "I'm in a bit of hurry."

"Well, Mr. Jenkins," Hardesty replied, smiling faintly, "it would help if we knew where we were going."

"Someplace in Bosnia," Mike said. "Just head for Sarajevo and I'll try to get a better read when we're in-flight. I'm expecting some calls."

Mike looked out at the tiny airport that served the town of Herzjac and thought about its recent history.

Herzjac was on the border of Serbia and Bosnia-Herzegovina, just over the Bosnian side. The Bosnian civil war had raged for years, with the various factions gaining and losing ground. As soon as it broke out, the UN, with the connivance of the Russians and certain European countries, notably France and Germany, had slapped a weapons embargo on the entire region. The problem with that was that the Serbians had, traditionally, held most of the military bases and production in their areas. Tito had been a Serb, and while forcing everyone into a "pan-Slavic" society, he had ensured that some Slavs were more equal than others. Since Russia and France had long running ties to the Serbian factions, it quickly became clear that rather than being a "humanitarian" move, the weapons embargo was designed to disarm, and keep disarmed, the "other" sides of the multisided war.

This meant that the Serbians had an immediate jump-start in the war and they had pressed their advantage home mercilessly. Thousands had been killed in the fighting and in "ethnic cleansing" in areas the Serbs overran. Of course, they were not the only perpetrators; when Croats or Bosnian Muslims retook regions that had been "ethnically cleansed" of their families, they were less than gentle with the Serbian inhabitants.

There had been various attempts to bring peace, but it wasn't until the U.S. stepped in, covertly, that peace had actually been possible. The U.S. had secretly supplied the Croatians with training personnel, equipment and even real-time intelligence. Using those assets, the Croatians had retrained their army along American lines and used American real-time intel and "shock" tactics, multipronged heavy armor converging columns, to entrap the main Serb field army and virtually destroy it.

The surprise of having the Croats, whom they had been forcing back left and right, suddenly show such massive competence, not to mention military intelligence and supplies, had driven the Serbs to the bargaining table. At Wright-Patrick Air Force Base, outside of Dayton, Ohio, the Serbs had been forced to sign the Dayton Accords, fixing the borders of their country and those of the Bosnians and Croats and permitting an "Implementation Force," IFOR, to enter the various countries and *enforce* peace on all sides.

So when IFOR arrived, the obvious place for it to set up was Herzjac, one of the most embattled towns in the war.

IFOR consisted of an American mechanized infantry or armor division, depending upon what was available to deploy, along with a large number of "allied" support personnel. When the Americans arrived, as Americans do, they had first set up a large and virtually impregnable camp in a manner very much like the Roman Legions. But they were in the country to do far more than just enforce peace. The "nation builders" among the State Department, and the military, quickly went to work trying to "rebuild the local economy." Besides letting contracts to local firms for everything from laundry service to construction, they set up a market outside the base. Since the base was named Eagle Base, they naturally named it Eagle Market. It was something of a flea market, initially selling everything from cheap Southeast Asian electronics to shoes. Security was provided by the U.S. military and it quickly was recognized as the most secure such market in Eastern Europe.

It was that security that drew the slavers. Just like drug dealers, slavers had their conflicts. Fights over bad deals, fights over the girls, fights over "turf," fights over bad blood between different ethnic groups or clans. But in Eagle Market, they were on neutral territory. The U.S. military prevented the conflicts from getting out of hand.

The military quickly became aware of what was going on and a very covert discussion broke out. On one hand, the chain of command was horrified. Slavery, especially slavery of rather young and almost invariably pretty to beautiful girls, was against everything the U.S. military believed in. The motto of the Special Forces is *De Opresso Liber*: To Liberate the Oppressed. But it was a motto that *any* American fighting man, or woman, would agree with. However, short of eliminating the slave trade, there was no way to stop the dealing from going on. And at least in Eagle Market the military could prevent the worst of sins being committed against them.

So a tacit "ignorance" existed, with American MPs strolling past men with strings of girls, bluntly, for sale. It was uncomfortable on many levels, especially since many if not most of the hookers

in Herzjac, whose primary customer base were the enlisted men and officers of IFOR, had passed through Eagle Market. But the situation was still maintained.

As the plane rolled to a stop outside of an outlying hangar, a Mercedes sedan pulled up alongside. Before the customs vehicle could reach the plane, a man in a suit stepped out carrying a briefcase.

Mike saw the sedan inbound and by the time the plane stopped he had the hatch undogged. As the man reached the plane, he flipped down the stairs and stepped back.

"Mr. Duncan," the man said, stepping up into the plane and setting his briefcase on the front seat. "I'm Charles Northcote, the IFOR liaison at the American embassy in Sarajevo."

"Pleased to meet you," Mike said, frowning curiously.

"I have your documents here," the man continued, pulling out a manila envelope and handing it to Mike. "I think you'll find they're all in order."

Mike frowned again and opened up the envelope, spilling it out on one of the seats. There was a diplomatic passport in the name of Michael Duncan along with various secondary IDs. A Florida driver's license, American Express, Visa and hotel "frequent user" cards. All the usual things that a frequent traveler would carry.

He dumped out his pockets and started changing out materials as Mr. Northcote continued to speak.

"You're checked in to the Hotel Krcelic. It's a pensione in Herzjac on a side street. I'll take you there and drop you off after I deal with customs. Mr. Dukhovic is going to meet you there this evening. He's a former slaver who now does various odd jobs for the embassy."

"An intel source?" Mike asked. "I don't want to burn one of your sources."

"Your cover is that you're a State Department official investigating the slave trade," Mr. Northcote said. "It's well known that Mr. Dukhovic is a source for us. He also is a source for the French, the British, the Russians, what have you."

"Well, we're not investigating the slave trade," Mike said, finishing switching his documents and putting his "real" stuff in the open envelope. "Are you briefed on what I'm here for?"

"Fully," Northcote said, smiling faintly. "I'm the Bosnian Station Chief. And I've got my other sources looking as well. I think it's a long ball play, but sometimes they go right. Oh, and on that subject," he continued, dipping back into his attaché case and pulling out a device covered in wires. "This is a Geiger counter. There's an earbud that can be run up through your clothing. Not entirely invisible, unfortunately, but unobtrusive. The detector goes down your arm and the counter clips to the waist."

"Perfect," Mike said, taking the device.

"I'll go talk to customs while you get the rest of your gear in order," Northcote said, handing him a card. "By the way, technically diplomats are not to be armed. But since you also cannot be arrested, or even detained, carrying is not an issue. Just don't carry anything that can't be concealed. If you run into shooting trouble, call me and I'll call in IFOR. They have an alert team standing by in support, and we have nuclear specialists who are currently in Germany but can be here in a couple of hours. I'll go take care of customs."

Mike dumped the detector in his jump bag and took the envelope to the cockpit.

"The gentleman is going to be clearing me through customs," Mike said to the pilot. "Hang onto this for me and put it in a secure location on the plane. As long as it doesn't leave the plane, it doesn't come to the attention of customs, right?"

"Yes," Hardesty said uncertainly.

"You've got a manifest, right?" Mike said. "The name of the passenger is now 'Duncan, Michael.'" Mike handed him his new passport and smiled thinly. "Bosnian customs will know damned well that's not my name and not make an issue of it. But from now through the end of the charter, that's the name."

The pilot regarded the passport warily, but opened it up and noted the data on a pad.

"This is . . . rather irregular," he said, then shrugged. "But you don't jolly well get diplo passports if you're a drug dealer."

"Nor do you if you're CIA or any of the rest of the alphabet," Mike said, taking his passport back. "I don't know when I'm going to be leaving. Give me a number I can call you at and you'll have to be on call. So . . . stay off the sauce, if you will."

"We'd planned on that, lad," Hardesty said, handing him a card with his cell phone number on it. "No idea at all where we're going next?"

"Hopefully I'll find out here," Mike replied.

CHAPTER THREE

The Hotel Krcelic was similar to other pensiones Mike had stayed in. Pensiones were somewhere between a "regular" hotel and a bed and breakfast. Most resembled ancient inns and many of them dated from the Middle Ages. This one was in an old limestone-block building with vaguely baroque architecture that probably dated to the seventeenth or eighteenth century. The interior was heavy wood and dark, but the second-story room, one of only six in the whole "hotel," was well lit by a southern window. The bed was heavy wood with two eiderdown mattresses; in cold weather the upper mattress acted as a quilt and sleeping in one was like being wrapped in silken warmth. Mike looked at the bed longingly—he was on about forty hours of straight ops at this point—then hooked up the Geiger counter with the receiver run down his left arm and went down to the bar.

He'd just ordered a Johnny Walker Black, bourbon being unavailable, when a man sat down next to him.

"Mr. Duncan," the man said, holding out his hand, "I am pleased to finally meet you. Janus Dukhovic." The man was just above six feet tall, heavy-set, with close-spaced eyes and a thin face that stood out oddly from his heavy girth. He had black hair and black eyes that were cold and hard.

"Mr. Dukhovic," Mike said, shaking his hand and waving at the bartender. "Would you care for a taste to cut the dust?"

"Of course," Dukhovic said. "I'm always willing to drink for free."

When the drinks arrived, they moved to one of the booths and toasted.

"To IFOR," Dukhovic said dryly.

"To peace between nations," Mike replied just as dryly, taking a sip of the scotch. "What were you told?"

"That you want to look at the slave trade," Dukhovic said, shrugging and pulling out a Marlboro. As he lit it he continued. "I have toured many people around the slave trade. Most of them, I think, enjoy the sight," he added, smiling brutally and blowing out smoke. "I had two congressmen once that were so excited I think they nearly came in their pants."

"I'm sure," Mike said coldly. "I'm less interested in the girls than in how they are transported. I understand that the vehicle of choice is a nine-passenger Mercedes van, usually white, usually with tinted windows."

"This is true," Dukhovic said, puffing on the cigarette nervously and reevaluating the man across from him.

"I need to find as many of those vans as possible," Mike continued. "And walk near them. Ones that are carrying girls are lowest on the list. The girls are usually traded at Eagle Market, right? But they don't stay there overnight, true?"

"True," Dukhovic said, blowing out a smoke ring. "There are various houses in the town that their protectors keep."

"Where are the majority of the vans going to be?"

"During the day at the parking lot at Eagle Market," Dukhovic said, shrugging. "They tend to be clustered in the southwest quadrant."

Mike looked at his watch and frowned.

"We're going to be at this for a while," Mike said. "Maybe the rest of the day and well into the night. Are you up to that?"

"Of course," Dukhovic said, putting out his cigarette. "When do you want to start?"

"Now," Mike replied, downing his drink.

▲   ▲   ▲

"There are dozens of protectors in the town," Dukhovic said as they drove through Herzjac in his ancient Peugeot, the springs complaining at the rough ride. Much of the town was paved with asphalt, but it was sketchily patched and sometimes seemed to have more potholes than pavement. "And dozens of houses. And all of the dealing does not occur in Eagle Market. Some of the finest girls never go there, but are traded at the houses."

"Van," Mike said, gesturing with his chin down an alleyway.

"You wish to stop?" Dukhovic said, looking for a parking place. The street was lined with cars, however.

"Just drop me off and circle around to the other block," Mike replied. "I'll walk down the alley and meet you there. Be aware that I'm, we're, probably going to be walking as much as driving."

Mike slid out of the Peugeot and through a couple of cars to the street. There were shops lining the street, some of them starting to close, and a few pedestrians. He strolled to the alleyway, then turned down it, looking around in interest. Most of the buildings in Herzjac were built of limestone block like the pensione, with a scattering of Soviet-era concrete. As they had driven, he had seen still visible signs of the fighting in the area, mostly bullet pockmarks, but also some homes that had clearly suffered from artillery shelling. There were a large number of tree stumps, a clear sign of a town that had been under siege.

The alleyway was cobbled, with many of the cobbles missing, and stunk of garbage and shit. There was debris scattered through it, mostly newspapers and garbage.

The van was parked by a side door to a three-story building on the far street. The door was metal and well set into the frame, not that he particularly cared. He was more interested in whether he could be observed as he walked past the van and casually raised his hand towards it, lifting it further to scratch his head. Nothing. He needed to get a radiation source to test it.

He kept walking to the far block and looked around for the Peugeot. Dukhovic had passed his position and was pulled in to a free parking place, so he strolled over to the car and got in.

"What I just did is what I'm here for," Mike said. "You're the expert, tell me the best way to do it."

"Over in Serb town is where most of the houses are," Dukhovic

replied, thinking. "I'd suggest we get dinner, wait for the girls to start coming back to the houses and then walk around. It might take most of the night, maybe part of tomorrow, but we can cover all the vans that way."

"Security issues?" Mike asked as Dukhovic pulled out into traffic.

"There are some robbers in the area," the Croat said, lighting a cigarette as he drove. "And if it becomes obvious the protectors may get upset."

"Can you cover us on it?" Mike asked, looking around as they drove. The girls in this town were just as awesome as in the rest of Eastern Europe. Maybe it was something in the water?

"No," Dukhovic said shortly, blowing smoke out the window. "When the market was first set up, the routes had every nation plying their trade. Bulgarians were prominent, but they didn't dominate or anything. But about five years back, the Chechens started getting into it in a big way and there was . . . call it a slave war. Lots of killing. Not as bad as the real wars, but very bad and very bad for the trade. Anyway, now most of the protectors are fucking Chechens. I got out when I saw it coming, but a bunch of my friends who stayed in the business are dead from the damned Chechens."

"Same thing happened in the U.S., twice," Mike said. "The cocaine trade in the southeastern U.S. used to be mainly internal. They received their shipments and distributed, but the guys who ran the internal distribution were mostly American background. Heavy Mafia influence, but even that wasn't dominant. Then, well, there was this thing called the Mariel Boatlift in the 1970s, under that bastard idjit Carter. Castro agreed to let people who were 'longing for freedom' come to the United States. What he *really* did was empty out his prisons. Not even the *political* prisons, just the prisons with all his real criminals in them. Burglars, murderers, rapists, armed robbers. So south Florida got about ten thousand criminals dropped on it, really brutal ones. They quickly took over the drug trade. Anyone who got in their way they just eliminated without making any fuss about it at all.

"Then in the 1980s, when the crack wave hit, the Columbians came in, heavy. They had soldiers who were trained in their civil

war and it was even more brutal than when the Marielitos took over. Lots of use of automatic weapons, which had been fairly unusual up to that time. They're still in control. So I know what you mean."

They had dinner in a small restaurant, eating a sort of stew that wasn't too bad. There was dark bread with it that was particularly good, as was the red wine. Mike wasn't sure what the meat in the stew was but he'd learned not to ask too many questions about foreign food. Fortunately, Europe wasn't into dog and cat the way the Orient was.

After finishing off the bottle of wine and a pastry something like baklava, they got back in the car and headed for "Serb town," Dukhovic chain-smoking the whole way.

Mike could tell right away that this was one of the older parts of the town. The streets were narrow as hell and the alleys were overhung by the buildings. Some of them were simple enough to date back to the late medieval period. There were some Soviet architecture buildings as well; the cheap concrete the Soviets used was famous for being cracked and worn by time.

They found an open parking place, got out and started walking.

There were a few people walking the streets; from their hurried walk Mike guessed that they were on the way home and just hoping to get there before being mugged. The muggers and drug dealers were in evidence, standing on street corners or in the shadows of the alleys. But Mike and Dukhovic were clearly not their sort of target. Mike was on full orange alert as he walked, and his attitude was easy enough to read. It was a sort of crackling tension that said: "This may be your turf. But I'm a big dog and just passing through so don't get busy." Even the junkies they saw gave them a wide berth.

Besides the drug dealers, junkies, losers and thugs, there were lots and lots of white vans. They seemed to be everywhere, parked on the streets, parked in the alleys, sitting in lots by apartment buildings. Many of them had license plates from other countries: Russia, Georgia, Bulgaria, Ukraine. Mike got tired of trying to keep up, but he also didn't want to double up, so he wrote down a bit of the tag number of each as they passed.

They stayed at it all night, covering just about every street in Serb town, watching the street people gradually fade away into the night.

"I am getting quite tired," Dukhovic said towards dawn.

"I've been up for about fifty-six hours," Mike replied. "If I can keep going, so can you. Have we covered the whole area?"

"There is a section of small warehouses," Dukhovic said, yawning and pointing. "That way, about two kilometers. Usually not many protectors over there, but they sometimes use the houses along the river."

"Well, I'm willing to ride," Mike said, looking around. "The car's about three blocks that way, right?"

"Yes," Dukhovic replied, heading towards the car. "What is it you are looking for? I see that you are waving a device at the vans."

"The Chechens stole some radioactive isotopes from the Russians," Mike lied. "Not enough to make much of a radiological bomb, but we think they're planning something like it. The device is a radiation detector."

"Don't they have those sorts of things on helicopters?" Dukhovic asked, confused and tired.

"Yeah," Mike said. "But nobody thinks they're coming here except me. I guess the detectors are all being used in Russia."

They got in the car and drove around the section of warehouses, looking for white vans. These buildings were almost all Soviet-style architecture, running close to the river, which had a small port. Finally, Mike spotted a van on a side street and waved Dukhovic to stop.

He got out and walked down the street, casually, as he had at least a hundred times that night. As he waved his arm at the van, though, his ear was practically blasted by a screech from the Geiger counter. He could vaguely see into the van as he passed, and it had had the seats removed. It also had a Russian license plate. Pay dirt.

He continued walking to the far end, though, just another night person on the way home. Or, as it may be, going down to the river. The warehouses petered out short of the road that paralleled the river and there were more of the "older" buildings

along there, these showing particular abuse from the war. He waved Dukhovic into a parking place and got in.

"What time do they start to move the girls?" Mike said, looking around. There were a few cars starting to move on the streets as the day people went to their jobs.

"A little after eight," Dukhovic said. "That van doesn't make sense where it is, though. These houses might hold girls; there's a brothel down the street," he added, pointing. "But all there are up that street are warehouses."

"Well, it's radioactive as hell," Mike replied, thinking. "If I don't come back, call Northcote and tell him to send in IFOR."

He got out and walked back up the street, examining the warehouse without really looking at it. There was a small personnel door and a much larger roll-up door. The personnel door was metal and probably locked.

However, SEALs had access to some pretty obscure schools and one of them had covered "discreet entry." He didn't see any signs of life in the warehouse, no lights, no sound, so he slipped up to the door and slid out a set of picklocks.

It had been years since he'd really practiced with picklocks and it took him forever to get the door open. But finally the lock clicked over. He put the picklocks away and drew his sidearm, carefully screwing on the suppressor. That done, he slid it into the back of his pants and stepped through the door.

The room had a large crane system rolled over by the back wall, a large forge on the far left-hand side, several large metal tables, a drill press and an office on the right, near the door he had entered. There were five men in the room, cleaning up. Two of them were wearing heavy rubber gloves and appeared to be picking up bits of metal off the floor while two others were sweeping up the floor. The fifth turned and regarded him balefully for a moment, shifting so as to be behind one of the metal tables. There was a strong smell in the air that he couldn't quite place, but it reminded him of shooting rooms. Melted lead, that was it. It made him feel quite at home.

Nadhim Medein looked up in surprise and annoyance as a Westerner walked in the door. Nadhim was from Yemen and had

been a member of one terrorist group or another since he was a teenager. He had first joined the Popular Front for the Revolutionary Jihad in Yemen then traveled to the Tribal Areas in Pakistan where he attended jihadi madrassas. Eventually he was picked to aid the Taliban in their jihad for control of Afghanistan. He had been in the Taliban in Afghanistan on September 11, 2001, when the Great Martyrs had brought down the Towers of the Great Satan and had danced in joy with all the other Taliban at the news. He loved, still, to watch the video of the towers falling.

But he had also experienced, firsthand, the vengeance of the Great Satan and eventually fled Afghanistan to continue the jihad where it might bear less bitter fruit. He had fought in Fallujah with Al Islam and had been in Syria when this mission was formed. All he knew about the mission was that a bomb had been constructed in this building and he was to clean up so that IFOR would have no evidence of what had been done there. It was not the fiercest job in the world, but one that had to be done quickly and surely. Nadhim Medein was a soldier of the jihad who was known to be quick and sure. So he had been asked to participate and, after ensuring that it was a mission that would be useful to the work of Allah, he had agreed.

And he was *sure* he had locked the front door, but the man just opened it up and walked in. He was unarmed, apparently an American from the dress and walk. Nadhim was sure they had been discovered, but he tried to dissemble.

"How did you get in here?" the fifth man said as the others stopped what they were doing.

"Is Mr. Budak here?" Mike asked, ignoring the question.

"There is no one called Budak here," the man said, reaching down. "How did you get in here?"

"The door was open," Mike said, stepping forward to place himself by one of the tables. "I'm looking for Dzore Budak. He said he would be here."

"Well, he's not," the man said, his hands out of sight behind the table. "You need to go."

"What are you doing?" Mike answered, looking puzzled. "This is the warehouse of Dzore Budak, isn't it?"

"Get out," the man said, lifting up an AK as the others began diving behind tables and the large forge.

Rifles are hard to lift quickly but pistols are very quick indeed, and before the AK could come up all the way the silenced pistol had targeted the man's chest. Mike put a round into either side of the chest and dropped behind the table, turning it over with a massive heave as the others pulled out rifles from their hiding places.

Asfaw Rabah watched in shock as Nadhim was cut down by the American, then reached under the worktable and pulled out his AK. He could not believe that Nadhim had been killed so easily. Nadhim was a legend in the Jihad and his stories of fighting the Dar Al Harb throughout the world had passed the slow times on this mission. It made Asfaw incredibly angry that so great a man had died in such an ignominious way.

Asfaw was from Saudi Arabia, the only son in a family of five. His parents were not particularly devout, to his way of thinking, and did not support his choice to join the jihad. But when he was fifteen he had gone with some friends to hear the words of the Mullah Yahya Mahad, one of the many Wahabbist preachers who made their living bringing the Word of God to the Dar Al Islam along the road to Mecca. At the time the forces of the Great Shaitan were still infesting the Holy Lands, their main base within a few hundred miles of the Holy City. Until that time, Asfaw had never thought what a sin against Allah it was to have the Crusader forces so close to the Holy City. The mullah, though, had thought long and hard upon it and he pointed out how very angry Allah must be.

From that day forward, Asfaw had pledged himself to rid the Holy Lands of the Crusader forces, wherever that might be. He had been picked up by the Saudi police in a demonstration against the Crusaders and, while his family had managed to get him out of prison, he had been forced to leave his home country. He had added to his pledge the vow to eventually throw down the corrupt House of Saud who had allowed the Crusaders into the Holy Lands and had joined the Jihadi Al Islam with that purpose in mind. With the fall of the kaliphate in Afghanistan he had been

forced to go to Syria, and it was there he met Nadhim and been recruited for this mission.

Asfaw held the AK by his hip, as Nadhim himself had taught him, pointing it at the table the cowardly infidel had ducked behind and blasting the top as the weapon bucked in his hands. The weapon, stupidly, ran out of rounds and he reached under the table again for his spare magazine. He had his head down and never saw the American peek around the table...

Mike heard the rounds hit the top of the heavy working table and one punch through as he rolled to the left side of the table and peeked out. One of the terrorists was standing in the middle of the room, reloading after a "spray and pray" so Mike targeted two rounds right through his breast bone, spaced no more than a quarter's width apart.

Asfaw felt the rounds in his chest like two punches and a sharp pain in his back. His legs gave out from under him as the spinal cord was severed, and he dropped the AK and the spare magazine as he fell, his face striking the ground, hard. His nose was broken, he was sure, and, as his vision faded, he thought that his mother would be very angry at him for breaking his nose...

One of the terrorists was running to the right, heading for the crane for a better vantage point. Mike shot at him but missed as the target dove behind the crane. He reloaded, considering the situation, then popped straight up.

This received fire from behind one of the tables, also turned over, from the forge and then from the crane. He burst out of cover to the left, rounds cracking around him as the terrorists fired off most of their clips, and slid to a stop on his stomach behind the last table in the room. As he did the Geiger counter started screaming: the metal shavings on the floor were hot as blazes. At that realization, he popped up to his feet, quick. He duck-walked forward, trying to keep his balls away from the shavings. The Geiger was still screaming from the dust and shit on his clothes, so he yanked the earbud out and ignored it, then leaned out, looking for targets.

▲   ▲   ▲

Zuhair Adil put his last magazine in the weapon and considered what to do. Nadhim and Asfaw were probably dead. He had seen Nadhim shot and had heard the chuffs from the American's silenced weapon and the sound of Asfaw's weapon clattering to the ground. It was a great thing to die in the Service of Allah, but it was a greater thing to kill the infidel at the same time. Killing, in this case, meant staying alive long enough to do so.

Zuhair was seventeen, a Bosnian Muslim who had been too young to join the jihad against the Serbs. But after the war was over the Wahabbists had come in to rebuild the mosques of Bosnia that the Serbs had defiled, bringing with them their extremist brand of Islam. Zuhair was an orphan of the war; his father had been a shopkeeper killed by the Serbs and his mother had disappeared when they were refugees. He had been taken into a madrassa funded by the International Council for Muslim Charities, a Wahabbist charity funded primarily by Saudi oil money, and it was there that he had been taught the truth of Islam, that Mohammed had declared that the whole world must be in submission to the will of Allah and that the way of jihad against the Dar Al Harb was the highest calling of the Muslim.

He had been recruited by one of the mullahs of the madrassa to assist in this mission, which was simple enough: clean up the warehouse and make sure no one got into it until the clean-up was complete. He was told that there might be trouble, but he had thought they would have some warning. And he very much would prefer not to die. He realized that as he considered what to do. Dying for Allah was all well and good to shout at the madrassa. But facing it, in real life, was a different thing. He would gladly kill a Serb if he had a chance. They had killed his mother and father, after all. But this was no place to die and no way to do it. All he wanted was *out*. But to do that meant either surrendering, which would look very bad, or making it to the door. To do that, he had to know where the American was. So he leaned around the forge, searching for him. As he did, he saw the American, around the side of a table, doing the same thing, and he lifted his rifle in terror, pointing it at him and yanking the trigger . . .

▲   ▲   ▲

The tango by the forge was leaning out, also, and fired at him as he came around the side. But all the rounds went high, so Mike put a round through his exposed forehead, spreading the terrorist's limited brains all over the back wall. He slid back, then lifted himself straight up over the barrier. None of the terrorists were in sight, so he reloaded, thinking . . .

Imad Al-Kurbi was annoyed. He had fired off two full magazines at the American, carefully holding the weapon with one hand on the pistol grip and the other on top of the barrel to keep it on target as he had been taught. But he still could not hit the slippery infidel.

Imad was from the Tribal Territories of Pakistan, one of seven children, three sons, of a small mountain farm. He had been raised with an AK in his hand and considered himself a good shot, so it was doubly annoying that he had been unable to hit the American. He had left the farm when he was fifteen, entering a Wahabbist madrassa in Islamabad. There was no work in Pakistan and the madrassa fed him both food and the Word of Allah. He had left the madrassa at seventeen and, paid by the jihad, had traveled first to Afghanistan to fight the Crusader invaders, then to Iraq where he had met Nadhim who was another veteran of Afghanistan. They had planted bombs to fight the Crusaders for a year before the Crusaders flooded the country with heavy forces and began destroying the jihad in that country. When it was clear they were going to be caught soon, Nadhim suggested that they travel to Syria where jihadis were being recruited for international missions.

This mission was *supposed* to be simple. But it was clear that the Americans had discovered them and he had to kill this one before the word got out. However, he was out of rounds. Nadhim, though, had never gotten off a shot, so he should have a full weapon.

With that thought, Imad quietly set his empty weapon on the ground and lifted himself on fingers and toes and leopard-crawled around the table he had been using for cover. He could hear faint sounds from the American, a magazine being slid out and then

another into the weapon, and he thought about sight angles. If he crossed the open area and around to the far side of the table Nadhim had been using for cover, he would stay out of sight. He got to his feet and, crouching over, darted across the gap, ducking behind the far side of the table.

Mike duck-walked sideways, keeping the room covered as he sidled over to the forge. He bent down and picked up the terrorist's AK and switched it for his pistol. There were ten rounds left in the magazine and no more mags. That meant the other terrs might be out of rounds.

Imad listened to the faint sound of the AK magazine being removed and then either it or another being reinserted and considered what to do. Nadhim's weapon was on the far side of the table, maybe in reach. He lay on his stomach and stretched his arm out, hooking at the trigger guard of the weapon . . .

There had been one of the terrorists behind the overturned table, but he was gone. His weapon was on the ground but he wasn't there. Mike had moved left, so the terr had probably moved right. That meant he was behind the drill press, one of the overturned tables or in the office. It was unlikely he had made it to the crane. And there was the one left behind the crane, of course.

The back side of the drill press was just out of sight, so Mike sidled that way, AK at tactical present, and peeked around the corner. No "Middle Eastern Male" there. He quietly peeked over the table to see if the terrorist was on the far side, keeping half an eye on the crane. He should have taken fire from there by now, but he hadn't so the terr was probably out of rounds.

There were two more sides to the drill press and Mike checked those, wondering where the target had hidden himself.

"Olly olly oxenfree!" Mike called tauntingly. "Come out, come out wherever you are!"

Imad didn't speak English very well, but he recognized the taunting tone. Let the American taunt; by sliding his body almost fully under the table, he had managed to get one finger

on Nadhim's rifle and he could *see* the American's legs from his current position. He began to slide the AK slowly to him and winced at the metallic scraping sound...

Mike heard a magazine being surreptitiously removed then reinserted by the crane; he ducked down behind the table, waiting. As he did that he heard a metallic sound where the first terrorist had been standing: the tango he lost track of had been out of rounds and had snuck over to the leader type to get his full weapon. Most of the head terrorist's body was in sight, so the target must be on the far side of the table on his stomach, reaching under it for the weapon.

Mike dropped to his own stomach, looking under the table and, sure enough, there was the tango. He was half covered by the body of the leader and snatched the weapon to him when he saw Mike's sudden movement. They locked eyes for a moment, the terrorist raising the AK to fire under the table and then Mike shot him between the eyes.

All Majali Fu'ad wanted was *out*. Majali was from Egypt and had been a student in Germany until the money for college ran out. He hated Cairo, where there was no decent work for a college-trained young man and very few distractions unless you were married. So he stayed in Europe, doing odd jobs, until he ended up in a madrassa in Bosnia of all places. The madrassa fed him, and if the food came with a healthy dosing of the Word of Allah he was willing to accept that as long as his bowl was filled. He'd taken this "mission" because it was just another odd job, like dozens of others he'd done over the years since college. He'd only fired at the American because everyone else did so, and it gave him a sense of security to shoot the weapon. But now he was out of bullets and a long way from Cairo. If he managed to get to the door he was going back to Cairo, finding a job, any job, and never, ever leaving again. And if anyone said the word "jihad" in his presence, he was going to punch them out. He crouched down, his eyes fixed on the door, and as more firing broke out, he sprinted for the door...

▲   ▲   ▲

Mike lifted up to the top of the table as he heard pounding feet, putting the last three rounds from the AK into the running terrorist who slid to a halt, leaving a trail of blood behind him. His arm twitched a bit and then he was still.

Majali lay on his face, feeling the blood flowing out of his chest, and tried to crawl to the door. It was a long way to Cairo, but he would crawl if he had to. He was cold and it would be warm in Cairo . . .

Mike lifted up and looked around, then switched the AK for the one the leader had had, checking the leader. The leader had probably lived for a few seconds based on the blood trail, but he was dead.

Mike checked the office, cautiously, then moved from one body to the next until he was sure they were all Dead Right There. And they were.

"I really could have used a prisoner, you know," Mike said, shaking his head in frustration. "One of you could have bothered to survive!"

CHAPTER
FOUR

"Well, I threw sevens," Mike said, sitting down and pulling out his phone. "Where are we?"

"Corner of Levakonic and Miskina," Dukhovic replied. "I heard shooting. Automatic rifles?"

"Northcote?" Mike said, ignoring him. "Corner of Levakonic and Miskina. Up Miskina street. Warehouse with a white van outside. Van's hot, so's the warehouse and I took fire when I entered. I think we have the site; site is secure. Yeah, full response and get the Nuclear Emergency Search Team moving." NEST was the premier group in the world at detecting, analyzing and, if necessary, taking apart, nuclear wepaons. "No prisoners, unfortunately, they all croaked on me. Make contact with Dukhovic; he's going to be at the corner. I'm going to go get some sleep."

"There was shooting," Dukhovic repeated nervously.

"Yeah," Mike said. "There won't be any more. That brothel. Think they're open this time of day?"

"Yes?" the pajama-wearing man at the door said in an irritated tone. It had taken Mike three minutes of hammering with his pistol grip to get the door open at all.

"I'm looking for a girl," Mike replied. He'd gone back to the pensione, changed out of his mildly radioactive clothes and taken

a shower first. Then had Dukhovic drive him back to the warehouse and kicked him loose.

"It is too early," the pimp said, starting to close the door. He was about fifty, even heavier than Dukhovic, with a receding hairline and heavy jowls that were tracked with sleep lines. "Come back this evening."

Mike jammed his foot in the closing door and pulled out a wad of hundred-euro notes, waving them in front of the man's nose.

"Money talks, bullshit walks, as we say in America," Mike replied.

"The girls are all asleep," the man said, watching the money wave back and forth. "It will take some time to wake them up."

"Fine, you can serve me breakfast," Mike said, pushing the door open. "What I'm looking for is a young blonde, nice breasts. I'm going to treat her extremely roughly, but not leave too many marks. Then I'm going to sleep with her most of the day. Three hundred euros to you. You throw in breakfast."

"Deal," the man said, following Mike into the room. "I am Ivo Kovacic."

"And I'm nobody you want to remember," Mike replied.

Mike was dipping bread in rather decent coffee when Kovacic came into the kitchen leading a very pretty young blonde. She was wearing panties and a camisole that revealed a tight stomach, long legs for her height—she was quite short—and very large breasts that were still high and full. She had a gorgeous face, long, curly hair and beautiful Tartar eyes. He couldn't quite get a look at the color since she had her head down in a very submissive posture that he found immediately alluring. Of all the whores Mike had seen in all the countries he had visited, she was close to the best looking, if not the top. If she wasn't so short, no more than five four, she could be a supermodel.

"This is Magdelena," Kovacic said. "She is a new girl here, but I think you will find her to your tastes. Do not strike her in the face hard, if you will. Other customers will get the idea that she can be used as a punching bag."

"I won't," Mike said. "As long as she does what I tell her to do. Come here, girl," he said, grabbing her wrist and pulling her

onto his lap. "Let me see your eyes, look at me." He grabbed her chin and lifted her face so he could look her in the eye. When she looked at him he could see that her eyes were wide and frightened, and she kept trying to drop her head, her chin pulling against his fingers like a trapped bird.

Mike was, briefly, troubled, his conscience nagging at him. But the whole stinking mission had raised his frustration level to a fever pitch and his demons had hold of him firmly. He slid his hand up under the camisole and felt her breasts, roughly. They were tight as if she had just finished growing them and he reevaluated her age; she couldn't be more than seventeen and fifteen was probably closer. Again, his conscience twinged, but he ignored it. Her youth and relative inexperience was too exciting.

"I'll take this one," Mike said, standing up and taking the girl by the hand. She tried to pull away and he shifted his grip to her wrist. "Where's her room?"

"Upstairs," Kovacic said. "I think that payment up front would be good, however."

Mike pulled out the wad of notes and peeled off three, handing them to Kovacic.

"Show me your room," Mike said to the girl, pulling her forward and slapping her on the ass, hard. "Now."

The girl walked into the main living room of the house, then up the stairs. Her room was down the hall on the left. It had a double bed, pushed up against one wall, a small wardrobe, a nightstand and a chest of drawers. When she entered the small bedroom, Mike closed the door, then grabbed her by the hair, pulling on it brutally.

"You speak English?" he snapped, pulling her around to look her in her frightened eyes.

"A little," the girl whimpered. "Please, no hurt."

"I *like* hurt," Mike said, twisting her hair and watching as tears formed in her beautiful eyes. "You do what I say, I won't hurt as *much*. Understand?"

"Yes," the girl said in a terrified tone. "Please . . ."

"Down on your knees, bitch," was his reply, pushing her down. "Pull out my dick and suck it. Suck it good, or I'll hurt you."

The girl quickly unzipped him and pulled out his cock, sticking

"I've raped you," Mike said brutally, pulling out her gag. "Now I'm going to sleep with you. And if you try to run, or steal anything, I will wake up. You will sleep right here, with me, until I'm ready to get up. If you try to get away, you'll be beaten. Do you understand?"

"Yes," the girl said, pulling herself up against the wall and as far away from him as she could.

"Get over here," Mike said, pulling the covers back, then lying down on the bed and pulling the girl to him. He forced her to spoon with him, facing the wall. "Don't try to run," he said in her ear, wrapping an arm around her possessively.

The girl was gently crying, but she nodded. She smelled of fear and he still found that incredibly exciting, his member briefly engorging to touch her on the ass. Other than in agreed-upon "scenes" he had never been so brutal to a woman in his life. And she had, no question, not been a willing participant. It had been paid rape, pure and simple. His conscience was still nagging at him, but he was ignoring it. He slid his hand up to cradle one lovely breast and fell asleep like he'd been drugged.

Mike woke up, once, when the girl tried to slip out of bed. He simply grabbed her by the wrist and pulled her back to spoon, then went back to sleep. The second time he woke to the sound of his phone ringing. He pushed her into the corner of the bed and picked it up, checking the time as he did. It had only been four hours, not nearly enough time for NEST to have arrived and done a full survey.

"Duncan," he said after a moment; he still wasn't used to his cover name.

"Northcote," the man said. "Go scramble."

Mike punched in the code on the phone and hit scramble.

"Be aware," Mike said. "I'm in an unsecure location."

"That's fine," Northcote said. "The IFOR team has finished a preliminary evaluation. They've found traces of plutonium, uranium and tritium. There's also a container that probably held new tritium, which is one of the things . . ."

"Look," Mike said, "this is all fine and dandy. But call me back when a full sweep has been completed including information from

the area. I need to sleep; I've been on continuous ops for a while. I'll probably be over there this evening; I'm not far away."

"Okay," Northcote replied, nonplussed. "Will do."

"Bye," Mike replied, hitting the disconnect. He tossed the phone on his clothes on the floor and pulled the girl to him, entering her dry and pumping her hard. It clearly hurt and her face was screwed up in pain. After raping her for a while, he pulled out, then grabbed her camisole from the floor, forcing it into her mouth as a gag and entered her again. She tried to fight him this time, but he was much stronger than she was and there was no way for her to stop him raping her. He slammed her, brutally, holding her hands above her head with one hand gripping her wrists and twisting at her nipples with the other as she cried out in pain against the gag.

That wasn't enough, so he turned her over again, using her panties to tie her to the bedstand and tying the camisole around the back of her head. He put on another condom, then pulled out his belt and whipped her ass red as she cried in pain. Finally, when he was so full of cum he felt he would burst, he mounted her, hard, pounding her lovely ass brutally, while kneading her breasts and pinching her nipples. He still held back, though, giving her a full, hard fucking, before letting himself release into her ass.

When he was done he threw the condom away and untied her.

"Lick me clean," he said, pushing her head down to his crotch. "Clean me all up."

The girl did as he said, then he pushed his cock into her mouth.

"Suck it," he ordered, lying back. "Suck me back to life."

She blew him and played with him until he was engorged again, and then Mike threw her on her back and started pounding her again.

"I love raping you," he said, looking at her face that was screwed up in fear and pain. "Look at me," he ordered. When she opened her eyes a crack he laughed at the fear in them and they shot closed again at his expression. "I love raping you. I'm going to do it over and over again until I have to leave."

He'd already come several times, so he could fuck her for

her, playing with her tits and only pulling her nipples a little bit, until he came.

"You've been a lot of fun," Mike said, throwing the condom away and dipping into his pants. He pulled out a wad of euros and tossed them on the crying girl's back. "I'm going to tell your pimp that that is for you. And I'll check up, make sure he hasn't taken it from you. I'll also tell him that unless you want, you're off-duty tonight."

The girl rolled over and pulled the money from behind her back, her tears drying and eyes widening at the sight of the bills. He wasn't sure how much was in the fold, but it was probably half a year's pay for the girl. Most of the money she made, usually two or four to one, went to her pimp, even "tips" like Mike's. She flipped through the roll then looked at Mike, quizzically, for the first time without fear in her eyes.

"I'm not particularly proud of that side of me," Mike said as he pulled on his clothes. "It comes out from time to time, but I don't like it. That," he added, gesturing with his chin at the money, "doesn't make up for what I did to you. But . . . it helps. Both you and me. And I'm sorry for how I treated you, but I was at a point where it was do what I did or kill somebody. And, unfortunately, right now there's nobody left for me to kill."

"Is okay," Magdelena said, pulling the clip off the roll and counting the money. "Not like, much hurt, much . . . bad memory." She got to the end of the quick count and looked at him again, curiously. "But for this, is okay. Would do again."

"Yeah," Mike said as he holstered his piece and picked up his jump bag. "But then you'd be acting. It wouldn't be the same."

The brothel had a few customers checking out the girls when he walked downstairs, but he spotted Kovacic talking to somebody on the door who must have been a bouncer. He waved him over with a lift of the head as he headed for the door.

"I gave Magdelena a tip," Mike said, cocking his head to the side. "A very large tip." He dipped into his pants and came up with another hundred-euro note. "This is your tip. Her tip is hers. I'll be checking up. And just to be clear, I'm tight connected with

IFOR. Do *not* think you can have part of her tip, or you'll end up sorry and sore as she is. Am I being blunt enough?"

"Yes," Kovacic said, pocketing the money.

"She's off for tonight unless she wants to work," Mike said. "That's for her share of tonight. We okay on that?"

"Yes," Kovacic replied. "I could hear some of what was going on. She won't be good for much tonight, maybe tomorrow."

"She's got some strap marks on her ass from my belt," Mike said, shrugging. "No bruises. A hand print on the face that is mostly faded. I may be back later for . . . fifths I guess."

"It will not be on the house," Kovacic said. "I normally don't let my girls be treated like that."

"You're such a sweetheart," Mike said, walking out.

CHAPTER
FIVE

There was a large cordon set up down the street. Mike walked up to the line of soldiers securing the area and pulled out his diplomatic passport.

"Michael Duncan," he said. "I'm here to meet Mr. North-cote."

"I have to clear it with the sergeant of the guard, sir," the private said, swallowing nervously. "Normally that would get you past, but we have a serious security issue here and . . ."

"Fine," Mike said, grinning. "I know where you're at, son. Follow procedures, I've got time."

It took a visit from both the sergeant and the officer of the guard before he was past, the officer of the guard escorting him to the warehouse. Even then he wasn't allowed to enter until Northcote was called outside. The van was gone, he noticed. He wondered, idly, if they'd loaded it on a tow truck or if some poor bastard had had to drive it. It had been, radioactively, hot as hell. *He* wouldn't have wanted to drive it.

"There you are," Northcote said, exasperated. "I was wondering when you'd bother to show up."

"I figured it would take most of the day to get a full read on the situation," Mike said, yawning. "And I'd been up for about sixty hours. What do we have?"

"Thank you, Lieutenant," Northcote said, dragging him into the warehouse through the personnel door. Mike noticed that the lock had been knocked out by a door-knocker. "We've got a briefing set up . . ."

"Spare me the Powerpoint," Mike said, looking around. About half the warehouse was now covered in a set of plastic bubbles with guys in clean-room suits waving detectors around and using small vacuums to pick up dust. The office had apparently been converted back to being an office. There were at least thirty people in the room outside of the investigation area, standing around and looking worried. "Just the facts, as they say. And you're on pins and needles. Why?"

"Besides the fact that a nuke slipped into my AO and back out?" Northcote asked exasperatedly. "Maybe it's the fact that the last call I got was from the Office of the White House asking about you. What or who the hell *are* you? I'd pegged you as a CIA Office of Special Actions guy, but the White House doesn't call about them as a rule. And they asked for you by name; I had to tell them you were sleeping."

"I am not now, nor have I ever been, CIA," Mike said bluntly. "I do favors for the United States government and they, in turn, do favors for me," he added, tapping the pocket where he had his "official" passport.

"Contractor?" Northcote asked.

"Not even that," Mike said. "A contractor signs up for a specific payment. I consider myself more in the field of . . . salvage operations." He grinned and then shrugged. "What do we have?"

"This is Todd Jameson," Northcote said, leading him over to one of the groups. The guy he addressed was a big blond in a blue jumpsuit with NEST printed across the back. The other people were military, ranking up to a bird colonel. "He's the head of the nuke team."

"You must be Duncan," the NEST leader said, shaking Mike's hand.

"Mike," Mike replied, shaking his head. "Duncan's a name that gets you into fights and I hate getting in fights."

"Mike, then," the guy replied, smiling humorously. "Well, the nuke was definitely here. We got the isotope signature from the

Russkis and the remnants we picked up are a match. Whoever was working on it knew what they were doing, too. There's remnants of wiring and the detonator circuit had been pulled. It would have degraded from radiation by now, so it was one thing they had to replace."

"Wouldn't they have had to reshape the explosives and the plutonium?" Mike asked.

"No, these older nukes are remarkably stable that way," Jameson said, shrugging. "They had to replace the tritium; it would have degraded. And the plutonium might be a little degraded. But I'm ninety percent sure, based on the evidence, that we're going to get some sort of nuclear reaction. What gets me is the rest of the evidence."

"What's that?" Mike asked. "The lead smell?"

"Yeah," Jameson said, leading him over to the side of one of the bubble tents. "See those?" he asked, pointing to some metal pieces on one of the tables. "Those are metal bars that have been cut with an arc welder. And there were large bolts sitting on the floor." Jameson waved to one of the space-suited guys and made a motion like turning a wrench. The person in the bubble went over to another table and picked up a bolt, turning it back and forth.

"Can I see it up close?" Mike asked. "How hot is it?"

"It's not hot enough to bother about," Jameson said, walking over to the entrance and waving for the bolt to be brought over. "About like a tritium watchface. The shavings that were on the floor were hot as hell, though."

"Yeah, I ran into those," Mike said. "Slid through them, to be precise."

"Jesus," the NEST team leader said, his eyes wide. "You need to be decontaminated!"

"I took a shower," Mike said, shrugging and turning the bolt around and around. It was familiar, but he couldn't place it. "I'll survive. I've survived worse, trust me. A little radiation's good for you. So we've got metal bars and big bolts. Anything else?"

"Well, they were melting and pouring lead," Jameson said, looking at him askance. "And there's a big crane," he continued, pointing to the device. "That's cold as snow. It wasn't in contact

with the live weapon. For the rest, I'd suggest you talk to the forensic guys."

Mike walked back over to Northcote, who was talking with a civilian in a rumpled suit and a major with an IFOR MP brassard.

"You the forensics guys?" Mike asked.

"Major Forester," the major said, shaking his hand. "And Agent Wilson with the FBI."

"Pleased ta meetcha," Wilson said in a thick New York accent. "What do you think?"

"They encased the nuke in lead," Mike said. "That way it can't be detected as readily. Probably rigged it to blow. Maybe a timer, but more likely a cell phone. Maybe more than one. I'd want the ability to turn it off."

"My guess, too," Wilson said, looking at him sharply. "But what did they move it in?"

"Big engine," Mike said, holding up the bolt. "But what kind? Any read on the bolt?"

"Used in various systems," Wilson said, shrugging. "Engine blocks, mostly."

"That's where I've seen it," Mike said. "When we had to strip down the engine on my boat. A Volvo diesel."

"That's one of them," Wilson said, nodding. "Also Mercedes. But if the nuke is stuck in an engine cavity, the engine isn't running. So we're looking for a big truck with an engine that's not running?"

"Doesn't make sense," Mike said. "Major, what do you have?"

"There was the proverbial little old lady," the major said, pulling out a pad. "One Branca Obilic, eighty-three. She's lived in this area since, as she put it, the good old days when Tito was in charge. Never been run out, not even by the war. Was a refugee for a few days and came back. One hard-nosed bitch of a Serb, too; she only talked to us because nobody else would listen to her. But she knew something different was going on here and kept an eye on it. She said that about two days after the van turned up, and it was never moved, a large white truck pulled into the warehouse. It was here for about three hours, maybe more, but she's sure of at least three hours. That was three days ago. It was

an odd vehicle. It had a tractor front end but a short rear with doors on the side and back. Personnel doors on the side and double doors on the back. We've got the description out to IFOR, the Bosnian police and Interpol. It shouldn't be hard to find."

"Yes it will," Mike said, frowning.

"It's a pretty unusual vehicle," Forester protested. "There can't be many vehicles like that in Bosnia. Europe for that matter."

"What you just described is a press van," Mike said, sighing. "There are thousands of them in Europe. And if we start stopping all of them, somebody is going to figure out what is going on."

"Shit," Forester said, angrily. "Why didn't I think of that?"

"You've been too close to the problem," Mike said, thinking. "Okay, but what is the engine? Generator."

"There's one of those in those press vans," Wilson said, nodding. "Good call."

"Okay," Mike said thoughtfully. "They put the nuke in the engine, holding it in place with the bars, then poured hot lead around it? That doesn't make sense."

"There are some bits of stainless steel around, too," Wilson said. "I'd wondered what those were. They must have enclosed it in a sleeve, then poured the lead around it."

"That is going to make it a bitch to disarm," Forester said.

"*Nicht scheiss*," Mike replied. "No shit. What's going on in Europe right now?" he asked rhetorically.

"There's always something being covered by the press," Northcote said, shrugging.

"Any American officials going to a summit?" Mike asked. "Anything like that?"

"The G-8 meeting in Zurich!" Forester said, slapping his forehead. "Shit, that's in a week!"

"Could be that," Mike said. "Let's not get too tightly focused. But it's a good beginning. We need to start looking at potential targets and make it clear what we're dealing with. The nuke is in play and prepped." He pulled out his cell phone and looked at the time. "Okay, I'm going to go find someplace that has a TV. Is there . . . well . . . a 'real' hotel in town?"

"Not really," Northcote said. "Not something like a Hilton or whatever. There are some in Sarajevo."

"Okay," Mike said, sighing. "Northcote, get somebody coming up with a target list. But I'm going to go watch TV in Sarajevo and try to go on hunch. It's been working so far."

He keyed his cell phone and punched in the number the pilot had given him.

"We're going to Sarajevo next," Mike said. "Just a hop. We'll probably be going somewhere after that."

Mike walked out of the warehouse thoughtfully, then down to the brothel.

"You again," Kovacic said. The brothel was in full swing and Mike could see several military uniforms in the room.

"We need to talk," Mike replied, putting his hand on the man's arm and leading him to the back rooms.

"I want to buy Magdelena," Mike said when they'd entered his cluttered office. Apparently running a brothel was like any business, because most of the clutter was paper and there was a computer on the desk.

"You won't be able to take her out of the country," Kovacic said, frowning.

"Yeah, I will," Mike replied. "Trust me."

"And she is very expensive," the pimp added. "I had to pay very much for her."

"How expensive?"

"Fifty thousand euros," Kovacic replied.

"Pull the other one, it's got bells on it," Mike said, laughing. "I can buy a girl just as good in Eagle Market for five thousand. And younger. I'll give you ten."

After a good bit of dickering, with Kovacic referring to Magdelena as his daughter and Mike threatening to leave twice, they got the price down to twenty-five thousand euros.

"Fine, fine." Mike sighed, lifting his bag onto the desk and dipping into it. "Go tell her to get ready to leave."

When Magdelena came in the room, her eyes widened in fear at the sight of him. Which wasn't anywhere near where he was going, but it would work for the time being. She was carrying a small duffel bag and the hand holding the strap on her shoulder twitched nervously.

"Here you go," Mike said, pointing to a pile of mixed dollars and euros. "The dollar is over the euro at the moment, but I went with even so you're a bit ahead."

Kovacic pulled some of the notes out at random and checked them for counterfeit, then pulled apart a couple of the bundles and started counting.

"Can we go?" Mike asked. "I have a plane to catch."

"I suppose," Kovacic said, frowning at the pile. "You were planning on buying girl?"

"No," Mike replied. "I tend to carry a good bit of cash on me. It's not as if anyone was going to take it. They can feel free to *try*." He took Magdelena's hand and led her out of the office and out of the brothel to the street, then looked around for a taxi.

"Magdelena, I treated you horribly," Mike said, not sure if the girl was understanding what he said or not. "I can't take that back, but I can try to improve things for you. I won't do what I did to you again. But you have to promise me not to try to run away. Not right now. If you want to leave once we're out of Bosnia, you can. But if you stick with me, I'll try to do the right thing by you."

"Where we go?" Magdelena asked, confused.

"Right now, Sarajevo," Mike said. "I need a hotel with a decent TV connection."

He finally managed to get a taxi and directed it to the airport. Once there he went to the plane and was pleased and surprised to find that the pilot had gotten there before him.

"We've completed preflight," Hardesty told him, nodding as Mike stepped to the plane with Magdelena's hand still in his. "Pick up a girlfriend?"

"Something like that," Mike replied. "I saw a TV in the plane. Can it get satellite?"

"Of course," Hardesty said, as he boarded. "Use the remote for channel changing. Anything from the Playboy channel to CNN."

"CNN is what I'm interested in," Mike said. He settled Magdelena, her eyes wide at the sight of the plane, in one of the rear seats, then sat down opposite the large TV mounted in the rear bulkhead. He keyed it on as the plane's engines began to whine

and had found Headline News, Fox and Skynews by the time the plane was finished taxiing. His interest was Europe, and Skynews had more about Europe than Fox or Headline News. He switched around, looking for current updates.

"I need an Internet connection," he muttered. "I don't suppose you have a laptop with an Internet connection on it, do you, honey?" he asked rhetorically.

"No," Magdelena said. "What are you do?"

"You understand more English than you let on," Mike replied. "I'm trying to figure out what event a terrorist attack is most likely to be against," he continued, flipping back to Headline News. It was at the top of the hour and he listened to the news, ignoring most of the underlying commentary. President Cliff did this, what a horrible person, deaths in Iraq, Syria swearing it's not a source of terrorism, the pope visiting Paris . . .

"Wait," Mike said, swearing, as the seven seconds devoted to the pope's visit cycled off. Apparently the pope had suddenly become aghast at the state of Catholicism in European countries and after traveling the world had decided to work nearer home. But that was all that Mike could get in the brief bit that Headline News mentioned. And there wasn't anything on the other channels about it, just commentators nattering about how horrible President Cliff and America were, except on Fox, where they were nattering about how horrible the other channels were.

"Crap, crap, crap," Mike muttered. "I need info." He picked up his cell phone and called Northcote, but all he got was voicemail. The pope would be a perfect target; Catholics from all over France would be gathered to see him. Sure, France was increasingly an Islamic country; Muslims made up about ten percent of the population with an enormous immigration and birthrate while ethnic "French" were barely reproducing themselves. But he was sure that the incidental few hundred thousand Muslims that would be killed in a nuke strike would be of no real issue to Al Qaeda, if that was who was running the show. He thought about the terrorist "engineer" who was at the top of the list to have refurbed, and likely armed, the nuke. He wouldn't bat an eye at killing a few hundred thousand Muslims if he could take more Christians with them. They would simply be martyrs to Allah.

He thought about it some more and decided that his gut was telling him this was the target. So he picked up the sat phone again and dialed OSOL.

"Office of Special Operations Liaison, Colonel Johannsen, Duty Officer, how may I help you, sir?"

"Go scramble," Mike said, punching in his code.

"Scrambled."

"This is Mike Jenkins," Mike said. "Pull up my file if you don't know who I am. I need somebody to brief me on where the pope is going to be in Paris and when. I also need access to France in a private jet for myself and one undocumented female." He felt the jet begin to reduce power, as if preparing to land, and stopped. "Wait one." He keyed the intercom for the cockpit and whistled.

"Sorry about this," Mike said. "I don't suppose we have fuel to get to Paris?"

"We do, sir," Hardesty replied. "I take it I should divert?"

"If you please," Mike said. "I have to get back to the other line.

"Sorry about that," he continued. "We were landing in Sarajevo. Can you get somebody to run point for me by the time we get to Paris? We'll probably be going into DeGaulle, at a guess."

"I can do that," Johannsen said. "Is this about the item?"

"Yes. I'm running on gut. Everybody else can run around to whatever event they want, but I'm guessing it's the pope. The timing is right, the target is right. So I'll need high-level access."

"What's the name of the undocumented female?" Johannsen asked.

"Magdelena Averina," Mike said, pulling the first Russian name that came to mind. "And I'm under the cover name, Michael Duncan."

"Got that, too," Johannsen said. "I'll put out the word that you're headed there and give a heads-up to the locals."

"Thanks," Mike replied. "Out here."

"We are not go Sarajevo?" Magdelena asked.

"Nope," Mike said, leaning back. "We're on our way to the City of Light."

CHAPTER SIX

"The pope is going to do a large audience at the Stade de France and a high mass on Sunday at Notre Dame. The high mass is the culmination of a seventeen-country European tour."

Colonel Mark De'Courcy was one of three military attachés in the U.S. embassy in Paris. He had graduated from the United States Military Academy at West Point, served as a junior officer in the Twenty-Fourth (later Third) Infantry Division, then up the chain, mostly in staff positions, until he had managed to wangle this assignment. And as with everyone associated with military or security work in Europe, he hadn't gotten a lot of sleep in the past two days. So he was less than thrilled about meeting some high-level, no-real-names-I'm-special agent at two in the morning at Charles DeGaulle.

"French police are all over both events like flies," he continued as he, the agent and the agent's Russian hooker-girlfriend walked to the waiting embassy car. It was a Peugeot with diplomatic plates. "We've got the call on the van and they're looking for it. So why are you here?"

"Because I've been lucky every step of the way," Mike replied. The colonel was a starchy regular Army SOB who clearly thought he was hot shit for getting such a choice assignment as military attaché to the French. Of course, the French military had sunk

to such a low ebb, they'd be hard pressed to defend their country from a troop of well-trained Cub Scouts. So being a military attaché was less than impressive to Mike. "I got lucky in Russia, I got lucky in Bosnia and if this is where it's coming, you'd better hope I get lucky here."

"Well, we put the word out to the French security guys that you were inbound," De'Courcy said, sighing as they got in the car. "They're less than thrilled but willing to work with us. What are you planning on doing?"

"The events are tomorrow, right?"

"Yeah," De'Courcy said. "The audience is at noon and the high mass is at four PM. Then he goes on to Berlin. That's closer to Bosnia, I might add."

"I know that much geography," Mark replied dryly. "But the longer this item is in play, the more likely we are to pick it up. And if they didn't know we were tracking, they do now with the way that IFOR took down the warehouse; that stood out like a sore thumb. I'm surprised it's not all over the news."

"There was a squib about it," De'Courcy said. "We covered it with a suspected bomb-making facility."

"Like that's going to hold with NEST running around in coveralls that *say* NEST," Mike said irritably. He thought for a moment and then shrugged. "Where's this stadium?"

"Southwest of Paris, out in the suburbs," De'Courcy replied, pulling a map out of his briefcase. "Where are we going?"

"Somewhere *away* from the stadium," Mike said. "And away from Notre Dame. Northeast of Paris is there a good hotel?"

"There's a Hilton up there," De'Courcy said. "Will that do?"

"I dunno," Mike said. "Is it outside the radius of a ten-megaton blast?"

De'Courcy shot a look at the girl and his jaw worked, but he nodded. "Yeah."

"Suits," Mike answered. "Leave the map, give me some contact info and I'll cut you loose. Where do you want to be dropped? I take it I can keep the car and driver?"

"At the embassy," De'Courcy said grumpily. "It's going to be an all-nighter. And, yeah, the car's yours."

▲   ▲   ▲

Mike checked into the Hilton, taking a suite that he insisted be on the north side, and led Magdelena upstairs. They attracted looks from the late-night staff, especially since he was pretty travel-worn and both of them were carrying single bags, but he could care less about the looks.

When they got to the suite, and got rid of the entirely unnecessary bellhop, Mike showed her the two rooms.

"You can have either one you like," he said.

"Which one will you use?" she asked, confused.

"The one you don't," Mike replied. "Look, I know I messed up in Bosnia. I'm sorry. I'm not carting you along to use you again. Maybe we'll have time to get together. If we do, I'll try to show you the more pleasant side of me. But for right now, I have to get moving. Stay in the room. Order room service if you want food. Don't go out. You can run away if you'd like, but I don't suggest it. And don't call anyone. Just . . . watch TV or something. Okay? If we get a chance I'll take you shopping. But I don't think we'll get a chance."

Mike put his dirty clothes in the bag provided, called down and asked the management to try to get them cleaned by tomorrow, and walked out.

"Where to?" the driver said, leaning his seat upright as Mike walked to the car.

"You know this stadium the colonel was talking about?" Mike asked.

"Yes, sir," the driver said, putting the car in gear. "There?"

"There first," Mike replied, looking at the map. The stadium was circled in red. He first checked the legend, then made some circles with his fingers. Unless he was much mistaken, a blast there would take out the stadium and some of the burgeoning suburbs around it. But that was about it. However, a blast near Notre Dame would completely gut Paris. And the bomb was a big one, one of the nasty "city busters" from the 1960s before the era of Multiple Independent Reentry Vehicles.

"You're American," Mike said, putting the map away and leaning back.

"Yes, sir," the driver said. "I'm one of the diplomatic protection drivers. They figured you might have to have secure conversations."

"You know what we're looking for?" Mike asked. "And what is your name, O genie? I'd hate to have to call you James."

"Bruce Gelinas," the driver said with a chuckle. "And, yeah, I know what you're looking for. The colonel briefed me on the way to pick you up. You really think it's coming here?"

"This is the target I'd pick if *I* was a terrorist," Mike replied, frowning. "The French are big into appeasement of the rifs. But you'd think they'd have learned from 1939 how well that works. Yeah, it might be headed anywhere in Europe; the American option is pretty much out the way they rigged it. But the pope is the right target in the right place at the right time. They don't have nearly as much of a hard-on for the Germans as they do the French. And waiting for Berlin just gives us more time to find it. So, yeah, I think it's going here."

"Great," the driver said. "And I suppose I have to be there while you look for it."

"Well," Mike pointed out, "if it goes off at Notre Dame, it's going to get the embassy, too. So sitting on your butt there won't get you anything. You don't have any family in town, do you?"

"Nope," Bruce said. "I'm single and fancy free, now that my last wife filed the papers. And she's in Texas."

"I think I'd rather be in Texas," Mike admitted, picking up his phone. He dialed the number for the pilot and was answered in a rather surly fashion.

"What do you bloody want now?" Hardesty snapped. "Sorry, sir, I'd just laid my head down. Are we up again?"

"No," Mike said. "But in the morning, get the plane up and to a dispersal field away from Paris."

"Might I ask why?" the pilot said curiously.

"No," Mike replied. "But you can come to your own conclusions. At least sixty kilometers from Paris. To the south or east."

"Very well," Hardesty said cautiously. "Given that information, perhaps I should move it now."

"Up to you," Mike replied, hitting the disconnect. "I'd hate to have my wings shot off by this."

"That wasn't exactly the most secure conversation I've ever heard," Bruce said. "You could get your ass in a sling over that."

"You'd have to find someone with a big enough sling," Mike said, leaning back in the seat and folding his arms.

The more Mike looked at the stadium, and the area surrounding it, the less enthusiastic he became about it being the likely target. Yes, if they hit it they would get international coverage; that was guaranteed with any nuke. But the only people they would kill would be sixty thousand or so attendees, the pope, and a few hundred thousand people in the surrounding area. And the closest dense population was high-rise "low-income housing" that was mostly populated by Muslims. They'd definitely kill more Muslims than Christians. And it wouldn't gut the City of Light.

TV vans were already setting up, with Klieg lights running and the works. He regarded them balefully as the sedan drove past. There were dozens of the damned things, any one of which could hold the nuke. With the lead wrapped around it, there was no way that there'd be a radiation trace. There was a small particle given off by nukes, a nucleotide or somesuch. That would get through the radiation shielding. But the detectors for it were huge, giant tanks of cleaning solvent of all things. He wasn't sure there were any that were mobile. He'd have to ask NEST. On the other hand, if there were any, he was sure they were in use.

"This isn't it," Mike said, shaking his head as they passed through the security cordon. "Or if it is, I'll take the hit. Head to Notre Dame."

By the time they got there the sun was rising and they had to fight traffic. French drivers weren't the worst in the world—Italians had them in Europe, and the entire third world had Europeans for bad driving—but they were pretty damned bad. Bruce negotiated the traffic expertly, however, with only an occasional curse, and got him to the security cordon alive.

Security was tighter here than at the stadium, but their plates, and especially Mike's passport, got them into the area and he had Bruce park. He looked around at the buildings and nodded. This was a much superior target.

Notre Dame was a magnificent Gothic cathedral completed in 1345 after nearly two hundred years of construction. It was built on the Ile de la Cite, an island in the Seine River near the

center of Paris which joined the Right and Left Banks through a series of four bridges. But it was only the last of several religious structures on the island. In turn there had been a Druidical grove, a Roman temple to Jupiter and a Romanesque church occupying the same island over the millennia.

Notre Dame, including its nave and secondary buildings, occupied only about half of the large island, with the rest taken up by two hotels of nearly the same antiquity. The island, thus, had little in the way of parking; the multitudes of attendees were anticipated to be brought in by bus while the press were relegated to an adjoining island, Ile Saint Louis, which had a far too small parking lot for the purpose.

Security was tight, with French police wandering all over the area, most of them carrying submachine guns on friction straps. Mike regarded the press area balefully. There were, if anything, more press vans here than at the stadium.

"This is the command post over here," Bruce said, pointing to a set of police vans as they got out of the Peugeot. "You'd prob-ably better get a security badge if you're going to be wandering around the area."

He led him over to the command post, Mike's diplomatic passport getting them through another layer of security and up to the rear of one of the vans.

"I take it you are the American who thought we would let a nuclear device slip into Paris," a woman said as they reached the rear of the van. She was a narrow-faced brunette holding a cup of coffee and wearing a very pissed-off expression.

"That would be me," Mike said, smiling. "And you are . . . ?"

"This is Madame Gabrielle LaSalle-Guerinot," Bruce said hastily. "She is the French minister of security."

"Madame," Mike said, bowing slightly. "A pleasure. I'm not sure I can get the whole last name. Can I call you Gabby?"

"No you may not," Madame LaSalle-Guerinot responded angrily. "And if it wasn't for the Cliff government making a stink of things, I would have you thrown out right now."

"Pity," Mike replied. "I thought we were getting on splendidly. But unless you are the clerk that hands out badges, I think we're looking for someone else."

Madame LaSalle-Guerinot started to reply, thought better of it and stomped off.

"You did not make a friend there, I think," a French colonel sitting at the rear of the van said dryly.

"Well, I don't think getting laid was in the cards, anyway," Mike replied. "And I don't think you are the clerk I need to see, either, Colonel . . . ?"

"Henri Chateauneuf," the colonel said, languidly sliding out of the van and handing Mike a badge. "Call me Henri. And I *am*—I am the clerk. So Madame LaSalle-Guerinot informed me but minutes ago."

"I suspect you don't have a friend in the good madame either," Mike said, taking the badge and hanging it around his neck on a lanyard.

"*C'est la vie*," the colonel said, shrugging, then taking Mike's arm and leading him towards the cathedral. "I doubt that I shall, as you say, get laid, either. It is a terrible world. The madame was appointed after the last election. She was an academic with copious papers to her name, explaining how the French security apparatus, including its military, oppressed the poor Muslims of our fine country. Since the Muslims are an increasing voting block, we inherited Madame LaSalle-Guerinot, a woman who has not once seen the inside of a refractary building except on carefully guided tours."

"Refractary," Mike said, frowning. "The low-income Muslims?"

"Indeed," the colonel said, sighing. "She is very much against being 'high-handed,' as she puts it, with the refractary. Even when they riot, as they often do. May all the saints forbid that we, for example, make random sweeps for any who are holding guns or drugs. That we enforce French laws against battering women. She is a feminist, yes? But this is simply their 'culture.' Something that we have to learn to live with, as a multicultural society."

"Has that interfered with this investigation?" Mike asked.

"Many of the drivers of press vans in Europe are of Middle Eastern or North African origin," the colonel replied tightly. "Make your own conclusion."

"Is she *mad*?" Mike snarled. "We're talking about a nuke, here."

"Calmly, calmly," the colonel said, stopping and turning to regard him with lidded eyes. "The item has not come here, of course. The Muslims of the world are angry at the Cliff Administration, not France. It was not we who invaded Iraq. It was not we who staged a raid on Syria, who detonated a nuke over their territory. We did not set forces in Saudi Arabia and Qatar. This was all America, so naturally the Muslims are angry at America, only. France has done so much for them they would not think to attack us. We are good friends to the Muslims here in France. And the way that we will continue to be friends is to treat them gently, as we would fellow Frenchman. Better, in fact. So we have not, for example, conducted a van-to-van search for a generator that does not run. Such would be intrusive, both to our Muslim brethren and to the news media. In the latter, I agree, she has a point. If we start searching vans, one by one, if the nuke is here, they would simply detonate it."

"So *that's* the way it is," Mike said, breathing out. "In that case, I'm glad I came here."

"As am I," the colonel replied, turning to walk again. "With your diplomatic passport, Mr. 'Duncan,' the most that can be done to you is expulsion and making you persona non grata. And with the pressure the Cliff Administration exerted on your behalf, you have access to the full area. But I repeat; letting them know the van has been spotted, if it is here, will likely cause them to detonate the item."

"It would have been nice if it had been stopped before it arrived in the middle of Paris," Mike pointed out.

"Perhaps it will be," the colonel said, shrugging. "Perhaps it is not here. Perhaps it will be found on some road somewhere else, and it will be their headache. And, then again, perhaps it is."

"You have a suspicion?" Mike asked.

"No, simply the same deductive reasoning I assume you used," the colonel said, stopping at the edge of the press area. "And here we must part, alas. I have many things to attend to, as do you. Feel free to stop by the van again; we have a superior coffee I would have you try."

"Now you tell me," Mike said, chuckling. "But onward and upward." With that he passed through the security cordon around the press area.

The area set aside for parking the press vans was packed. Everyone in the news industry appeared to be there. There were vans for CNN and Skynews, all the major American networks, BBC and all the rest of the European networks. Most of them seemed to have more than one van. Mike quickly zoomed in on the larger ones, which were, he determined, mostly satellite uplink vans. All of them had dishes on top and he recognized that, if their van was there, they'd had to have been retrofitted somewhere. Most of the dishes were up and pointed at satellites, but not all.

He wandered around the area for about an hour, looking for anomalies and finding none. Part of that was the controlled chaos of the environment. People were moving around doing things about which he knew nothing. There were people arguing by the vans, people sitting around tapping at laptops, people eating breakfast.

He checked a couple of vans that were from networks he'd never heard of, and looked closely at the Al Jazeera van. That one had the usual collection of Middle Eastern types, including a woman, probably a reporter, who was a real looker. But he could hear the generator as he passed. He'd already determined that the generators were for providing power to the satellite links and all the rest of the equipment in the vans. But if they were running, they couldn't contain a bomb.

After a while he got frustrated and headed back to the command center, cadging a cup of very good coffee and a couple of stale croissants. He hung around the command center for a bit, thinking, until he'd finished off the croissants, then headed back to the press area, sipping his coffee.

He was walking down the line of vans when he saw a lone person sitting outside of one from ABC. The guy looked like an American, blond hair cut short on the sides, American clothes, so Mike wandered over.

"How's it going?" Mike asked, sitting down on a spool of cable.

"Purty good," the guy replied in a thick Southern accent. "Gonna be a nice day."

It was, too. There had apparently been a cold front through so the air was crisp and felt washed clean. The sky was clear and deep blue and the sun shone on Notre Dame perfectly.

"What's your name?" Mike asked, continuing to look around. He saw a cluster of Middle Eastern types, probably drivers, and honed in on them for a second.

"Steve Edmonson," the ABC guy said. "I'm from Tuscaloosa, Alabama. You?"

"Michael Duncan," Mike replied. "Florida."

"You don't have a press badge," the guy said.

"Nope," Mike replied, turning back to look at him. He was eating a piece of pressed meat with a side of rice. In the Dari areas of Afghanistan, Mike had eaten the same thing. They called it chelo kebab, but it was what people in the U.S. put in gyros. Mike blinked for a second as something bothered him, but he mentally shoved it away. "I'm with the U.S. embassy. Just keeping an eye on things, you know. Making sure everyone has all the credentials they need and whatnot. You been over here long?"

"Nope," Steve said, finishing off the last of the meat and rice. "Born and raised in Alabama. Went to UA. Roll Tide and all that. Got a degree in video tech and a job with ABC. Been all over the U.S., but this is my first overseas assignment. Sitting in Paris, nursemaiding a broken van."

Mike watched as Steve set down his fork, and it hit him. Americans, almost invariably, will cut a piece of meat with the fork in their left hand and then change back to holding it in their right. Steve had been eating with the fork held, almost the whole time, in his left. It was the "Continental" style of eating. And he'd done it smoothly and flawlessly. It wasn't just that he was trying to pick up local manners, it was his normal mode of doing things.

"What's wrong with the van?" Mike asked disinterestedly.

"Generator's broke," "Steve" said. "We've got a call in to a tech, but I can't get it running."

"You got any other problems?" Mike asked, taking a sip of coffee.

"Other than the generator, nope," Steve said.

"Well, if you do have any, call the embassy," Mike said, standing up. "They'll know how to get in touch with me."

"Will do," Steve said, smiling. "Good to hear American again."

"Same here," Mike replied, grinning back. "It's gonna be a good day."

He wandered back out of the press area, stopping from time to time to chat with the American crews, then over to the command post.

"Colonel Chateauneuf?" he asked one of the sergeants at the main van.

"He is around," the sergeant said, shrugging.

"Call him," Mike said in a command tone. "Now."

CHAPTER
SEVEN

"You, as they say, rang?" Colonel Chateauneuf said, strolling up.

"I hope like hell I didn't hit pay dirt," Mike said, pulling him over to where they could talk quietly. "But I think I did. There are three ABC vans. One of them has a 'broken' generator. The guy nursemaiding it says he's American, and he's got a good accent, but he's not."

"And you know this, how?" the colonel asked, carefully.

"The way he eats?" Mike said. "Word choice? He's not."

"Does he know that you suspect?" the colonel asked.

"I'm pretty sure not," Mike replied.

"So . . . and so . . ." the colonel said, blowing out and grimacing. "How to do this?"

"I have an idea," Mike said.

"Hey, Steve," Mike said, walking over to the ABC van. "Your country needs you."

"What?" the man said, standing up from where he'd been tapping on his laptop.

"I've got a situation I need help with," Mike replied, closing the laptop and pulling on his arm. "Quick. CBS has managed to

really piss off the French. Something about camera angles. I don't know for camera angles so I need a third party to interpret."

"I've got to watch the van," Steve said desperately, his accent slipping.

"Look, this won't take more than five minutes," Mike replied, stuffing the laptop into the man's case and hanging it over his shoulder. "It's locked, right?"

"Yeah," "Steve" said, allowing himself to be led away.

Mike led him out of the press area and over to an area that was near the command post and out of sight.

"So," Mike said as they rounded a corner and "Steve" found himself confronted by three sub-gun wielding police and Colonel Chateauneuf, "care to tell me who you really are?"

"Steve" let out a grunt of surprise and plucked his cell phone off his hip.

"Not happenin'," Mike said, grabbing his hand and twisting it so hard he heard a crack.

The man let out a cry and dropped the cell phone, cradling the wrist as one of the police officers stepped forward. The officer slid plastic cuffs on him, broken wrist and all, then a hood over his head. The man was hustled into a police car, which drove sedately away.

"I think you may be right," Chateauneuf said, blowing out and picking up the cell phone gingerly.

"May I?" Mike asked. When the colonel handed it to him, he scrolled through the speed dial list. Most of them were names, all European sounding and almost certainly false. But one was listed as "Fire" and one as "Ice."

Mike noted down those two numbers and handed the phone back.

"And now," Mike said, "I think you'd better call your very *best* EOD people."

"We cannot afford to move it," the senior EOD tech said.

The hurried meeting was taking place in one of the police vans. It included Madame LaSalle-Guerinot, who was looking pissed as all get out, the colonel, a couple of senior police officers and Mike, who had forced his way in through sheer chutzpah.

"There could be tremblor switches," the tech continued. "There could be a locator system. They could be watching, for all we know. It could be detonated at any time."

As he said that, the terrorist's cell phone, which was in the middle of the table, began to buzz.

Most of the people around the table looked at it like it was a snake. Mike just leaned forward and picked it up.

"Yep?" he said in his very best Southern drawl.

"How is it going, Steve?" a man said. He had a faint British accent underlaid with something else. Mike recalled that the "engineer" had been trained in British boarding schools. He was talking loudly since there was music in the background. Mike recognized the tune as being a current dance hit. He mainly recognized it because it was the sort of thing you heard in strip joints a lot.

"Turr'ble," Mike answered, half shouting. "Jist turr'ble. Generator's still broke. D'ju call that technician?"

"Yes, I did," the man said in a puzzled tone.

"Talkin' to a guy from the embassy 'bout it now," Mike drawled, rolling his eyes. "Hope he gits har befur the pope."

"Ah," the man shouted understandingly. "He will, I'm sure. Or about the time the pope arrives. When he gets there, you can go, of course."

"Weel thankee," Mike yelled, his eyes cold. "Thankee kindly. Gotta go now. Later."

"Later," the man said.

Mike hit the disconnect and counted.

"One, two, three . . ." He closed his eyes and waited and then sighed. "I think he bought it. One Southern accent sounds about the same as another to a foreigner. They can't tell the difference between Alabama and North Florida."

"Are you INSANE?" Madame LaSalle-Guerinot shouted. "He could have decided that the operation was blown and blown us all sky-high!"

"Oh, higher," Mike said. "Which was exactly what he would have done if the phone wasn't answered. With, more or less, the correct voice. I know this bastard. He loves to see things go boom. He set the timer on the nuke in Andros, for example, rather than

have it fall into our hands. If he gets a sniff that there's anything wrong, he'll set it off just to see the pretty lights on TV.

"Look," he continued to the EOD tech. "Go in looking like repair technicians. That is what everyone in the area is expecting. Enter the forward part of the van; I've *seen* him use the door, so it can't be rigged. You have his keys. Set up in there, out of sight. Do your magic. Get cracking, though. It's going to be a tough nut."

"That will work," one of the senior police said, to nods. "We can give you cover clothing. You'll have to pack your gear so it is out of sight."

"Don't bother with carrying pads," Mike said, chuckling. "If it goes up, you won't need them."

"*You* need to leave," Madame LaSalle-Guerinot snapped, turning to the senior inspector. "I want him out of this area in fifteen minutes," she continued, standing up. "I am going to go brief the president."

"Well, I wonder what got her titties in a twist," Mike said, sighing. "And who, exactly, is going to answer the phone if I leave?"

"You are," Colonel Chateauneuf said, standing up. "She said you have to leave, not that you couldn't take the phone with you. Does anyone have a specific use for it?"

"We'd like to check the directory," one of the civilians at the table said. He had a faintly military bearing and Mike had pegged him as DGSE. "Run down some of the phone numbers."

"We have a list of all of them already," the senior inspector said.

"Does that mean you don't want me to keep it?" Mike asked, waving it in the air.

"Oh, no," the DGSE agent said, smiling. "By all means. And . . . try to be as convincing as you just were."

"Will do," Mike replied in a Southern accent. "Gentlemen, much as I respect the capabilities of the French security establishment, you wouldn't mind if I watch the goings-on from, say . . . twenty klicks away or so, would you?"

"Not at all," Colonel Chateauneuf said somberly. "I will escort you to your car."

"I take it you're not leaving," Mike said as they walked to the sedan.

"No," Chateauneuf said, shrugging. "My place is here."

"Been there, done that, got the T-shirt," Mike said. "I've got to introduce you to a song called 'Winter Born.'"

"Crüxshadows," Chateauneuf said, grinning. "A very good band. You will not tell people that I Goth, I hope? It is so hard to retain respect when people know you Goth."

"Of course not," Mike replied as he got in the car. "When it comes down to popish time, give me a holler and give me a play by play, okay?"

"I shall," Chateauneuf said, holding out his hand. "*Adieu.*"

"Even I know that much French," Mike said, shaking his hand. *Adieu* meant *Go with God*; it was a permanent farewell. "Let's go for *au revoir.*"

"So what did you find out?" Bruce asked as they drove away.

Mike didn't bother to answer, just picked up his cell phone and dialed OSOL.

"Pierson."

"Go scramble."

"Scrambled."

"It's here, Bob," Mike said, breathing out. "Notre Dame. The embassy driver and I are getting the fuck out of Dodge."

"We heard," Pierson replied. "Along with a very sharp message about your encounter with Madame Two-names."

"Gabby LaSalle-Guerinot?" Mike said. "What a nice gal. We got along so well."

"So I heard," Pierson said dryly. "I believe the term 'insufferably arrogant' was used."

"What? About the French?" Mike said.

"No, about you," Pierson observed. "But, yes, arrogant is a good word. Not to mention lacking in leadership skills. The entire government is quietly evacuating. The president and Madame Two-names are already gone, taking their families. The president was *supposed* to be attending the pope's high mass, but he sent his regrets. Some minor stooge, clearly not in the loop, is going instead."

"Ah, French heroism at its finest." Mike sighed. "All joking aside, we've got ourselves one fucked-up situation here. I don't know for beans about EOD, not at this level, so I'm leaving it up to the experts. And, as I said, getting the fuck out of Dodge; I don't see how they can prevent it from detonating."

"Your phone call was intercepted by NSA," Pierson said. "They were aware of the number before we were and traced the call to Amsterdam."

"That's nice," Mike said. "The bomb's scheduled to go off in about six hours . . ." He paused. "You want me to go to Amsterdam?" he added incredulously.

"Up to you," Pierson replied. "The voice match was Assadolah."

"Yeah," Mike said thoughtfully. "I was pretty sure it was him. That English/Pakistani accent. But I've got to sit on the phone."

"NSA has it covered," Pierson said. "Calls to that phone will be transferred to your sat phone. And they can feed in artificial background noise from the event at Notre Dame. When a call comes in from the same phone, it will read 'Assadolah.'"

"Gotta love modern technology," Mike said sourly. "Bruce," he continued, "about face. Charles DeGaulle. Step on it."

On one level Mike loved Amsterdam's red-light district. He'd stopped through on his European tour and sampled the wares, and lovely wares they were. But it was, in a way, just too "in your face." As he walked down one of the narrow alleyways of the district, the curtain behind a plate-glass window moved and a very attractive young woman, a redhead wearing a green teddy and high heels, stepped out and reclined on the pillows in the window. She smiled at him as he passed and he smiled back distractedly. Pretty as she was, she wasn't who he was looking for.

The street was lined with brothels, like the one he'd just passed, their "wares" casually presenting themselves in the windows, topless bars that doubled as brothels, brothels that doubled as bars, and "sex clubs" that were some of each.

"The call came from somewhere around cell tower 4793," Colonel Fagan said. The colonel was another military attaché, in civilian clothes, but much less stuck on himself than Forester

had been. With Mike's haircut and build they just looked like two soldiers out for a good time. "That services the red-light district and some of the areas around it."

"Assadolah's into women," Mike replied. "And the sounds that were behind him were from a bar, probably a topless joint from the music." He paused at the first one they came to and shrugged. "What a horrible job we've got." He paid for both their covers with a fifty-euro note, getting back forty euros in five- and ten-euro notes and a handful of one-euro coins.

The strip joint ran to form, dark with the only light coming from the three stages. In the middle of the room was the main stage, a long walkway with a pole at both ends and a swing in the middle. A blonde was dancing on it, down to nothing but her platforms and money-filled garter, doing a pole dance that Mike had to admit was spectacular. The women wandering around the room were equally spectacular, mostly blonde, long-legged with large breasts. You could tell the fakes from the real ones, even the very good fakes, and it was apparent that mostly they were real.

The two of them split up on either side of the stage, wandering casually to the back, then retracing their steps on opposite sides. There were two side rooms, one a "champagne" room where for probably a ton of money you could sit and talk to one of the girls while sipping champagne, and the other a "dance" room where for less the girls would perform "lap dances" for their "gentlemen friends." When they got back to the front, Mike sat down in one of the chairs along the wall and shrugged.

"I don't see him," Mike noted. "But he could be getting a lap dance. Or a blow for that matter; it's Amsterdam."

"I'll take the champagne room," Fagan said, grinning. "But the U.S. government is going to have a hard time keeping up with my tab."

"Uncle Sam can afford it," Mike replied, handing over a wad of hundred-euro notes. "Keep an itemized tab and we'll submit an expense report."

He grabbed a passing blonde and smiled at her.

"Care to dance?"

The lap dance room turned out to have several curtained

cubicles in it. Mike rather obviously twitched several aside, getting angry looks from the men in the cubicles, one of whom, sure enough, was getting a blowjob, and causing the girl with him to pull him along to an empty one.

"Sorry," Mike said, sitting down in the chair. "I like to watch."

"It is very much against house rules," the girl said, sitting down next to him. The previous song hadn't finished, so they had to wait for the next one. "I am Hanne."

"Pleased to meet you, Hanne," Mike said. "I'm Mike." It made just as much sense to use his "real" name as a cover. The girl didn't give a shit who he was.

"Is twenty euros for a lap dance," Hanne said, taking off her halter top. "Is fifty euros for blow. That is two songs. If you don't come by end of second song, well, I do my best."

"I'll just take a dance," Mike replied. "Do I get to touch?"

"You can touch," Hanne said gravely. "If you touch too hard, though, I will tell you to stop. If you don't stop, you get sent out."

"I can live with that," Mike said as the previous dance ended and the next began.

The girl slid to her knees in front of him, spreading his legs and dragging her hair over his crotch, then slowly slid up his body, humming as she did so.

Mike slid his hands down her back and along her sides, then up her stomach to her high, firm breasts. She clearly hadn't been dancing long, since they were natural and had hardly a hint of sag. He continued to run his hands over her body, gently, teasingly, as she teased him in turn.

"You are very good with hands," Hanne said huskily.

"Maybe you should be paying me," he replied, smiling into her eyes.

"Is very nice," she whispered in his ear. "I like."

"I'm glad," Mike said, licking her ear lightly. "But all you get is one dance. I have to save my strength for all the other girls in the district."

She giggled at that and slid her head back down, rubbing her face in his crotch. Then she slid back up and licked at his ear.

"I think maybe you wish you'd paid for blow, yes?"

"You're very nice," Mike said, nipping at her earlobe. "But I have promises to keep, and miles to go before I sleep."

The song finished and Hanne backed away slowly.

"Wooo," she said, holding out her hand for the money. "That was more than usual fun."

"I'm glad you liked it," Mike said, handing her thirty euros. "You take care."

He walked back out to the main area and looked around for Fagan, but the colonel was nowhere in sight.

"Come on, man," Mike muttered. "One dance is enough."

When two more dances, six minutes more or less, had passed, Mike walked over to the champagne room door, a curtain rather, and tipped the bouncer to let him in without a girl.

"Fagan," Mike said loudly.

"Coming," the colonel replied in a strained voice.

He exited one of the cubicles a moment later, zipping his trousers.

"I don't care what that comedian said," Fagan noted. "If he thinks there's no sex in the champagne room, he's never been to Amsterdam."

They had hit two more strip joints, where Mike very pointedly had the *colonel* go for a single lap dance while he took the champagne room, and were headed to another when Mike's phone rang.

He stepped into an alley to cloak the street noise and hit the connect.

"Ay-yup?" he said.

"The technician is on his way," Assadolah said. "All is well?"

"Turr'ble," Mike replied. "Jist turr'ble. Been sittin' here watchin' the cops go by for the last few ahrs. Jist a wond'rin' when that techie'd show."

"He will be there soon," Assadolah said. "You can go, now. How is traffic?"

"Baid," Mike said. "But Ah figur Ah kin git back in plenty of tahm fer the evenin' shows."

"That is well," Assadolah said. "Have a safe trip."

"Bet on it," Mike replied, hitting the disconnect. He immediately dialed OSOL and went through the scramble routine.

"Got a call," Mike said.

"We were listening in real time," Pierson replied. "One hour until the pope's mass."

"He cut it kind of close," Mike said. "That tech, whoever he is, isn't going to have much time to get out of town."

"The tech turned out to be a former IRA member," Pierson said. "The bomb is not only encased in lead, it's filled with booby traps. The French had never seen anything like it but the British had; it was a full IRA rig. IRA bombs are . . ."

"The toughest in the world," Mike finished. "Fuck, I hate those Provo bastards. Now they're selling their expertise to the mujahideen."

"We talked to the Dutch police," Pierson said. "They're willing to not flood the place to find Assadolah, for obvious reasons. But there are a couple of undercover cops moving around as well. And there's a tac team on standby if you need backup."

"Nice to know," Mike said, walking back to the street. "I have to keep looking."

"Terrible job, I know," Pierson said, chuckling blackly. "Nero only fiddled while Rome burned."

"You wouldn't believe the tab that Fagan is running up," Mike agreed, looking over at the colonel. "I'm surprised he can still stand with all the blowjobs he's been getting."

"Oh, thanks very much," Fagan said, shaking his head. "You realize all those calls are recorded."

"So is most of what goes on in the lap dance rooms," Mike replied. "I wish we could get access to the tapes; it would make this a lot quicker."

CHAPTER
EIGHT

They crossed the street, dodging traffic, and headed to the next strip joint. This one was rather seedy: the cover was only three euros and the girls were pretty worn out. The crowd was also different, running a lot more to Middle Eastern males. Mike spotted one that looked a bit like Assadolah and did a double take. But he was pretty sure it wasn't him. And there was no evidence of a phone on the guy. He looked like a day-laborer and was staring at the girl on stage like she was the Holy Grail.

He passed around the stage and back to the front, meeting up with Fagan, who had also noticed the guy and dismissed him, then headed to the champagne room with one of the halfway decent-looking women.

This champagne room had larger cubicles, with couches that were wide enough to be beds, and Mike caught more than one guy going at it when he looked behind the curtains. Most of them didn't notice, but the girls under them did. In the third cubicle he saw the target. He was sitting on the couch, lying back with his eyes closed, being fellated by a naked redhead. Her hair was obviously out of a bottle since her exposed pubic tuft was dark brown and flecked with gray.

Mike dropped the curtain disinterestedly then took one step forward, drawing his sidearm, and stepped back to the cubicle.

He stepped through the curtain, took a double-handed grip and carefully shot Assadolah Shaath in the right shoulder, covering the whore in front of him in blood-splatter.

The whore backed away, screaming, as Mike crossed the room and grabbed the terrorist by his shot arm, dragging him to the floor, face-down, as he screamed in pain.

"Which one is the disconnect code?" Mike growled, stepping on the terrorist's wounded shoulder to hold him down and socketing the .45 into his ear. "Which one?"

"Fuck you!" Assadolah shouted, then switched to Arabic for a long, solid, curse.

Mike plucked the phone off the terrorist's belt and pitched it across the room as the first bouncer came into the cubicle in reaction to the shot and screams.

"Back off," Mike said, pulling out his diplomatic passport and holding it up. "This is a terrorist we've been looking for. Call the police, they know all about it."

"Put the gun down and I will," the man said, drawing his own sidearm.

"This is a diplomatic passport," Mike said, waving it at him and then tossing it across the room. "You shoot me, for any reason, and you're going to jail for the rest of your life. Put your own gun down, call the police, and in the meantime I'm going to *talk* to this gentleman." He leaned his weight into his foot as the terrorist screamed, and then shifted his pistol to the other shoulder. "I can go for two. Which one is the disarm code?"

"ICE!" Assadolah screamed. "Ice. Fire for the explosion, ice for the disarm. Ice."

"Thank you," Mike said, lifting up his weight. "Don't try to move or I'll gladly shoot you some more."

"He said 'Ice' was the disconnect." Mike was back in the airplane, his chair reclined, a drink in his hand and the headset of the sat phone plugged in his ear. The Dutch police had been less than happy about the shooting, not to mention the torture of the suspect. But it was amazing how well diplomatic passports worked. He was, however, persona very non grata at the moment. Which was why he was sitting in an airfield in France, well away from Paris.

"So we heard," Pierson said. "Along with how you got the information. You're a regular one-man coalition breaker, you know that?"

"Hell, the Dutch couldn't even hold Sbrenica," Mike said. "What do we need them for?"

"What's the chance the information was good?" Pierson asked.

"Zero," Mike admitted. "I just wanted to see what he would say. Look something up for me on the Internet, will you? Google: 'Some say the world will end in fire.'"

"Robert Frost," Pierson replied. "I know the poem: '*Some say the world will end in fire, Some say in ice.*' That one?"

"That's it," Mike said musingly. "Both of them could be a disconnect, but I don't think so. If the pope got held up, if something happened to slow down the crowds, they'd want to wait. There's probably a timer, with the cell phones as backup controls. The output isn't going to him, is it?"

"Nope," Pierson said. "It goes to a phone in Germany which is connected to a webserver. Then it posts a text message to the webserver. Anybody can view it. NSA cracked the server and took a look at who was visiting. All the links have been coming out of Iran. But we know some of the Al Qaeda leadership are still there. The circuit on the phone is set to detonate if the phone doesn't connect to the right number. The French are talking about spoofing the server and the phone output system, but it's a bit tricky. Frankly, they don't want to fuck with it if they don't have to."

"I looked at his cell phone before it got taken away by the Dutch," Mike said. "He'd only called the sentry on the bomb and he hadn't received any calls in two days. So I don't think the take-down is going to cause a problem. Sunni bombers. Shia supporters and fighters. Who says the Sunni and Shia can't get together to fight the jihad?"

"Democrats," Pierson said. "Academics. The Council on American–Islamic Relations."

"Wise people, all," Mike said. "We're down to less than a half an hour. I'm calling Chateauneuf." He hit the disconnect and dialed the colonel.

"*Mon cher*," Chateauneuf said after they were on scrambler. "I understand you had an interesting time in Amsterdam."

"I'd like to say it was enlightening," Mike replied. "But it wasn't. How goes it?"

"Oh, it goes so very, very well," Chateauneuf said lightly. "The bomb is clustered with antitampering devices. There were movement detectors, X-ray detectors, ultrasound detectors and even a motion detector inside the casing. They managed to find a part that wasn't covered with some sort of detector and have now managed, finally, to get a drill into the inner casing of the bomb. This is as far as they have gotten. We have less than thirty minutes until the pope arrives. And he has refused to forego his arrival, stating that if all of his children must die, then he shall go with them."

"Nobody ever said the pope was a coward," Mike replied, picking up the sentry's phone and regarding it with interest. "Where are you?"

"Oh, I've moved to the press van," the colonel said. "It won't matter if I am here or at the command center. So I thought I would watch the proceedings. The men are very cool. They know how perilous is what they do. But they proceed. Ah, the senior technician tells me they have gotten to the stainless steel. Now they must change drill bits, yes?"

"Yes," Mike said.

"They begin to enter the bomb casing," Chateauneuf said calmly. "They can only drill slowly. It will take some time. Perhaps as long as ten minutes."

Mike looked at the time readout on his cell phone and shook his head. It was seventeen minutes until four.

"So, you got any family?" Mike asked.

"A wife, Josee, and three children: Claude, Colette and Danielle," Chateauneuf replied as if discussing the weather. "They, fortunately, live well outside Paris. Josee was going to come into town to go shopping, but I managed to dissuade her. Danielle is just starting school. They study English in the primary, yes?"

"Probably learning whatever the equivalent of '*Frere Jacque*' is in English," Mike said, just as calmly.

"It is, I believe, 'Yankee Doodle,' " Chateauneuf said, sighing

painfully. "At least, she was singing it a great deal when I was home last."

"That makes sense," Mike said. "Although I've always wondered about the macaroni line. I don't think macaroni was a major food group in colonial America."

"I would think not," Chateauneuf agreed. "It was probably another word and got changed. Do you have any family?"

"No," Mike admitted. "I was married, once. It didn't work out."

"That is unfortunate," the colonel said sadly. "With what you and I do, it is always possible we will not be able to leave children behind if we do not do so early."

"Well, I've got some people that don't like me very much," Mike pointed out. "I'd hate for them to take that out on any kids, if you know what I mean."

"I do," Chateauneuf replied. "Your exploits in this adventure alone would cause some angry reactions."

"I've done worse," Mike said, looking at his time readout. Six minutes. "Where we at?"

"They are through the casing," the colonel said. "They are inserting a camera into the hole." There was a pause and Mike heard the colonel sigh. "It is never a good thing when you hear a bomb disposal expert curse."

"Nope," Mike agreed lightly. "What's the problem?"

"There are more antitamper devices," the colonel said to a background of muted, and remarkably calm, French. "And a timer. It has less than four minutes to go. Three minutes and forty seconds."

"Wonder why they set it so early?" Mike asked, humming a Pat Benatar song.

"Perhaps they mistook the time zones?" Chateauneuf said, chuckling grimly. "The Palestinians did this once. They had the timer set for Palestinian time and it went off as the bomb was being carried to the target. Very sad."

"Terrible," Mike agreed, mentally adjusting the time left. "*Mon Colonel*, you'll forgive me if I don't stay on the line? The static . . ."

"I understand," the colonel said. "I have a call to make as well. *Adieu*."

"*Au revoir*," Mike said, killing the call and picking up the terrorist's phone. He brought up the speed-dial list and hit the "Fire" number.

Cedric Jalabert had been an EOD technician for ten years. He had been chosen as the "point" disarmer of the device due to his experience and the fact that he still had "it." There were techs that had been working with demolitions for longer. But those with real world experience, handling actual explosives, tended to lose the edge after a while. They had seen too many of their fellows blown to bits over time. He knew of one Brit bomb tech who had stood up in the middle of a disarm, walked far enough away to be outside the blast area and then had a complete, raving nervous breakdown. So it was always a trade-off between experience and edge.

Cedric still had the "edge," but he knew he was losing it as he watched the timer count down. He had to penetrate the arming device to disarm the bomb, but it was loaded with antitamper devices. The visual timer was totally unnecessary. Whoever had put it in place had done so purely to screw with any technician who got this far, as it was screwing with him.

He put the countdown out of his mind and manipulated his driver, which was at the end of a long, mobile wand, into place on the first screw to remove the control panel. He had several of the wands running through the narrow hole they had drilled in the lead and steel surrounding the bomb; it was somewhat like trying to disarm it through a straw. He loved pressure—he ate it with a spoon. He also knew he didn't have time; the timer was down to less than two minutes. But he was going to keep working the problem until the device detonated.

"Incoming call," Master Sergeant Mimoun said. He was the team leader, but not the point, and he had been watching the various monitors double-checking Jalabert's progress. "The 'Fire' circuit."

Jalabert froze as the phone rang. They had been unable to disconnect it, due to its output, and now, it seemed, the terrorists had jumped the gun. Perhaps they had finally become aware that the police had the bomb.

"It's the sentry's number," Mimoun snarled. "The phone we gave the American agent."

Jalabert switched to watching the countdown timer as the phone in the bomb, audibly, rang once, twice . . .

"The timer has stopped," he said, reapplying his screwdriver to the screw.

" 'Fire' was the disarm code," Mimoun said, sighing. "But it can still be detonated on the other circuit."

"Not anymore," Jalabert replied, switching to another tool and cutting the appropriate wire. "We have ten minutes, maximum. But I can finish in that time."

Mike walked into the suite and looked around.

"Magdelena?" he called, tossing his jump bag on the table in the living room.

In his room, on the bed, he found a note written on the hotel's stationery.

> Dear Mr. Duncan,
>   I met a nice older gentleman down at the pool. He is very sweet and likes me very much. I have agreed to travel with him. I thank you for getting me out of where I was.
>
>   Magdelena

"Well," Mike said, letting out a breath. "That's one problem solved. I had *no* idea what I was going to do with her."

He pulled his sat phone off his belt and dialed a number.

"Hardesty? Spool 'er up. Since Amsterdam is out, we're headed back to Russia."

EPILOGUE

"Michael Duncan is very not welcome in Holland and France," Pierson said. "And they're well aware that it was a cover identity, so I'd suggest staying out in your own person."

"Wasn't planning on going to either," Mike admitted, negotiating his way around a pothole. He had his earbud in his ear and both hands on the wheel to negotiate the lousy Russian roads. "Well, maybe Amsterdam. I've got a date with a hooker there."

"The President, however, is pleased, despite the diplomatic repercussions."

"Glad to hear it," Mike said tersely.

"He wondered how you knew it was the Fire circuit," Pierson said.

"Tell him to read Robert Frost," Mike replied. "Or listen to Pat Benatar."

"Seriously," Pierson said.

"Honestly it was less than fifty-fifty," Mike replied. "But it was going to go off, anyway. So I thought about Assadolah's interests. More than the poem, the song caught me. In the song, the guy comes on with fire, but the cutting part, the damaging part, is ice."

"That's it?" Pierson asked, aghast.

"That's it," Mike responded. "Paris was doomed, anyway. I probably would have let the damned thing go off if it wasn't for the kids that would get killed. And, hell, Chateauneuf is the exception that proves the rule that all Frenchmen are bastards."

"Well, there's more money coming your way," Pierson said, wondering at the response. "Another five mil. Arguably, the French should be paying it, but they're unwilling to admit that you kept Paris from being obliterated."

"Normal for them," Mike replied.

"And I don't suppose there's any chance of an after-action report, this time?" Pierson said diffidently.

"Nope," Mike replied. "Don't care for them. Staff officers pee in them."

"Where are you now?" Pierson asked, sighing. Just once, he'd like an AAR out of Ghost. Was that too much to ask?

"Russia," Mike said, glancing at the sky, which was gray and pregnant with snow. "But the weather is really getting crappy so I'm headed south. Probably to Georgia. There are lots of cute hookers from Georgia. I'm going to go see what the original quill looks like."

"Switzerland of the Caucasus," Pierson said, a grin in his voice. "I was there for a few months training their local commandos and the girls are, yeah, spectacular. Try not to get caught in that border war that's building down there. The Chechens use Georgia as a base of operations against the Russians, and the Russians are getting tired of it."

"I'm going to stay well away from the Chechen area," Mike agreed. "As well as Ossetia and all the rest. I'm actually sort of looking for someplace to settle down for a while. I liked the Keys, but the action was just too hot for me."

"Gotcha," Pierson said, his grin evident over the circuit. "So you're heading for a country that's on the edge of war with Russia, to an area where terrorists move freely and through which both weapons of mass destruction and lesser evils are transported. Too hot. Gotcha."

"No, really," Mike protested. "I'm just looking for a safe place to lay my head."

"Whatever," Pierson said, chuckling. "Take care."

"Don't I always?" Mike asked, hitting the disconnect.

He was on a small back road that was headed in the vague direction of Georgia, according to the Michelin map. But what he was mostly looking for was peace, quiet and aloneness. Finally, he

spotted a barely graveled road that headed into the interminable birch forests that had been covered in an early winter snow.

He turned the late-model Mercedes sedan down it until he was fairly sure he was completely and totally alone. Then he pulled it over to the side, got out, and started pulling out supplies, tossing his sidearm in the back of the sedan.

First there was a comfortable reclining chair. Then a cooler with some cold Pepsis. Then a poncho liner, since it was bloody cold. Next he pulled out a couple of plastic cups and a bottle of Maker's Mark bourbon. He filled one of the cups with ice, then poured Pepsi over it, setting it in the holder of the chair. Then he sat down in the reclining chair, pulling the poncho liner over his legs and tucking it in. Last, with shaking hands, he removed the cap from the bottle of Maker's Mark and put the bottle to his lips, chugging.

"Why the fuck do I do these things?" Mike asked quietly. "I go charging in to save some girls that could care less about 'my kind.' I get shot up stopping a nuke for a country that doesn't even know I exist? I took it on myself to DESTROY PARIS! WHAT THE FUCK WAS I THINKING?" he ended in a shout that was very near a primal scream.

The woods were lonely, dark and deep and did not answer as the snow began to fall.

GHOST SONG LIST

Book One: *Winter Born*
   Crüxshadows: Winter Born
   Warren Zevon: Roland the Headless Thompson Gunner
   Warren Zevon: Lawyers, Guns and Money
   Heather Alexander: March of Cambreadth
   Crüxshadows: Citadel
   Guns and Roses: Knockin' on Heaven's Door
   E Nomine: Per L'Eternita

Book Two: *Thunder Island*
   Jay Ferguson: Thunder Island
   Jimmy Buffet: Margaritaville
   Jimmy Buffet: He Went to Paris
   Glen Frey: Smuggler's Blues
   E Nomine: E Nomine
   Bruce Springsteen: Thunder Road
   Richard Wagner: Flight of the Valkyries
   Blue Öyster Cult: Don't Fear the Reaper

Book Three: *On the Dark Side*
   John Cafferty and the Beaver Brown Band:
      On the Dark Side
   Warren Zevon: The Envoy
   Natalie Imbruglia: Torn
   Metallica: One
   Queen: Another One Bites the Dust
   Nickelback: How You Remind Me
   Metallica: The Unforgiven
   Blue Öyster Cult: Veteran of the Psychic Wars